JILLIAN HART

Heart and Soul

Almost Heaven

Steeple
Hill®

Published by Steeple Hill Books™

STEEPLE HILL BOOKS

Steeple
Hill®

ISBN-13: 978-0-373-65199-3
ISBN-10:   0-373-65199-6

HEART AND SOUL AND ALMOST HEAVEN

HEART AND SOUL
Copyright © 2004 by Jill Strickler

ALMOST HEAVEN
Copyright © 2004 by Jill Strickler

www.SteepleHill.com

Printed in U.S.A.

CONTENTS

Books by Jillian Hart

Love Inspired

Heaven Sent #143
*His Hometown Girl #180
A Love Worth Waiting For #203
Heaven Knows #212
*The Sweetest Gift #243
*Heart and Soul #251
*Almost Heaven #260
*Holiday Homecoming #272
*Sweet Blessings #295
For the Twins' Sake #308
*Heaven's Touch #315
*Blessed Vows #327
*A Handful of Heaven #335
*A Soldier for Christmas #367
*Precious Blessings #383
*Every Kind of Heaven #387

*The McKaslin Clan

JILLIAN HART

makes her home in Washington State, where she has lived most of her life. When Jillian is not hard at work on her next story, she loves to read, go to lunch with her friends and spend quiet evenings with her family.

HEART AND SOUL

And the most important piece of clothing you must wear is love. Love is what binds us together in perfect harmony.

—*Colossians* 3:14

Chapter One

Senior Special Agent In Charge Gabe Brody shucked off his motorcycle helmet, still straddling the idling Ducati M900. He waited on the graveled turnout along the country road while the cell phone connected. The hot Montana sun felt good, and so did the chance to rest. His first time on a motorcycle in years and his thighs and back muscles hurt immensely.

He prided himself on being the best agent in his division, but the truth was that the hours spent in the gym couldn't prepare a man for the rigors of a mission.

Even if that mission involved riding a powerful motorcycle in the middle of a summer afternoon with heaven spread out all around him. He breathed in the fresh air that was sweetened with the scent of seeding grass and wildflowers from the surrounding fields.

Not much different from the kind of place where

he'd been as a boy. The countryside was peaceful and he didn't mind looking at it while he waited to be connected with his commander. Finally, he heard his direct supervisor bark out his usual gruff salutation.

"Agent Brody here, sir. I'm on assignment in Montana and good to go."

"Watch your back, agent." Captain Daggers was an old-time agent who believed in a job done right. And who'd seen too much in his years at the Bureau. "The Intel we've got says this McKaslin fellow is a wild card. We can't predict what he's gonna do. You keep your head low. I don't want to lose my best agent."

"Don't worry, sir. I'm cautious." He patted his revolver tucked in its holster against his left side and ended the call.

He was ready to make his move. His first objective was to make contact with McKaslin. Brody figured that with heaven on his side, he'd soon have enough evidence for a team to move in on an arrest warrant.

Please, Father, let this mission be a safe one, fast and clean. It was his last assignment for the Bureau. He wanted a textbook case, a solid evidentiary trail and an arrest without incident, as he was known for. He'd built the last ten years of his reputation on working hard and smart, and he wanted to leave the same way. Without a single blot on his record.

What could go wrong in paradise? Brody breathed in the fresh country air, once again taking in the scenery that spread out before him in rich fertile rolling hills. The beauty of it was deceptive. As if injustice never happened here. As if criminal activity could not exist where the wide ribbon of river sparkled a brilliant and perfect blue.

Mountains jabbed upward, rimming the broad valley spread out before him. Larks sang, a few cottonwoods rustled lazily in the breeze and the hum of tractors in a distant field sparked a memory of his childhood.

He'd been a farm boy in the quiet hills of West Virginia. A lonely childhood and a hardworking one, and sometimes he missed it and his parents who had passed on when he'd turned twelve. When his happy country life had come to an abrupt end.

Enough of that. Brody shut off the sadness inside with a shake of his head. He yanked on his helmet and drew down his shades. What sense was there in looking back?

Life was in the here and now, he'd learned that the hard way. Now was the only thing that mattered. He'd leave the worry over tomorrow to God, and make the most of what he had today.

And today he needed to get rolling. His stomach rumbled something fierce—he'd skipped lunch again. A sign of too much on his mind.

He'd find a room, grab a bite, right after he made a pass through the McKaslin property. Get a feel for the lay of the land and what he'd be up against.

The swish of an approaching vehicle on the two-lane road was a surprise. He'd been sitting on the pullout of a dirt driveway for eight minutes—he checked his watch—and no one had passed by. Until now. Was it too much to hope that it was Mick McKaslin speeding along in his truck?

Brody took one look at the ten-year-old Ford Ranger that had seen better days judging by the crinkled front bumper, the rust spot in the center of the hood and the cracked windshield. Nope, he didn't recognize the vehicle from the workup in his file. It wasn't Mick's truck.

He waited until the vehicle whipped by before he revved the Ducati's sweet engine, released the clutch and cut out of the gravel with enough spin to spit rocks in his wake.

He hadn't been on a bike since the counterfeiting bike gang down in Palm Springs five long years ago, and he felt rusty. He needed to practice, put the bike through its paces. Dust off his motorcycle skills so that when he drove up and asked old man McKaslin for a chance at a job, his cover would be flawless.

No one would see one of the top agents in his field, but a drifter on a bike who, like so many others across America, was looking for temporary work.

With the wind on his face and the sun on his back, Brody lost himself in the power and speed of the machine.

He intended to make this last case his best job. No matter what he faced.

Was it wrong to love shoes so much? Behind the wheel of her little blue pickup, Michelle McKaslin considered the three shopping bags crammed beside her on the bench seat. It was officially summer, so she needed the right shoes. The styles this summer were *so* cute—strappy flats and sassy mules and the softest suedes a girl just couldn't say no to.

Even if her credit card was significantly maxed.

Well, nothing good came without sacrifice. It was a tough job, but someone had to sacrifice themselves for fashion, right?

Her cell chirped out the melodious strains of Pachebel's Canon in D. That was the song she'd picked out for her trip down the aisle—not that she was getting married any time soon, but a girl had to hope. Besides, how could she sit through two of her older sisters' weddings and not imagine one of her own?

She dug in her purse with one hand, keeping a good hold of the wheel because she'd already run into a fence post while she'd been searching for her phone and had the dent to prove it. She'd learned her lesson. She kept her eyes on the road and on her mirror. There was a motorcycle buzzing up behind her. A bright red one. She didn't recognize the motorcycle or the broad-shouldered man whose face was masked by a matching red helmet. He wasn't anyone she knew, and she knew everybody. That's what you got for growing up in a small farming town. It was just the way it worked.

So, who was this guy? Probably someone passing through. She saw it all the time—drifters, travelers, tourists, mostly tourists. This guy looked young and fit.

Hmm, it never hurt a girl to look. She found her

phone, hit the button and held it to her ear. "Hey, Jenna, talk to me."

"I'm dying and my shift isn't close to being over." Jenna, her best friend since the first grade, sounded absolutely bored.

Of course she was. What other way was there to be? They were living in the middle of nowhere. In the middle of rural Montana where growing grass was *news*. Where exciting headlines like the current price of hay, wheat, soybeans and potatoes dominated the radio stations' airwaves and headlined the local paper.

Her life was so uneventful it was a miracle she didn't die of boredom. Her life was good and she was grateful, but a girl could use some excitement now and then.

"Check this." Michelle leaned forward just enough to keep the biker in her side-view mirror.

Of course, he was passing her because she always drove the speed limit; one, she couldn't afford a ticket and two, she felt guilty breaking the law. "There's this really cute guy. At least, I think he's cute. Kinda hard to tell with the helmet. He's passing on the straight stretch like right down from my driveway and—"

"He's not a gross scary guy, is he?" Jenna was never too sure about men she didn't know.

With good reason, true. "But this is a daydream, Jen. We've got to make it good. He's got these broad shoulders, strong arms, like he's in command of his bike."

"In command of the road." Jenna sighed, picking

up on the game they'd played since they were freshmen in high school. "He's a bounty hunter, wrongly accused. A good man, but hunted."

"That's an old TV show," Michelle reminded her, taking her attention completely off the road as the man and his bike swept past her window. She caught a good profile, a strong jaw and the sense of steady masculinity. "How about a spy on the run, disenchanted?"

"Or how about a star hockey player. A man of faith, a man of integrity, taking a trip across the country looking for that piece missing from his life."

"The love of his life," Michelle finished and they sighed together. It was a nice thought—

"Oh! No!" She saw the tan streak emerge from the tall grass along the side of the road. A deer and a fawn dashed onto the road and turned to stare at the oncoming bike and Michelle's truck.

The phone crashed to the seat as Michelle hit the brakes and turned into the skid with both hands trying to figure out who was going to move first—the biker or the deer—and which way everyone was going to go.

A little help, please, Father, she prayed as time slowed down like a movie running too slow. Her vision narrowed. Only the road in front of her mattered. The biker had turned too fast, hit his brakes too hard and was going down. One strong leg shot out trying to break his fall, but all he was doing was wiping out right in front of her.

She aimed for the deep irrigation ditch, crossing

the double yellow, bracing herself for the impact she knew was coming. She put both feet on the brake and prayed. The deer and fawn skipped safely off the road and disappeared into the field of growing alfalfa.

The man and bike fell in a graceful and final arc to the pavement and skidded. She heard the crash of metal and the revving engine rise and then cut off. Her feet on the brake didn't seem to do any good. She was skidding toward the deep ditch and a solid wood telephone pole on the other side of it.

Then, as if angels had reached down to stop her, the truck's brakes caught and the vehicle jerked to a stop.

Silence.

Thank you, Lord. Michelle tumbled back against her seat, grateful that her seat harness had secured her tight. The truck's engine coughed and died. In the space between one breath and another she saw the man on the ground. He was as motionless as a rag doll sprawled on the two-lane county road.

She grabbed her phone only to hear Jenna sobbing. "Michelle? Can you hear me? Are you okay? I'm calling the police—"

"I need an ambulance," she said in a rush. "Not for me. The motorcycle guy. Tell them to hurry."

She ripped off her seat belt, leaped from the truck and flew across the road. Dropped to her knees at the fallen man's side.

He was so still. All six feet of him. His black leather bomber jacket was ripped at the shoulder where blood streamed through a tear in the seam of his black T-shirt. His chest rose and fell in shallow breaths.

Good. That meant he was alive. *Thank God.* She leaned over him, careful not to move him. "Mister? Can you hear me?"

"Seraphim for the win" came a muffled response from behind the shaded visor.

Seraphim? He was talking about angels? He *must* be at death's door. *Oh, please don't die on me, mister.*

"Mister, hold on. Help is coming." She lifted his visor with her fingertips. His eyes were closed, but those dark lashes were perfect half moons on the sun-browned perfection of his face. A proud nose, high cheekbones. No obvious signs of injury. "Mister, do you know your name?"

His eyelashes flickered, giving her a glimpse of dark brown eyes before those thick black lashes swept downward.

Where was the fire department? Michelle glanced up and down the road. Empty. There was no one! Even the deer had fled the scene and there was only her to help him—like she knew what to do!

He clearly needed help. A big drop of blood oozed from beneath the left side of his helmet, over his left brow. She yanked down the sleeve of her faded designer denim jacket that she'd gotten on sale for an unbelievable one hundred and twenty dollars, and wiped away the trickling blood. Was it a head injury? What if he was suffering from head trauma? She was a faithful TV watcher of medical dramas, but what did she know about intracranial hemorrhaging?

He moaned, still unconscious, and moved into her touch as if he needed her comfort. Tenderness rolled through her. She watched a shock of his dark hair dance in the wind, brushing her knuckles. Her heart tugged at the brief connection. He dragged in a shaky sigh and his dark lashes fluttered again.

Please, Father, help him. He looked so vibrant and strong, so fit and healthy, like a mighty dream of a man who'd fallen to the ground before her.

Except his skin was warm and he moaned again. He was no dream but a flesh-and-blood man.

She slid two fingers down the warm leather of his jacket's collar to feel the steady pound of his pulse. He was breathing. His heartbeat was strong.

"Hold on, mister."

His eyelashes fluttered again.

"Help is coming. I promise."

Who was speaking? Brody wondered as he struggled against the dark. He flashed back to scuba school, when he'd been underwater without air, training for every disaster, fighting off fake enemies and holding his breath. The moment he'd been free, his lungs had been close to bursting as he surged up, up, up toward the glowing light. Once again fighting with all his might, he broke through the light and opened his eyes.

"Why, welcome back."

Her voice was light music, and his vision was nothing but brightness and a round blur of a shadow directly overhead. The bright light speared pain through his skull. Dimly he registered the pain but his body felt so far away.

Who was talking to him? It was that silhouette before his eyes. Wait, it was no silhouette but an angel kneeling over him, golden-haired and radiating light. A light so pure and perfect, he'd never seen the like.

Where was he? A fraction of a memory flashed into his mind. The rumbling vibration of the bike's engine, the kiss of the summer wind on his face, the rush of the asphalt beneath him as he shifted and the deer and fawn leaping onto the road in front of him.

He was dead. That's what happened. The crash had killed him and he was looking at heaven. At an angel who watched over him with all of the good Lord's grace.

Boy, his captain was sure going to be disappointed, and Brody was sad about that, but he'd never seen such beauty. It filled his soul, made insignificant the pain beginning to arch through his body—

Wait. He was in pain? That didn't seem right. And he was lying on something hard—the road. And where was St. Peter? No pearly gates, no judgment day.

Pain slammed against him like a sledgehammer drilling into his chest. He wheezed in a breath, alive, on earth and gazing up into the face of the most beautiful woman he'd ever seen.

"Lie still." Her voice was like the sweetest of hymns. Her touch was like a healing balm as she eased him back onto the ground.

He hadn't realized he'd even lifted his head, but he

was breathless as he rested against the road. His senses cleared, and he could feel the breeze shivering over him, the heat radiating off the pavement. See the blue of the flawless sky and the peaches-and-cream complexion of the concerned woman gazing intently down at him.

"The paramedics are coming." Relief shone in her deep blue eyes. "You just lie still and have faith. You're going to be fine."

She said those words with such force that he believed her. Even with the pain rocketing through his head and jabbing through his ribs and zipping all the way down his right leg. He knew he was going to be fine.

The siren shrilled louder, closer, magnifying the pain in his throbbing head. He gritted his teeth, refusing to give in to the inviting darkness of unconsciousness. He *could* hold on. He *would*.

She laid her hand against his unshaven jaw, and it was as if light filled him from head to toe.

Who *was* she? Why did she affect him this way? Maybe it was shock setting in or how hard his head had hit the pavement, but when he looked at her, his soul stirred.

Boots pounded to a stop. Men dropped equipment and a uniformed man—a local fireman—dropped to his knees.

"Had a spill, did you?" Kindness and wisdom were written into the lines on the man's face. "No, don't try to sit up. Not yet. What's your name, cowboy?"

"Brody," he said before the fog cleared from his brain and he realized he was in big trouble.

He'd blown his cover. He hadn't been on the job more than five minutes, and what did he do?

Blow it all to bits. He'd given his real name instead of the cover name he'd been given. And this was his final mission. When he wanted to go out with a bang, not hanging his head.

It's not over yet, he realized, biting his tongue before he could say his first name. He had to think quick.

"Brody," he repeated. "Brody Gabriel."

It wasn't the name that matched his false ID and social security card, his insurance information and the registration papers to the bike, but he'd worry about that later.

This mission could still be salvaged.

"Don't worry about your bike," the fireman reassured him, the name Jason was embroidered in red thread on his shirt, "It's still in one piece. Sure is a beauty. How'd you wipe out on a straight stretch?"

"A deer."

"Rough, man." The fireman shook his head and patched in his equipment.

Brody tried looking around again. Where had his rescuer gone? All he knew was that he couldn't see her. He tried to sit up and nausea rolled through him. He sank weakly to the pavement and let the medics check his pulse and blood pressure.

While they did, he took a quick inventory of his

pain. His ribs were killing him. But his right ankle hurt worse.

Lord, Brody prayed, *please don't let my leg be broken.* That would be an end to everything. He'd worked hard to prepare for this mission. No one was as primed and prepared as he was. He refused to hand over his hard work to a junior agent. This was supposed to be the mission he'd be remembered for.

"I'm good," he told Jason. "I just need to sit up, get my bearings. I hit pretty hard going down."

"You've got a mild concussion to prove it, is my bet." The fireman flicked a flashlight and shone it into Brody's eyes. "Let us take care of you. Sometimes you can't tell how bad you're hurt right off. It's good to go to the hospital, let 'em take their pictures and run their tests. Make sure you're A-OK. Now move your fingers for me. Can you feel that?"

"Yep." Brody's relief was tempered by the cervical collar they snapped around his neck. His toes moved, too. Another good sign.

That's when she moved into his line of sight. His golden haired rescuer leaned against the front quarter panel of the sheriff's cruiser and crossed her long legs at the ankles.

My, but she was fine. Tall, slim and pure goodness. Her long blond hair shimmered in the sun and danced in the breeze. Her blue eyes were now hidden behind sunglasses, but her rosebud mouth was drawn into a severe frown as she gestured toward the road, as if describing what had happened.

She wore a faded denim jacket over a light pink

shirt and stylish jeans. The sleeves were rolled up to reveal the glint of a gold watch on one wrist and a glitter of a gold bracelet on the other. Her voice rose and fell and he was too far away to pick up on her words, but the sound soothed him. Made longing flicker to life in the middle of his chest.

He'd never felt such a zing of awareness over a woman before. He was on duty. He was the youngest senior agent for the Federal Bureau of Investigation. He knew better than to take a personal interest in anyone when he was dedicated to a case, to upholding the laws of this great land.

What he ought to do was put her out of his mind, ignore the sting of longing in his chest and concentrate on his job.

Then she turned in profile to gesture toward the side of the road, and that's when he recognized her. The perfect slope of a nose, the delicate cut of cheekbone and chin. She was one of the McKaslin girls. Michelle.

The youngest daughter of the family he'd come to investigate.

Chapter Two

In the harsh fluorescent lights of Bozeman General's waiting room, Michelle stared down at her new toe-thong, wedge sandals that went so perfectly with her favorite bootleg jeans.

It was a perfect sandal. And on sale, too. She'd been wanting a pair of wedge sandals for over two months now, salivating each and every time she saw a model wearing them on the pages of her beloved magazines. So, when she'd saw them in the window display at the mall on her way to the Christian bookstore, she'd bought them on impulse.

An hour ago, she'd felt rad. Better than she'd been in a long time. Tapping across the parking lot to her truck with her shopping bags had given her great satisfaction. As if all her problems in life were solved with six pairs of new shoes.

Until she'd seen the medics working on the motorcycle guy, their faces grim. Their equipment had reflected the sun's harsh rays in ruthless stabs of light that had hurt her eyes and cut straight to her soul.

She could still see that man wipe out right in front of her. The drag of his body on the pavement, the ricochet of his head hitting the blacktop, the deathly stillness after his big body had skidded to a stop.

She shivered, horrified all over again. It was by God's grace he'd opened his eyes, she decided. A miracle that he'd survived. She'd never realized before how fragile a human life could be. Flesh and bone meeting concrete and steel...well, she hated to think of all that could have happened.

Or all the catastrophic ways the man the firemen called Brody could still be hurt.

"Go on home," Sheriff Cameron Durango had told her at the scene.

Go home? She hadn't caused the accident, but she felt responsible. She couldn't explain why. She just was. From the moment she saw his big male form sprawled out on the road, the rise and fall of his chest, the ripple of the wind stirring the flaps of his jacket, she'd been involved.

When she'd lifted his visor and saw the hard cut of his high cheekbones, the straight blade of his nose and the tight line of his strong mouth, he looked strong and vulnerable at the same moment.

She'd *seen* him crash. She'd seen him bleed. She couldn't just walk away as if it hadn't happened. As if she didn't care. As if she didn't have a heart. She couldn't have left a wounded bird in the road, let alone a wounded man. Even if she'd been waiting for hours and hours.

Where was he? What was taking so long? Okay, the waiting room was crammed with people coughing and sneezing and one man was holding a cloth to his cut hand—the nurse came out and took him away quickly. They were busy, she got that, but what about Brody? Was he so hurt that he was in surgery or something scary like that? Maybe she ought to go up to the desk and ask.

She grabbed her purse and tucked her cell safely inside. With great relish, she abandoned the hard black plastic chair that was making her back ache. She wove around sick people and some cowboy's big-booted feet that were sticking way out into the aisle.

The line behind the check-in window was long. She fell into place. But when she looked up, she nearly fell off her wedge-sandals at the sight of Brody limping down the wide hallway toward her.

Alive. Walking on his own steam. He looked bruised but strong, and her spirit lifted at the sight. Relief left her trembling and weak, and wasn't that really weird because he was like a total stranger?

He was holding his helmet in his left hand and a slip of paper in the right. The white slash of a bandage over his left brow was a shocking contrast to his brown hair and sun-golden skin.

His eyes were dark, shadowed with pain and his

mouth a tight unhappy line as he strolled up to her. "I remember you."

He could have said that with more enthusiasm. Like with a low dip to his voice, the way a movie star did when he was zeroing in on his ladylove for the first time. He'd say, with perfect warmth in the words, "I remember you," and the heroine would flutter and fall instantly in love.

Yeah, that would be better than the way Brody said it, as if she were a bad luck charm he wanted to avoid. "They're letting you walk out of here, so that must mean you're all right."

"My ankle's wrapped. I've got a few stitches and I'm as good as new."

"I'm glad. I mean, like, you really crashed hard. I couldn't go home until I knew for sure that you were all right."

So, *that's* what she was doing here.

Brody stuffed the pain prescription in his pocket and mulled that little piece of information over. According to his research, Michelle McKaslin was the spoiled favorite of the family, the youngest of six girls. The oldest had been killed in a plane crash years ago. She was working two jobs, one at the local hair salon and the other at her sister's coffee shop, and still living at home. The Intel he had on her was that she loved to shop, talk on the phone with her friends and ride her horse.

"You came here to see a doc, too," he said, not believing her. Nobody sat in a waiting room for hours without a good reason. Unless she suspected who he was. What had he muttered before he'd come to? Had he given himself away? "I saw your truck skid to a stop. Hit your head on the windshield, didn't you?"

Her big blue eyes grew wider. "Oh, no, I was wearing my seat belt. It just looked so scary with the way they put the neck collar on you and took you off in the ambulance. I can't help feeling responsible, you know, since I was there. I'm really glad you're not seriously hurt. I started praying the minute I saw the deer leap onto the road."

There wasn't a flicker of dishonesty in her face. Only honest concern shone in her eyes, and her body language reinforced it. None of the paperwork he had on her had indicated she'd be sincere. That surprised him. He didn't run into nice people in his line of work.

Unless the niceness was only a mask, hiding something much worse inside.

"Let me get this straight. You drove all the way back to the city to sit in a waiting room for two hours just so you knew I was all right?"

"Yep. This is Montana. We don't abandon injured strangers on the road."

She seemed proud of that, and he had no choice but to take what she said as the truth. He relaxed, but only a fraction.

"Wait one minute!" the clerk behind the desk shouted at him, forcing him to abandon Michelle and approach the window where intimidating paperwork was pushed at him. "Your insurance isn't valid."

"Not valid?" It figured. None of his ID matched his new name. His cover was supposed to be Brad Donaldson, and that's what his Virginia driver's license said, his new insurance card, everything.

"We can make arrangements if you can't pay the entire bill right now." The woman with the big, black rim glasses and the KGB frown could have had a job at the Bureau intimidating difficult people.

Brody glanced at the total. Blinked. His heart rate skyrocketed. "Are you sure you billed me right? I didn't have a liver transplant."

The woman behind the window turned as cold as a glacier. "Our prices are so high because of people who do not pay their hospital bills."

Great. Why did that make him feel like dirt? He paid his bills. Not that he had eight hundred dollars in his wallet to spare.

The woman, whose badge identified her as Mo, lifted one questioning brow. She glanced at his biker's scarred bomber jacket, the right shoulder seam torn, and the unshaven jaw as if drawing her own conclusions.

Michelle stepped discreetly away from the scene to give Brody his privacy. She probably should go home now that she knew he was all right and could go on his way. She'd tell him where his bike was, and hand over his bike's saddle pack. Yep, that would be the sensible thing to do.

"Are you able to pay the bill in full?" Mo demanded.

"Yes, but I need an ATM machine."

"Do we look like a bank?"

The big man sighed in exasperation as he rubbed his brow. His head had to be hurting him.

Just walk away, Michelle. That's what her mom would say. *Sure, he looks nice and he's handsome, but he's still a stranger.*

A stranger stranded in a city without his own transportation, she remembered. The sheriff had called the local towing company to have the bike hauled away.

What should she do? Maybe the angels could give her a sign, let her know if this man was as safe as she thought he was. He didn't fit the stereotype of a biker, if there was one. He was youngish, probably in his late twenties. He wore a plain black T-shirt and a pair of Levi's jeans. But it was his boots that made her wonder.

They were special order, handmade and cost more than she made in three months. Not just anyone could afford those boots to ride a motorcycle. Just who was this handsome stranger? Maybe he was a software designer on a vacation. Or a vice president of a financial company getting away from the city on an always-longed-for road trip.

There she was, off on her romantic daydreams again. The question was, did she help him or not?

As Brody leaned forward to thumb through the contents of his wallet, a gold chain eased out from beneath the collar of his T-shirt. A masculine gold cross, small but distinctive, dangled at the curve of the chain.

He was a man of faith. It was all the sign she needed. Michelle stepped forward, intending to help.

"Are you going to pay or not?" Mo demanded.

"I'll give you what's in my wallet, how's that?" One-hundred-dollar bill after another landed on the counter.

He had that much cash? Michelle's jaw dropped. Didn't he have credit cards? It was a travesty. "I'll take you to the bank, if you need a ride."

Brody shoved the pile of bills at the somewhat mollified Mo and pivoted on the heels of his boots. His dark eyes surveyed her from head to her painted toenails. "You'd help me out, just like that?"

"Sure. I don't think you're dangerous and you *are* in need. I don't think you should walk very far being hurt like that." She reached into her purse and started rummaging around. Where had her phone gone to? She pushed aside her sunglasses and kept digging. "Oh, here it is. Is there someone you should call? To let them know you're okay?"

He stared at the cell phone she offered him. "No, thanks. I've got my own phone. Besides, there's no one waiting for me."

"*Someone* has to be concerned about you. A mother? A wife?" Since he wasn't wearing a gold band, it didn't hurt to ask. "A girlfriend?"

He blushed a little and stared at the ground. "No, there's no girlfriend."

"There used to be one?" Okay, call her curious. But she had to know. Maybe he'd had his heart broken. No, wait, maybe he'd been jilted at the altar, and he'd taken off on his bike not knowing where he was headed only that he had to get away and try to lose the pain.

The shadows in his eyes told her that she was close. The poor man. Anyone could see how kind he was. How noble. It was in the way he stood—straight and strong and in control of himself. A real man.

She sighed as she stuffed her phone back into her purse. "Which bank do you need to go to?"

"I don't care. Nearest cash machine is good enough." Brody crumpled his receipt and jammed it in his coat pocket.

"No problem. Do you want to get your prescription filled, too?"

"No. Where's my bike? My pack?"

"The town mechanic towed your bike to his shop in town, but I thought to grab your bag. I told the sheriff I'd look after you. Since I feel responsible."

"It wasn't your fault."

"I know, but I was there. I saw you fall. I've got to know that you're all right." She had the energy and grace of a young filly, all long-legged elegance as she led the way toward the electronic doors. "You've got to be hungry, too. And you'll need a place to stay. Unless you have reservations nearby?"

Things couldn't be working out better if he'd planned it this way. What seemed like a disaster was a godsend. How many times had that happened in his missions over the years? Brody knew, beyond a doubt, that's what happened when a person followed his calling. The Lord found a way to make everything work out for the good.

Brody decided to ax his plans and improvise. Go with the flow. "No, I don't have a place to stay."

"Then we'll find you something."

Excellent. He couldn't ask for more. He didn't mention the local classifieds he'd pored through on the Internet at his office in Virginia. Or the fact that he'd already chosen a place to stay in town not far from the McKaslin ranch. A dirt-cheap hotel with convenient kitchenettes that rented by the week. What a biker like him would be expected to afford.

What would Michelle McKaslin suggest? This opportunity was too good to turn down and adrenaline pumped through his blood. He forgot that he was hurt. That pain was shrieking through his ankle and up his leg. With Michelle McKaslin willing to help him, it could only help his mission.

He fell in stride beside her, only to have her dart away from him in a leggy, easy sprint. Where was she going?

"Oh, I'll be right back," she called over her shoulder. She trotted down the brightly lit sidewalk in front of the emergency area.

Away from him. What was going on?

He watched Michelle dash up to a gray-haired, frail woman. The two spoke for a moment. The elderly woman dressed neatly in a gray pantsuit and a fine black overcoat looked greatly relieved.

Someone she knew? Brody wondered. From his records he'd already ascertained that Michelle had a grandmother. But the woman Michelle was speaking to didn't look anything like Helen, whose picture he'd seen in the local paper as a member of the Ladies' Aid.

To his surprise, Michelle escorted the older woman toward him and pointed to the wide doors to the desk where Mo was now collecting information from another patient. "Right there, she can help you," Michelle said.

"Oh, you are a good girl. Thank you so much." Looking seriously grateful, the older woman made her way to Mo's counter.

"She was lost. It *is* confusing around here," Michelle said easily as she hopped off the sidewalk onto the pavement. "They need more signs."

Brody was speechless. Michelle really *was* a sweetheart. She'd stopped to help an elderly woman find her way with the same good spirit as she was helping him tonight. Unbelievable. Yet, true. He didn't see that often in his line of work.

He recognized the somewhat rusty and slightly dented 1992 Ford Ranger as the same one he'd been passing this afternoon. Dust clung to the blue side panels and someone had written "wash me" on the passenger door.

"That was probably one of my sisters," Michelle commented as she unlocked the door for him. "When I find out which one, she will regret it."

Michelle looked about as dangerous as a baby bunny. Still, he recognized and appreciated her sense of humor. "A cruel retribution?"

"At the Monopoly board, of course. We play board games every Sunday night. Fridays, when we can manage it."

"How many sisters do you have?" Although he already knew the answer.

"I have four older sisters." She didn't mention the oldest sister, although she sounded sad as she walked around the back of the truck to the driver's side. "They are great women, my sisters. I love them dearly. They are so perfect and beautiful and smart. And then there's me."

He settled in on the bench seat. "What's wrong with you?"

"What isn't?" She rolled her eyes, apparently good-natured about her shortcomings and dropped into place behind the steering wheel. "First of all, I didn't go to college. Disappointed my parents, but I've never liked school. I got good grades, I worked hard, but I didn't like it. I like working with hair."

Michelle yanked the door shut with an earsplitting bang. "I like my job at the Snip & Style. I'm fairly new at it, and it takes years to build a clientele, but I'm doing pretty well.''

''You're a beautician?''

''Yep.'' The engine turned over with a tired groan. ''What do you do?''

''I used to ride rodeo,'' he lied, and his conscience winced.

It was his job, and being dishonest had never bothered him like this before. He'd justified it all knowing it was for the greater good. He was trying to bring justice, right wrongs, catch bad guys.

As he gazed into Michelle's big blue eyes, where a good brightness shone, he felt dirty and ashamed.

''Rodeo? Oh, cool. I used to barrel race. I was junior state champion two years in a row. I'm not as good as my sister, though. Her old room at home has one whole wall full of her ribbons.''

''You have a horse?''

''Yep. Keno. I ride him every day. I've been riding since I was two years old.''

''I was eighteen months.'' Brody couldn't believe it. Not everyone he met had been riding nearly as long as they could talk. ''My dad was a cattleman. He'd take me out in the fields with him as early as I could remember. I'd spend all day in the saddle on my pony, Max. I rode better than I could walk.''

''Me, too. All my sisters had horses, and so I *had* to ride, too. My mom has pictures of me sitting on my sister's horse, Star, when I was still a baby. I got my own pony for my fifth birthday.''

"I traded in my pony for an American quarter horse. My dad and I would pack up after a day in the fields and head up into the mountains. We'd follow trails up into the wilderness, find a good spot and camp for the night. Just like the mountain men used to do. Those were good times."

"I know what you mean. Before my oldest sister died, my family used to take trips up into the mountains. We'd ride up into the foothills and we'd spend a few days up there. Catching trout and having the best time. Real family times. We don't do that anymore."

Sadness filled her, and Michelle stopped her heart because it hurt too much to think about how the seasons of a person's life changed. It wasn't fair. She missed the closeness of her family. It seemed like everything she'd ever known was different. Her sisters had moved out on their own. Karen and Kirby had gotten married. Michelle couldn't believe it. She was an aunt now.

"That's what I like about taking off on my motorcycle."

"Camping?"

"Yep. That's what I've been doing, but not tonight." Brody's rumbling baritone dipped self-consciously. As if he were embarrassed he'd wiped out.

No wonder. It took a tough man, one of determination and steel and skill, to survive on the rodeo circuit. One who wouldn't like to be seen crashing his motorcycle, even if it was practically unavoidable. "You're probably a little sore from hitting the pavement so hard."

"That's an understatement." His grin was lopsided, and the reflection of the dash lights made him impossibly handsome. "It sounds as if you miss going camping."

"Not so much. I'm sorta fond of hot water and plumbing." It was hard to talk past the painful emotion knotted in the center of her chest. "I guess what I miss is the way things used to be. How close we all used to be. The fun we used to have. I know everyone grows up and everything changes, but it just seems sad."

"Some days I think the best part of my life is behind me. Times spent with my folks on the farm. Those were good memories. I haven't been that happy again."

"I hope that I will. One day."

"Me, too."

Amazing that this perfect stranger understood. That they had this in common. The knot of emotion swelled until her throat ached and her eyes burned. It was grieving, she knew, for the better times in her life. Pastor Bill had told her that the best was still ahead of her. To have faith.

Is that the way Brody felt? Did he look around at other people who were starting marriages and families or raising their children and see their happiness? Did he long to be part of that warm loving world of family and commitment the way she did? Did he feel so lonely some nights it hurt to turn the lights out and hear the echoes in the room?

Maybe Pastor Bill was right. Maybe life was like a hymn with many verses, but the song's melody remained a familiar pattern. One that God had written for each person singularly. And maybe she was starting the second verse of hers.

She had faith. She had no patience, but she had faith. And knowing that a perfect stranger, and one as handsome as the man beside her, was walking a similar path helped.

She pulled up to the well-lit ATM at the local bank and put the truck in Park. As Brody ambled up to the machine, rain began to fall. Small, warm drops polka-dotted her windshield and felt like tears.

Chapter Three

The plump woman behind the motel's front desk cracked her gum and tilted her head to the side, forcing her bleached beehive at an angle that reminded Michelle of the Leaning Tower of Pisa. "Honey, we're booked up solid. It's tourist season. There are no vacancies from here to Yellowstone, but I'll call around for you, if you'd like. See if there was a last-minute cancellation somewhere."

"I'd sure appreciate that, ma'am." Brody sounded patient and polite.

Michelle noticed he was looking pasty in the bad overhead lighting. He was in pain, she realized with a cinch in the middle of her chest. Much more than he was letting on. She remembered the prescription he didn't want to fill.

So, he was a tough guy, was he? She wasn't surprised.

But she was shocked at the dark patches in the woman's hair. Someone had done a bad job—a seriously sloppy coloring job. Shameful, that's what it was.

That was something she could fix. Michelle dug around in her purse and found a business card. This side of Bozeman wasn't far at all from the pleasant little town she lived and worked in, and so, why not?

God had given her a talent for hairstyling, and maybe she ought to do good where she could. She dug around for a pen, found one beneath her compact and wrote on the back of her card, "Free cut and coloring. Just give me a call."

"Maybe you'd better sit down before you fall down." Michelle eyed Brody warily. He stood militarily straight, but dark bruises underscored his eyes. The muscles along his jaw were rigid, as if it took all his will to remain standing.

"I'm fine." His terse reply was answer enough.

Yep, definitely a tough guy. Too macho for his own good. Michelle rolled her eyes and capped her pen. He wasn't her responsibility, not entirely, but what was she going to do? Just leave him? He obviously needed help and he didn't even know it.

"I'm sorry," the clerk returned. "I've called all the chains and independents around. The closest vacancy I could find was a room in Butte."

An hour away. Brody groaned. That wasn't going to work. Maybe he'd call his emergency contact at the local office. See if he couldn't crash on a fellow agent's couch for the night. Brody thanked the woman for her trouble.

"If you're interested," Michelle said as she handed something to the woman. "On the house. For your trouble tonight."

"Why, that's awful nice of you." She beamed at Michelle. "I'll sure do that. I've been needing to make an appointment, and gosh, just couldn't fit it into my budget."

"Then I'll be seeing you." Michelle joined him at the door.

Had she just given away a free haircut? Brody pondered that.

"What are we going to do with you, mister?" Rain dripped off the overhead entrance and whispered in the evening around them as she flipped through her key ring.

"Abandon me in the street?" He shrugged. "I'll be fine. Let me get my pack out of your truck before you go."

"I'm not leaving you here." With a flick of her hair, she marched toward her truck, fearless in the rain. "What are you standing there for? Hurry up. You're coming with me."

"As in, going home with you?"

"Isn't that what I said?"

No way. That was too good to be true.

"What are you going to do? Sleep in the rain? My parents have this big house. They won't mind a guest for the night."

An invitation to spend the night in the McKaslins' home. He was speechless at this rare opportunity. "They'd take a stranger into their house, just like that?"

"You can have the bed over the garage. Don't worry. It's nice. You can get a good night's sleep, and in the morning one of us will drive you to town so you can check out the damage to your bike." With a shrug, Michelle unlocked her truck and climbed behind the wheel.

He swiped rain out of his eyes and took refuge inside the cab. Unbelievable.

As the rain began falling in earnest, tapping like a hundred impatient drummers on the roof, he had this strange, sinking feeling. Just like the time when he'd been diving and his gear hung up on a snag, pulling him down against his will. "You shouldn't be offering perfect strangers rides in your truck. Or to stay overnight in your parents' house."

"I trust you."

"You shouldn't."

"You're a man of faith." She touched her own dainty cross.

"I don't suppose you realize some people pretend to be what they're not. To take advantage of others." When he did so, he did it for justice. To protect the innocent citizens of this country.

He knew for a fact there were bad people in this world. And those bad people kept him and his colleagues well employed. Didn't she have a clue? "I *could* be dangerous."

"But you're not. I have a sense about these things." Michelle's smile was pure sunlight—gentle and bright and true—as she turned her attention to her driving.

Unaware that she was about to bring a wolf in sheep's clothes into her family's home. A protective wolf, but one just the same.

The hard edge of his trusty revolver cut into his side, mocking him, concealed in the slim leather holder beneath his leather jacket.

"Besides, what else are you going to do? Walk all the way to Butte? You're injured and I told you, I feel responsible."

The way Michelle saw it, God might have placed her on that road at that exact moment just so that Brody wouldn't be alone when he crashed to avoid the deer and her fawn.

Maybe she was *meant* to help him. As a Christian, it was her duty. How could she *not* help? It would be wrong.

She didn't know if her mom would see it that way, but she was absolutely sure that her dad would, because he was cool. By now, her parents ought to be used to her habit of bringing home strays, right?

Even if she'd never brought home a stray this big before.

Or one so handsome he made her teeth ache.

* * *

The house was dark, except for the lone lamp in the entryway. It wasn't Mom's Bible-study night. Or Dad's grange hall meeting night. Where were they? And didn't they know she worried?

Maybe they'd gone out to dinner. Could it be? Afraid to hope, afraid to say it out loud, Michelle grabbed fresh linens from the hall closet. If her parents had gone out together, it would be the first time in six years. Ooh, the curiosity was killing her as she stole a pillow off Kendra's bed along with the plain blue comforter.

Brody. He'd turned down her invitation to come into the house and was checking out the apartment over the garage.

He sure was a courteous guy. Concerned about her safety. Maybe it came from the kind of life he'd lived. Always on the road with the rodeo. He'd probably seen a lot that she couldn't even dream of.

She liked that about him. That he was worldly. Experienced. But when he smiled, his eyes sparkled with a quiet kindness. She liked that. Which was too bad. Brody didn't have plans to stay. He was just passing through.

At least it didn't hurt a girl to dream.

She caught sight of him through the second-story windows. He stood gazing around the small apartment, wandering around to look at this or that. A zip of warmth flooded her heart, and she couldn't stop the sigh that bubbled up until she felt as if she were floating with it.

What a man. He stood like a soldier, alert, strong and disciplined, and so inherently good, it made her eyes glisten. She knew beyond a doubt that helping him was the right thing to do.

She closed the front door, skipped down the steps and dashed through the remaining splashes of the rainstorm. In no time at all she was bouncing up the steps and into the attic apartment where Brody turned to her.

And made her pulse stop.

"This is a nice place you've got here." Brody gestured around at the shadowed front room that led into the small kitchen.

But Michelle didn't bother to look around the place and admire it with him. How could she notice anything when he was so near? He'd taken his leather jacket off and folded it on the tabletop, leaving him in the black T-shirt where torn fabric gaped over another thick bandage.

Was her heart ever going to start beating again, she wondered as air rushed into her lungs and she could breathe. Maybe she'd waited too long to eat dinner—they'd grabbed takeout on the way out of Bozeman—and that's why she felt funny.

"Does someone live here?" Brody strolled to the wide front windows and closed the blinds. "Or do you just keep this place for random strangers in need of a good night's sleep and patching up?"

"The foreman used to live here until my dad had a cottage built down by the creek. Then my sister

Karen lived here for a long time, but then she got married, and my uncle lost both his job and his wife and needed some place to stay but he said it was too small...." Oh my, was she rambling? Yes, she definitely was. Stop it, Michelle.

"As it turns out, we don't have a foreman anymore, so my uncle took over the cottage last month. So, no one's staying here right now." Was she still holding the sheets and stuff?

Yes. What was with her anyway, staring at handsome Brody as if she'd lost her cerebral cortex? She dropped the pillow, sheets and comforter on the corner of the couch.

She still felt nervous. Why suddenly now? Because she was alone with him, and that didn't make any sense at all. They'd been all alone in the truck. This felt different. When was the last time she'd been alone with a guy like Brody? Had she *ever*?

"I appreciate the hospitality." He favored his injured right ankle as he ambled over to grab the set of floral-printed linens. "I can't say that I've slept on pink and blue flowers before."

"Flowered sheets are more restful."

"Is that a scientifically proven fact?"

"Absolutely."

They should have been teasing, but it was something else. Something that flickered in an odd way in her chest. A warmth of emotion that she didn't know how to describe because she'd never felt it before.

She turned away. Feeling like this couldn't be a

good thing. Vulnerable, that's what she was, and she didn't like it. She retreated to the open entry where a dark slash of the deepening night welcomed her. "The bedroom's through those doors. If you need anything, let me know."

"Thanks, Michelle. You don't know how much I appreciate this." He looked sincere. Strong. Like everything a good man ought to be.

Michelle fled onto the tiny porch, pulling the door closed behind her. She felt her face flaming and her pulse jackhammering. She was feeling a strange tug of emotion, longing and admiration all rolled into one.

Great. Had he noticed?

Probably. How could he not? At least he was leaving come morning. She could pretend she didn't think he was the coolest man ever for a few more hours.

It wasn't like she had a chance with him. He was too worldly, and he had a life. It wasn't as if he was going to drop everything and move to a tiny town in Montana that was a pinpoint on a detailed state map.

Be real, Michelle.

Common sense didn't stop the stab of longing that pierced through her chest. It didn't stop the pain of it.

She wiped her feet on the welcome mat on the front porch. She locked the door behind her. As she did every night, she hung her denim jacket on one of the hangers inside the entry closet. There was a note tacked to the message board in the kitchen by the phone. Her mom was the queen of organization.

"Michelle, went to supper and a show with your gramma. Make sure you start the dishwasher when you get in. Don't stay up too late."

There went the hope that her parents were out together. After all this time, she knew better than to hope. But it was one of those wishes that never died, that flickered to life new and fragile every day.

The message light on the answering machine was blinking and she hit the playback button. The old machine ground and hissed and clicked. There was a message from older sister Karen, calling to remind Michelle about her shift tomorrow at the coffee shop. A message from some old guy looking for Dad.

Michelle groaned at the third message. It was from Bart Holmes. The farmer who lived down the road. The same Bart who'd been mooning after her sister Kirby, until Kirby had married.

As if! In disgust, Michelle erased Bart's nasal voice. She was *so* not interested in going out to dinner. She'd do her best to avoid him in church. She was not interested in joining his Bible study, either, thank you very much! Couldn't he get a clue?

Just her luck. The guys she didn't want to notice her, pursued her. And the one that she *did* want to notice her was so far out of her league, she might as well be trying to jump to the moon.

Give it up, Michelle. She squeezed dishwashing soap into the compartment and turned on the contraption. She left the kitchen to the hissing sound of water filling the dishwasher, and hopped up the stairs.

Every step she took was like a glimpse at her past.
School pictures framed and carefully hung on the wall
showed the six McKaslin girls, all blond and blue-
eyed, alike as peas in a pod, smiling nearly identical
smiles.

As she climbed toward the second story, the pictures grew older, marching through the years. To high
school portraits in the hallway and Karen's and
Kirby's wedding pictures. Everyone looked so happy
and joyful, all the sisters crowded together in colorful
bridesmaid dresses in both sets of wedding photos,
but one sister was missing. Allison.

Nothing would ever be the same, she knew, as she
stood before the final picture in the photo saga of the
McKaslin family. Karen's newborn daughter, Allie
was named in honor of the sister who had died so
young.

What other pictures would follow, Michelle wondered? There would be more babies, more weddings.
She had no doubt her two currently unmarried sisters
would find love.

Would there be love for her? Or would she always
be like this, running behind, left in the dust. She'd
watched as her sisters were old enough to do what
she couldn't: ride horses, ride bikes, go to school,
become cheerleaders, go to the prom, go steady,
marry a great guy.

She'd always felt as if she'd never caught up as
her sisters grew up and left home. And in the grief
of losing Allison, she'd felt like she'd lost her family,

as well. The house that was once full now echoed around her as she made her way down the hall.

She supposed that's why she wanted to fall in love. To try and finally have what had been so wonderful and then slipped away. The warm tight cohesive love of a family and the happiness that came from it.

"Patience," Gramma was always telling her. "The good Lord gives us what we need at just the right time."

Well, how long would she have to wait? Her steps echoed through the lonely house that once had been filled with laughter and love.

She knew better than to hope that a stranger, a man passing through town on his way to a more exciting life, would be the one who could save her from this aloneness.

She was old enough to have stopped believing in fairy tales. But she wanted a happily-ever-after of her very own. She wanted a white knight on a fast horse with a heart strong and true.

That it was impossible. There weren't men like that in the world. Well, maybe the world, but absolutely certainly not in tiny, humble Manhattan, Montana.

She could see Brody's window from her bedroom. Just the corner of it, where a small light shone through the dark and the winds and rain. Her heart caught and remained a stark ache in the middle of her chest.

Brody would be moving on come morning. She knew it. That's why she was sad as she brushed her teeth, washed her face and changed into her pj's. The sadness deepened as she said her prayers and turned out the light.

It wasn't about Brody. That wasn't it. It was the promise of what he could be. Of what she wanted a man to be. Protective and disciplined and honest and strong. The kind of man who would never lie, never fail, never betray her and love her forever.

Were there men out there like that?

Only in fairy tales.

She drew her comforter up over her head and closed her eyes.

"I'm in." Brody kept the lights off as he sat on the little balcony deck, tucked beneath the awning just off the small apartment bedroom. "I took a spill on the bike, but—"

"Are you okay?" His partner sounded concerned.

"When haven't I been? I've crashed and burned before." He'd learned how to avoid serious injury during his training. He related the sequences of occurrences that had him bunked up in the McKaslins' spare apartment. "Banged up, but I'll survive. I don't have my pack with me, or I could start surveillance tonight."

"You're on the property? Man! Talk about Providence."

"No kidding." Hunter Takoda was a good partner, the best of the best, and they'd worked together for the past five years.

"Your footwork paid off. I'm going to head out

tonight, once the lights are out and everyone's bedded down for the night—''

He heard the crunch of tires on gravel, and high beams upon the driveway cast spears of light around to the back of the garage, where he was.

Because of years of being partnered together, Brody didn't need to tell Hunter that he had to check something out. Hunter waited patiently on the other end of the secure call while Brody limped through the dark apartment as fast as he could go, stubbed the toe of his injured foot on the leg of the coffee table, bit back the gasp of pain and crouched in front of the windows.

He heard the garage doors crank open as a big gray car—the one registered to Mrs. Alice McKaslin— drove into the garage beneath him and out of sight. He heard the engine die, and the garage doors eased downward.

A tidy, well-kept woman in her fifties, wearing a dress and heels, tapped down the walk to the front porch, opened the door and disappeared inside. Lights flashed on in the kitchen windows, but the blinds were drawn.

"I'm going out tonight. I'll rough out the property. There's got to be a few more service roads around here than I could find on the map. McKaslin's moving the money somehow."

"Think it's a family operation, like the last case we busted over in Idaho?"

Brody thought of Michelle's easy goodness. It was

hard to see her engaging in criminal activity. "I may just have to spend some time ferreting that out for sure." Wasn't that too bad?

"Oh, I know. All those pretty blond women." Hunter laughed. "Yeah, I did the original surveillance. I know what you're thinking. When was the last time we got to work with really pretty women?"

"Really pretty and really decent women don't have a tendency to garner the FBI's interest." Brody hoped Hunter wouldn't figure out the truth—that he had a personal interest in Michelle.

Interest. That's as far as it could go. He could secretly like her, what did that hurt? As long as he kept his objectivity. He was a professional. He was the best in the agency at what he did.

He'd finish this job the right way.

Chapter Four

As Michelle saw it, there were only two problems with having a horse. One was that she had to get up every morning at five to feed and water Keno and change his bedding. And the second problem was that the stable was in the *opposite* direction of the garage.

"Stop that, Keno." She flicked her ponytail out of his mouth and gave him a sharp glare; the one that said, cross me and you'll regret it.

Except that everyone, even her horse, already knew the real her. Ever playful, Keno shook his big head from side to side. The instant she bent back to work, he tugged on her ponytail again.

"All right, all right. I *know*." Michelle rescued her hair and leaned the pitchfork against the side wall of the stall. "I've got things to do, I don't have time to let you order me around this morning."

Keno, her best friend ever, knew when he had the

advantage and moved in to cinch the deal. He leaned the length of his nose against her sternum and stomach, as if to say he loved her. And what was a girl going to do about that?

Michelle melted like hot gooey chocolate left in the sun and gave her horse a hug back. "Okay, okay, you win."

The big dark bay shook his black mane and nickered in excitement. This is what she got for ignoring him yesterday. "It wasn't as if you were neglected, you big baby. You had the other horses to keep you company."

The poor, neglected gelding stood still while she snapped the blue lead rope onto his matching nylon halter and led him through the wide stall door into the pasture.

What a great morning for a ride. The morning was fresh and the breeze sweet and warm as the new sun welcoming her. As boring as it was living in smallville, *this* was worth it. Freedom sparkled all around her, and she laughed at the nuzzle of Keno's whisper-soft lips against her face.

She buried her left hand in his sturdy mane and braced the other on his back. She hopped on, pulled herself astride. Keno shifted with her weight, holding back all his power and energy until she sent him into an easy lope that made his mane dance and the meadow speed by.

She hadn't ridden him yesterday, and he stretched his legs now as she leaned forward, gripped him hard with her thighs, and urged him into a faster run. But to where?

She could nose him into the rays of the rising sun and take him on the river trail, as she often did, or she could circle him around along the fence line. Yep, that's what she'd do. Because from the rise near the house, she'd get a good look at the garage. She'd be able to see if Brody was up yet.

And if he was, she'd invite him in to meet her parents. And since she had several clients this morning, she'd take him with her on her way to town and connect him up with his bike. That way she'd at least be able to say goodbye to him before he rode off forever.

Speaking of goodbyes, there was her dad's truck. The old tan-and-white pickup lumbered down the driveway and kicked up a soft plume of dust into the clean morning air.

Dad was going to town? He was usually in the fields this time of morning, checking the crops and irrigation equipment. There were always a thousand things to keep him busy.

But to head to town? Nothing was open, not even the coffee shop.

Brody. The realization pierced through her chest, leaving a physical pain. Surely Mom and Dad found the note she'd left, detailing the events that led to the stranger staying the night in the garage apartment, and Dad was taking charge, like always. He was taking Brody into town.

What? Without getting to say goodbye to him? As if!

Michelle signaled Keno to stop. At the crest of the knoll closest to the house, she could see the garage and the windows above it. The blinds were open, so that meant that Brody was obviously up. Thanks to the low angle of the sun, she could see right into the apartment. No one was there.

Sadness ripped through her, sharp as a razor blade. And how could that be? She'd only know Brody for what, like thirteen hours, and most of those she'd been asleep. So why did she feel so sad? As if she'd lost something of immense value? It made no sense.

He was gone. She laid the heel of her palm over her heart, wishing the sadness would stop. *Watch over him, Father. Keep him safe on his journey. Help him find whatever he's searching for.*

Michelle swore she could hear the faintest answer, but the wind gusted and the seed-heavy grass rattled before she could grasp the words.

It was as if the sun had gone down on her, and how much sense did that make? But that's what it felt like as she walked Keno back, cooling him off before she brushed him down in the gentle warmth of the rising sun.

Maybe it was the promise of a man like Brody. The hope of what she wanted in her life. A big strong man who was a little tough, looked a little dangerous, who was unique. A rugged individual. A good man of faith with a gentle heart.

There had to be men like that *somewhere* in the world. All she wanted was the right man. The best man. Someone she could love with all her heart.

Yeah, like they just fell out of the sky like rain.

She checked the water in the trough, poured grain, forked fresh alfalfa into the feeder and gave Keno one last hug before she locked the stall gate after her. She hadn't felt this lonely in a long time, so why now?

Her steps echoed in the stable, melancholy sounding. She remembered when the stalls were full, and her sisters were always around, coming and going, cleaning stalls or grooming their horses. Now there was only the brush of dawn at the open doors as she stepped out into the morning alone.

Meeting Brody had done this. It made her wish—for one impossible second—that her life could change. That she could find love and a family of her own. That she would be able to be loved and to love, to give her soul mate all the love she'd been saving up in her heart just for him.

Whoever he was.

Well, not Brody. That was for sure.

At least it was Friday. She'd better remember to give her sisters a call—well everyone but Kristin because she lived in Seattle—and set up a game tonight. It was her turn to host. What was she gonna do for food?

They could barbecue, but then she was a disaster when it came to Dad's propane grill. She'd set the cobs of corn on fire last time. She wasn't the best cook, so she didn't want to torture her sisters with some lame casserole. Wait, maybe she'd pick up a take-and-bake pizza from town. Perfect.

Feeling a little better, she kicked off her boots at the back steps and skidded to a stop in the threshold.

There, seated at the round oak table in the kitchen's sunny eating nook was a dark-haired man. She recognized the tousled shanks of hair and the long powerful curve of his shoulder and back.

Brody. He was here? He hadn't left?

Her knees felt unsteady, so she leaned against the door frame realizing too late that she'd swept her sleep-rumpled hair into a ponytail, and she hadn't showered. Without makeup, and wearing a pair of old cut-offs, she had to look totally gross. She had to smell like her horse.

She was afraid Brody was going to leap out of his chair in horror and run on his injured ankle for the hills.

She couldn't blame him if he did.

"Here, Michelle, honey." Her mom noticed her first as she turned from the stove. "You're just in time. Do you have a full morning at the Snip & Style?"

"Yeah." Somehow she managed to talk like a normal person—with consonants and vowels and words and everything. "I'm, uh, didn't know Brody was here."

It was the nicest surprise *ever.*

He twisted in the chair, hooking his arm around the

ladder back, looking like a dream come true as he smiled. Slow. Steady. "Your mom offered me breakfast and I'm not about to turn down a home-cooked meal. Mrs. McKaslin, I can't remember when I've had such a privilege."

"Goodness, you're awfully well mannered for a biker." Michelle's mom tried to look stern, but pink blushed her face as she set two more plates on the table. She was pleased with the compliment. "Call me Alice. Michelle, I put your plate in the oven to keep warm. Mick's is in there, too."

"He's not with Dad?"

"He's not up yet. He's not answering his phone, anyway."

Michelle knew better than to say anything more. She grabbed a hot pad from the hook on the wall and found her plate in the oven. Uncle Mick was a sore point in the family. Her stomach tightened with worry over it as she headed to the table.

"Who's Mick?" Brody asked, absently, as if to make conversation in the suddenly tense silence.

"My uncle." Michelle dropped into the chair closest to him. "He's going through a divorce and lost his job, so Dad hired him on to help out this summer."

"Hmmph!" was the only comment Alice McKaslin made as she switched the burners and set the frying pan heavy with hot grease on a trivet to cool.

Brody quirked his left brow.

Michelle *knew* his question. She didn't even need

to ask. How weird was that? "Uncle Mick is Dad's favorite brother. I was named after him. I was supposed to be a boy, so they named me Michelle instead of Michael. Anyway, Uncle Mick's not the most responsible of men. He's a rad uncle, but he's—"

"—never grown up, and that's not attractive in a forty-nine-year-old man." Her mother's stern look said everything. "Now, it's time for grace."

Michelle clasped her hands and bowed her head during the prayer. As she whispered an *amen,* she looked at Brody and wondered. Was it chance that he'd landed here? Or was he part of a bigger plan?

He looked noble with his high proud cheekbones and the slant of his straight nose. He sat straight in the chair, head bowed forward as he added a silent prayer to the end of her mother's grace.

Okay, she *had* to like him even more for that—if it was possible to like him any more than she already did. He was so sincere and faithful as he muttered an *amen* and reached for his fork. He looked a little sheepish as he caught her watching him.

"I always say a prayer for my mom and dad. They're in heaven." He shrugged as if a little embarrassed.

Could he be more perfect?

"Brody," Alice said as she poured a glass of milk, "where are you from? That's some accent you've got."

"Me? I thought I'd gotten rid of that. I've lived in the West so long, it's practically gone." He shook his head when Alice offered him the creamer. He lifted the steaming cup of coffee by his plate and sipped. Savored. Swallowed. "Sure is good, ma'am. I'm from West Virginia."

"Goodness. That sure is a long ways from here. Did you live there long?"

"Born and raised." Brody dug into the delicious-looking hash browns—so buttery and golden crisp and made from real shredded potatoes. He took it as another sign he was on the right path. "I'm a country boy at heart, even though I moved to the city when I was twelve."

"Was that in West Virginia, too?"

"Yes, ma'am." He felt the steel around his heart harden. There were a lot of things he didn't like to think too much about. Spending his teen years in a boys' home for lack of foster care was one of them. He cleared his throat, tried to keep his mind focused. To not let the sadness of his past effect the quality of his present life.

"Mom, you're being nosy again." Michelle's eyes sparkled with those little glints of blue sapphire that could captivate the most professional, dedicated agent. "You don't have to give us your life history. Where are you headed next when you get your bike?"

"I don't rightly know." That was the truth. He was ready to go on about how he'd be heading up to Glacier, that was the background story he'd hatched up, but the truth sidetracked him.

He had vague ideas about what he wanted to do

when he left, but he didn't have a set plan. It bothered him. The past ten years at the Bureau had been demanding work—long hard hours, constant travel, tough assignments and dangerous missions.

It wore on a man. Chiseled at his soul.

He believed in the power of prayer. He figured he'd leave it in God's hands. That the good Lord would point him in the right direction.

"Surely you have family back in West Virginia. You're eventually headed back there?" Alice McKaslin prompted.

"I don't have any family."

"What? No family?" Tenderhearted Michelle sat wide-eyed, watching him carefully.

His heart stopped beating. Why was he reacting to her this way? Just because she looked like everything right in the world, with her hair tied back in that bouncy ponytail and her honest face more beautiful without a hint of makeup, it didn't mean that he should notice her.

He was on a mission. He needed to stay focused.

Right. His mission. Where was he? What did he need to do? Oh, that's right. You'd think he was a green agent getting his feet wet on his first assignment with the way he was acting. Good thing the surveillance equipment wasn't installed yet or Hunter would be getting a good laugh about now.

Focus, Agent Brody. Focus. He took a big bite of delicious scrambled eggs, getting a good rein on his thoughts while he chewed.

Alice McKaslin focused on her daughter. "You be sure and tell Nora that I say hello. I've missed her at the Ladies' Aid. I hardly see her now that she's busy with her new grandbabies."

"Here it comes again." Michelle rolled her eyes, as if she knew exactly where her mother was going with this. "I know, only two of your daughters are married, with only one baby between them."

"It's not right, that's what! I raised you girls better than that. I want grandchildren." Alice McKaslin's eyes were twinkling as she held back a dignified smile. "Nora has three grandchildren of her own, and three step-grandchildren."

"It's a hint. Like I'm supposed to be desperate enough to marry Bart, the farmer guy next door, who keeps trying to ask me out. Just so she can have a few more grandchildren to cuddle. As if!"

Alice gave him the eye. "And tell me why it is you haven't married? You'd think a man your age would want to settle down and have a family."

"I haven't met the right woman yet." Why did his gaze flick to Michelle?

"So, you're looking?" Alice gave him a careful nod, as if he maybe—just maybe—might pass muster with her.

"Looking, but it's tricky to find the right match. Someone who is right for you in every way." And wasn't that a little too personal? It took all his will-power not to look at Michelle, even though he felt the power of her presence as tangible as the floor at his feet. As the bandage on his forehead.

Time for a change of subject. "So, Michelle. I bet you're a good stylist."

"I do my best, but as I mentioned yesterday it takes a long time to get a good clientele built up. Especially in a town where you grew up in and everybody remembers every dumb thing you ever did."

"You don't look as if you could do one dumb thing."

Alice coughed delicately into her hand. "You don't know our Michelle."

Michelle rolled her eyes in mock agony as she scooped her serving of eggs on one slice of toast. "You turn your sister's hair green once and nobody forgets it. Three years later, and people are still saying, 'Now don't you go turning my hair green like you did your sister's.'"

Brody struggled not to laugh. That wasn't in his Intel report.

"And these are people of faith! You'd think they'd know how to forgive. I'm never going to live it down. When I'm an old maid of sixty-nine trying to build up to full-time, people are *still* going to be talking about it."

"Haven't I always said a girl's reputation is beyond price?" Her mom actually smiled.

Michelle's fork tumbled from her fingers. Her mother had had a difficult time with depression since

Allison's death. And to see her looking almost happy made Michelle want to jump up and give thanks.

She recovered her fork instead, choosing to thank the Lord quietly, and she rolled her eyes again when she saw Brody watching her with a quirked brow and a crooked grin. "All right, I am a little klutzy. I've been rumored to be a walking disaster, but those tales are largely exaggerated."

"I'm glad to hear it. When I was driving up this way, folks would warn me about this blond-haired woman who lived north of Manhattan who was an F-5 tornado disaster. To keep clear of her. I can see I wasn't spared, even when I was trying to pass you on the highway."

"Ha ha. I had nothing to do with your accident."

"Tell that to my lawyer." He winked.

"I'll settle out of court, as long as you agree to let me keep my shoe collection."

"That's her entire net worth," her mom quipped.

"That's not true. Well, almost." Michelle thought of her impulse purchases upstairs, still in their original boxes. What a shame she hadn't time to add them to her closet. She felt a pinch of remorse, but she'd worry about her budget later.

"Speaking of which, I've got to shower and change if I don't wanna be late!" Michelle stuffed two strips of bacon on her eggs on toast and folded it over into a sandwich.

Well, there was no more procrastinating, no way to draw out the morning. There was a handsome stranger

at her kitchen table and she had to go. It was her
Christian duty, of course, to help him as much as she
could, right? "Do you want to ride to town with
me?"

"I'm not so sure. I was hoping that before your
family booted me out on my ear, I'd be able to repay
their hospitality." Brody wiped his plate clean with
the last of his toast. "Is there anything I can do
around here, Mrs. McKaslin? Something your husband is too busy running the farm to do for you?"

"Oh, my dear man. You have no idea!" Her mom
lit up like a thousand-watt bulb. "But you're injured.
You couldn't possibly do much."

"My ankle's wrapped. I'm a quick healer."

Brody's wink made Michelle shiver. All the way
to her toes. Wasn't it just too bad he might be hanging
around for a little while longer? "Put him to work
and make him suffer, Mom. I have a feeling he de-
serves it."

"Me? What did I do?" But he was chuckling, a
warm rich wonderful sound that could make a girl
dream.

"Later." She escaped while she could, dashing up
the stairs and trying not to think of the…possibilities.

Chapter Five

Hunter didn't bother to say hello, he picked up the phone in the middle of the first ring. "You're late checking in, buddy."

"Sorry about that. Unavoidable." Brody, with the phone tucked in one hand, carried the full can of paint out of the corner of the garage and into the shade outside. "Mrs. McKaslin has me busy. I've changed lightbulbs, repaired a window blind, fixed the ice maker on the refrigerator and now I'm painting their garage."

"All of that, and it's not five o'clock yet?"

"Their day starts at 4:30 a.m."

"Wicked." Hunter laughed. "Still hangin' in there? How's your ankle?"

"Killing me, but that's okay. I'll ice it tonight. It's endeared me to Mrs. McKaslin. She baked me a chocolate cake."

"Couldn't do better. Look, I've got the drop taken care of. The surveillance equipment is in a storage place just east of town. I'll leave a starter bag on your balcony some time after dark."

"Good. It sounds like most of the family is going to be gone. It's Friday night. The missus has a church function, which her husband will be showing up to later. Michelle probably has a date. The way Alice talked, she worried that I'd be on my own."

"We shouldn't have any problem. If you can handle it on your end, I'll set up a tail on Mick. I'm pulling some agents from the Bozeman office to help me out."

"All two of them?" It was a small office, and in a small population base they had to worry about being recognized. A stranger's face stuck out in a small town. So did a strange vehicle tailing a suspect on a road with no traffic for miles. "I called the mechanic in town. He's got a part coming overnight, and I should have my wheels back soon."

"That's one problem solved. Be careful tonight, Brody." Hunter turned serious. "Remember the Misu Flats case? Started out like this, nice as pie. Sweet grandmother type who surprised us by sending two hired hit men to kill us in our sleep."

"I get the hint. You be careful, too, buddy." He heard the sound of a rattling engine and he signed off. Tucked the phone in the back pocket of his cutoffs and went to work removing the empty can and replacing it with the full one.

Michelle, he figured, without turning around, and wasn't surprised when her vehicle pulled into the carport on the other side of the garage.

"Careful!" He called out when he heard the hinges of the truck's door squeak open. "Wet paint."

"Mom has been putting you to work. Are you sure you're up to this?" Michelle's sandals clacked on the concrete. The sound of plastic bags rustling had him looking up.

And admiring the prettiest girl he'd ever seen. He'd seen beauty—who hadn't?—but deep down loveliness, the kind that came from within, was something a man didn't come across every day.

Her hair was tied back in a single decorative braid, and her short, wispy bangs framed her face. She wore little makeup, just on her lashes so thick and long, and a hint of color on her lips. Fresh-faced and lovely, she smiled her genuine smile.

The kind without guile. Without guilt. Without falsehood. The kind he didn't see too often in his line of work.

He snagged the empty paint can and headed her way. "What? You're concerned about me now, are ya? Wasn't it you who said that I deserved to be put to work and made to suffer?"

"Sure, what man doesn't?" Trouble twinkled in her eyes.

He could be trouble, too. "I suppose it's a woman's duty in life to make a man suffer."

"Sure, it is. What else are men for?"

"Changing lightbulbs. Painting garages. Making credit card payments."

"Exactly. Oh, you missed a spot."

"Thanks. I wouldn't have noticed that spot being half of the entire wall without you."

"Happy I could help." She slid her sunglasses on and clicked away, her shopping bags rustling.

"Got any food in there for me?" he called after her.

She didn't even turn around. "Nope. We planned on starving you."

Why was he laughing? Why was he feeling like he was not on assignment?

Get back to work, Brody, and stop flirting with the pretty lady. That was easier said than done, he thought, as he climbed the ladder. But he had painting to do, and a counterfeit money ring to break.

Was that the phone? Michelle tugged off the towel wrapped around her head. Her hair was still wet from a quick shower, and the terry cloth made it hard to hear.

The loud *brring* from downstairs confirmed it. In bare feet and with her hair all tangly and without a speck of makeup, she tore down the hall and down the stairs in time for the ringing to stop.

That's why the good Lord had invented caller ID. She checked the number on the little white box in the kitchen. She dialed and waited, figuring that Karen, her older sister, had called to ask what to bring tonight. Karen was like that, conscientious and wonderful, and Michelle missed having her around all the time. She didn't see Karen as much now that she'd had the baby and was only working part-time at the coffee shop, which she owned.

Karen answered on the first ring. "There you are! I was just about to try the coffee shop."

"Nope, I closed up. No problems." Michelle planted her elbows on the kitchen island and leaned forward, trying to get the best view out the window. If she looked just right, maybe she could see Brody. "Are you ready to get the socks beat off you tonight?"

"I wish, but that's why I'm calling."

"What?"

"I just got back from the clinic with the baby. Allie's got an ear infection and we can't come tonight. I'm sorry."

"Is she all right?" Michelle tried to set aside her disappointment. Her baby niece was ill, and that was what truly mattered.

"I've got some medicine in her, and Zach's rocking her. She's almost asleep." Affection and concern warred in Karen's voice. "The doctor assured me she'll be fine. I just worry."

"Me, too." Michelle thought of her precious little niece, so tiny and vulnerable. It was really something how families were made, children grew up and the cycle continued; sure, it was obvious, but the reassurance of it was like a piece of beauty in her life.

"Do you need me to do anything? I could run to the store, if you need me to. Come over if you need a volunteer to rock her."

"Thanks, sweetie. I'll let you know if we need you. Have a good time tonight and know I'm missing you all."

"Not half as much as we'll miss you. Give Allie a kiss for me."

The beep of the phone's off button echoed in the too-quiet kitchen. It was a big room. It was a big house. She felt so alone in it.

If she listened hard enough she could hear the echoes of memories, of good times. The morning sun streaking through the window as six girls dashed around the kitchen. Mom at the stove shouting orders. Dad trying to read his paper in peace.

There were arguments and chaos and laughter and inevitably a spilled glass of milk or juice. The squeals when Mom shouted out the time. "The bus'll be here any minute. You girls are going to be late if you don't hurry up!"

And they'd all squeal again, racing to find shoes, hair ribbons, library books or whatever else in the last flurry before they all shoved out the back door.

And now the house was so quiet. Sadness ached like a sore tooth inside her as she headed back upstairs, taking the phone with her. For everything there is a season, the Bible said, but the changing of those seasons brought with it a loss. Was what lay before her as good and as happy as the times behind?

As if in answer, the back door thudded closed, and the sound drummed through the house. Was it Kirby? Or Kendra? Maybe it was Brody. She couldn't let him see her like this. Not again. She had to at least get her hair combed!

Yep, it was Brody, she figured, when no sister paraded through the house in search of her. In her room, Michelle ran a brush through her tangled locks, took some curly gel stuff and scrunched it into her hair and went in search of her favorite lipstick. Of course, it was downstairs. With her purse. She'd have to make do with Plum Sunrise. She grabbed the tube and applied it, hands trembling.

Okay, she had to admit she'd been hatching a plan all day. It had undergone many revisions, but she'd settled on one. To invite Brody to join them tonight, of course. She'd gotten an extra pizza, with the works on it, because he didn't look like a plain-cheese-pizza kind of guy.

Brody rinsed out the sprayer hose, put away the ladder and groaned on his way toward the family's two-story ranch house with the wide front porch and Victorian charm. Although Alice McKaslin had run off to her church meeting, she'd promised there were leftovers in the refrigerator he could help himself to. To make himself at home, use their large-screen television with the satellite dish. She'd said he'd certainly earned it with all his work today.

Work? Well, he was pleasantly tired as he rapped

his knuckles on the back screen door. No answer, but
he went in anyway. Michelle was probably upstairs.
He'd grab some ice and put up his feet and rest his
ankle for a bit. See what happened from there.

He heard the phone ring, shrilling in the empty,
spacious kitchen. The handset was gone, so he sidled
close to where the base sat tucked at the end of the
kitchen's breakfast bar. He peeked at the caller ID
box. Kirby and Sam Gardner. He recognized that
name. Another one of Michelle's older sisters, married and living in town.

The ringing stopped. He could hear the distant rise
and fall of Michelle's cheerful voice from her room
upstairs. He knew the name because he'd gotten a
good look at the house while doing handiwork for
Alice McKaslin today. Curious, he hit the caller ID's
back button and read the list of names. There were
names he recognized; one was the name and number
on his suspect list. Lars Collins.

The question was, who had made that call to Lars?
He'd requested phone records, and he was still waiting on the warrant. He knew there were possibly other
calls. Mick had so far made no long-distance calls
from his current phone. Were more of the McKaslins
involved? Or was Mick using this phone, wise enough
to use different phones.

Brody didn't need to write down the list and numbers. He memorized them before taking a step toward
the refrigerator. He spied Michelle's purse tossed on
the counter. Keys, a few greenbacks, her wallet and

a tube of lipstick had spilled out of the open zipper, as if she'd tossed it there in a hurry to unload the grocery bags he remembered that she'd been carrying.

When it came to Michelle, he remembered a lot. The way she walked—quick and fluid, like liquid gold. And how quick she was to smile. He was impressed by how nice she was, and she didn't even seem to be aware of it. That was a rare woman, in his experience.

He closed off bad memories of terror and cruelty he'd seen over the years, and the weight of it hurt inside him. Like a wound too often reinjured to heal. It was heartening to see goodness, for a change. He knew that during the course of his investigation he would find nothing to incriminate Michelle. She was too good. And it made something in his closed-off heart brighten. As if touched by sunshine for the first time.

Maybe he'd spend some time here. Figure out if Michelle had any plans for the evening. She'd brought food home; she didn't have a date? He hoped not. The center of his chest warmed with the intensity of a grow light, and it was an odd thing.

He reached into the top cupboard for a glass. Sure, he used to date, but he was never in one place long enough to keep a relationship going. It had always made him sad, but he'd known he wouldn't be doing investigative work forever. It was a noble cause he served, and he figured there would be time later for love and commitment and family. If he was ever lucky enough.

Not that he was thinking in that direction, but—

He looked down. A serial number caught his attention. The folded twenty-dollar bill had only part of the sequence visible, poking out of Michelle's wallet the way it was.

His jaw dropped. The blood in his veins turned to ice. The warmth in his chest faded into darkness. He inched the twenty-dollar bill out enough so that he could verify the number. Grabbed his cell phone, glanced over his shoulder to make sure he was alone and that the lilting mumble of Michelle's voice was still coming from her bedroom overhead, before taking a picture with the camera on his phone.

Documented. He felt sick in his stomach, sick in his soul. He carefully checked the rest of her cash stuffed haphazardly in the expensive leather wallet. There was one other twenty, hidden between a five and three crumpled ones, but it was legit.

Just because she had a counterfeit bill didn't mean she was guilty. It could have been passed to her in a number of ways. Those bills were in circulation around town and around Bozeman. Both places where she'd been recently.

Be real, Brody. You just don't want to believe Michelle could be a criminal. Innocent-seeming Michelle, who made even his battle-scarred heart begin to feel.

Evidence. That's what he was here to discover. And he'd just found a big piece of it.

Michelle just knew it was bad news. "No, don't even tell me. You're going to cancel tonight. Again."

"I'm sorry. You know Karen has the same problem."

"I know." Michelle rolled her eyes. She wasn't mad or anything, but she couldn't be more disappointed. "It's the husband factor. I know. You have to spend some time with him. It's ridiculous, and I *can't* understand why—"

The way she said it, with just enough teasing to hide her true feelings, made Kirby laugh.

"I know I cancelled last week for that very reason, but I have a much better excuse this time." Kirby turned serious. "I received a medi-vac call about a half second ago. I'm on my way to the airstrip. Sam's holding the chopper for me."

Someone was seriously ill or hurt. How could Michelle begrudge them her sister? "You two fly safe. Call me tomorrow when you get up, okay?"

"I promise. Gotta go!"

At least Kendra was still coming. Michelle realized it would just be the two of them—the old maids of the family. And she'd bought two whole pizzas. That was wrong. Pizza couldn't go to waste. Wasn't it good that she intended to do the right thing and invite Brody to join them?

That made her smile as she blow-dried her hair,

and chose a new pair of sandals to go with her favorite carpenter shorts and her new eyelet, V-necked top. She grabbed the phone and clipped on her gold bracelet her dad had given her when she graduated from high school as she headed down the hall.

Should she pick a movie or music for background noise? A movie, definitely, she thought as she descended the stairs. She'd pick a favorite romantic comedy, one they'd seen a few times before so they could listen without having to watch.

She walked into the living room. The TV was on. Did she do that? She couldn't remember turning it on, but then she forgot a lot of stuff.

The chair moved and she squealed. For one split second fear paralyzed her and then she recognized the man's chiseled form sitting half hidden in her dad's recliner. "Brody! You scared me to death. I didn't know you were here."

"I didn't know I was so scary just sitting in the recliner."

He sat calm and self-possessed as he took a drink from one of her mom's flowery brown-and-yellow glasses. Ice cubes tinkled as he drank long. The strong column of his throat worked as he swallowed and set the glass aside. All he had to do was smile, and her pulse was still racing. She couldn't slow it down. How crazy was that? As if her heart rate was ever going to be normal around him!

But she could try to *seem* normal. She spotted a

bag of frozen green peas draped over his propped-up ankle. "How's your ankle feeling?"

"It's protesting, but I'm tough."

"And the bag of green peas is, what, a fashion statement?"

He shrugged one wide shoulder but he looked away and not directly at her. "I didn't want to snoop in the drawers looking for a zipper-seal plastic bag, so I borrowed this from the freezer. What are you up to?"

"No good, as usual."

"Is that right? A nice girl like you?"

"Yep. I'm planning a night of wild partying and reckless wrongdoing. Are you interested?"

She *had* to be kidding, Brody figured. With the way she knelt in front of the entertainment cabinet and studied the very wholesome movies there. "Sure. Count me in. I'm a wild kind of guy."

"Even with that ankle slowing you down, huh?" Michelle leaned forward to study the titles, golden hair tumbling forward, shiny and beautiful. After some debate, she selected a movie. "How do you feel about pizza?"

"I've been known to eat a slice or two. Or three. Or twelve."

"Pepperoni?"

"What other kind is there?"

"Ah, a man after my own heart." Michelle felt her face flame. Could she have said anything more embarrassing? She tried hard to act casual. "How about sausage?"

"Onions, green peppers, you name it. I'll be glad to eat it and give thanks."

"Good. I understand if you're not interested, but if you're a courageous man who isn't afraid of danger and intrigue, then you can join me and my sisters for our weekly gathering. Dinner and, since it's my turn to pick the board game, a rousting round of Scrabble."

Brody's ankle slipped off the pillow and he sat up with a bang. The bag of peas dropped to the floor. "I'm a Scrabble buff."

"You're kidding."

"No." Who would have guessed this? He forgot about his sore ankle, the revolver tucked in the back of his Levis and that Michelle was in possession of counterfeit cash he was here to investigate. Excitement seized hold of him. "I've played since I was a kid. My brother and I, we were just a year apart—"

He stopped as a dull ache tore through him. How could he have forgotten? How could he be getting carried away like this? He hadn't thought of Brian in years, and on purpose. He'd been killed in the car accident that had taken their parents.

It was easier to focus on the mission, and keep the pain in his heart locked behind closed steel doors. He took a steadying breath and rescued the sack of vegetables from the carpet.

Think about the mission. Remember where you are and what you are doing. He studied the bag of peas in his hands, still cold. *I need to get close to Michelle because she could be a criminal. Got that?* This was his opportunity and he intended to make the best of it.

"I got a knack for Scrabble, and I've played all my life. A buddy of mine—" really his partner "—and I play a couple times a week when we can. I've gotten pretty good over the years. It's only fair to warn you. I'm a dangerous man."

"Oh, like I'm scared." She turned a pretty shade of pink as she straightened, a movie case in hand. "I hope with that huge ego of yours that you'll survive losing to me."

"I won't lose."

"Okay, believe what you want. Cling to desperate hope if it makes you feel better." Michelle tried to pretend like she wasn't totally losing it around him, even though her hands were shaking as she set the movies on the top of the big screen TV her dad had bought to watch football.

She could see Brody perfectly. "Do you mind if I turn this on?"

"Go ahead." He stepped closer and watched her.

She could see him out of the corner of her eye, the way he stood as immovable and as impressive as a marbled statue. A wing of dark hair tumbled rebelliously over his forehead, making him look like a dangerous man gone good—barely.

Was he something or what? He made the room feel different, and she felt as skittish as her father's favorite mare during a thunderstorm. Brody's just a guy like any guy, she argued as she searched for the DVD remote.

Wrong. Brody was different from any man she'd ever met. He was the ideal dream of a man she saw when she closed her eyes in prayer asking for the perfect man to love for the rest of her life. Her palms were damp and she felt tingly in the middle of her spine. Looking at him made her hear Pachebel's Canon in D and envision the bouquet of roses and lilies she intended to carry the day she walked down the aisle. What good was that?

He was going to leave tomorrow on his sleek, expensive motorcycle and speed right out of her life forever.

There was the remote! She unburied it from beneath the TV schedule and clicked on the player.

"Your family has a few pictures on the wall."

"A few?" Michelle knelt in front of the entertainment center and inserted the disc. "More like thousands."

"There aren't that many."

"Okay, hundreds."

"You were pretty cute in that one without your front top teeth. And pigtails."

"Great. Thanks for mentioning that."

Brody still couldn't believe it. He'd seen the counterfeit bill with his own eyes, and it was hard to believe Michelle would be involved in something like that. It wasn't just because she was beautiful, it was something more. Something deeper.

He was wrong to want her to be innocent when he needed to keep his cool. Stay objective. Stick to his mission objectives. It was his duty to find evidence if she was involved and send her to prison.

He watched Michelle hit the play button, and in a few seconds the big black FBI warning flashed on the TV screen, and he took a step back.

Maybe beneath that girl-next-door freshness lurked the mind of a conscienceless criminal. It was his job to find out.

Then she straightened, and her big innocent eyes focused right on him.

"I'm sorry. I grabbed a romantic comedy out of habit. Kendra has been wanting to see this one again—like for the tenth time." She waved a DVD box with the picture of a smiling couple in the air. "I could check the dish listing and see if there's something more macho on. Like action adventure. But one without any blood and gore and violence. Ooh, and anything embarrassing. I guess they don't usually make those PG."

"Not usually."

She blushed, as if the prospect of the stage intimacy on screen embarrassed her beyond all belief. He turned away while she put the movie on Pause and switched the screen over to the local station. A friendly news anchor was announcing the future on wheat and soybeans.

The phone rang, and Michelle reached for the handset she'd left on the coffee table. "Hello?"

She cradled the receiver against her left ear, and she cocked one foot, listening with care. There was elegance to her and an understated class. There was no mistaking her wholesome beauty.

Everything within him beat with longing. When she breathed, he breathed. When her smile faded, so did his. She folded a golden lock of hair behind her ear. The glint of sunlight on the curve of her hoop earring was nothing compared to her beauty. He shouldn't be noticing her beauty.

Sadness touched her porcelain-fine features. Whom was she talking to? She was so expressive, how could she be hiding a life of crime?

"I understand, Kendra. Don't worry. I'm fine. Call me when everything's okay, will ya?" Michelle's chin dipped as she ended the call. She looked vulnerable, while trying not to show it. And failing.

His conscience was bothering him, and why was that? He'd never had this problem before. He'd done nothing wrong. He was doing his job. He didn't need to feel bad about suspecting a nice, sweet girl, who looked about as guilty as Marcia Brady.

"That was Kendra, my other sister." Michelle's smile was bright, but her eyes remained shadowed. Sad. And so was the false note in her voice. "She's bailing, too. One of her prized mares is having a hard time foaling, and Kendra has to stay. I'm praying mother and baby will be fine."

"What about the other sister?" He gestured to the framed group picture on top of the end table between the recliner and one of the couches. A family picture from last Christmas, he figured, since all five sisters were crowded together in front of a decorated tree. "She's not coming, either?"

"That's Kristin, and she's moved out of state. The only one of us with any sense." Her attempt at a joke failed, but at least it gave her time while she crossed the room and pulled the movie disc from the player.

As she placed it into its case, Michelle prayed for her sisters tonight, for her niece who was ill and her sister who was flying in turbulent weather and for Kendra's beloved mare.

All things change, she told herself, and so would this loneliness, too. One day there would be a husband of her own and a busy life to manage.

"You said that your sister's the only smart one," Brody asked. "Do you think that she was smart to leave? You don't like living here?"

"I thought about moving to L.A. or New York City, but after living here watching the grass grow all my life, I thought those cities might be a little dull for me."

"I've lived in those cities. They have their pluses and their minuses. But here—" He gestured to the wide picture window that offered a stunning view of the rugged Rockies with their jagged lavender peaks stabbing into the harsh gray of threatening clouds. "It's a piece of paradise."

Yes. In that moment, it felt as if her heart opened

up. As if the secret wishes within her shimmered like stardust begging to be revealed.

How did she tell Brody? How would a man like him understand? He boldly followed his whims. Whenever he wanted to travel, he hopped on his powerful bike. He was a man of the world.

Sure, he hadn't said a single thing about it, but it showed. She could see he was a rugged loner. If he knew the truth about her, he'd probably just laugh at her. Like everyone else would. He might look out of her living room window and see heaven, but he wouldn't understand.

She had dreams. She had passions. She had goals she wanted to reach. And they mattered to her. She doubted a world-wise man would understand.

She stalked out of the room and away from Brody, leaving both her sadness and her dreams behind.

Chapter Six

Did he stay in the living room? No. He had to follow her into the kitchen when she wanted to be alone. His gait might be uneven due to his injured ankle as he padded over the carpeting and onto the linoleum, but there was no mistaking the confidence of his step and his sheer masculine power.

Why was it that when she *wanted* a handsome, intriguing dream of a man in her kitchen, there wasn't one to be found anywhere.

But the one time she *didn't* want one in her kitchen, there he was, stalking toward her like a predatory lion while she was wrestling with the stubborn wrapping on the pizza.

"Need some help?" His deep baritone rumbled over her.

She wouldn't look up. He was not her dream. He was just some guy. That's what she was going to tell herself over and over until she believed it. "I'm doing just fine, thank you very much."

"You don't look fine to me."

"That's because I'm hungry."

He splayed his wide, sun-bronzed hands on the breakfast bar, leaning closer.

Her awareness of him doubled. It was as if there were no barriers, not even flesh and bone, and her heart was out in the open and vulnerable.

Why did he make her feel this way?

"I know you don't *need* my help, but I'd like to lend a hand just the same," he offered.

The way Brody was leaning against the counter seemed to shrink the entire room. Make her senses zero in on only him.

A new emotion she'd never felt before sparked to life in her chest. Something painful and powerful and life changing. Just like that, she could feel places in her heart she'd never known. Vulnerable and still bearing the scars from her last relationship.

Please, Father, she prayed as she yanked open the drawer in search of the scissors. *Help me to be wiser. Help me not to confuse friendliness with affection.*

She wanted a great man to marry. She didn't want to make the same mistake she'd made with Rick. That in the wanting, she got carried away with the dreaming of what could be and didn't see the signs in front of her. The small clues that should have warned her Rick had his own motives.

But what motives could Brody have? He was here by chance, not by design.

"You could dig out the pizza stone." She freed the pizza from its shrink-wrapping. "It's in the bottom drawer beneath the built-in oven."

"Sure thing."

He sounded happy to please, digging through the bottom drawer as if it were a perfectly natural thing to do.

Her dad didn't do anything in the kitchen. Uncle Mick, her favorite uncle ever, sat at the table and good-naturedly expected to be waited on.

Brody retrieved the stone and laid it on the counter as she read the instructions to find the right temperature for the oven and turned it on. "I've been on the road a long time. I've forgotten what a real home feels like."

"I told you. It's pretty boring here."

"You don't seem bored."

How could he know? "It's not a life people think is all that interesting. But I ride my horse every day. I watch the sun rise every morning. I go to bed at night on this land my great-grandfather homesteaded. And I feel…"

She dumped the pizza on the stone and turned away. It was dorky and she wasn't going to say it.

As she grabbed the pizza stone, his big hand covered hers. Held on. The link she felt was like touching a live wire, a zapping vibration of emotion. Of understanding.

It was in his heart, and she *felt* it.

"Complete," he finished her sentence.

The exact word she would have used. How could this be happening?

"It's really something, what you've got here." He removed his hand from hers and stepped away.

Taking a part of him with her. How could that be? It didn't make any sense, but that's how it felt. The deepest part of her being throbbed with too many emotions to name—loneliness and longing and loss mingled with hope and love and wishes.

Brody had done this, opened a door to a room in her heart, one she'd never known existed. Now it was all she could feel.

He crossed to the big bay window behind the table, and he somehow still had a hold of her.

A torrent of feeling flowed through her, as cold as snowmelt in a spring creek. And it was as if she could feel his loneliness. Feel how he longed for dreams, too. It was as tangible as the oven handle in her hand.

She slipped the pizza into the oven, the draft of heat attempted to dry the tears on her cheeks, but she feared nothing could. She swiped at the wetness with the backs of her hands and hoped the slap of her sandals on the floor hid the sound of her sniff. What was happening to her? Did Brody feel this, too?

He jammed his hands into his back pockets, and he stood as straight as a soldier. "Which horse is yours?"

"The dark bay is my Keno. Look, he's lifting his head, watching the house. He knows tonight is Friday, and I'm not going to be taking him for a run until later, and it always makes him cranky."

"He's keeping watch for you."

"Yep. We're old friends."

"I know how that is." Brody could hear the affection in her voice. Feel it like sunshine on his skin. "A horse can be your best friend."

"Keno and I have been through a lot over the years. It's a bond I can't explain. We grew up together. Keno is a part of nearly every good memory I have. We know each other so well."

"It's a good way to grow up."

"It sure is." She didn't add how she'd loved her childhood. How one day she wanted to give that kind of life to her own children. To blond-haired little girls riding their horses in the vast meadows. "It's a good way to live now."

Longing. Brody didn't know why he felt it so strongly within. His personal feelings had no place when he was on the government's clock. He wanted to tell himself he'd do better pushing the line of questioning to find out what he needed to about Michelle. To uncover her as a clandestine participant in her uncle Mick's money printing scheme.

But he knew beyond a doubt she was no criminal. His heart told him so.

* * *

"*Ring.*" Proud of herself, Michelle slipped the tiles from her tray onto the crowded board. "Ooh, and a triple score square."

"Good, solid move." Across the dining room table, pizza crusts on their plates pushed aside and forgotten, Brody studied her with unflinching eyes. A predator's gaze.

Sure, he may have come up with a few good words, but he was probably just lucky. He didn't know whom he was up against. She'd been playing since her sisters let her sit on phone books so she could reach the table.

"Take your time. No hurry," she told him.

"A good player never hurries." He winked at her. "It's the secret to winning the game."

"Sometimes a stall tactic means you don't have a word to play."

"Are you doubting me?" He quirked a brow in a challenge.

A challenge? She wasn't afraid of him. "Show me what you've got, Mr. Scrabble Expert."

A killer grin tugged at the corner of his mouth. He dropped two tiles on the board to spell *gun.*

"That's the best you can do?" Boy, weren't some men all ego? She pulled new tiles out of the bag and arranged them on her tray. Piece of cake. She was going to win hands down.

"I'm not through yet," he said, fitting two more letters on either end. "*Gunship.* That means I'm ahead."

Michelle's jaw dropped. That was more than luck.

Her admiration for him rose a notch higher. "You show some skill."

"I tried to warn you." He held up both hands as if he were innocent.

So, this was a serious game. Fine. She could rise to the challenge. She slid *vow* into place. "Top that, mister."

"No problem." He added *loner* to the board. "I need more tiles. Hand me the bag."

Their fingers brushed, but it was more than the callused warmth of him she felt.

She'd been in love before, and it hadn't felt like this. Being with Rick had made her feel happy. Being with Brody was overwhelming. Why was that? What was it about *this* man? She kept thinking about him, and she had to stop herself from dreaming about him.

"Having trouble?"

No. She pushed a *c* in front of *rush* on the board. *Crush.* That's what she had. It was like she felt in high school, before Rick ever noticed her. That innocent hoping, that rush of longing for the ideal.

"Michelle, I think that move of yours proves than I'm superior." He laid down the missing tiles to make the word *superior.* "And a bonus square, too."

"This is war. Wait. Give me a minute." She studied her letters. As if she'd let him win. "There. Take that."

"*Bride?* And a triple score." Brody quirked one brow. "Impressed, but I'm not intimidated."

He was already moving his pieces into place. *Wolf.*

She took more tiles and organized them on her tray. She built *romance*.

Why did she keep coming up with the same theme?

Because she was enamored by the rogue Scrabble master across the table from her.

As if he could hear her thoughts, he frowned. Not an unhappy frown, but it was a thoughtful one. His tiles spelled out *bachelor*.

She studied her letters. She added three more. *love*.

He spelled *freedom*.

Wed.

Single.

They each wrestled in the bag for the last of the tiles.

"I'm ahead by two points." Brody arranged and rearranged his letters. "Just thought you should know. You're going to lose this match, Miss McKaslin."

"Pride goes before a fall, Mr. Gabriel." She sounded confident, but her tiles were an unfortunate combination of the dregs in the bag: *ULASOMT*

"Can't do it, can you?" When his words could have been triumphant, they were low and rumbling and intimate.

She shivered down to her soul. There was only one combination. Her mind was blanking. Sure, she could use a word like *mat* or *lout*, but it wouldn't give her enough points. The question was, did she want to save her dignity or win the game?

How could she let him win? There was no way

Michelle Alice McKaslin lost a game of Scrabble to a man! *Think, Michelle. Think.*

"I just need a minute," she said.

"Take five. Take ten. You still aren't going to beat me."

Did he say that just to provoke her? It worked. "Now I have no choice. Here it is."

She pushed the letters onto the board, shifting them next to an *E*, until they spelled *soulmate*.

Could she be any more embarrassed? With the way Brody's eyes were gleaming and the way he cleared his throat, she wondered if he had a better word.

He reached across the table and pushed a stray hair out of her eyes and tucked it behind her ear.

A sweet and caring gesture. Everything within her stilled. Had he guessed? Did he know she had a crush on him?

Then he chucked her chin, just like her dad used to do when she was sad. A platonic gesture.

Oh. The open door inside her closed. She watched, swallowing hard to hide her disappointment, as Brody spelled his last word.

"For the win," he said.

She looked down to see he'd spelled *zero*.

As in her chances of having him fall in love with a girl like her.

She smiled with all the dignity she had left. Nothing had ever cost her so much.

Brody couldn't get the sick feeling out of his stomach as he headed up the flight of stairs to his temporary home above the garage. Tonight was going great.

Right up until he'd blown it.

He shouldn't have touched her. It sure seemed to upset her. After he'd won the game, she'd offered him a gentle congratulations, adding that she never lost and it had been an honor to play with a player who challenged her. All the while deftly packing away the game.

He'd helped her—at least, he thought he did. He couldn't remember. There was a moment in time where all he'd been aware of was the glide of her gold chain bracelet along her slim, sun-bronzed wrist. The swing of her hoop earrings against the delicate curve of her face.

The way she made him feel forever in a single moment.

"You gotta stop this, man," he muttered to himself as he put his hand over his weapon, ready to draw it. Training, and ten years of habit, had him checking the apartment before he relaxed. Mick McKaslin was so far a no-show. Not at his house. Not on the McKaslin land. Not at his usual places in town.

Had someone tipped him off? The usual spotters were in place—airports, train stations and rental car agencies. Maybe they'd do a sweep of license plates at hotels. Try to track him down that way, unless he'd gone to ground. Either way, his mission was clear. He had surveillance to do on Mick's place. Brody pulled out his cell and fired off a text message to Hunter. "Be here at midnight."

He opened the blinds that had been closed tight against the afternoon sun. The sun had disappeared behind dark thunderheads blanketing the sky. A movement in one of the windows caught his attention.

Michelle. She was yanking at the cord of her blinds, which appeared to be stuck. She unraveled them, yanked on them, untwirled them some more and pulled again. The blind went unevenly down and she gave up, turning the vinyl slats closed against the coming twilight.

She'd taken the movie upstairs with her, and he figured she had a television in her room.

He felt oddly sad that she'd retreated from the living room instead of staying there with him.

And was that professional?

Not one bit. He'd better get his head on straight if he wanted this mission to be a safe one. Things could get out of hand quick.

There was a pickup lumbering up the driveway, kicking up dust in its wake. Pete McKaslin. Brody watched and waited while the man who'd greeted him with reserve early this morning stopped his truck and climbed out.

"Dad!" Michelle must have heard his truck because she darted out of the house. "Did you get supper while you were in town? I can put a pizza in the oven."

"That'd be great, honey." Pete gave his youngest

daughter a reserved nod. "Smells like we're gonna get lightning. Did you put up the horses?"

"I was just going to." Michelle traipsed back up the steps and hesitated on the wide old-fashioned porch. "Do you want me to put coffee on for you, too?"

"Later, honey." Pete opened the hood of the trunk. "I've got some trouble. Got to get it figured out. Now go do your chores, sweetie."

Pete seemed out of sorts, his brows deeply furrowed and his frown intimidating as he bent over his work.

Nothing like a perfect opportunity. Brody couldn't see an industrious farmer like Pete being involved in a counterfeiting ring, but he'd seen more unbelievable things. He'd keep an open mind.

"Want me to help troubleshoot?"

Pete looked up. "Hey, Brody. Glad to see you're still here. The garage looks good."

"I told Alice I'd do the trim first thing in the morning."

"Sure do appreciate it. This time of year I'm working from dawn until dusk. Get behind on what needs done around here."

"I appreciate the place to stay. Your son-in-law Zach said my bike will be ready about noon, so I'll be out of your hair."

"You ain't in the way, son. You're more of a helping hand than that brother of mine. Did he show up here tonight?"

"Nope. Is this the uncle Mick I've been hearing about?"

"That'd be him. Everybody loves Mick." Pete's frown returned and he stared at the engine. "Now this is a problem I can solve. I hope."

"Need this for work tomorrow?" Brody understood.

"I've got hay to cut. It can't wait. This storm'll blow over, you can feel it, but might not be so lucky tomorrow night. You know something about mechanics?"

"Enough to get by on." Brody gave thanks for the assignment where he'd worked undercover in a repair shop in Boring, Oregon. "What kind of problem are you having?"

"Overheating. Went to town this morning, got my son-in-law to open up his garage for me to check it out. Nothing. He changed my hoses, flushed out the radiator, replaced a fuse and such, but figured I might have to take it to the dealership. All those fancy computer chips they've got now days."

"Yep." Brody had to give high marks to the mechanic's work he saw. Neat and very competent. "An electrical problem?"

Pete wiped his face, as though the thought of it made him profoundly weary. A farmer's life was one of long hours and hard work, and it showed on this man who, by the look of it, had done it all his life. "Be right back."

Brody leaned against the truck while Pete disappeared into the depths of the roomy garage. The rising wind gusted across his face, hot and humid and bringing with it the fresh scent of mown grass. Of drying hay. Memories, unbidden and unwanted, whirled up. Those when he was a boy, standing on the floor of the tractor between his father's knees, while his dad drove the tractor through the fields, cutting hay beneath the summer sun.

"When you're a grown man, this will all be yours, son." His father's voice, even in memory, was something he hadn't let himself hear in a long time.

He closed off the memory, but it didn't stop it. His father's voice, the hot rush of summer wind, the faint scent of mechanic's grease and hay brought it all back, as clear as that day twenty years ago.

"This land will be yours, son, and I'll teach you how to take care of it. It's a sacred thing, this land God made, and being a farmer is a great responsibility."

A month later, when the second cutting of hay was growing thick and hopeful in the fields, his father hadn't been there to cut and bale it. Brody's family had been laid to rest in the small town's cemetery, and Brody had never seen his father's land again.

The darkness around him strengthened, drawing his attention to the family's house, where the curtains had not yet been drawn against the coming night. He caught a glimpse of Michelle in the kitchen, the phone cradled on her shoulder, as she opened the oven and slid in a pizza, like the one they'd shared for supper.

Still talking, looking as graceful and elegant as goodness could be, she shut the door and swept from his sight.

It was as if a string linked his heart to hers. And as she walked away, she drew that string taut, pulling his chest wide open.

What was it about this woman? He'd been on hundreds of assignments. He'd dated women, trying to find The One, but no lady, no matter how beautiful or kind or successful, had a hold on him like this one.

Floodlights blinked on overhead, lighting up the entire concrete pad in front of the three-car garage. Brody whipped his attention away from the house just in time as Pete ambled into sight. There was an unmistakable air of integrity about the man, a hardworking, down-to-business attitude. No, he couldn't picture Mr. Peter James McKaslin aiding and abetting his brother's illegal activities.

"If you follow the wire, I'll check the lead." Pete cast his glance at the house, as if realizing where Brody had been looking and who he'd been looking at. "Know anything about electronics?"

"Some." Brody reached into the engine compartment to separate the mass of wires and got to work. Testing the charge of each. Working methodically and slow, feeling Pete's curious and finally approving gaze.

"You sure know a lot for a drifter on a bike."

"I'm not a drifter on a bike." Brody didn't feel like lying to this man. Carefully saying as much of the truth as possible, he stopped to follow a negative wire back around to its fuse. "I've been gainfully employed for the last ten years back in Virginia."

"Now and then I hear an accent. Got a decent job? Let me guess. As a mechanic?"

"No. You could call it white collar."

Pete considered that. "Had yourself a fancy corner office?"

"It wasn't a corner, but it was good enough. But I've put in my notice. I'm taking time to decide what I want to do next."

"Wise. You made good money in that office?"

"I did." Brody straightened up. "Here's your problem. The fuse the mechanic changed blew again."

"He said it could."

"Have him order in a new chip, he'll know which one. I can fix this with a pass. It'll be enough to get you by."

"Appreciate it, son." Pete nodded, his brows furrowed not with fatigue but with thought. "Good thing you came along when you did. I'd been asking for help, what with my brother makin' things complicated."

"Ah. Hired him to help and he's not showing up?"

"He works when he does show up. But it's the showing up that's the problem." Troubled, Pete swept off his Stetson and mopped his brow. "Storm's about to break. Best start headin' in."

"This'll take me a minute." Brody hauled his knife

out of his pocket and bent to work. "How about you? You've been farming a long time, by the looks of it. Have you ever wanted to do anything else?"

"Never. Working the land is what I'm meant to do." Pete gazed at the sky where the first bolt of lightning fingered across the leaden sky. "'Course, some days I have to ask the Lord if He ever meant for me to retire. Seeing as He didn't see to send me a son, I'm not sure what I'm to do with all this land. 'Course, I've got some fine sons-in-law, but they're not farmers."

"Daughters can be farmers." Brody noticed how Pete tensed. His hands fisted.

"Seein' as you and Michelle have struck up a friendship, I don't mind tellin' you that she's had a hard time of it, what with the way her last boyfriend treated her."

So, that's where Pete was going. To warn Brody off his daughter. Another sign of Pete McKaslin's decency. He loved his family and protected them. Brody knifed through the wire and peeled back the coating. "Some men don't live up to their word."

"That's the truth. Turns out Rick figured this was a real valuable spread I had. Thought he'd get himself a rich wife, but he thought wrong."

Brody heard the unspoken warning. He straightened and closed his pocketknife with a click.

"Some people don't know what's important in life. They think the shortcut to easy money is worth anything, no matter what laws they break. It doesn't matter who gets hurt. When the truth is, what's important and valuable on this farm isn't the property, but the family you raised inside that house.'' Brody met Pete's gaze. Stood tall and straight while the older man took his measure.

Finally Pete nodded. ''That'll do.'' He headed toward the house.

Always on the outside looking in, Brody took his time, keeping a close eye on the house. He watched the kitchen window as Michelle greeted her dad with a smile and waltzed out of sight, only to return with a big glass of iced tea.

There she was, tugging at his insides again, as if his heart was still on that string.

What *was* it about her? He didn't know. He only knew this was wrong on many levels. A highly trained, decorated senior agent did not spend his time on a mission watching a woman serve her father a glass of iced tea.

The trouble was, he couldn't look away. His gaze kept drifting back to her, to her gentle smile, her willowy grace and the way she made him feel. As if she were the answer to every question he'd ever had.

His next thought was torn away by the squeak of brakes and the crunch of tires breaking on the gravel. An older red pickup that had seen better days veered around the parked truck and skidded to a stop.

A truck he'd been hoping to see. The same license plate, make and model that was registered to a Michael M. McKaslin, according to the Department of Motor Vehicles.

Brody figured he deserved a demotion for being distracted while undercover. His captain would have his head for this, if he knew. Ashamed, Brody shut the truck's hood to get his first look at his counterfeiter. They had a fuzzy picture of him from a convenience store tape and another from the bank in Bozeman where he had an account, but nothing had prepared Brody for how much the man had changed in the last few months.

His combed black hair had turned salt and pepper. Bags sagged under his bloodshot eyes. His lifestyle was catching up to him, and he had to figure he was here because they'd been tailing him all across Montana. Where there would be no lease, no utility bill, nothing to let the Feds know where he was.

"Hey, who are you and what are you doin' here?" Mick's suspicious gaze slammed hard into his.

Brody could smell the fear. Yeah, Mick was on his guard. The former rodeo rider motorcycling his way through Montana didn't know Mick McKaslin so he had to keep his cover intact. Brody held out his hand, friendly and easygoing. "I'm Brody Gabriel."

"I bet you're Michelle's new beau."

"A friend." Brody had to set aside everything he knew about Mick McKaslin, on the job, at full alert. "Not a boyfriend. Yet."

Mick chuckled, and the suspicion melted away.

"Oh, she's a great gal, my little Michelle. And hey, there she is!"

"Uncle Mick!"

Brody stepped back as Michelle raced across the yard and into her uncle's benevolent arms.

After a quick hug, she stepped away, bright and sparkling. "Where have you been? We were starting to worry. I've got pizza hot from the oven. Want some?"

"You know I do, darlin'. Would it be too much trouble?"

"No way. You know I'd do anything for you."

Brody's stomach turned to ice. What did she say? There was no way she meant it literally. No way. He wouldn't believe it. It was an expression, that was all—

"Here's a little something for my favorite niece." Mick reached into his shirt pocket and pulled out a twenty-dollar bill. "You go buy something nice for yourself next time you're in town."

Brody relaxed. The adrenaline quit squirting into his bloodstream. She was innocent, just as he'd believed.

"Oh, Uncle Mick. You can't keep spoiling me like this."

"What else is my namesake for? Now git on up to the house. I'll drag your new beau in with me. Would like a chance to talk with him."

"*Uncle Mick!*" Michelle turned a bright shade of pink. "Brody, don't pay him any attention."

A sudden gust of wind lifted a dust devil from the driveway and preceded another flash of lightning that seared the sky and seemed to make the ground crackle at their feet.

"It's time to head for cover." Mick whipped off his cowboy hat, gazed up at the sky and then looked straight at Brody. "You can never tell how safe you are. It's always best to be cautious."

An unsettling feeling slid into Brody's stomach. He followed Mick toward the house, glad he had his revolver tucked in his boot. He was determined to banish every thought of Michelle from his mind tonight.

Mick was right. A man could never be too careful.

Zero. It's the last word Brody spelled during their Scrabble match. It was also a number she needed to pay attention to. She had to be losing her mind, because all common sense told her to look the other way when Brody stalked into the room, a predator in black boots and denim, but what did she do?

Look right at him.

He was ignoring her. Following Uncle Mick to the table where her father was rifling through the morning paper he hadn't had time to read. Brody straddled a chair, the way the tough macho heroes did in Western movies, and she felt the knot of emotion harden into an aching ball.

He was a little older than she was. He was well traveled, wiser, worldly and tough. His hands were marked with scars from old cuts—probably rodeo injuries.

She set two empty glasses on the table and filled them from the iced tea pitcher. Brody didn't look up; he merely nodded his thanks.

Disappointment twisted around her, like a lasso yanking her so tight she couldn't breathe. Yep, he was fully aware of her crush. Of every word she'd created on the Scrabble board because romance had been on her mind. And what had he written?

Loner. Freedom. Single.

Yeah, she got the clue. Michelle left the pitcher on the table. "Dad, I'm going out to put up the horses."

"Thanks, sweetie." Her father answered absently, the way he did when he was preoccupied.

"Can I see the classifieds, sir?" Brody asked in that intimate wonderful baritone of his.

Hearing his voice made her long a little more.

She headed outside, where rain wet her face and washed away her tears.

Chapter Seven

Michelle burst into the kitchen and startled her mom, who turned from the cutting board. "Good morning, sweetie. Where are you off to in such a hurry?"

"Town. I'm meeting Jenna at the diner for breakfast."

"Make sure you eat a well-balanced meal, now." Smiling her approval, her mom returned to dicing potatoes for the frying pan. "Will you be here for supper? Kendra's coming."

"Oh, I've got a late appointment at the Snip & Style, and then I'm going to do Jenna's hair."

"Dear, I guess I won't see you until bedtime. You call me if you're not home by ten, you hear? A mother worries. Oh, and did you hear the good news?"

Michelle stole a raw slice of potato from the pile

on the counter. Its sweet crispness exploded over her tongue as she chewed. "You mean about Kendra's new foal?"

"No, dear. Although that reminds me, I need to call her. She's bringing potato salad to supper today. I need her to bring dessert, too. Anyway," Alice continued, as she returned to her slicing, "Uncle Mick's going to buy us out."

"What?" Michelle's keys tumbled from her fingers and crashed on the linoleum at her feet. She knelt to retrieve them, but the shaking didn't stop. Sell the land? Dad was selling the land? Her stomach twisted into knots. "When did you all decide this?"

"Your father's been looking to retire for some time, you know that."

"Sure, but—" Michelle bit her bottom lip before her thoughts could escape. "You'd let Uncle Mick have this place?"

"Your father wouldn't take a contract on the land, Mick's offered us cash. Of course, that doesn't include the twenty acres the house and stables are sitting on. We'd be staying here, so don't look so alarmed, sweetheart."

Michelle's head was spinning.

Sell the land? How could they have done something so drastic without even mentioning it? Her feet felt unsteady as she headed toward the door. Numb inside, she was on autopilot, turning the knob, pulling open the door, stepping through the threshold. "Are you sure you want to sell?"

"We're seeing the lawyer this week." Her mother sure seemed happy at the news. Done with her chopping, she grabbed a bowl and slid the big heap of diced potatoes into it, using the edge of the knife. "Don't worry. You'll always have a home with us."

Michelle tried hard to smile. This was good news for her parents. They had been tied to the land for so long. And now that their family was raised and they were reaching their retirement years, they would have enough money to do anything they wanted.

This was a lot better for them than if they'd been offered a real estate contract. A cash-out deal was a great opportunity for them.

"You have a good day, okay, Mom? Give me a call if you need me to pick up anything in town for you."

"That's a good girl. I might just have to do that. Goodness, your grandmother and I had the best time last night. Holly Pittman's wedding was such an event, I tell you."

"I'm glad." Michelle managed to make it to the back porch.

Since her knees were quaking, she took it as a sign she ought to sit down. The porch step's boards were rough and weathered, but warm from the sun as she settled onto them.

The sweet morning air breezed over her face like a kiss, and Keno grazing with the other horses in the white fenced paddock lifted his head and whinnied a greeting.

This land was her life. She'd lived here every one of her twenty-two years. Her childhood was here. She'd thought that her future might be here, too.

A shiny quarter landed on the flagstones at her feet.

Brody strode around the corner. He wore a simple white T-shirt and faded Levi's. "Hey, I'd pay you a penny for your thoughts, but you looked so serious, I figured it would cost me more."

"I *was* deep in thought, but then someone interrupted me." She managed to smile. And tried hard not to think about how he wasn't actually looking at her but at the nail beginning to pop up out of the bottom step.

"Sorry. I'm here to fetch breakfast and paint the final coat on the garage. Is your mom inside?" He stuck his hands in his front pockets as if he didn't know what to do with them.

"Yep." She stared at her fingernail polish that was starting to chip. She'd have to fix that. "I hear you get your bike back today."

"Yep."

That meant he'd be leaving. To each thing there is a season, she knew. The Lord had meant for Brody to cross her path. Surely, He had his reasons. "I hope you have a safe journey. That no more deer leap into your path unexpectedly."

"I appreciate it." He started up the edge of the steps, as far away from her as the banister would allow. "It looks like I might not be leaving yet. You know that ad your father put in the newspaper?"

"For seasonal help?"

"That would be the one. I'm thinking of staying, if your dad will have me."

"There's a reasonable chance of that." When she smiled, he'd never seen anything so lovely.

"I never thanked you for everything you did for me that night when I was hurt. I was lucky I was just banged up. If I'd been really hurt, it was good to know I wouldn't have been lying in the road alone."

"No problem. I'm glad you're all right, Brody. Really. That you're able to go on your way, healthy and all in one piece." She felt her stomach clench, because she knew from her older sister's death how final an accident could be. How precious everyone's time was here.

That she shouldn't waste it pining away for something that wasn't meant to be. "I'm glad I could help out. But why would you want to stay here?"

Did he tell her the truth? Not about the mission, but *his* truth? He hesitated, so that one foot was on the top step beside her. "I'd like to work on a farm again. I've been thinking about getting some land. I have a little pocket money saved up. Listening to your father and uncle last night got me to thinking about wide-open spaces."

"Land." Michelle turned wistful. "I'd like that someday, too, but it's way expensive. So that's why I live at home. Okay, the card debt is another, but that's not the only reason. As exciting as big cities must be, I can't imagine living forever bound by concrete and steel.''

''You're happy here.''

''It's what I am. A country girl.'' She bowed her head and shrugged, as if she'd confessed too much.

Why was it that he could see her dreams? Brody knew without asking what she wanted.

He saw it all in an image, as if it were a thought of his own. Horses grazing in all these carefully groomed paddocks, which were empty but for a few animals. Hay and alfalfa in the fields, riding a green tractor over the rolling hills, cutting and baling and praying for good weather.

To know the freedom of the wind, the sun and the land.

''I know what you mean.'' He cleared the gruffness from his voice. ''I guess it's hard to take the country out of the boy. Or the farmer.''

''Is that why you're retiring from the rodeo?''

''The best part of my life sometimes feels like it's behind me. I don't know if I'm trying to find my past.''

''Or your future?''

''Exactly.'' How could she know? Brody knew full well he ought to be heading inside; he had work to do.

He couldn't seem to step forward, so he sat beside her. ''Some of the best memories I have are of being on the tractor with my dad, held safe on his lap, riding out to check on the livestock. Companionable, just the two of us.'' He gazed into the distance.

''Guess I want to bring back those memories of my dad. Maybe I'll get lucky and find the right woman to marry, so I'll have a son of my own to take out on the tractor. Guess I'm looking for a new life.''

Michelle could hear the longing in his voice. How amazing they had this in common, too. Her heart squeezed. There it was, that connection again, unseen but tangible. Gazing into his eyes, feeling the warmth of his understanding, she was afraid to move for fear of breaking the fragile bond.

It was as if they were breathing together, and she'd never felt so close to anyone. Not physically, but emotionally. It felt as if a string stretched from her heart to his, like those homemade mittens her mom had made her wear when she was in kindergarten. The kind with a string of yarn sewn from one mitten to the other so they wouldn't get lost in the snow.

''I know what you mean,'' she confessed. ''When I was born, I guess my dad always figured out that after six girls he'd never have a son, so I think I sort of was his. I hung out with him, rode in the tractor and the combine. When I was old enough, I helped bring in the crops. I drive a harvester better than anything else.''

''Judging by the dents in your truck, I sure hope so.'' He tossed her a wink and made her laugh.

''I know. You're like everyone else. As if a dented

truck and the 411 on the latest fashion trends is the most that you can expect from me.''

''That's not what I think.''

''It's not?''

Please, Lord, help me find the strength to hold back the truth. Brody knew if he said the words he was thinking, he'd tell her what a good and kind person she was. Wonderful and unique. So fresh and untouched and amazing, different from any woman he'd ever met.

He would tell her that when he was back home in Virginia, in his two-bedroom town house and he closed his eyes on another day of hard work done, he was alone—as he'd been for all his adult life.

He would tell her that when he looked inside his soul, she was what he'd been dreaming of.

He was on a mission. He had a job to do. But not forever, he realized. Soon, he would be free to find a whole new life.

Maybe, he reasoned, dreams could come true.

He didn't say another word as he climbed to his feet and ambled into the house. Leaving her wondering. Yeah, he could feel her wondering.

He was wondering, too.

''You look worse than you did last night, and that was with face paint.'' Hunter surveyed Brody up and down as he was covered in the shade of a cottonwood grove. They were halfway between town and the

McKaslins' ranch. "Looks like they've been working you to death."

"I had to really push hard to get that second coat of paint on the garage before noon." Brody, astride the repaired Ducati, whipped off his helmet and let the puff of breeze from the river cool his hot skin.

"Did you bring up the ad in the paper?"

"I waited until Alice was driving me into town to pick up the bike. She was happy with my work, she didn't see why Pete wouldn't hire me on for a while. It could take some time, judging by the way Mick looked me over." Brody told Hunter about Mick's cash offer for the McKaslins' property.

"He'd cheat his own flesh and blood." Hunter looked disgusted. "That may be one way we'll nail him. He's been lying low."

"Think someone tipped him off?"

"Anything's possible. How's that ankle of yours?"

"I heal quick. The sprain was minor. The bike took the worse damage. It turns out the town mechanic is married to one of the daughters. Zach. He offered to show me some riding trails, if I stay around."

"Sounds like a good opportunity. As close as you can get to the family, the better information we can get."

Brody checked his watch. "I've got to get back. Are we still on for tonight?"

"Midnight." Another night of watching Mick's bungalow. Of lying stomach down on the earth letting the snakes hiss at him. "I'll meet you there."

Brody strapped in the small pack, containing the laptop computer he needed and a few extra gadgets. ''Take care, buddy.''

After he was back on the two-lane road heading north, he spotted a set of tire marks on the pavement where Michelle had skidded to a stop when he'd wiped out. They'd met right here, he thought, and figured it was a sign that he'd even thought about that moment.

He was getting soft. Tough successful agents didn't get distracted by sappy stuff like that.

What he needed to do was to put all thoughts of her aside until the job was done. Then he could start to wonder if she was his future. If there was a chance…

No, he wouldn't think about it. He'd wait until the case was closed and his loyalties were undivided.

That sounded simple. Right?

Wrong. Brody sat in the front room of the second-story apartment and watched the McKaslin house. He'd picked up groceries at the local store and had a package of frozen pizza pockets picked out for dinner tonight, but right about the time he was going to nuke it, he heard a car door slam in the carport below.

Michelle? He'd missed her all day. He'd finished painting the trim on the garage, and accepted Pete's offer to work the next few weeks, just until the first cutting of hay was in. He'd gotten in a hard afternoon in the fields, where Mick worked with the determination of a man on a pilgrimage.

He was lying low. Had Lars Collins gotten word to Mick before Lars was arrested? It had been quiet, they'd made sure of it, but just in case, Brody made sure his revolver was within reach.

He was a patient man. He knew how to wait. And when to move. He'd earn the family's trust, and Mick's as well.

"You did a good day's work, son," Pete told him on the way in from the fields. "I'm glad to have you working for me."

It felt good to have the man's respect, and Brody thanked him for it.

The sun was setting, and family that had gathered for supper at the McKaslin house were leaving. Maybe he'd just pop his head out the door and see if Michelle had come home without him noticing.

Brody opened the door. Michelle's parking spot was empty. But there was Zach helping his wife into a new SUV. He would have been a friend under different circumstances. Zach looked up and asked how the bike was running. Brody could only compliment the mechanic's work.

"Working for Pete this time of year," Zach told him, "you won't get much time off. Sunday, I'll show you those trails I told you about. Give me a call if you want."

It was an offer of friendship. But he was working. They could not be real friends. Wasn't that too bad?

What he did accept was the chance to get closer to all the family members. "I sure will."

He felt horrible as he returned to the silent apartment.

Michelle hadn't come home as twilight lengthened and night stole the last of the shadows from the hills. When Hunter's small rock tapped against the glass window, Brody noticed Michelle's truck still wasn't in her covered parking spot.

"She's in town at the diner eating ice-cream sundaes with a girlfriend," Hunter told him the minute they were away from the house. "Don't think I haven't noticed a change in you. She's a pretty girl, but don't get distracted, man. This is serious business."

"You don't have to tell me." He slung the rifle over his shoulder, shrugging the strap into place. Professional. That was what he was.

Then why was she lurking in the back of his mind? How she'd looked this morning sitting on the porch step, not cheerful and sparkling as she usually was, but quiet. And filled with a longing he could feel. Dreams he could see.

Had the Lord brought him here for a reason? While he was lying belly down in the fields with Night Vision binoculars watching Mick's bungalow, he had time to wonder. Was there a greater reason why he'd met Michelle?

As the hours passed, and her truck's headlights cut

a bright path through the night, it was as if the stars flickered more brightly.

He felt the answer deep in his heart. *Yes.*

''He's coming!'' Michelle whipped forward, nearly knocking her Bible from the pew beside her. She caught it before it tipped, pulse pounding. She'd figured her mom would invite Brody along, but she'd had to get to the coffee shop early and hadn't been able to know if he was coming for sure.

It had been killing her all morning, wondering if she'd see him today.

He was staying. He didn't have to do that. His bike was fixed, his wounds were healing. He could hop on his snazzy red motorcycle anytime he wanted.

But he wanted to stay.

Sure, because he wanted to work on the land again. She knew he hadn't stayed here for any other reason—like for her. She understood how powerful a dream could be.

If she couldn't have her dream, then maybe Brody could find his. Maybe that was why he'd come into her life. To work on her family's ranch. To find both his past and his future, so that when he left them, he knew what would bring him happiness.

I want that for him, please, Lord, she prayed.

She knew the moment Brody spotted her in the crowded church. She could feel the sharp hook of his gaze on her back. Why was he coming after her? Mom and everyone were on the other side of the church. *That's* why she picked this side, where she could hide with Jenna—they were both short enough that they'd been hard to find behind the Pittman family, who were very tall except for Mrs. Pittman and she always wore a hat.

Michelle had hoped she would be perfectly camouflaged, but no. Her life could not go as smoothly as that.

Jenna twisted around in the pew. "Is that Brody?"

"Don't look right at him!" Then he'd know she'd been talking about him. He'd guess her crush was turning into something much more powerful. What would she do if he knew how she felt?

She was trying not to feel anything.

How was she going to deal with him? She'd be cool. She'd be in control. She would not blush or see the dreams he'd told her about in the early morning light. Dreams so like her own.

Friendly. That's what she'd be.

"Michelle! You didn't say you rescued the most gorgeous guy ever! No wonder you have a thing for him."

"I don't have a thing for him."

"Then can I have a thing for him?"

"Jenna!" Then Michelle realized her friend was teasing. "Go ahead. He's a nice guy."

"Sure, you're just head over heels over him. And why not? He's rad. No, don't deny it. You can't fool me."

"Shhh! He's going to hear you."

"Why not? Maybe you should tell him—"

"No, there's no way he can know. He probably already does—" A black leather boot halted at the end of the row. "Oh, hi, Brody."

Just how much of their conversation had he overheard?

She looked up and saw the dark gleam in his eyes. The questioning crook of his brow left no doubt.

Yep. He'd heard.

Was she ever going to stop humiliating herself around him? "This is my best friend, Jenna. Are you trying to find my parents?"

"No, actually, I was looking for you. It's nice to meet you, Jenna." He offered a polite nod to Jenna and moved into the row. "Michelle, would you scoot over?"

"You're going to sit here and torture me?"

"Sure. Besides, you've got good seats."

"This isn't NFL." She waited for Jenna to shift over, so she could, too, taking her Bible and her purse with her. "Why are you avoiding my folks?"

"I was the topic of conversation at breakfast, when I came by to ask which church they attended. They were arguing with Mick about letting me stay. He's insulted your father hired me."

"I love my uncle, but he's unreliable." It was the nicest thing she could say. "I can't believe they're selling him the farm."

"Your parents are selling?" Jenna sounded shocked.

"No one really knows yet." Michelle's stomach soured at the thought. "At least it stays in the family, I guess, but Mick isn't a hard worker. I just think Dad wants to retire. He's a farmer with no sons to take over."

"He has five daughters," Brody added. "Not one of you wants the land?"

Michelle swallowed and looked down at her Bible. There was a pen mark on the cover and she rubbed at it with the pad of her thumb.

Brody's shoulder bumped against hers and remained a steady pressure of hot steel. "Oh, I see. Your father doesn't know."

"No." She'd never had the nerve to ask him. "How do you know what I want?"

"You're easy to read, I guess."

Oh, so this wasn't the same for him as it was for her. This feeling. The way she'd seen his dreams so clearly as if they were projected in front of her on a big screen TV. What did it mean? How was she supposed to help him?

"Are you sure you don't want to sit with my sisters? Karen said you and Zach have struck up a friendship."

"Friends are good. I need more of those, but I'd rather sit incognito with you."

"Sure, you could *try* to go incognito, but you're going to have to work for it because—"

"Of my good looks?"

"Sadly, no. Because you're not a short man. Slump

a little, and no one might notice you behind Mrs. Pittman's hat.''

"You've done this before?''

"Gone incognito? Sure. I'm always in one kind of trouble or another.''

"Shocking, because you *look* like a law-abiding citizen to me.''

"Oh, not that kind of trouble. What kind of person do you think I am?''

The nicest person he'd ever met. "I bet you speed. That's breaking the law.'' He knew because those two tickets were all he'd found on her record. All paid promptly.

"Both times I was talking on my phone and didn't notice I'd crept over the limit. I haven't done that in an entire ten months. I'm very responsible. And why am I defending myself to you? What about you? What kind of laws do you break?''

"Every one.''

That made her cover her mouth with her slender, soft hands to hold back genuine laughter. He liked the sparkles that glittered in her pure blue eyes. The rosy color her cheeks turned, and her sweetness. He felt as if he could talk with her and make her laugh for every day to come.

You know I'm looking for a new life, Father. Since he was already in church, the good Lord felt a little closer. *Is this woman supposed to be my new life?*

The choir chose that moment to begin a sweet harmony of reverence that felt like an answer.

Speechless, Brody felt frozen to the pew. Gentle music filled the air, but even more reverent was his awareness of the woman at his side. The brush of her arm against his sleeve and the faint fragrance of strawberries from her hair. They were breathing together, in and then out, the same rhythm, the same *everything*.

Distance, Brody. Remember your duties. Stay distant. Keep your objectivity.

As worshipers shuffled into place and hurried down the aisle to join their loved ones, he reached for the hymnal the same moment Michelle did. Their hands touched, and he felt as if the light of the sun warmed him for the first time.

Making him wish. Making him see the future that was to be.

Chapter Eight

Michelle thought of Brody all through the service. She tried to concentrate on Pastor Bill's sermon, but her mind kept drifting off, even when she was trying to stop it. She knew exactly who to blame: the man at her side. Who'd come under friendly terms, and the last thing she wanted to be was his friend. Why else had he bantered with her, not as a man interested in courting her but a man with strict boundaries in place.

Friends. Was that something she could accept?

He was like a hero who stepped out of the movie screen and into her life. A man who seemed to *fit*. He loved horses and Scrabble and wide-open spaces and—

Stop thinking about him! She was in the Lord's house of worship. As if she should be even thinking of a man, even in the most chaste and respectful way.

What she should be doing was filling her mind with pious thoughts. Pondering the deep spiritual significance of the minister's words. *That's* what she should be doing.

One day, when she arrived at the pearly gates, St. Peter was going to shake his head at her in disappointment and say, "You should have been paying attention! There's a demerit section, you know. And that's where you're heading, missy!"

She concentrated on today's chosen passage from Chronicles. "Worship and serve Him with your whole heart and with a willing mind. For the Lord sees every heart..."

And she felt assured the Lord could see hers. He had a plan for her, she had to stop worrying about what was to come. To accept each day the Lord gave her and cherish it. She would do the best she could with this day.

And what about Brody? She couldn't help it. There she was, thinking of him again. He appeared to be the model of respect as he bowed his head for the final prayer.

She did, too, concentrating hard on the minister's words. She was so grateful for every blessing in her life. She wanted the Lord to know that. She wanted Him to know she did her best to follow her faith and live by His word.

And as the service ended and shuffling filled the sanctuary, Brody turned to her. "That was a good service. I sure like your minister."

"He's been here since I was in middle school. He's like a second father to everyone." She felt peace deep within her. Because now she had her answer. She knew what she was going to do about Brody.

She was going to forget that he'd guessed she had a crush on him, and she would trust the Lord's purpose in bringing Brody here. She would be his friend.

Whatever path unfurled from that would be the best one, for it was in the Lord's hands.

"Rick alert!"

Jenna's urgent whisper cut through Michelle's thoughts. She jerked to attention.

Two choices. She could stand here and smile with as much dignity as she could manage, or she could leave. If she got in the aisle far enough ahead of him, then she could avoid him entirely.

That was another problem about living in a town so small, you couldn't hide from anyone. You couldn't hide from the man who'd broken your heart.

Brody had risen, all six feet of him, blocking her only escape. Unless she wanted to take on the rest of the Pittman family at the other end of the bench, who were all busily trying to gather shoes and purses and children, then she was trapped.

Brody was such a gentleman, but he was blocking her only escape by politely waiting for the other worshipers to file down the narrow aisle first.

Michelle leaned close to whisper and inhaled his fragrance. Spicy and manly and, hmm, really nice.

"You don't have to wait. There's an opening. Just push your way out there."

"What's your hurry?"

"I've got places to go, people to see." Old boyfriends to avoid. "Please."

"I guess." He waited until there was a clear opening before stepping into it and stood for Michelle to ease out in front of him.

"Thank you, you are such a good shield!" She sparkled up at him with the kind of gratitude he'd expect to see if he'd saved her life.

Then she pulled her friend to her side. Why was Michelle rushing off with her friend? They were like two impatient salmon swimming upstream, careful not to crowd anyone, but making a clear run for the door.

He followed her. He was on the job, of course it was his duty to observe members of the McKaslin family. Mostly, he wanted to know more about this woman who, he figured, might be the one woman on earth who would always keep him guessing.

Michelle glanced over her shoulder, looking down the aisle, and Brody turned, too. He saw a river of faces he didn't recognize. Was she trying to avoid someone? Who?

She'd slipped away from him. He could just make out the top of her golden head in the crowded vestibule. He muttered, "Excuse me," and tried to keep up with her, but she was out the door before he could step foot near the exit.

Then, when he finally made it into the hot blast of noontime sun, he saw her, the white eyelet dress swirling around her as she helped an elderly lady down the last of the narrow steps.

"You're a dear, you know that?" the woman said, safely on the walkway and settling back on her cane. "I'm looking forward to my appointment on Tuesday."

"Where we'll make you even more beautiful." Michelle flashed the woman a genuine smile.

And like a bullet to his heart, he felt the shock of it. The finality of it. This woman of quiet country goodness and unshakable kindness was the woman he was going to marry. And why? Because what lay lodged in his heart was no bullet at all, but a love so hard and strong, it felt as if it were made of steel. Unbreakable. Unalterable.

Families surged around him, kids running loose away from family members or back again. Real life, bright in the sunshine and as tangible, was everywhere he looked.

They were the people he'd served so long and hard to protect. Whom he'd made enormous personal sacrifices for. Long, lonely years of hard training, harder work and heartbreaking consequences. Friends he'd buried. Innocence he'd lost. Crimes and horror and death that haunted him. That had changed him.

Soon it would be his turn to pass on the weight of responsibility and live a life like this. Where plans for family barbecues were talked aloud and carried on the wind. Where children laughed, arguing over the window seats, where polished and well-kept cars, be they new or old, ferried away their passengers to homes and restaurants and barbecues.

"What are you doing just standing there?"

He looked down to see Michelle at his side, fingering her long bouncy hair out of her eyes with her slender, sun-browned hand.

Tenderness filled him, sweet and heavy like honey. "Figuring out what I want to do next. I have the afternoon free. The weather's good, and your dad's taking the whole day off."

"You start haying tomorrow?"

"Looking forward to it."

To Michelle's surprise, he did seem excited by the idea. The crick at the corner of his mouth was a grin spreading from one corner to the other, showing even white teeth. His relaxed stance said he was comfortable and happy.

Good. She truly hoped he would find what he was looking for. "I'm free, too. Jenna has a family thing she's roped into going to, but I could use company over at the diner. There's a cheeseburger with my name on it."

"What a coincidence. I think there's a bacon burger waiting for me."

"And the best tartar sauce on the planet. Trust me." Michelle took the first step toward the street, wondering how to do this. She'd never had a friend quite like Brody before. Sure, high school guys who were buddies, but friends?

Brody stalked after her and shortened his stride to match hers. "The best tartar sauce on the planet? How do you know? Have you ever been out of Montana?"

"Sure. Loads of times. Family vacations," she explained. "You know, the pile in the car, road songs until Dad couldn't take it anymore, are-we-there-yet kind of vacations?"

She dazzled him when she smiled, and he could see it, as though the memory were his own. A carload of kids, parents wondering if they'll survive the trip, while trying not to laugh at the antics of their kids but trying to appear stern at the same time.

It was a hope. A vision of what the best of a family could be. But it wasn't Michelle's past he was seeing.

It was the secret wishes within him. The ones he'd never dared to pull out and examine too closely. It wasn't macho. It wasn't tough. He was used to being alone. And to think there could be a place here for him in her life.

It was more than a prayer answered. It was a prayer answered before it was asked.

He stayed by Michelle's side down the length of the old uneven sidewalk, shaded by trees and watched over by tidy bungalows. Brody made sure his pace matched hers. That he stayed at her side—not one step ahead or one behind—all the way.

* * *

"No, I can pay for my own." Michelle began digging into her purse for a five-dollar bill. This was no different than going out with Jenna. Friends split the check, right?

"That doesn't sit right with me." Brody reached past her and tossed a fifty-dollar bill on the counter. "I'm the man. I pay."

"Oh? Well, that sounds awfully bossy of you, *plus,* I don't want to scare you off or something, thinking that makes this a date. I know how commitment shy you male types are."

"Me? I'm not commitment shy." He grabbed the white paper bags the teenager behind the counter thrust at him, along with his change.

Michelle grabbed the drinks. "Where do you want to sit?"

"I'm not sure I want to sit with you. I'm still stinging from that commitment comment."

"Well, Mr. Drifter on a motorcycle, if the shoe fits…"

He put the bags down on the nearest available booth. "You mean the boot, don't you, darlin'?"

Oh, his accent was smooth, and it ought to come with a surgeon general's warning. Dangerous. Can cause weak knees and blurry vision. Michelle dropped to the plastic bench seat.

Brody sat down across from her. "At least during a game of Scrabble men don't spell *bride* and *wedding* and *romance*."

"You had to bring that up!" Her face felt so hot it had to be glowing. "It's just…"

"I know, the way women think. Married women, single women, elderly women. It was different playing with you, that's all, instead of crusty old buddies of mine that don't often see the softer side of life." He took a big bite of his burger. Good and juicy. "Different, but nice."

Across the table, Michelle took a bite of her cheeseburger and they ate in companionable silence for a while.

"What was that back at the church? You know, when you made me knock down women and children so you could dash out into the aisle and leapfrog over people to the door."

"You have a knack for exaggeration. There was no pushing or shoving, let alone knocking people down and leapfrogging over them."

"I swear I saw a few bodies left in the aisle. In the church. Seems like St. Peter would take notice of that."

"Stop teasing me." She flicked a French fry at him. "Behave."

"I'm being a gentleman. Just sitting here finishing my vitamin B burger."

"Vitamin B?"

"Bacon. It's an essential daily requirement." He grabbed his soda, ripped off the plastic lid and drank deeply from the cup. "Stop lobbing food at me because it isn't going to distract me. Who were you trying to avoid?''

"An old boyfriend. While I know he is one of God's children, he is currently disguised by a very greedy facade. There he is." She started, turning her head away as a medium-height, medium-build, blond-haired man approached the counter.

Tan trousers. Tan riding boots. Matching shirt, buttoned up to the collar. A new looking Stetson shaded his face. Standing too straight and talking down to the teenager taking his order.

Brody didn't like him. "He can't be the brightest bulb in the pack if he let you go."

"I let him go." She took another bite of her cheeseburger, pretending as if everything was fine.

It wasn't. Brody could feel the pain inside her as if it were his own. Whatever that man did to her was bad. What kind of man could hurt Michelle? She was the kindest person ever.

Protective anger tore him inside out. But he didn't act on it. He crushed the hamburger wrapper in his fist until it was a small, crumpled ball.

What he ought to do is head back to the ranch. He had files to study on his laptop and surveillance data to analyze. There was always the chance that Alice would invite him over for supper and give him a better opportunity to earn their trust. Not to use them, but to protect them.

That's what a responsible, seasoned senior agent would do.

But that isn't what he wanted to do.

He had to be crazy as he held out his hand. "Ever been on a motorcycle?"

"No." Delight sparkled through her like sunshine through the finest of diamonds.

Flawless and pure and unreachable, that's what she was, and she was *his*.

"Are you saying you'd take me for a spin on your bike?"

"Sure. For the right price." He stood, holding out his hand, palm up, to help her from the seat.

Her palm settled against his, a perfect fit. When she smiled up at him, he saw eternity.

It wasn't like riding a horse at full gallop, not in the least. It was more like flying low, Michelle decided as she clung to Brody's solid back. The pavement swooshed into a black blur whenever she looked down. So she didn't look down.

Did she worry about them crashing? No. Brody felt so in control. Competent. She had no problem trusting him completely. He was just that kind of man. Strong, inside and out. Of will and character. With her arms wrapped around his back, she could *feel* it in him.

She'd never met a man like Brody. He was perfect, like knights of old in their tarnished armor, strong and gallant and wise. She longed to lay her cheek against the hard plane of his shoulder blade and just hold on to his goodness and strength.

Of course, the helmet he'd made her wear prevented that. Plus she'd be acting like a forward schoolgirl with a crush and then he would know for sure that she wanted so much more than the friendship she was destined to have with him.

All very good reasons, but they couldn't stop the longing inside her. *I wish he loved me. More than anything. I wish he wanted me forever.*

Some things weren't meant to be. She accepted that. But deep in her heart she would always love him. Always.

She was grown up enough to accept the Lord's wisdom in guiding her life. Some things weren't meant to be for a greater reason. She believed that the Lord would take both her and Brody on the best paths for each of their lives.

Sure, it would be separate paths, but for now, for His reasons, their paths had crossed. And she would enjoy this rare time with Brody while she had the chance.

Wasn't every moment in this life a gift? Every loved one a great blessing?

Brody was one of those wonderful gifts, and she savored the minutes that sped by like water through a sieve—so fast that she hardly had time to cherish the closeness of being with him. Of holding him tight before he took the last exit off the freeway at the mountain pass and circled back.

As they rode beneath the cheerful blaze of the summer sun toward home, she fought a heavy sadness that grew with each mile. When the ride ended, she would have to let him go.

Brody hated the sight of the McKaslins' driveway, marked by the well-groomed gravel turnout and the red barn mailbox planted neatly to one side.

He downshifted, kicked out his foot to keep the bike well balanced as he made the sharp turn. He felt Michelle's arms tighten on his shoulders.

On the return trip, she'd been inch by inch loosening her hold on him. He missed the warm band of her arms wrapped around his back. Tenderness burned within him, sharp and aching.

He'd never known any emotion like this. Made of respect and awe and wonder. It felt more powerful than any physical force on earth—and it was inside him. A fierce devoted love that felt as if it were in the very center of every cell and the very essence of his soul.

The McKaslins' two-story house came into sight amid the green fields and rolling hills. He saw a familiar SUV in the driveway and another motorcycle parked next to it. A man was taking off a helmet— Zach. He was a little early for their agreed upon time. Brody hated having to say goodbye to Michelle even five minutes sooner than he had to.

He stopped the bike. Killed the engine. Felt Michelle's hands lift away from the curve of his shoulders. Moving away from him. Taking a part of him with her.

"That was fantastic!" She whisked off his helmet and shook her hair so that silken strands breezed against his arm. "I want one of those, but Dad would put his foot down."

"So hard, it would make a tunnel to China." Zach walked up, swinging his helmet by the chin straps. "I see you've had Michelle as a tour guide. Maybe you don't need me. I could always head on home. Karen's got everything set up for a get-together tonight. Brody, you're invited, by the way."

"Hey, thanks." He'd like that. But did that mean he wouldn't get to spend the evening with Michelle? Or was she part of the get together?

"I'm bringing my Monopoly board. Ooh! I have to remember to call Karen and tell her." As if in answer to his unspoken question, Michelle let him steady her as she climbed off the bike.

A surge of love washed over him as he enfolded her hand in his. How could he hold back this powerful tide within his heart?

Unaware of his feelings, Michelle flashed him a smile, the kind that came from not just surface beauty, but from within. "I had the best time, Brody. Thanks. I'll remember this always."

"Me, too." I love you, he wanted to say. But how could he? They weren't alone. He was on assignment. And she appeared to have no obvious feelings for him.

He thought of something less revealing to say to her instead. "This sure is some beautiful country here. The more I see of it, the more I can't believe my eyes.''

"That's how we all feel." She finger combed her tangled hair with her free hand and spun away, with as much energy as a young filly, all legs and lean lines and spirit. "Oh, here's your helmet. Like I need it in the house."

"You never know. A falling meteor might crash through the roof. A sudden tornado might roll by."

"It's a clear sky." She brought with her the scent of strawberries and goodness as she handed him his headgear. "I won't hold you up. I know you two handsome dudes have hills to conquer. Trails to blaze. See ya later!"

"Later." Brody revved his bike, cutting off the sound of his voice, keeping his emotions private.

He waited until she'd skipped up the steps and disappeared inside the house before he released the accelerator and the engine quieted down to a low rumble.

"So that's why you're sticking around." Zach was buckling his helmet's chin strap. "You're sweet on Michelle."

"Sweet on her? Nah." That was only the truth. He was to the marrow of his bones in love with her. "I'm just short of cash, and working for Pete seemed like a good idea."

"Sure it is." Zach's chuckle was warm, not censuring. "I could always use another brother-in-law. And before you deny it, I saw the way you were look-

ing at her. A man only has that expression on his face
when he means business. She's a real nice person.
She'd make a good man a fine wife.''

"I know. I'm not out to hurt her, if that's what this
is about.'' His resolve was steel. He loved her. He
would never hurt her. He'd die first.

"I'm not worried. You're more than you seem,
Brody. I like that. C'mon. I'll show you some of the
best trails you've ever ridden.''

Already missing Michelle, Brody turned his bike
away from the house and followed Zach's dust trail
down the dirt service road that spliced the ranch in
two.

He might have left her behind, but his thoughts
remained faithfully on her. As they would be for the
rest of his life.

He was here on false pretenses. That was the problem. So, how was he going to make her believe his
heart was true?

Well, he *was* one of the best agents in his division
for a reason. He was capable. He was determined.

He'd find a way to make her believe in his love,
with the Lord's help.

Chapter Nine

Michelle tapped along the new cement driveway and up the walk to the front steps of the brick front two-story house and rapped on the glass panel of the screen door. She didn't want to ring the bell in case baby Allie was asleep.

There was no answer, so she juggled the grocery bags and the huge straw bag she'd thrown all her stuff in, and opened the door. "Karen?"

She heard footsteps overhead and sure enough, there was Karen popping around the corner newel post on the landing. "Thanks for not ringing. I just put Allie down. She's actually *sleeping*."

"Oh, that means I have to wait to snuggle her." Michelle laid her bag and sacks on the breakfast bar. "I picked up dessert. Look. Whipped cream. Ice cream."

"I've got syrups and sprinkles." Karen whizzed

past her, balancing a laundry basket on one hip, and opened the laundry room door. "When Zach gets back, we'll barbecue. He was glad to have someone to go trail biking with."

"Oh, so he told you about Brody?" *Act cool, Michelle. Chill.* There was no reason to let everyone know about her crush on Brody. She piled the container of Neapolitan ice cream into the freezer as if finding enough space on the wire racks was what really mattered. "I guess he's working for Dad or something."

Karen set the basket down on top of the washer with a thunk. "I guess so. Mom pointed him out to me in church. Sitting right next to you."

Remember, be calm. "He's only a friend. I hardly know him."

"Mom made it sound as if you'd saved his life when he'd crashed on the road, avoiding a mother deer and her fawn." Karen cast a sideways glance, like a detective after the truth.

No way! Michelle thought of Bart, the neighboring farmer who kept trying to ask her out. Maybe a mental picture of him would help. "He got scraped up and hurt his ankle. He's fine. He was nowhere near death."

"Mom sings his praises."

"Oh, really? I guess he's nice enough." Michelle closed the freezer door and wadded up the plastic grocery sacks for Karen's reuse container under the sink. "Did you want me to set up the game?"

"Sure. Kirby called. She's on her way. Kendra should be here any minute—" A light rap rattled on the screen door. "There she is now."

As Karen rushed off to let Kendra in and inform her of the sleeping baby, Michelle felt horrible. It was the first time she'd ever been dishonest with her sister. She hadn't meant to lie. She'd only been trying to protect her heart.

And why? It was already too late. She'd never had a chance with Brody. She never would. He was...*Brody*. Everything she'd ever dreamed a man should be.

They were friends, that was all. In that, she'd told Karen the truth. As hard as it was, Michelle accepted it. Brody treated her like a friend. He could have taken that friendship to a new level this afternoon, on their trip together.

But he hadn't. No. She knew he never would.

Setting aside her disappointment, Michelle greeted her sister and concentrated on unpacking the game.

Michelle tried to pay attention as Kirby rolled the dice across the crowded board.

"Ha!" Karen's cry of victory echoed in the high ceilings of the kitchen nook. She'd apparently already counted ahead and was consulting her property deeds for the amount of rent due, even though Kirby hadn't moved her token yet and Allie was yawning, just awake, on her lap. "Let's see, since I own all three properties and I have houses, you owe me seven hundred and fifty dollars.''

"I'm going to go broke!" With a good-natured laugh, Kirby counted out her play money, handing over one butter-colored hundred bill after another. "Michelle, want to partner up with me?"

"No, I want to win, thank you very much." Her sisterly teasing made everyone laugh and neatly covered up the fact that her thoughts had drifted off to Brody. Again.

Kendra stole the dice, rolled and gave a victorious "All right! Ventnor Avenue. I'll buy it," she said of the last few available properties.

The image of Brody, powering the motorcycle over the lush grass hills flashed into Michelle's mind. Even though he'd been riding away from her...

"Earth to Michelle!" Karen thumbed through the property deeds and tossed the one marked in yellow across the board to Kendra. "I don't think she's paying attention. I wonder where her thoughts could be?"

"And on whom?" Kirby asked, as if she already knew the answer.

"I was wondering if I should buy more houses." Okay, that was a lie; the second one she'd told in two hours! Horribly guilty, she grabbed her assortment of deeds and thumbed through them. Now she would have to think about what to buy to make an honest woman of herself.

Kendra gathered up the dice and slid them across

the Free Parking square to Michelle. "I don't know. I haven't met the man, and I know Mom and Dad are singing his praises, but that Brody looks like trouble to me."

"That's what we like about him," Kirby added.

"Not *that* kind of trouble. The bad kind." Kendra refused to budge on her opinion. "I just think Michelle should be careful."

"Why should I be careful?" Michelle grabbed hold of the dice and shook.

She let go of the dice and they somersaulted across the board and into one of Karen's hotels. She hadn't breathed a word to anyone how she really felt. But if they already suspected she had a major-league crush on the guy, then how could she act as if he were no big deal? If she admitted it, then she'd never hear the end of the teasing from Karen and Kirby and the scolding from Kendra, who was very suspicious of men in general.

"Brody is just some guy Dad hired to help with the haying, right? No big deal."

"You just keep telling yourself that," Kirby told her.

"Uncle Mick doesn't like him," Kendra added.

No big deal. Just keep saying it over and over again, Michelle. Brody Gabriel was just an average, ordinary, no-big-deal kind of guy.

Wrong, her conscience reminded her. *Everything* about Brody was a big deal. The palm of her hand, when he'd helped her off the bike, still tingled from his touch, as if he'd left stardust there to shimmer with a warm glow.

She wasn't going to pretend that she hadn't had a wonderful afternoon with him. She had. Did she hope for more? Yes. Did she expect more? No.

Sure, he'd charmed her today with his humor and his gentlemanlike behavior. It was probably easy for a man of the world like him, who'd traveled all through the south and southwest, and probably most of the country, rodeoing and probably winning one championship after another, to know what to say to a sheltered, small-town girl.

The fact that she was in love with him wouldn't matter when it came time for him to fire up his polished red motorcycle and ride away forever.

She looked up at the sound of giggling. Kirby was moving the little silver shoe, Michelle's token, all seven squares according to the number indicated by the dice.

"No, she doesn't like Brody at all," Karen commented wryly.

Michelle's face turned hot. She'd been caught. Okay, so she was a terrible actress. But she was trying to keep her head on straight, thank you very much, and that wasn't always easy.

Kendra consulted her deeds. "Michelle, you owe me seventy bucks."

Michelle blinked. "How much?"

"I'll just take it." Kendra tugged a fifty and a twenty out from where Michelle had tucked them beneath the edge of the board. "You're in big trouble if you're that far gone on him."

Michelle knew her face had to be bright red. Her skin felt hot enough to cook eggs on. "Can't we change the subject? What about Uncle Mick buying out Mom and Dad?"

"I don't know. Uncle Mick is great and everything, and he's always been good to us, but he's declared bankruptcy twice." Karen searched for the dice. "I'm afraid he'll let Dad down. What if he breaks up the land and sells it off to development?"

"That's the kind of thing he'd do," Kendra agreed. "He's always looking for easy money."

At least that worked, although the new topic wasn't any better. She loved her uncle. They all did. He was fun and sent great presents and always doted on them. But he had problems, just like anyone else. A lot of them.

"At least Dad's making Uncle Mick work this time." Karen rolled the dice. "Of course, he had to hire Brody to pick up the slack."

Kendra looked troubled. "Mick's not pulling his fair share *and* he's moved into the bungalow rent free. It's hurting Dad. What if Brody is just another man cut from the same cloth Mick is?"

"He's not. I *know* it." Michelle bit her tongue. Had she really said that? Had she really leaped to his defense with that much oomph?

Across the table, Kirby sparkled with delight. "I saw him in church, too. Of course he was hard to see behind Mrs. Pittman's impressive hat. He's not a bad-looking man. Not as handsome as my Sam, but then, who could be?''

''Or my Zach,'' Karen agreed. ''But Michelle's Brody is a close third. What do you think, Kendra?''

''He's not my Brody!'' Michelle protested. This was why she didn't want them to know!

''His looks may be all that he has going for him, but Dad did say he was a hard worker,'' Kendra conceded. ''Still, it takes a long time to know a person. People have many layers. Everyone has things they don't want you to see.''

''That's not necessarily a bad thing,'' Kirby added.

Pain flashed in Kendra's eyes from past experience, and Michelle guessed that whatever had happened to her sister wasn't something she ever talked about. It had been something that changed her opinion of men forever.

Kendra stood her ground. ''Look at Rick. We all thought he was a good guy, but he was lying to Michelle. To all of us.''

It hurt to remember how gullible she'd been. How much she'd trusted him. But what else should she have done? Approach the potentially most important relationship in her adult life with suspicion and a closed heart?

''Take your time if you're interested in this man, this Brody,'' Kendra advised. ''Promise me. There's no hurry to fall in love. No hurry to trust someone until you're sure they deserve it.''

"Love?" Karen's mouth dropped open and she searched the board for her token.

"I didn't say I was in love with him!" Michelle tipped over her iced tea.

Kendra jumped up with a napkin and came to the rescue. "Awfully defensive, aren't you?"

"No! I'm not in love with him!"

"Yes, you are. Ooh, it sounds like my husband is back from his ride." Karen looked up at the sound of a motorcycle pulling into her driveway and seemed to remember she had a hold of her token, and so she moved it. "Not so good. I'm in jail."

"Yeah, you derelict." Michelle had enough talking about Brody so she bounced out of her chair and wanted possession of her niece. "Allie can't stay in jail with you. She did nothing wrong."

"Not Allie, the most perfect baby ever," Karen agreed as she lifted her infant with one hand on her bottom into Michelle's waiting arms. "Perfect timing. She needs changing."

"Fine. That's the price I pay to get away from you guys and all your gossiping and making up wild stories about me." Michelle cuddled Allie, who promptly grabbed a handful of Michelle's hair and pulled.

"We're not imagining the blush on your face," Kirby called out. "Karen, you get to roll again."

"I'm not blushing!" Michelle said it with enough force, hoping it would make the heat on her cheeks fade. Of course it didn't. She cradled Allie close as she made her escape while she could. "And I'm not in love with him," she called over her shoulder, just to have the last word.

Did it work? No.

"Are you at least *starting* to fall in love with him?" Karen asked.

"No!" Her denial echoed in the stairwell as she started up the carpeted steps to the second story.

"Liar!" Kirby accused.

"Okay, I admit it. Just don't tell anyone else." Michelle paused on the landing where she could just see her sisters at the kitchen table around the polished newel post. "*Maybe* I've got a little bit of a crush on Brody. Okay, a *huge* crush."

She hadn't taken two steps before she heard the screen door rasp open and a man's boots hit the wood floor. Did Zach hear what she'd said? Her face flamed again. How could he have missed it? The back door had been open.

Then a second set of boots struck the kitchen floor. A tingle crawled along the back of her neck. Brody? *Please, Lord, don't let that be—*

"Hi, Brody."

"It's Brody."

Her sisters sounded way too pleased.

He'd had to have heard what she'd said. Ready to die, Michelle hugged Allie harder, glad her beautiful little niece was giving her an excuse to never go downstairs again.

* * *

"Root beer or cola?" Zach asked from behind the open refrigerator door.

Brody tried to force his stunned mind to function. Michelle's words were still ringing in his head. *Maybe I've got a little bit of a crush on Brody. Okay, a* huge *crush.*

She did?

He felt the weight of three women, Michelle's older sisters, watching him and wondering. He might be a seasoned agent, trained to handle any situation, but he wasn't prepared for this. For two women smiling at him like he was the best joke they'd ever seen, and the third looking at him as if she expected him to have a rap sheet twenty pages long.

"Uh, root beer." He was relieved when Zach handed him a cold can over the top of the refrigerator door.

He almost dropped the can. His fingers didn't work. What was with him? All he could think about was Michelle's voice replaying in his head like a recording. *A* huge *crush.*

He could see his new friend's amused response as he took a soda for himself and shut the door. Zach seemed amused but not accusing, as if they were only two men and outnumbered, so they had to stick together.

"Hey, Brody." Zach gestured with the liter bottle of soda he carried to the round table where Michelle's sisters were watching him over their Monopoly board. "Meet the rest of the gang. This incredible lady is my wife, Karen. Kendra is the horse lover of the family, and that's saying something. Kirby, here, is the sister we pretend we don't know.''

"Yeah, I'm out on five different warrants. It's shameful.''

"Says the quietest one of all,'' Zach interjected. "Would any of you ladies like a refill?''

"Such service. Thank you, handsome.'' Karen rewarded her husband with a sweet and affectionate kiss.

Brody popped the top of the can and sucked down a couple gulps of soda. The fizzy sweetness wasn't enough to wash away the ache of emotion in his throat. This nice new home with the roomy kitchen and large bay window eating area, with its warmth and simple charm and framed pictures of family on the walls. It was a house filled with love.

It amazed him that families existed like this. So one family was raised in love, and now those daughters were making homes and families of their own. Little baby things were everywhere. A swing in the family room by the sofa. A scattering of toys on the floor. It was like something out of TV.

It was new to someone who'd been alone for all his adult life. The man in him ached for what these people had. Family. Love. Friendship. The agent in him acknowledged they weren't criminals. He didn't need more surveillance to know it.

"C'mon and join us,'' Kirby invited as she started collecting up the colorful play money. "We'll start over. Everyone was about to lose to me anyway. You guys come join us.''

''I'll pop corn,'' Zach volunteered as he added soda to the rest of the glasses on the table. ''Kirby, give Sam a call. See if he's done at the airfield. What do you say?''

A round of feminine ''yeahs'' filled the room, and the warmth and coziness left Brody spinning.

An evening of Monopoly? He'd done a lot in his line of work. He'd lain on his stomach in mud and rain in the cold foothills of the Cascade Mountains surveilling an extremist group gone bad. That hadn't been pleasant.

He'd been in shoot-outs and riots. And there was the time he spent three months in east L.A. as a homeless man. That had been a tough assignment. He'd handled escaped felons, drug dealers, gang members and murderers, but never something like this.

Television shows were made of this. Not experiences in his life.

He ached with a need he couldn't name. A need he'd never paid attention to before. It overwhelmed him as everyone in the kitchen watched him expectantly.

''Sure.'' He shrugged in agreement. ''A game of Monopoly won't kill me.''

''No,'' Karen agreed, ''but Michelle might kill *you*, Kirby, when she realizes you invited Brody to stay after—'' She lifted her brows suggestively.

Michelle's words played through his mind again. *I've got a little bit of a crush.*

It blew him away. Michelle had feelings for him? He wanted to shout so everyone would know how incredible that felt. How impossible.

He couldn't—and not because it would make him look like a nut. He was on assignment—undercover, with the objective to observe the family and gather evidence to either indict them or clear them. Tonight would be an agent's dream of infiltration. They'd extended an invitation and their trust.

But there was nothing typical about this assignment or this family or this girl. No, Michelle was amazing. One of a kind. Even though she'd left the room, he could feel the echo of her heartbeat between his own. He could feel a tug of connection like an unseen string binding them together.

He felt alive for the first time in his adult life.

These feelings were new and they weren't because he'd been alone for nearly two decades. Or because he'd lost his family long ago. He knew these feelings weren't because the years since had been solitary and colorless, like a black-and-white photo with no vibrancy and no life.

He felt this way because of Michelle.

Zach brought in two chairs from the dining room table, and Brody moved to help him. Karen scooted her chair over so there was room for him right next to Michelle. The tall, silent sister, what was her name? Kendra, glared at him with warning in her eyes. He couldn't blame her. In a good family, a big sister looked out for her little sister.

"Which token do you want?" Kirby asked him as the sisters handily restocked the money and turned in the houses and hotels and property deeds. "Michelle always takes the shoe."

"Doesn't matter." He didn't care. He hadn't played Monopoly since he was a boy.

Kirby picked the top hat for him before she tossed the car at Zach.

Everybody seemed used to the routine. Zach began popping the corn. Kendra gathered up the houses and hotels. Kirby divided the play money by color.

What should he do?

Karen leaned close. "Someone's going to have to tell Michelle to come down. I could do it, but she's going to resist my best efforts. If I know Michelle, she'll find a way to stay up there forever. She's a little embarrassed."

All eyes turned to him, and Brody could feel their amusement. And their expectations.

"Go on up," Kirby urged with a wink.

Don't you do it, the seasonal agent in him ordered. There was no sense spending more time with Michelle. Not until he could close this case and come to her a free man, his work done.

But the man in him, who'd been alone for too long and saw an end to it, couldn't help it. He looked in the direction of the stairs and along the polished wood banister leading up and out of sight. If he followed that path, would it change his future?

He had evidence to find. A case to investigate. The Bureau depended on him to do his job and do it well. And to do that, he had to stay focused.

It wasn't his loneliness, he realized, that he felt so keenly here among this loving extended family. It was something greater. Something as powerful as gravity that kept the planets in alignment around the sun and the stars in place in the galaxy, and the power of it lit up his soul. Made him see what he'd been fighting so hard to ignore. For like gravity holding the moon to the earth, and the earth to the sun, so his soul was bound to Michelle's.

He set his soda can on the table and his feet led him to the stairs. Inexorably, it felt as if every moment in his life had happened for the sole purpose of bringing him here. To this place and time.

He took the first step and the next, rising up to the second story, where Michelle was. He wasn't sure his boots were touching the carpet.

Fear gathered in the pit of his stomach. He felt numb. He felt as if the love that bound them was pulling him forward, like a boat in a strong current. This was a different kind of fear than he'd known before. He was used to shoot-outs and takedowns and violent criminals. Life and death situations.

As he followed the low murmur of Michelle's voice, he felt abject terror. There was more than his life at stake. It was his future. It was his soul.

The murmur became music and he waited outside the doorway. Just looking at her. She was enough to fill his senses and his heart for eternity.

He'd never seen any woman look so beautiful. Sunshine slatted through the blinds in the big window seat behind her, cherishing her as she sat in a wooden rocker holding her precious niece. She gazed down at the infant while she sang a lullaby he didn't recognize, singing the melody so quietly, he couldn't hear the words. The gentle grace wrapped around his heart and held him captive. Opened him wide.

All he was, all he would ever be was hers. It wasn't a decision.

It just was.

As if the angels had brought him here to find the woman he was destined to love for all time.

"She's asleep," Michelle whispered to him without looking up, changing to a soft hum as she stood with her lithe elegance and carried the child to her crib.

He watched captivated as Michelle gently laid her beloved niece in the polished and well-appointed crib. Love shone in this room from the coordinated wallpaper and window coverings to the mobile and sheets. Love shone, too, on Michelle's face and in every gesture as she brushed her hand over the infant's soft blond head.

She'd make a great mom. Brody had never let his thoughts wander in that direction before. No woman had ever inspired that thought in him until this moment.

"What are you doing up here?" She didn't look at him as she stepped into the hall and she drew the door nearly closed behind her.

"I was sent up to fetch you. They're starting a new game and they're waiting for you."

"No, I mean, what are *you* doing here? In my sister's house?" She deliberately moved in front of him so that she didn't have to look at him. Because then she'd see the horror on his face. She'd see the rejection. Because he *had* to have heard her. Had to have overheard her confession.

"Zach invited me, remember?"

Great. She just knew who to thank for her humiliation. Michelle walked fast as she could down the hall, but Brody kept a pace behind her.

Thank heavens he wasn't going to bring up what he'd overheard. He wasn't going to make an issue of it. Okay, so she was clued in. There was no way that a great guy like him with the world at his feet was going to fall in love with a small-town girl like her.

So what did she do now? She felt unsteady, so she grabbed the banister railing for support. The wood was cool and smooth beneath her hand as she kept ahead of him so that it didn't feel as if they were going down the stairs together.

She took one look at her sisters, all smiling and happy for her—except Kendra, who never thought falling in love was a good idea. Even Zach was beaming. There was a rap on the screen door and through the mesh she could see Kirby's husband, Sam, a big hulk of a man, flash her a knowing wink.

They all thought it was so cute, the way she had a crush on Brody. She did *not* think it was cute. At all. Not when everyone knew about it.

"We've saved your place, Michelle." Karen gestured to two empty seats beside her. "And one for Brody. We decided to seat you two together."

Wasn't that special? Oh, this was going to be so uncomfortable! Could anything be more embarrassing than this? She didn't think so. Everyone acted as if Brody had proposed, and how crazy was that?

Well, *he* was acting as if nothing had happened. Good call. That's exactly what she was going to do, too. Just erase that comment she made so she could pretend it never happened. Hit the delete key. Press the back button and rerecord. Erase the chalk from the blackboard.

She dropped into her chair as Zach rescued a popping bag from the microwave. Sam took a seat next to Kirby, Kendra got up to get napkins, Karen asked about Allie, and through all the activity, as loud as it was, it was merely background noise to the fact that Brody was easing into the chair beside her.

Love filled her. Gentle and sweet and life changing, making her all shivery and tingly and lifting her up, as if she were sitting on a big fluffy cloud.

She was only distantly aware of Zach setting two popcorn bowls on the table. The buttery good fragrance might be one of her most favorite on earth, but not even popcorn could tear her attention away from Brody. His iron-hard arm brushed hers.

A place in her heart opened. A place she'd never known before. And it filled with a love so pure and great, she felt as if it changed her. Completed her.

"Michelle, it's your turn." Kendra nudged her. "Stop daydreaming and roll."

"Daydreaming?" She hadn't been daydreaming. This was no dream. This was real, and she was full and floating. She hadn't even got to dreaming yet.

She grabbed the dice and rolled, barely paying attention as Brody took the dice next and rolled. Did she notice what happened next? No. She was only aware of his scent, the rhythm of his breath, the brush of his skin to hers, the shift of his body, the beat of his heart within hers. The overwhelming love that left her dazed.

Kirby's husband, Sam, rolled high and started the game. She heard the tumble of the dice on the board and the groans as he dropped his token on a property.

"I'll buy. The railroads always bring me luck." Sam slapped his money down in front of Kendra, who was in charge of the bank.

Kendra separated the play bills. "Michelle, you're in charge of the properties."

"I am?" She hadn't even noticed the stack of cards someone had placed right in front of her.

Somehow she thumbed through the cards. Luckily, someone had put them in order and she didn't have to go far to recognize the deed. "Sure, like you got the first railroad, but I'm going to get the other three."

"That's what you think, kiddo," Sam threatened with a teasing wink.

"Is that a challenge?"

"More like a declaration of intent."

Kendra rolled and the dice tumbled across the board and into a tumbler of soda. She squealed when she got doubles. She moved her token onto Vermont Avenue. "I'll buy, and I get to roll again. Okay, dice. I need a seven so I can take the next railroad."

"Kendra, how's the new filly?" Zach asked.

"Shh, I'm trying to concentrate." Kendra cupped the dice, as if to exert her will on them.

Brody felt Michelle's fingers brush his wrist. "Do you think you can stand my family? Are you ready to run for the door?"

"Nah, I'm going to hang around. People who act like this need to be kept under close surveillance. Soda and popcorn and Monopoly. I saw Zach stoke up his grill on the back deck. My guess is barbecued hamburgers."

"Kendra brought the potato salad." When Michelle looked up at him, it was with a new light in her eyes. A radiance that matched the glow he felt inside.

As if a dream inside him had been brought to life. A chance for real love. For a real life. A secret wish he'd been too afraid to pray for all these years. But it had lived inside him all the same. The hope that one day he would find not what he'd lost as a boy, but what he needed as a man to make him happy. What he'd never figured he'd find—a woman of goodness and gold and spirit.

God had planned this all along. Brought him here on his last assignment.

The last thing I can do is fall in love now. In the middle of an investigation. *Please, show me what to do next, Lord.*

It felt more than wrong to be investigating these people. They were good, kind, decent. A real family with a bond that wrapped around him. Without question. Without judgement. Including him in their good times. Trusting them with their beloved youngest sister.

She sat next to him, spine straight, feigning disappointment when her sister landed on and bought Pennsylvania Railroad. Apparently it was a long-standing family battle for those properties.

"My turn!" She rolled the dice and watched them roll. "No! Oh, no."

She hid her face in her slender hands. Her gold bracelets clicked. Her earrings brushed against the soft skin against her jaw. She was so delicate and feminine and so amazing. He loved her so much that he hurt.

"I can't believe this!" Good-naturedly, Michelle laughed at herself, too, moving her little silver shoe to the Reading Railroad. "I can't believe I owe you, Sam. Yeah, I know, twenty-five bucks."

"Hand it over." Sam seemed like a good guy, holding out his hand for the rent payment. "Hey, too bad this isn't real money."

"Yeah, Michelle, you could pay off your credit cards," Karen piped in. "And buy my half of the coffee shop."

"I don't want to own your coffee shop. I love working there, don't get me wrong, but owning a business just isn't for me." Michelle gathered the dice and pushed it in Brody's direction. "I have other dreams."

Brody didn't mind the way the sisters exchanged questioning looks and amused comments. No. He knew about dreams. Because he was sitting right beside one. A dream, rare and perfect, that God had placed within his reach.

Brody vowed right there and then, as he rolled the dice and landed right next to Michelle on Reading Railroad, that being stuck beside her was exactly where he wanted to be.

For the rest of his life.

Chapter Ten

"This is so like a movie or something," Jenna said, as she loosened the reins to let her horse drink from the creek.

"Definitely a movie," Michelle agreed as she gave Keno his head so he could drink from the cool water, too, on what felt like the hottest day they'd had so far this summer.

It had been exactly a week since she'd spent time with Brody. Between her work schedules, she was gone long hours. It was a peak time for both the salon and the coffee shop. Between people getting their hair done before going on vacation and tourists spotting the coffee shop and stopping by for iced drinks and a bite to eat.

Brody had spent long hours with her dad in the fields. She'd spot him every morning when she fed and watered the horses. He'd be already hard at work, a speck against the distant fields, at her dad's side. She'd come home after dark every evening this week, and Brody's lights had been off in his apartment. Probably sound asleep from the long day of manual labor.

She missed him. It was as simple as that. And today, he hadn't been at church. He hadn't been at his apartment afterward. His bike was missing from its usual place in the carport. Where had he gone? Or maybe—she hated to think it—he'd been trying to avoid her.

The Monopoly game had been fun, with Sam and Kirby teaming up to defeat Karen and Zach. Zach had grilled burgers and they'd eaten on the shaded deck outside, talking about nothing, really. But every moment, Michelle had been aware of what she'd said. Of how he'd overheard her. Of how he didn't react at all.

The first available chance he'd gotten, he probably decided to avoid her. Keep his distance because it was easy to see what she wanted. A man to marry. A man to love. She wanted that man to be him.

"It's too romantic for words." Jenna sighed. "The mysterious stranger comes to town and falls in love with one of the locals. It's a happy ending all around. An idyllic courtship. A heartfelt proposal. A wedding of her dreams. And a husband to die for."

"Heck, why stop there? Let's make him financially well off. And he has to be happy living in a small town."

"And never leave the love of his life again."

It was too good to be real. Michelle knew that. And it hurt. "Keep dreaming, Jenna. Maybe one day it could happen."

"Dreams happen all the time on TV. You just have to know which shows to watch."

Jenna was teasing, sure. But what about real life? Michelle shifted in the saddle at the sound of a motorcycle. It was only a kid on a dirt bike revving along the public trail. Not Brody.

She shouldn't feel so disappointed. "I'm talking real life here. Sure, romance is nice, but do you know what? The problem with romantic dreams is that they involve men."

"They are *supposed* to involve men," Jenna said.

"Yeah, but men are…*men.* You know. Maybe there are fewer good ones than we think."

"I know what this is about." Jenna drew solemn as the horses, having their fill of the cool water, lifted their heads and splashed back to the trail. "This is about Rick."

"No, this is about reality. Good men don't just fall from the sky. Or fall in front of you in the road. There's always a catch." She knew he didn't want her. *That* was the catch.

"Are you saying Brody isn't a good man?"

"He's a great man. I've never met anyone like him." Longing punched inside her. "But I'm not going to let this crush turn into anything else."

It was too late, she knew. But it was her story, and she was sticking with it.

"Because he's like such a mystery? A stranger? You hardly know anything about him. He just shows up in town. That would make me nervous, too, if it came to risking all my heart." Jenna was completely sympathetic, one hundred percent understanding.

Even so, Michelle still couldn't say the words out loud. She loved Brody. If she kept it silent and to herself, then maybe it would hurt less when he broke her heart. "Mr. Wonderful, Dark and Handsome is going to leave one day. And this time around, I'm going to keep my dignity."

"This *is* about Rick!" Jenna sounded so distressed. "You can't let someone who lied to you influence the rest of your life."

"I know. I believe that, too. This is about me. If Brody doesn't know how I really feel, he can't hurt me as much."

"You don't know that. You might have to give him time. You'll get to know him more and maybe he'll get a crush on you."

"I wish." But she wasn't holding her breath. She'd probably faint from lack of oxygen.

The truth was, Rick had shattered her. He'd been her first big love. He'd come with flowers and promises and praises that made her feel cherished and special. She believed him. And when he'd betrayed her, when she found out the kind of man he truly was, she'd felt worthless. She hated to admit it, but she did. She'd let a man who didn't respect her make her feel as if she'd never be good enough.

And how bad was that?

But he was one man. Not Brody. Brody was the genuine thing. A real man. One who worked hard, lived with integrity, who had never lied to her. Never pretended.

She respected him for that. Admired him even more.

The thought of trusting a man, really trusting him, made her shake down to her soul. But when she thought of Brody, she wasn't as afraid. He was one man worth trusting. She knew it down deep.

That's how much she loved him.

They'd reached the part of the trail where the public river trail bordered her family's property. As they'd done since they were six years old, Michelle drew her horse to a stop at the path that trailed through the alfalfa fields. Her way home. "Did you want to come over and have supper with us? Tonight we're at Kirby's house."

"Nah. I'd love to, but it's my brother's birthday. We're having a dinner over at my gramma's house. I'll call you later?"

"'Kay." As they had done for almost twenty years, Michelle nosed Keno down the path that would take her home, waving a final goodbye to her best friend.

She wasn't going to think of Brody. She wasn't. What she had to do was find a way to keep the love she felt for him locked away and hidden. Her very own secret.

If only he wanted her. If only he loved her. She'd wished for a lot of things in her life, but nothing with as much genuine longing as this.

Nothing had seemed so impossible.

Keno nickered, stalling in the middle of the path. His ears swiveled and he lifted his nose, smelling the sweet-scented breeze. An odd flickering began at the nape of her neck and rose up over the back of her head. Her pulse began to pound not from fear but from recognition.

She stood up in the stirrups and saw the familiar palomino. What was their horse doing tied up out here. And wait, there was something moving in the grass. A shock of dark hair, a hard curve of steely shoulder—

Brody.

"You were right, buddy," Hunter's voice crackled in Brody's ear. "Mick may be lying low, but he can't keep away from the blackjack tables."

"It about killed me today to watch him go and I couldn't tail him." Brody had spent the better part of the afternoon coordinating the operation that kept Mick under surveillance. "Did we get him on the cameras?"

"I'm with the head accountant right now. She came in just to help us. We've got the casino's security cameras watching his every move. He hasn't passed one of his twenties. *Yet.*"

"He will. With the setup I saw today, he'll use the cash. He can always make more."

"You were in his house?"

"Yep. And the captain is going to like what I found." It was exactly what he'd been expecting, but better. Much better. "How's the warrant coming?"

"I've got to check my e-mail. Daggers was going to let me know as soon as he gets it. I'll call you. Hey, and be careful."

"You, too, buddy." Brody clicked off the phone and shoved it into his back pocket.

While he was here, he'd change the battery packs in the hidden surveillance cameras he and Hunter had set up during their after-midnight missions.

The snap of breaking grass made his blood freeze. He'd been keeping an eye the road, and he was pretty well hidden by the crest of the gentle rise of the land. So if someone was sneaking up on him, from the fields rather than the road, he was in trouble.

In a flash he saw it all: his cover blown, Mick stalking him through the grass. Years of training had him reaching instinctively for the revolver tucked in the back of his jeans.

Instinct made him hesitate, too. He didn't draw his weapon. There was *too* much noise. Something felt off. Wrong. There wasn't a threat in the air. The larks were undisturbed, squawking happily. He heard the seed-heavy grasses rustling in the ever-constant breeze and the sudden low, *whoof* as a horse exhaled loudly.

Not the horse he'd saddled up to ride out here, but another one. His horse stood at attention, ears swiveling, nickering a greeting to an approaching horse.

He felt a shock of emotion. Soft and gentle. Without thinking he swung in the direction of the river where he'd noticed a path leading to the public riding trail.

He already knew who was taking a shortcut through the field. He knew because he could feel her. He eased up out of the grasses and spotted the brim of a lady's Stetson, the bounce of a ponytail and her perfect profile. The wink of gold jewelry in the sun.

Michelle. His entire being filled with tenderness. That was the woman he was going to marry. It was the only thought in his mind.

That was wrong. It was dangerous to be this distracted. He couldn't help himself. The cowboy hat she wore was small, just enough to shade her eyes, but not the soft beauty of her face.

"Brody, is that you?" She squinted at him because of the distance. "What are you doing hiding in the grass?"

"I'm up to no good." He swiped the bits of grass and dirt from his jeans and climbed to his feet, thankful the small knapsack he'd carried camouflaged well with the grass and dirt. He'd come back to get it later. "Just out riding and took a break."

"Dad gave you permission to ride Jewel? I can't

believe it. *I* don't get to ride his favorite horse. How did you get so lucky?''

''She'd come up to the fence when I was passing by and I petted her. We seemed to strike it off.'' He gathered the mare's reins and untied them from the low bush he'd tethered her to. ''Your dad said I had a way with her, and how hard I've been working for him. So he said since I had the experience to handle her, that I might as well ride her.''

''He's a tough taskmaster, you know.''

''He likes a job done right and done well. So do I.''

''So *that's* how you won him over.'' Michelle knew the admiration showed in her voice. Her dad did have high standards, and he liked Brody. That said something about the kind of man Brody was.

''I like your dad.'' Brody pulled a mint candy from his pocket and let Jewel lap it from his palm. ''Pete and I found out we have a lot in common. One is a respect for horses. We started talking, and one thing led to another. I wound up telling him how much experience I've had in the saddle.''

From the rodeo, of course, and being around horses growing up. Michelle gave her Keno a pat on the neck, and a ''good boy'' for standing so patiently.

She swung down, the creak of the leather saddle as familiar as the ground at her feet. The mild wind, scented by the ripe grass and maturing alfalfa in the field, swept over her, as those smells had every summer of her life.

What wasn't familiar was the man striding through the grass to meet her. Even with Jewel's reins in his hand, he moved with the predatory might of a hunting wolf.

Everything about him, from his intense gaze to the indomitable set of his unshaven jaw to the hard bunch of his muscles beneath the denim fabric, made her want to run.

Every time she saw him, there was more to see. More of his strength. His power. His integrity. Like a cornered doe with no out, she tensed—too paralyzed to fight the inevitable. The secret love within her doubled, expanding through her whole being.

Stop gawking at him, Michelle. You can't let love grow for him, remember? He knew she had a crush on him, but he didn't know the truth. He didn't know the depth of what she felt. The force of it.

She needed to act as if he didn't matter. As if they could still be friends. Sure, and exactly how did she do that? It was impossible to shut off the feelings inside her. To deny her heart. Especially when he was striding through the grass with a fiercely intense look on his face.

He was coming after her like a man used to dominating everything around him. Someone who was in control and forged his own path.

That was scary, not because it was threatening, but for a whole different reason. She quaked inside, deep in her spirit, where she was the most vulnerable.

Could she let him know that? There was just no

way. "What were you doing out here? Wait. I know. You were keeping the snakes and the flies company."

He didn't crack a smile. "I'm on the lookout for the nosy female who just interrupted my nap."

"Hey! I'm insulted. I'm not nosy."

"Then what are you doing out here?" He looked intimidating, but a spark of trouble glinted in his dark gaze. "Come to spy on me, huh?"

What *was* he up to? "This is my family's land. I was passing by and decided to see what kind of varmints were infesting the field."

"No varmints here. Just an upstanding guy out for a little peace and quiet."

"Then I guess I'll just have to leave you here in the grass with the rest of the snakes," she said kiddingly, but that was not how she felt. Not at all.

She wanted to keep the conversation light, but inside she felt as if her sadness weighed a ton. Maybe two tons. Brody wasn't looking at her. He had to be thinking what he had done to deserve a woman's schoolgirl crush?

You captured my heart, that's what.

Maybe she ought to mount up and save what little dignity she had left. "Are you headed back to the house?"

"No destination, really. Just enjoying the day. Well, almost evening." His stony expression softened and he tossed her a sheepish, lopsided grin.

It was devastating. She wanted him to love her. She longed for it with her entire being.

She needed to face the truth: he didn't want her. *Stop doing this to yourself.*

She couldn't help it. Just as she couldn't stop the warm glow of tenderness within her. The most she could do was deny it. She lifted her chin, prayed for strength and the wisdom, and made her decision.

His shadow fell across her, shielding her from the sunlight. Standing before her without saying a word.

What was he thinking? He wasn't mocking her. He wasn't making fun of her. He wasn't running for the hills. Instead, he met her gaze and the impact of it felt like a great intimacy. As if he intended to see everything within her. Every gleam of love. Every burn of adoration.

It was as if there were only the two of them in the entire world. Her vow not to let herself love him any more crumbled apart and her heart split wide open.

She was defenseless against him. She'd never experienced anything as fearful and thrilling all at once—as if the solid earth had fallen away beneath her feet and she was falling down a mile-high cliff with nothing to save her from a hard and lethal fall.

Nothing, except Brody.

"I'd like to head back with you." His rumbling baritone wrapped around her like the comfort of a warm electric blanket.

"You would?" *Wow, that was brilliant conversation, Michelle. Impress him, why don't you?*

He didn't seem to be paying attention to her lame

words. He was staring at her. Did she dare to hope that was tenderness she saw in him?

No, she didn't believe it. If he loved her, wouldn't he have said something about it by now?

She turned away, moving on autopilot, inserting her foot in the stirrup. She hopped up into the saddle, pulled her leg over and settled into the seat.

Why was she on autopilot? Because she was watching Brody. He rose into the saddle like a pro. He was masculine grace and quiet control as he held the leather reins in his left hand, loose and low, just over the saddle horn.

Like a true horseman, he balanced easily between the stirrups, his weight shifting effortlessly as he placed pressure with his heels and Jewel eased forward.

What a man. Her entire being sang with the praise.

What was she going to do now? She loved Brody. More with every passing second. How was she going to hold back her heart?

Without an answer and with no defense, Michelle kept Keno a few paces behind Jewel.

Brody made his horse fall back and into place beside her.

Great. Now she had to talk to him. The longing within her was so powerful, it hurt like a gash from a sharp blade.

"What is a pretty lady like you doing unescorted on a Sunday afternoon?" His deep voice resonated along her skin like the wind, like the sun.

She wished he didn't affect her that way.

"I was out riding with Jenna."

"You do that a lot?"

"Since we were both in first grade."

"Practically lifetime friends. That must be something, to have a friendship like that. To have a life like that."

"I'm grateful." She knew that was a lame response but it was all she could think of to say. Nothing else came to mind.

What was she going to talk to him about? About how she was falling for him? *Thank you very much, but no!*

Brody cleared his throat. "Does she live very close?"

"The next farm on the back side of our land. We always meet at the fork at the river, halfway between our houses and ride for miles and miles. And talk."

"Women talking. There's a surprise." Brody's grin was slow and mellow.

His smile made her ache all the way down to her soul.

Why his smile? Why this man? Feeling this way was torture. To know that he didn't love her in return. He was unaware how much he was hurting her, but he was doing it all the same.

"You think all I do is talk on the phone and shop, right?" She braced against his answer, already knowing what he was going to say.

"That was my first impression of you."

There, she *knew* it. Was this the place where he broke her heart? Told her with a gentle hint that he wasn't interested? She braced herself for the worst.

"Then I took a closer look at the pretty girl who rescued me, and guess what I saw?"

His warmth had her looking up. Had her noticing there was no derision on his face, no disdain the way it had been on Rick's, the only other man she'd let this close. No. What she saw was something as rare and as tender as the love in her heart.

"I saw one of the most lovely women I've ever met." He gruffly cleared his voice and Jewel sped up the pace.

Michelle urged Keno forward. "*What* did you say?"

"I said it's a sorry state when circumstances force a man like me to be rescued by a woman like you. I thought you were an angel, you know. With all your golden hair. The way it shimmers like platinum in the sun."

Was he serious? Michelle's jaw dropped. She couldn't think of a single thing to say. Tears burned in her eyes. This couldn't be real, could it? Why wasn't he letting her down gently? Why was he making her love him even more? No one, *ever*, had said such nice things to her.

"Of course, you didn't know that you were helping a renegade like me."

Oh, so *this* was how he was going to let her down. By telling her all his faults, that he wasn't good for her, and so she shouldn't want to harbor romantic feelings for him. Okay, she could see what he was doing.

She could handle it. She was ready. Why wait? Her heart was already breaking. "You're a renegade, huh? I suppose you're going to say next that I shouldn't get mixed up with a bad guy like you. Is that it?"

He winced, as if he were in pain. As if she'd hit the mark. He cleared his throat, but his voice remained gruff and gravely. "You're right. I shouldn't be here with you. You shouldn't trust me."

"Why? You've made no promises. You've had no reason to lie. You work hard. Dad *compliments* you. I actually heard him."

"Well, so, I painted his garage. I fixed his tractor when it broke down in the field. I know how to hay."

"Do you know how rare Dad's compliments are? They are like the Olympics. It only comes around once every four years. Well, until they started doing it every two, but still."

She charmed him. Brody hid his chuckle because he didn't want her to think he was laughing at her. Her beautiful and buoyant spirit drew him like the moon to the earth, and she pulled at the tides within him.

He ought to be resisting her. Keeping this strictly professional. And what did he want to do? Hold her hand. Kiss her. Tell her how he truly felt. It was wrong, but he couldn't help it. He couldn't stop how he was feeling. It was like trying to stop the earth from revolving around the sun.

His love for Michelle was tugging at him, tearing at his resistance. Making him wish for a future.

Maybe he didn't have to choose. Maybe he could love her and do his job. He was a good agent. He was a strong-willed man. He could separate the personal feelings from the professional.

It hadn't escaped him that Friday night she'd planned an evening with her sister. Or last night, Saturday night, another big date night, she'd spent talking with girlfriends over ice cream and hot chocolate in the back booth of the town's diner—Hunter had noticed when he'd been tailing Mick.

Here goes nothing, he thought, and prepared for rejection. "I noticed you haven't been dating anyone. A pretty woman like you must have men knocking at your door all the time."

"I don't date random guys."

Good. Okay. That's what he would have guessed, but he had to make sure. "You *do* date, though, right?"

"I've been known to say yes now and then."

"I suppose you'd like to get married one day. I mean, don't all women?"

"I don't want to marry some farmer guy just to get married. I especially don't want to marry anyone who can't see me."

"What does that mean? Who couldn't see you? You're lovely and charming and amazing. All a man has to do is look.'' Couldn't she see that? Couldn't she see how much he loved her?

She bowed her head, and the brim of her hat hid her expression. She seemed sad. ''You don't have to compliment me. I'm all grown up. I know what you're trying to say.''

''You do?'' That didn't bode well. He knew for a fact she liked him. What had she called it? A major crush. That was a good place to start building a relationship, right?

''I don't want to marry just anybody.'' She said it with certainty, and she sat tall in her saddle. Chin held high, she sent her horse into a faster walk. ''I don't want some man who sees what you probably see.''

That confused him. What was she getting at? She didn't want some man like him? No, that couldn't be right. ''What do you mean?''

''You see a ditz with a cell phone and credit cards.''

Is *that* what she thought? Hadn't she been listening? What was hurting her? He could feel her pain as if it was *his* heart that had been broken. His trust. His belief in himself. What had happened? This had something to do with the old boyfriend. That wrinkle-free, self-impressed Rick.

She whipped away and urged Keno into a full gallop. Before Brody could react, she was far ahead of him. All he could see was the back of her horse, Keno's black tail breezing out behind him as he galloped faster, poetry in motion. Michelle balanced in the saddle, her spine straight, her shoulders square, her golden hair streaming in the wind.

"Michelle!"

She didn't draw her horse to a stop. No, she sent him into an all-out run.

He pushed Jewel as fast as she could go, eating up ground, flying over the worn path through the field. Gaining distance. Focused totally on Michelle. On closing the distance between them. Her horse was fast. A good strong Arabian, but his mount was faster. He asked her for more, and the mare gave everything she had.

He was helpless. Until he reached Michelle's side, he couldn't do anything for her. She was in pain. He could feel it. Was she as afraid as he was? Afraid to risk everything for the chance at real love?

He had to tell her. He was terrified, but he was brave. He was strong. He couldn't let her hurt like this for one moment longer. He had to reach her. He had to stop her before she went through that gate and into the yard. Or he felt as if he'd be losing everything. This was his only chance.

He was almost there. She'd stopped Keno at the gate and was reaching down to unlock it from her lofty position in the saddle. He had time, he would get to her before she went through. He nosed Jewel directly toward the gate and used the horse's body to block it.

Michelle didn't look up. The brim of her hat hid her expression, but he didn't have to see her to know she was crying. He could feel her emotion in his own heart, as if she were a part of him.

How amazing was that? Before he met Michelle, he didn't believe in soul mates. He didn't believe in love at first sight. He didn't believe in true love.

Brody knew this connection he had with Michelle and the infinite love he felt for her couldn't be by chance. God had meant for this to be.

So he shouldn't be afraid. And neither should she.

He had to make this better. He had to fix her unhappiness. Show her there wasn't one thing to be afraid of because he'd die before he said one word to hurt her.

As if it were the most natural thing in the world, he cupped her lovely face with the palm of his hand. How soft she felt, like the finest silk. The glow within him strengthened, warming the cold places in his soul. His love for her was phenomenal, stronger than steel, unlike anything he'd ever known.

And he knew that's what God meant love to be.

Risking everything. His heart. His future. His soul. He simply told her the truth. "You are lovely. Like a fairy tale come true in my lonely life, and I love you."

Her eyes filled with tears. She didn't move. She didn't breathe. Brody went ice-cold. She didn't love him?

Then he saw the smile radiating across her beloved face.

And into his soul.

Chapter Eleven

Would it be another long week of not seeing Michelle? Brody hated to admit it, but not being around her was killing him. And why?

Because he'd risked everything. He'd stood out on a limb and told her how he felt. She hadn't said the words in return, and now the next step was hearing her say that she loved him. She cared about him. Was it too much to hope for more?

What about his mission? Working beside Mick wasn't helping to gain the man's trust. If anything, he was earning the counterfeiter's *distrust*. Mick had warned him twice about breaking Michelle's heart, that he wasn't going to stand for that as if he were a tough guy who could take Brody down.

All Brody needed was his thumb to put the overblown man on the ground and in handcuffs, but he didn't mention that. He merely tried to reply honestly, that he had no intention of hurting Michelle. He respected her too much.

And while his words and his hard work earned Pete's approval, Mick kept his distance. It wasn't hard to see why. Mick did as little as possible, and Pete wasn't happy with him.

"Is that what you're going to do when this is yours?" Pete would ask. "I don't want this land to go to ruin, Mick."

I'll buy it from you. It was all Brody could do not to blurt out those words. He would bite his bottom lip and keep working. But he could buy the land. At least, his nest egg would go a long way toward a down payment on property like this.

Mick had wandered off with some muttered excuse and after twenty minutes passed, he was missing. Was the man just ducking out of field work? Or was he sneaking off to meet his contact?

Please, Father, help me to end this mission well. But quickly. How could he keep this up for much longer? Keeping secrets from Michelle, spying on her family, having everything he'd ever wanted so close, but he couldn't seize it.

His phone vibrated—Hunter left a text message. Mick had been spotted leaving the ranch on the back service road.

What was Mick up to? Itching for some action and eager to bring this case to a close so he could get on with his life, Brody almost walked away from the fieldwork. He felt it in his guts—this was the break they'd been waiting for.

The cutter jammed and clattered to a dead stop.

"I'm askin' the Lord to help me hold my temper, because that's the only way I'm gonna stay calm with a thunderstorm headed this way." Pete tossed his hat to the ground. "Brody, think you can help me? Where's Mick, that's what I'd like to know."

My partner could tell you, Brody thought as he crouched down on his hands and knees, eating dust and shredded bits of grass. He bellied under, careful of the dangerous blades, and took a look.

"You've got a length of wire caught up in here. Must have picked it up with the grass."

"And with a storm coming in, too." Stress hardened Pete's voice. His face wore the brunt of it. He looked worn and tired. He studied the seasonal workers he'd hired—a handful of teenagers. "I've got hay to put up before the hail hits. The rest of us can load if you'd run to town. Take my truck. I'll give John a call at the hardware store. He'll have the part waiting for you."

At least it would give Brody a chance to get away and give Hunter a call. Find out what was going on. "I'll take care of it. We'll have that part in and running after lunch."

"Son, you're a good man. Let me grab my phone so I can make that call." Pete yanked open the truck door, found his cell phone on the floor. "I sure thank the Lord for sending you my way."

"I thank Him for sending me here."

Pete nodded in approval as he waited for the phone to connect. "You stop by the diner and ask Jodi to pack us up lunch to bring back with you. She'll put it on my tab."

"Will do." Brody hopped in Pete's rig and headed straight to town.

He called Hunter first thing and found out that it looked as if Mick was heading for the closest casino. They already had sensitive mikes in place, in case Mick was doing business while he gambled.

"If you are right, Brody, if Mick's exchanging the money he's printing, we may end this case tonight, tomorrow morning at the latest."

"The bearer bonds I found in his safe were a huge clue." Those midnight excursions had paid off. "We're a good team, Hunter. Buzz me if you get anything else."

"No problem."

The second he put away his phone, his mind went back to Michelle.

How wrong was that? He couldn't seem to help it. This case was almost in the pan, he could feel it. He'd never wanted an assignment to end so fast. He couldn't waste another minute.

How was she going to feel when she found out why he was really here? Troubled, he didn't notice the reduced speed sign at the edge of town. He hit his brakes, but the town sheriff must have been patrolling somewhere else.

Maybe he'd drive on by the hardware store, see if Michelle was busy at the hair salon. Then he'd circle back for the part. When he spotted her car in the lot, the warm glow in his chest brightened.

He couldn't wait to see her. He'd missed her smile and her quick humor and her spirit.

There she was! A wave of excitement washed over him. He was about to undertake a new mission. The most important of his life. The quest to make Michelle his wife.

Fully aware Brody was standing outside the salon's wide front windows, Michelle kept her back turned. She focused her full attention on her newest customer. Just the right shade of a handsome dignified blonde bounced in a sassy layered cut. Michelle was happy—she'd done a great job, if she did say so herself. Fran, the clerk from the hotel that first night Brody came to town, stared unblinking in the large mirror.

"That's me? Why, I haven't looked this good since I was thirty."

"You're beautiful. Look at you."

"Honey, I feel like a whole new woman." Smiling broadly, Fran reached inside her purse. "What do I owe ya? I insist on paying. I haven't been this happy with a cut and style since I don't know how long."

"I said complimentary and I meant it, and we're not done yet." Michelle caught her co-worker's eye in the mirror. "Cassie is slow today. Why don't you let her treat you to a manicure? She includes a hand massage to die for."

"Oh, I've always wanted those French-tipped nails. Thank you, Michelle." Fran grabbed her into a hug. "You are just a doll. I feel so good, I swear I could bust."

Michelle heard the door behind her jangle as she led Fran to Cassie's table. Confident boots tapped on the other side of the partition. Michelle didn't have to look around to know who those boots belonged to.

Before he opened the door, she could sense his presence, as tangible and as certain as the breeze from the air conditioner against the back of her neck. The tiny hairs at her nape prickled and her entire being felt as if it were blossoming, like summer's first rose.

I love you. His words were inside her, and she felt so vulnerable. Afraid and thrilled and uncertain.

The love so new to her heart was deep. What was going to happen? What if he let her down, the way Rick had? Or what if Brody decided the open road and his life elsewhere had a greater hold on him than his love for her?

So many doubts crowded together in her mind.

No, don't think that way. She stopped the doubts, but the echoes of them remained. The uncertainty breaking her hopes a little. She grabbed the broom from the closet and swept up the hair clippings on the black-and-white tiled floor.

Could she stop thinking about him for even one minute? No. Even when he was in the other room, she could feel him. She wanted to turn to him. To her dream.

How could a man be so wonderful? It was as if the angels had looked deep into her secret wishes, the ones she dared not voice, and brought her Brody.

This was how dangerous love was? Sure, love was tenderness and commitment and joy. She'd learned the hard way that it was also confusion and doubt and fear. Despite her worries, the love within her rose so strongly, like a river flooding its banks, taking over.

She *did* love him.

"I came to town to fetch a part, and your dad said to stop by and order up lunch from the diner." Brody's voice. Brody's step behind her as she swept the clippings into the dustpan and emptied it neatly into the small garbage can by the supply closet.

Would it be too forward if she ran to him and begged to know the feel of his arms holding her close? *Yes.*

"Want to come with me?"

I'd follow you anywhere, and that's the problem. She decided not to clue him in on that little bit of information. She straightened and put the broom and pan away and tried to sound sensible, as if she wasn't so in love with him she couldn't think straight. "Fran was my last appointment for the day. I don't have to start my shift at the coffee shop for a few hours."

"Then come with me. I'll buy you lunch while we wait."

"Make it a milk shake and you have a deal."

"Excellent." It was there in the way he watched her. Tender. Respectful.

Was this longing she felt for him part of his longing, too?

She grabbed her purse and slung the thin leather strap over her shoulder. With keys in hand she called goodbye to Cassie. Brody held the door for her and, when he fell in stride beside her on the sidewalk, wrapped her hand in his.

Like a couple. Like a man saying, "This is the woman I love and I choose to be by her side." She was proud to be seen with him, not because he was a good-looking man. But because he was the best man she'd ever met. And to think that he loved her.

She loved him with all the joy in her heart, even if she trembled inside. Love was scary. It was opening up a part of herself that she'd protected for a long time. She trusted that Brody, so protective and good, would never hurt her.

Trust. It was hard to hand over to a man again. But to *this* man it was right.

She'd never loved another human being the way she loved Brody. Even walking beside him, she ached in ways she couldn't explain. She only knew that she'd never felt so much. Been so alive. It was invigorating to see the world like this, the brightness, the colors and the brilliance.

And to feel the depth of her heart—and his.

How could she not? He fit perfectly into her life. Her family loved him. After the Monopoly game, her sisters and brothers-in-law couldn't say nice enough things about him. And her father had given Brody rare praise numerous times for his hard work in the fields. Her dad wasn't as young as he used to be, and it was hard for him to depend on others to do the work he loved.

Brody opened the heavy diner door, a perfect gentleman. His hand found hers again as they stepped into the cool breeze from the air conditioner and looked around. Only a few booths were occupied. This time of year was a busy one in farming country, and only the old-timers were talking over food and coffee today.

The waitress circled around the counter with a pot of steaming coffee in hand. "Hi, Michelle, and is this the handsome Brody I've been hearing about? What can I get you two?"

"I'd like an order to go," Brody said. "Can I see a menu?"

"I've been doing to-go's all day. Here, take this, find a booth and just wave me down when you're ready. Would you like some coffee while you wait?"

"Something cool sure would be good. Got some iced tea?"

Michelle chose a booth in the corner right beneath the air conditioner vent and slid onto the cool padded seat. "You look beat. Dad's been working you hard."

"Yep, but I don't mind. It's honest work, and I admire your dad a lot. He's a good man." Brody settled across the table from her. He looked uncertain before he reached out and drew her hand into his. "I've missed you."

His hand was iron-strong, but he trembled, a tiny bit.

Or maybe she was the one who was trembling. "I've missed seeing you, too."

His fingers squeezed hers more tightly, as if holding on. As if he never wanted to let go. "Did I tell you how beautiful you look today?"

"Not yet. I'm waiting." She liked making him chuckle. He had a nice laugh—warm and deep and quiet.

"You do. But what about me? I'm covered with grass and dirt and grease. I'm surprised you aren't ashamed to be seen with me." Brody felt ashamed now that he realized he'd been so eager to see her he hadn't given a single thought to how he must look after being in the fields since four o'clock.

"I like the way the way you look." Her big eyes filled with admiration.

His throat closed up tight with emotion. She might not have said that she loved him, but the way she was looking up at him said it all.

He couldn't find the words, but he was grateful. He held her hand more tightly, wondering about her slender fingers. He had a hold of her left hand, and he figured that was no coincidence. How right his ring would feel on her fourth finger.

He felt a strange flutter as his stomach tumbled, but he was determined. He'd ask her tonight. He would find out one way or the other if she loved him. If he had a chance of making her his wife.

"If it storms, I won't be working." Did he really sound that awkward? He cleared his throat and tried again. "I was wondering if you'd like to spend some time with me—"

A shadow fell across the table, and it wasn't the waitress's. Michelle tried to pull her hand away, but he didn't let go. Even when the slick dressed man stared disdainfully at their locked hands.

"Oh, hi, Rick." Michelle didn't sound happy to see him.

Brody felt his defenses rise.

"Michelle." He nodded, his baseball cap shading his face. "Hear you have a new boyfriend. A biker boyfriend."

Brody took in the man's mocking tone and the tilt of derision of his upper lip. It took only a second for Brody to see Michelle's distressed look of pain.

He nearly leaped to his feet, overwhelmed with determination to protect her. Fierce with it. "Good to meet you, now move on."

"Fine. Here's a hint. Her father won't give you the land, and she's locked at the knees. Good luck."

Brody saw red. It all happened so fast. He heard Michelle's gasp of pain, and he was on his feet. His hands full of collar and quaking with fury.

"Apologize to the lady," he growled.

"S-sorry," Rick gurgled, and Brody released him.

"Now go." Adrenaline pounding as hard as his

fury, Brody stood protectively beside Michelle. It wasn't a peaceful response and it wasn't right, but his fury came from an honest place. From the need to shelter her. To keep her safe.

Rick straightened his cotton shirt, looked as if he were thinking over his options and then swaggered to the door.

Brody trembled, all fight, ready to keep defending her until the door closed tight.

The waitress bounded down the aisle with an iced tea and a strawberry milk shake. "Goodness, Michelle, are you all right? He didn't make you cry?"

He stepped aside, keeping his gaze on Rick through the long wall of front windows. Letting Rick know Michelle was his now. The woman he loved. He wasn't going to let anyone hurt her. Ever. On his life. On his honor.

"I'm fine, Jodi." Michelle's voice was wobbly, and her eyes were bright, but she wasn't crying.

Good thing, because Brody didn't think he could take seeing her cry.

"Some men have it all wrong. They think money is what's important, when it's the love of a good woman," the waitress soothed.

"Thanks, Jodi."

Brody heard Michelle's single sniff and she cleared the emotion from her voice. Rick had crossed the street and climbed into a brand-new sports car, red and polished and sleek. Brody might drive a sensible sedan and his town house back home in Virginia was

modest, but it wasn't the net worth that made a man,
but how he lived and how he treated his woman.

When Brody sat back down, his anger was fading
and he realized the waitress was gone and Michelle
was stirring the long handled spoon in her thick pink
shake. She looked unhappy. Regret kicked in his
chest.

"Sorry. I acted before I thought." He was a man
of faith. He didn't go around intimidating people.
What was wrong with him? He was an FBI agent.

"Thanks. No one's quite stood up for me before.
Not like that, anyway." It was in her eyes. Her appreciation. Her love for him. "I thought Rick was a
wonderful boyfriend. He seemed wonderful because
he knew what I wanted and he was careful to give
me the dream of it."

"Marriage?"

"Romance, marriage, everything." She blushed
and stirred the spoon around in her milk shake. "He
said that he respected me for wanting to wait until I
was married to, well, *you know,* but he was cheating
on me with another woman."

Rage thundered through Brody's blood with
enough power to blow him apart. The edges of his
vision blurred. How could anyone hurt Michelle?
How could anyone not want her?

"Rick did the very worst thing he could. He betrayed me. He deceived me. He was dating me because he was hoping to get his hands on my family's

net worth. He used me. He lied to me. He knocked my feet out from under me for a while.''

He leaned across the table and cupped her face in the curve of his palm. Wiped a single tear from her cheek with the pad of his thumb. ''Beautiful, he is the dumbest man alive to think the land was more valuable than you. You're the true value. The kind a man waits all his life to find.''

She fell even more in love with him.

He pressed a kiss to her cheek, so sweet and tender it brought tears to her eyes.

This man had protected her, defended her and loved her. She couldn't find the words, so she pressed her face against his palm. She gave thanks that he felt this connection, too, the way their hearts beat in synchrony.

The way he fit against her soul.

Chapter Twelve

The thunderstorm held off. The tall stack of thunderheads amassed on the northwestern horizon as if gathering strength, waiting to attack.

Brody could feel the threat in the air. When the storm came, it would be with a fury. They worked all out, as fast as they could go. When the first gust of wind blew in cold and mean, they worked faster.

Some of the hired teenagers hurried off to help at home, to prepare for the storm. Pete and Brody kept working, fighting the wind gusts as they covered the stacked bales with tarp. The rain came and turned to hail. Lightning split the sky. They kept working.

Brody didn't mind the miserable conditions. They were good for him. He didn't think of Michelle constantly—just almost constantly. He kept picturing the love on her face as she'd pressed her cheek against his hand. Kept remembering how silken soft her skin was. How luminous her eyes were.

How he'd give anything. Do anything. Risk everything to have the right to love her. To make her his wife.

"I've got this last knot and we're done. You did good, Brody. I appreciate your hard work," Pete told him just as lightning split the sky and thunder followed within seconds. "Now you best get in while you're still in one piece, or Michelle will have my hide."

"Thanks, man."

There was nothing else to do as the hail bounced like miniature golf balls. The sound was deafening, and the pellets stung as Brody ran to his bike, strapped on his helmet, wiped his seat with the swipe of his hand and climbed aboard.

Worry troubled him as he roared down what used to be the road. It was now mud and streaming water. Hunter hadn't called. Where was he? He was feeling antsy because the sooner they could wrap up this case, the sooner he could propose to Michelle.

He splashed and slid and churned up the incline, revving the engine, both feet on the ground to give the bike enough balance and pull in the thick mud. He felt his cell phone vibrate against him—two buzzes. It was business. It was urgent. He idled the bike at the crest of the rise and dug the phone out of his pocket. "Brody here."

Static crackled in his receiver. It was Hunter's voice. "It was tough getting the warrant, but we did it. We've got Mick's middlemen on tape and we've ID'd them. I'll send you the electronic file.''

"Great." That meant the end was in sight.

There was static and then Hunter continued. "We're moving in a team. Be ready to—"

Lightning ripped through the sky overhead. Thunder crashed with such fury the ground quaked beneath Brody's boots.

"Hunter?" The line was dead. After a few more tries, he gave up and jammed the phone into his pocket.

How soon would they move in? How long did he have? He had to get to a landline and see if—

A white fork of lightning jabbed from the sky to the earth, about an eighth of a mile from where he was. Deafened by the thunder, he watched sparks explode from a utility pole. Must have hit a transformer. That meant there was no power. Or phone. When he needed them most.

He sped into the wind, fighting the mud and hail until the ranch house came into sight. The windows were dark. Lightning flashed and thunder roared as night descended, stealing the last of the shadows.

There was a bob of light in the darkness ahead. A flashlight? he wondered. It was Michelle. Was she in trouble? His motor stalled, and he let it die.

He spotted her slim silhouette in the paddock. Now that he was close he could see that she was tacking a lantern to the side of the stable. The sharp terrified squeal of a panicked horse sounded like a scream. The hair raised on the back of Brody's neck.

"You need some help, beautiful?"

"If you care to lend a hand," she yelled to be heard above the storm. She waved a lasso at the panicked mare, the large coil bunched in her hand. "How good are you at herding horses?"

"At least as good as you are."

"Then come help me, cowboy."

How could he say no to that? It was Jewel who raced by, a dark flicker of motion and substance before she disappeared into the darkness. Lightning strobed overhead with the whip crack of thunder, and Jewel went wild. She reared, her powerful front hooves slashing the air.

Astride Keno, Michelle rode with a steady calm. Brody had to admire her for that. Her voice was a low hum that did not waver as the mare came down fighting, teeth flashing, wild to attack whatever was frightening her.

Michelle was in the way as the mare charged. Brody hurled through the board rungs of the fence, fighting to get to Michelle. He had to help her. She was in danger.

No, she was in control, he realized. She tossed the lasso, the same instant she sidestepped her horse out of harm's way and the noose slipped neatly over the mare's head.

Just as the horse ducked away before the noose could pull tight and escaped. Brody endured the hail chilling him to his bones. Lightning flashed. The storm swelled.

"Throw me that lasso," he shouted.

She tossed it, a perfect throw. He ran forward to snatch it before the wind stole it. She was left with the rope coiled over her saddle—he could see her as she rode through the gleam of the lantern, and then there was darkness.

They didn't need to speak. He knew what she intended to do, and he moved without question toward the far end of the paddock. The mare was between them; he could see Michelle's shadowed outline moving against the utter blackness of the night.

Brody and Michelle worked together, driving the mare forward. Lightning shattered the darkness, blinding and bright. As thunder answered, the mare reared up, and its powerful hooves ripped into the air. Aiming right at Michelle.

Back! Michelle yanked on the reins, willing Keno to move before the mare's front hooves began to fall.

"Michelle!" She heard Brody's warning a nano-second before the blow came.

Pain shot across the top of her shoulder and knifed down her arm, but Keno saved her, wisely moving as she directed. She wouldn't worry if she was hurt. She had to save her dad's horse. Jewel was going to hurt herself. She was beyond all sense.

Michelle shook out her noose and threw. The rope caught the mare neatly this time, and she was ready, pulling Keno back before Jewel could toss the noose.

Michelle wound the rope around her saddle horn as Keno sat back, keeping the rope taut until Brody's lasso sailed high and into place. They brought the mare in.

Brody closed the doors behind her and fetched the lantern to light the way to Jewel's stall. No longer able to see the lightning, Jewel's panic faded to a skin-prickling terror. Michelle calmed the mare enough to cross tie her safely in her stall.

"Is she going to be all right?"

"Doesn't look like she's injured, just scared." Michelle grabbed a currycomb from the shelf in the aisle and got to work, talking calmly. "You sure worked yourself up, didn't you, girl?"

Leaving her to the mare, Brody unsaddled Keno, grabbed a jug of grain from the barrel in the feed room and let the gelding lead the way to his stall. It was clean and fresh with sweet-smelling straw—all Brody had to do was fill the trough with grain and fork in some hay.

It had been a long time since he'd cared for a horse, and it felt good. Right. He took it as a sign he was right where he belonged.

He took the comb from Michelle's cold fingers. "You sit down. I'll towel her off. I want to look at your arm."

"It's just a scratch. Look, it's already stopped bleeding."

Brody lifted one lantern to see for himself. "That should be bandaged. Come upstairs with me."

"It's more of a bruise. She got me with the outside of her hoof. How about you? You're a muddy mess."

He looked down. She was right. From the dirt from the fieldwork and the mud from the paddock, he was covered from hat to boot. "I'll shower, you go home and change and meet me at my place. I'll entertain you with dinner, candlelight and Scrabble."

"You've said the magic words. I'll be there. The electricity is out. What are we going to do for food?"

"I'll start a fire in the fireplace and we'll roast hot dogs. Not romantic, but hey, I guess I'm a cheap date."

How he could make her laugh. Brighten even the stormiest evening. "It's a deal. I bet I can find the makings for s'mores in Mom's pantry."

"Can't wait to spend time with you." He thumbed away a speck of mud on her chin. "When I'm not with you, I miss you so much."

She couldn't think, so she couldn't answer. His touch was like heaven, like the promise of peace and adventure all at once. Like being thrilled. Like coming home.

"Because I love you." Tough words for a tough guy to say, but he did it. "Maybe I'll have to stay around when the haying's done. So I can be with you."

How would she respond to that?

He'd traveled the country hunting bad guys, computer hackers, terrorists and criminals. He'd been undercover in extremists groups, criminal crime rings and nothing—ever—had frightened him like this. Terrified him down to his soul.

Standing before her with his heart on the line, no gun would protect him. No SWAT team could swoop in and save him.

Michelle, with her sweet-spirited gentle ways, had done what no one else could do.

She'd terrified him, she enlivened him. She made him complete.

"Yes." She looked as afraid as he felt, for this moment was a changing point for both of them. "I love you so very much. It would be wonderful if you could stay."

Tenderness overwhelmed him. A warm liquid sensation filled up his heart. His soul. He reached out—how could he not want a deeper connection to her? To this woman he'd been waiting for all of his life?

He wanted to marry her. He wanted to propose to her, but he had to do it right. Had to think it through. He wanted it to be a special moment for her to remember.

Her hair was like wet silk and smelled of strawberries and rain. Her face was rain-damp and warm as satin. He cupped her jaw, delicate against his callused fingers and, heart pounding with the importance of what he was about to do, leaned down and claimed her with a soft, slow kiss.

"Oh, Brody." She sighed against his lips.

"I didn't do too badly, then?"

"Passable."

"Is that all? Maybe I'd better try again."

"Maybe." Michelle, breathless, lifted her face to his.

Passable? No. More like paradise. Her fingers curled into the front of his shirt, holding on for dear life. No man had ever kissed her like that. With all his heart. With all he was. She melted into his kiss.

How could a simple brush of a man's lips feel like a caress to her soul? She didn't know how a man's kiss could be so incredibly tender.

The storm crashed overhead, rain hammered the roof and the horses shifted in their stalls, neighing as lightning struck. The lantern sputtered and went out.

All she knew was Brody's touch, Brody's kiss, the hammer of his heartbeat with hers.

He pulled away and gazed into her eyes. For the first time, in the pitch dark, she could see.

He was hers to love. She no longer had to hold back her heart. Keep this great affection secretly locked away. She eased into his arms, laid her cheek on his chest and savored the wonder of his strong arms enfolding her.

Michelle watched in amazement as Brody began shifting the tiles into place on the board. "I don't believe it!"

"Believe it. *Quartz.* Triple letter score. So let's see, that's forty-four points." Candlelight only improved the look of him—caressing his brow and high-cut cheekbones, the way her fingers ached to. "That puts me in the lead."

"Not for long."

"A challenge. I like that. Okay, beautiful, let's see what you've got."

Sure, he had to go and say that. As if she could do anything with the letters she had. She had to think. And how hard was that? With the love of her life across the table from her, how was a girl to concentrate?

Then inspiration struck. "*Buzz.* There's a double letter score, so—"

"No!" Brody leaned forward, as if to see for himself. "You can't have it."

"I do." Triumphantly, she slipped the last of her tiles into place around his most recent word. "And that's thirty-four points. For the win."

"Way to go." He pushed away from the table, circling around in the shadows and knelt at her side.

She turned toward him, captivated by the shine of unconditional love in his eyes. This was happening. It really was. Brody was in love with her. And he was staying. She could already imagine their wedding— simple but elegant. And his gold band on her finger. She'd have a new name—Michelle Gabriel—and he would be her husband. Her family. And in time, there would be children. A little boy and a little girl to love and take care of.

Her life and her future were suddenly full. And fulfilling.

Because of this man kneeling before her. Because of his love.

"Come over here to the fire with me." His big hands were callused and rough textured but gentle as he led her to the crackling hearth. Soft orange light danced as if in celebration, and seemed to welcome them as she settled onto the floor, and he sat across from her. Never letting go of her.

"There are some things I want you to know about me." He looked noble, like a knight of old, a man of unshakable integrity. "I work hard. I'm an honest man. And I love you. Not for any other reason than because you are the most incredible woman I've ever met."

Could he be any more perfect?

"I'm not here because of your parents' land. Or because I'm in transition looking for a new place in life. I know you've been hurt, and you didn't deserve that."

"Everyone's been hurt." She drew his hand to her lips and pressed a tender kiss on the back of his first knuckle. "That's life. You don't have to do this, to tell me you're not like Rick. I already know that."

"You hardly know me."

"And that would take a lifetime."

How did he get so lucky? "You have no malice for Rick, do you?"

"No. I still believe in the goodness of people. Sometimes a person can get misguided, but in the end, I believe we're basically good."

That was what he needed to hear. Maybe then the twist of nerves in his stomach would calm down. "Do you know what you deserve?"

"Another s'more?"

"No. I'm serious, here."

"Sorry. I'll try to keep the jokes to a minimum."

"Thanks." He leaned forward and pressed his forehead gently to hers. He felt a flash of connection, his heart to hers. He had to let her know. Try to make her understand.

"You deserve a man with an honest heart. A faithful soul. A man who will love you with everything he is, heart and soul for the rest of his life. When a man loves a woman like that, she's the only thing that matters to him. Not money, not pride, not comfort. He would die to protect her. Give everything to her." Gazing into her blue, blue eyes, he saw his future. In this life and beyond. "Know how I know this?"

"N-no."

"It's how I feel about you."

Big silver tears filled her eyes but did not fall. It was obvious his love mattered to her.

"You need to know this." He wasn't done, and she had to understand. If the warrant came down tonight and there was enough solid evidence for an indictment, then everything would happen too fast. There would be no time to pull her aside and make her understand.

"Shh." She was done talking and leaned forward to capture him in the gentlest of kisses.

Tenderness so perfect and powerful swept through him and made the fury of the storm outside seem small. He curled his fingers around the nape of her neck and held on. Breathed in the light faint floral scent of her perfume, only to kiss her again.

Marry me, he begged silently. Let me love and protect you forever.

But how could he ask? She didn't know that he was a federal agent. She didn't know who he was. He was here under false pretenses. Good ones, true, but he *was* deceiving her. He wanted to explain it to her, but he was sworn to secrecy.

Would she understand when the arrest was made? Would she forgive him for gathering the evidence that put her favorite uncle behind bars?

Of course she would. Look at her. She was good, through and through. She was compassionate enough to understand. To see that while he was doing a job, his love for her was the greatest truth.

"I love you." It was as honest as he could be tonight. "I want you to remember that. Regardless of what happens tomorrow, I love you, heart and soul."

She leaned into his arms and buried her face in his shoulder. She gave a little satisfied sigh. Love overwhelmed him. A deep abiding affection that was as infinite as the sky and as true as heaven.

"I love you the same way." She pressed her lips to the hollow of his throat in a quick kiss. "I'm so glad you crashed in front of me that day. What would

I do if I'd never met you? I never would have known you.''

Grateful to God for leading her here, for giving her this man who was perfect in every way, Michelle was too overwhelmed to continue speaking. Peace settled around them like the fire's glow.

She breathed in the masculine spicy scent of his skin and the fresh laundry scent of his shirt. She held him, just held him. This wonderful man who'd fallen into her life. A man like no other.

Her own honest, protective, faithful man.

It was fifteen minutes after one, according to his watch, and he couldn't sleep. The electricity was still off. The phone lines remained down. His cell was dead. There was no way to contact his partner or his captain.

He was worried about ending this job neatly, with no casualties. He was worried about Michelle.

The apartment held the memory of her laughter. The faint vanilla scent of the thick chunky candles she'd brought to light their way. The Scrabble game was boxed up on the table. The evening had been pleasant and companionable and complete.

He never wanted it to end.

He didn't want tomorrow to come. But the night was ticking away and soon it would be dawn. The morning raid was going to happen. Michelle was going to find out he had deceived her. There was nothing he could do to stop it.

He could only believe in the power of their love. In the goodness of her forgiving heart.

After the raid, when Mick was in custody and Michelle knew the truth, would she understand? Or would he lose her love forever?

All he could do was pray for the strength to handle what was to come.

Chapter Thirteen

❧

"Are you up doing chores?" Michelle asked into her cell phone as she wielded her pitchfork in the dawn's first light.

"*Hello?* Where else would I be?" Jenna sounded about as thrilled as Michelle felt. "Do you have power yet? We don't. No lights, no phones."

"Bummer." Michelle gave a quick thanks that their lights had come on sometime in the night and that their cell phones were working. "No power means no electricity for the water pump. Are you packing water?"

"Oh, just a few dozen ten gallon buckets. My arms are stretched like a Gumby doll's. Really. Where's a generator when you need one? Or a big strong handsome hunk living over my garage to help me out?"

What news she had to tell Jenna. But not on the phone. With her luck, Brody would come walking down the stable aisle and overhear. Or one of her sisters would show up. Or her mom. Then everyone would know.

Besides, it felt too personal to talk about on the phone. She felt as if Brody's love was too good to be true, and if she dared to say out loud, "I found the one. The man I want to love the rest of my life," then he'd vanish. Or some disaster would naturally follow.

Disaster did have a tendency to follow her around, and so she saved the news for later. "So, do you want to go on a ride this afternoon?"

"I've got work, but I could ride by after supper and we can take the horses to Bible study?"

"Cool. Great idea!" That would give them all the time in the world to talk. Plus, they hadn't gone on that long of a ride in ages. "Call me."

"Later!" Jenna's connection went dead.

Michelle pocketed her phone and laughed when Keno gave a gentle yank on her ponytail. "Hey, what do you think you're doing?"

The big dark brown gelding nibbled on the back of her neck, an affectionate gesture, and she put down her pitchfork to pull him into a hug. She rubbed her fingertips along his warm silken jawline and cheeks and up under his mane. He leaned into her touch, closing his eyes, wuffling softly, a low contented sound that said it all.

Yep, it was going to be a great day. The world felt at peace after the storm. The dawn's golden light was like a gentle promise of good things to come. Larks greeted the new day. The wind was lazy, stirring against her skin.

And she was spending the morning with her very best friend, Keno. Soon, she'd ride him out to the fields to bring her dad a pot of coffee, just because. And then she'd see *him.* Brody.

The thought of him was all it took to make her feel as if she were floating. She couldn't believe it. He loved her. Not just a warm glow kind of a love, but the real thing. All the way to his soul, with he-would-die-for-her devotion.

What had he said? *I love you, heart and soul.*

The way she loved him.

Thank you, Father, she remembered to pray as she gave Keno one last rub under his chin.

She had a good life. It wasn't the excitement of a big city and it wasn't the thrill of an ambitious life, but it was all she'd ever wanted.

To wake up before dawn and watch the sun peer over the jagged edges of the breathless Bridger Mountains. To witness the day coming new to the world as she worked in the paddocks. To be with her best friends, the horses and to have her family close.

To feel the changes in the land—the planting seasons, the growing seasons, the harvest. To live where she had so many roots. This place was her entire world. She had everything her heart had ever desired.

But would she leave it for Brody? What if he asked her to?

What if he wanted to marry her, but he didn't want

to live in a small town on a farm and while away the hours on the front porch?

What if his dreams were different from hers? What if he could never be happy here?

Put it in God's hands. That's what Pastor Bill always said. So, that's what she'd do. She would pray and ask the Lord to guide her. To trust that He would work these questions out in His way and in His time.

Hadn't He brought Brody to her? Surely He hadn't done that without knowing it would work out. Right?

This was no different.

She poured grain in Keno's trough and latched his stall gate. When she was putting up the pitchfork she heard it; a different sound than she'd heard on any other morning.

She rushed to the main stable doors and skidded to a stop at the sight of three sleek black SUVs, with dark-tinted windows speeding toward her uncle Mick's bungalow.

Ten minutes after five, and they were moving in, ready to make the arrest. The SWAT team was in place, situated around the perimeter of the yard, ready to protect, if necessary, the agents climbing out of the vehicles.

It was a simple plan, to keep downwind from the house with the team members in the back to make sure Mick didn't run. The hope was to arrest him unsuspecting in his truck on the road, where he was less likely to be armed and there would be less chance of a shoot-out. Where there were no passersby by to step in the line of fire.

Brody hoped to take Mick quietly, without harm to anyone.

Not to *anyone,* Brody amended, thinking of Michelle as he remained crouched in the shadows of the draw with the creek behind him, his boots in mud. He was hyped, tense with anticipation. His every sense was alert to the unexpected.

He waited soundlessly, his rifle cradled in the crook of his arm. He was ready. Prepared for the worst. Praying for the best.

"Glad this is your last mission, buddy?" Hunter broke the silence.

"You know it." This mission had been the worst, eating at his conscience. He'd lied to good people, been someone he wasn't. That was wearing on a man of faith.

How was Michelle going to take this? It troubled him. Worry burrowed deep in his stomach and didn't let up. They'd had a good evening together.

Last night, basking in the happy glow of their evening together, he'd had hope.

But this morning, in the cool damp, he was filled with trepidation. Maybe it was because of the bitter tang of adrenaline in his mouth or the tension balled in his guts. For whatever reason, he'd misplaced that hope. Lost it on the way from being Brody—the man Michelle McKaslin loved—to becoming Gabe Brody, FBI agent, armed and dangerous.

"He's coming down the stairs," crackled in his ear. It was Dan Thomas from the SWAT team. "Our target is in the kitchen. Getting his keys. Okay, this is it."

Brody felt the familiar calm spill through his veins. They were good to go. Anything could happen, and he had to be sharp, focused and prepared. He forced every last thought of Michelle from his mind and concentrated.

He realized this was the last time he'd be in danger like this. The last time he would lay his life on the line for his country. He prayed for a peaceful end. He didn't want anyone getting hurt.

And while he was at it, he would pray for God to fill Michelle's heart with understanding.

The crackle over the earpiece was the first indication something was wrong. It wasn't Dan. It was Pierce. "We've got a civilian. A woman on horseback."

"Michelle!" He was on his feet before he remembered to stay down. He only knew he had to protect her. If she got in the way and bullets starting flying, she'd be caught in the cross fire. He growled into his com, "Pierce, get her outta here."

Dan again. "He's on the move. In his truck. Team one, move in."

Brody moved fast and low. Had Pierce gotten Michelle to safety? What if she was scared? What if she tried to warn Mick?

Thoughts of everything that could go wrong and

things that had gone wrong on other missions flashed through his mind.

Pierce can handle it, he had to remind himself. He calmed his icy, near-the-edge adrenaline. He was intensely protective when it came to the woman he loved.

Concentrate, Brody. Mick's rusted old truck was bouncing down the mud-puddled lane, coming closer. The window was rolled down broadcasting classic country music. Johnny Cash crooned as two vans tore out of the underbrush and skidded to a stop in the road in front of Mick. One more from behind.

Through the cracked windshield and the scope of his rifle, Brody read Mick's confusion. *C'mon, Mick, stop. Do the right thing. Make this a peaceful arrest.*

As if Mick heard him, the truck skidded to a stop, sliding in the mud toward the creek, where cottonwoods and the deep water blocked him on one side. The cut of the hill penned him in on the other. He was trapped.

"This is the FBI. Hands up, Mick, where I can see them." Brody used the bed of the truck as a shield as he moved. Kept his weapon steady, site true and his finger on the trigger as Hunter threw open the truck's door.

"Brody?" Mick looked confused. "Is that you? What in blazes is going on here? I thought we were haying this morning."

"I'm not your friend, Mick. Now keep your hands up. Slide out nice and slow."

"Hey, I've got no beef with you. What is this about?" Mick took one look at all the weapons pointed at him, the very determined men in flak jackets and, holding up his hands, climbed out of the truck.

Two agents helped him to the ground.

Brody stood, feet apart, gun aimed at the back of Mick's head as the handcuffs snapped shut.

Around him men were shouting orders. The teams were moving in, the unit peeling off to search Mick's house. His safe, his computer, all his personal records would be confiscated and everything inside the house turned upside down.

It's over. The mission was done. The enormity of it sank in, and Brody removed his weapon once Mick was secure. He was free now. He'd leave Hunter in charge and find Michelle—

Wait. She'd found him. He felt her presence as surely as the sun on his back and the earth beneath his boots. A tingle of apprehension settled in his midsection. Something was wrong. *Very* wrong.

Michelle. She'd dashed onto the road, up from where Pierce had to have taken her near the creek. She stood in the muddy center of the lane, looking as fresh as the morning, as genuine as the countryside spread out around her.

She wore a pair of faded jeans and simple white T-shirt. Beneath the brim of her baseball cap, her eyes shone with tears. Her beautiful rosebud mouth, the one that had said, "I love you," to him looked as if she'd tasted poison.

That poison was him.

She scanned the huge FBI letters on his chest, then his gun that had been aimed at her uncle. Her lower lip trembled and she turned away.

She didn't need to say a word. Her silence was worse than if she'd started yelling at him, calling him every name he deserved.

She ran. Ran from him as if he was the worst thing that had ever happened to her.

Ran so he couldn't see her tears.

But he could feel her heart break. Because her heart was his, too.

She knew he was behind her, so she didn't bother to look over her shoulder to see it for a fact. She could feel him, sense him. And why? Because he was the love of her life. The man God meant especially for her.

It wasn't a surprise that she could feel the man who was meant to be a part of her forever, was it? No. And that made her even more mad. Made her hurt more.

Brody. He'd *lied* to her. He'd *used* her. She'd seen his jacket. His rifle. *FBI* had been blazed across his chest and his back.

"Michelle!"

She did not want to talk to him. After what he'd put her through! First, she'd been scared when she saw the black vans speeding toward her uncle Mick's house. It wouldn't be the first time old friends or people who'd loaned money to him showed up a little angry.

But when a gunman crept out of the brush by the creek and asked her to keep down for her own safety, and to come with him—

"Michelle! Wait up. I need to talk to you."

I don't care what you need. What *she* needed was a good hard stick to smack him upside the head with.

Well, not that she could actually hit anyone, but the thought of it made her feel better. Anger turned her bright red inside, and beneath that was the crumbling sensation of her being wrenched into pieces. It felt as if every part of her, heart and soul, was broken and bleeding.

"Michelle." His hand lighted on her shoulder, a silent offer of comfort.

And that was the problem. She didn't want his comfort. She wanted to hate him. She just wanted this pain inside her to leave, so she could curl up somewhere all by herself and cry until there were no more tears.

He'd deceived her. Pretended to love her. How could he do such a thing? And she'd thought he was perfect.

Too upset to speak, she did manage to shove his hand away. She walked fast, even though her vision was blurry. There were *not* tears in her eyes. Okay, there were. But they were *angry* tears. She was angry, not hurt. Furious, not betrayed. Outraged, not shattered.

"I'm sorry."

"I bet you are." She whipped through the grass, faster.

He stayed on her tail. "I was under oath. I couldn't tell you."

"I understand." Oh, she understood. She'd been the biggest fool of all, falling for his line. Another man telling her what she wanted to hear for his own purposes.

How dense was she? "For your information, I'm not some romantic sap of a fool. I see what you wanted. You needed to get on the property to arrest Mick and you tricked me."

"No, I never tricked you." He loped alongside her in his black jacket and gear. The white letters across his chest proclaiming his identity for the entire world to see. The FBI?

He'd used her. So he could arrest her uncle.

Keno looked up from grazing, nickered a welcome low in his throat. She yanked his reins from the low cottonwood she'd tied him to and knocked into Brody's arm as she turned.

"Out of my way."

"No. I want you to listen to me." He grabbed her with both hands, holding her so tight, with what felt like so much need.

Oh, he was good. Very good at playing his role.

Oh, yeah, she saw it all in a flash. The big white *FBI* on his chest said more than he ever could.

Whatever Mick had done, he'd done it big this time, and that's why Brody was here. That's why Brody had wormed his way into her family and into her heart. That's why he seemed so perfect, because he'd planned it all along.

And she, like the biggest fool ever, invited him right in.

"I can explain this, Michelle. Give me the chance. Please."

"What could you possibly have to say to me?"

"Everything. Let me explain."

"I think your gun says it all." He looked like some stealthy warrior, all dressed in black, with his semi-automatic weapon slung over his left shoulder on a strap. He was all steel as he held her, his grip an unbreakable band on her upper arms. "Let go."

"No, I can't. I told you the truth, everything but—"

"Let go of me."

It was the cool sound in her voice, the icy pain that shocked him enough to let go. Brody took a step back. His heart broke with her pain.

She was going to leave him. She wasn't going to understand. She wasn't going to give him a chance. And he'd hurt her. He'd gone back on his word and he'd made her cry.

He had to fix this. He had to stop those tears. Make her stop hurting. "Michelle, what I said last night.

That was the truth. I said regardless of what happened today, I love you. Do you remember that?''

She made a "huh!" sound and straightened the stirrup, fit her foot into it and rose up into the saddle.

This wasn't working. What should he say? He could see the sheen of tears on her face. See the pride in the straight set of her back.

He caught hold of her ankle. He had to get through to her. Had to make her see. "I love you, and that was as true yesterday as it is today. As it will be tomorrow.''

"You deceived me.'' She swiped at the tears on her cheeks with the back of her hand. Her eyes shimmered but more didn't fall.

He could feel her disillusionment. She was like a steel wall set against him.

He would give anything to take that wall down. To turn back the clock to last night, when he'd had the privilege of holding her close. "I never lied about the way I feel for you. That's the truth, Michelle.''

"You're not a rodeo rider. You weren't traveling on your bike to sightsee. You never grew up on a farm, did you?''

"That was the truth. The farms, my dreams, how I feel about you. That's me. You know what's real about me. From the moment I first saw you, I was captivated. I never hid who I really am from you.''

"You're an FBI agent. You hid that pretty well.''

"You have every right to be mad, but please, let

me fix this. I can't bear to know I'm making you cry."

"Oh, you're not. I'm crying because I'm mad at myself. I put my faith in you, and I shouldn't have. Shame on you."

She looked at him as if he were a stranger. A detestable stranger.

She was right. He didn't feel fit to stand on the ground in front of her. He wasn't good enough to breathe the same air.

Brody had never felt such shame. Agony squeezed so tight in his chest, he couldn't breathe as she turned her horse toward home.

"Can you forgive me?"

She turned in the saddle. "I understand. You were simply doing your job."

"No. I fell in love with you."

"Stop saying that." He was tearing her apart, and for what? So he could walk away from this with a clear conscience?

Didn't he understand that she still loved him? How wrong was that? He'd made her believe she was exciting enough and wonderful enough that a man like him could love her forever.

When all along he'd—

No, she couldn't think it, or she'd fall apart and there was no way she was about to let him know what he'd really meant to her. If nothing else, she was going to keep what she had left of her dignity.

Lord, help me find wisdom. She had to pull it together. She had to let him know she was just fine.

Dying inside, she firmed her spine, lifted her chin and looked at the man who'd used her and betrayed her. It was easy to see that he *was* sorry for it.

Sorry he'd made her believe something that could never be true. No matter how much it hurt, she held back her last tears. "Good luck to you in the future."

"Is there a chance—?" He looked like she felt—raw and bleeding.

Brody. Her heart cried out for him. Her love was so fierce for him, it tore her to pieces. She wanted him to be different. To go back to last night when he was her one true love.

How could she?

Her soul ached, empty, as she turned away. What else could she do? She urged Keno into a gallop as fast as his strong legs could carry them.

When Brody was just a lone figure on the distant field, she drew her horse to a stop. Slid from the saddle. Knelt in the grass. Let the tears come. Hot, wrenching, consuming.

She felt the soft velvet of her horse's nose against her jaw, nuzzling at her tears. Her best friend. Her trusty gelding she'd loved for most of her life. He loved her no matter what.

"Some males are pretty darn faithful and true." She leaned her forehead against his neck, grateful for his comfort. His friendship.

Not even his comfort could stop the horrible rending of her heart, of her soul.

Nothing ever would.

Michelle was on her knees and she was crying. Brody *had* to go to her. He'd vowed never to hurt her and look at what he'd done to her. To the woman he loved more than anything.

"C'mon, man, we gotta go." Hunter gestured toward the vans loading up. "Another mission done. It's your last."

Brody rubbed his hands over his face. This had gone terribly wrong. There she was, standing up. She was so far away, she was only a slim figure against the endless green.

If he went to her, would it make any difference? How could he change her mind? Repair the damage?

Hunter didn't relent. "C'mon, buddy. It's over. You've done your job and it's time to go. They're waiting."

How was he going to walk away from everything that mattered? Go home as if his time here hadn't meant everything.

"I can't believe this ended so fast," Hunter said. "Remember the Olympic Hills job? We lived in the mud and woods for a week."

"One miserable week. It rains every day of April in Portland."

Hunter chuckled. "I already knew that. Hey, this

case was a piece of cake. It was a good one to ride out on. What's next for you? The wide-open road?''

That used to appeal to him. To just take off, vacation. He'd never been good at vacationing. He was always too focused on work.

That wasn't his problem anymore. His time was his own. What did he want to do with it? He only knew one thing for sure. He wanted to be here. On this piece of land. With Michelle as his wife.

She hated him. She thought he betrayed her. How did he fix that? Surely the Lord didn't mean for things to end this way? Did He?

Hunter gazed in Michelle's direction. ''Don't tell me you've finally found the right woman?''

''That, my friend, is in God's hands. And hers.''

There she was, climbing back on her horse. She rode into the bright rays of the rising sun, golden and pure, and disappeared.

Leaving him alone. He'd lost everything.

Two agents were at the kitchen table, accepting Alice McKaslin's steaming fresh coffee with fervent gratitude as Michelle burst through the back door.

''Honey, there you are.'' Her mom looked relieved. ''I was worried. These men have questions about Uncle Mick. They need us to talk to him. He's got himself in some trouble now.''

''I need to change.'' She wanted to shower and find fresh clothes, but what she needed most was time.

Time to gather up the pieces of her shattered heart.

Find a place inside her to lock them quietly away. To pull herself together.

Then she could come back downstairs and face Brody's colleagues. Oh, how they probably got a good chuckle at the country girl who fell hopelessly in love with the worldly, mysterious Brody.

Michelle kept walking and headed for the stairs.

One of the agents was talking. "Gabe is on his way."

"Gabe?" Her mom asked.

"Gabe Brody," the agent clarified. "You don't know what your cooperation has meant. We want you to know your family has been cleared of all suspicion. We feared your farm and your one daughter's coffee shop were fronts for laundering counterfeit money."

"I just can't believe it. Mick! After all we've done for him. He was tossed out by his wife last year, you know. And I can see why! Counterfeiting. How could he think to do such a thing. And we couldn't bend over fast or far enough to help him."

Michelle hurried through the living room. Gabe. That was his name. Agent Gabe Brody with the FBI.

Of course he was a noble, distinguished, hard-working man. A hero that helped to keep the laws of their nation. She'd known all along he was someone special. More than a drifter on a bike in black leather.

"Everyone should have a supportive family like yours. Too bad Mick didn't make better choices with his life." The agent's words changed to a mumble as she started up the stairs.

She blinked hard. She was crying for Uncle Mick, that was all. Uncle Mick and his bad choices. Following the wrong paths. Making counterfeit money. Putting them all under the scrutiny of the FBI. Putting Brody right in the middle of their lives so he could use her for information.

Michelle stopped on the landing. There were the family pictures, all marching up neatly in carefully organized rows. Sadness wrapped around her. She'd hoped to add to the picture gallery, as Karen and Kirby had. She'd wanted that so much that it hurt.

She'd already envisioned her wedding pictures and her baby portraits. They would be framed in gold and hung at the top of the stairs, along with the others. A color documentary of the McKaslins' lives. A testimony to the abundant love they were blessed with.

Would that kind of love ever happen to her again? Brody had been pretending, but she hadn't.

Or was he her one true love, and there would never be another?

There she went, being romantic again. How foolish was that? Brody may have seemed like her true companion in this life. But it had all been an act on his part.

Maybe it wasn't.

Where did that thought come from? It was her heart still wishing for Brody. He *had* come to her afterward. He'd tried to explain. He'd said he was sorry. He'd said he still loved her.

And what if that was just an act, too?

What if it wasn't?

And if it wasn't, how did she open her heart, even crack the door, just to let in more pain?

There he was. She could see him climbing out of one of the black vans. He looked like a dream—better than a dream—dressed all in black, with his protective vest and his weapons.

He looked like a hero on the silver screen, and she had to close her eyes. Turn away from the man who'd blown her last dream apart.

He was no strong, protective, honest man.

She was done with Agent Gabe Brody.

"She won't see you, man." Hunter came through the door of the McKaslins' garage apartment and looked around. "Nice. This was a lot better than the trailer we were stuck in, remember that job in Tacoma?"

"Or the studio apartment in east L.A.?"

"Yeah. Good times." Hunter rolled his eyes. "Well, this is it. The captain says you might as well ride out the way you came in. You've got the surveillance equipment packed up?"

Brody pointed it out stacked behind the couch, ready to go.

It was hard to watch Hunter leave. They'd worked together for ten long years. It was tough watching from the window as the agents climbed in and drove away.

That was his life, and he'd been good at it. One of

the best. But it hadn't made him happy. It was the life of a loner, the life of an observer. He'd always been traveling, always been working. Being the hand of justice when necessary wasn't an easy thing.

He'd done his time, and it was over.

He'd trusted the Lord to show him what was next. To point him in the right direction.

And the Lord had.

He'd been all over the world in his work, and no place had affected him like this. No place whispered to him as if he belonged here, as if he'd been waiting for this all his adult life. And for the woman who lived in that house. Who owned his loner's heart.

Alice stepped onto the porch, squinted up at the apartment, frowned at him in the window and went back inside.

Yep, they were angry. It was a hard thing, knowing he'd duped them. He'd arrested their beloved relative. Despite his flaws, the McKaslins did love Mick.

He didn't have to be told he wasn't welcome. He left his business card on the table, in case they had questions, the office would know where to find him for a while.

It was hard to leave. Memories tugged at him. He'd told Michelle how much he loved her right here in front of the hearth. And she'd said the same.

How much did she mean it? Was she the woman he thought she was, that when she loved it was with everything she had? Heart and soul, the same way he loved her?

Only time would tell.

He grabbed his duffel, climbed down the stairs in the blistering sun and stowed his pack on the bike. No one came out to wish him well or offer their good-byes as he started the engine.

That was just as well. He wouldn't know what to say to them.

He took one last look at paradise before he released the clutch and drove away from everything that really mattered to him. The only home he wanted to have.

The only woman he would ever love.

Chapter Fourteen

"**O**h, I don't believe it. Tell me I counted wrong!" Michelle moaned as she dropped her little silver shoe on the hotel bearing Boardwalk.

"Looks right to me!" Kirby rubbed her hands together. "Two thousand dollars, please. If you hand over all your property and money, that should just about do it."

"I'm broke. Bankrupt." The phone rang and Michelle sprang out of the chair.

The past few weeks had been tough, but she was surviving. Tonight's game was Monopoly, because she couldn't bear to play Scrabble—her feelings were still fragile. It seemed everything reminded her of Brody. "Does anybody want anything from the kitchen?"

"Food!" Kirby called out.

"Lots of it!" Kendra seconded.

Michelle looked at the caller ID that read Federal Government and decided to let it ring. She'd blocked Brody's number on her cell and on the house phone. She did *not* want to talk to that man. She did *not* want to get a message from that man. Now he was resorting to playing hardball. How was she going to block all the FBI offices?

The answering machine clicked on while she was pulling a new bottle of soda from the fridge. Then there was Karen, blocking her way. Karen had that look in her eye.

Michelle knew just what it was, too. After the fall-out of discovering that Brody was an agent and he'd been deceiving them all, the shock had worn off and Karen and her husband were the first to be on Brody's side.

What was Karen going to do? Give her another gentle reminder that Brody had never outright lied. He had worked undercover in a rodeo. He was a good man. The face he'd shown them was authentic.

Michelle knew all that. She'd thought of nothing but Brody since she'd listened to his motorcycle rumble down their driveway, leaving her forever.

Leaving her so easily. And that's why she was certain he'd manufactured his "love" for her. Michelle doubted Karen would ever understand. How could she? Karen had the perfect life. A wonderful, trustworthy husband. A beautiful new baby. A comfortable home.

She hadn't been blown away by Brody's declarations of love. She hadn't been devastated by Brody's broken promises.

Karen headed toward the phone. "Aren't you going to answer that?"

"Nope. I'm screening calls."

"Are you sure you want to do that?" Karen stopped at the island, clearly waiting to see who was about to leave a message. "Brody called Zach last night. They struck up a friendship, you know, and Brody asked about you. He's been trying to get a hold of you. He wanted to know if you were okay."

"I'm sure." That was not a lie. She would be okay. She had to be. What she had with Brody was make-believe. What was the point in rehashing it? He'd done his job and he rode away.

Fine. Then he ought to stay out of her life. That's why she'd blocked his phone numbers and returned his letters. He was probably feeling guilty because he was a liar.

But a tiny part of her couldn't stop hoping that he wasn't. What had he said? Regardless of what happens tomorrow, I love you, heart and soul. Even now, she wanted it to be true.

How could it be? He left. If he'd loved her so much, then how could he ride away without looking back? And even if he was telling the truth about loving her, that didn't erase the fact that he'd deceived her once. Did that mean he could do it again?

She didn't know, but it ripped her in shreds to think about it.

Karen was relentless, even if she was the nicest person ever as she grabbed a new bag of potato chips from the pantry. "I like Brody. And so does Zach. He apologized for deceiving us. He was only doing his job and he did it well. He was as respectful to our privacy as possible."

"Oh, is that what he said." Making her want him didn't qualify for that, not in her book! "He made me—"

"Love him?"

Yes. She'd tried everything she could think of to purge this unbreakable affection from her heart. The abiding love that refuse to lessen, refused to fade and remained as bright as ever. Praying hadn't stopped it. Time hadn't diminished it.

What was she going to do?

There was sympathy on her sister's face. Karen had been there to guide her and protect her like a big sister should, all of her life. "What would you do? If Brody had been Zach, before you married him, wouldn't you have sent him packing?"

"You can never walk in another person's shoes exactly, so I don't know." Karen pulled out the stool at the breakfast bar and pulled the potato chip bag close so she could open it. "I only know that in a perfect love, there is room for forgiveness. And for mistakes."

"It wasn't a mistake. He deceived me on purpose."

"What choice did he have?"

"True." Michelle hated that one point of the argument, the one she kept going over and over again no matter where she was—whether she was riding her horse, chatting with Jenna, working at the Snip & Style and even when she was supposed to be studying her Bible.

The answering machine beeped and clicked. Karen had hit the play button and was turning up the volume.

It was a man's voice. "Yeah? Say, this is uh, Captain Daggers. I'm Agent Brody's supervisor and I'm trying to get in touch with Michelle McKaslin. If you could have her return my call, I would appreciate it. I want to assure her that my agent had no choice but to keep his mission from her, as it could have jeopardized innocent lives. Thank you."

As she ripped open the stubborn potato chip bag, Karen crooked one brow as if to say, *See? What else could the poor man do?*

Yeah, yeah. Michelle took her time searching for the tubs of dip. Since everyone liked something different, she had to make sure there was French onion dip or Kendra would complain. Ranch for Kirby. It was her sisterly duty. She wasn't trying to hide her tears or anything. Really. Her eyes were watering because it was cold inside the refrigerator. Really cold.

"Like I said, there is room in a perfect love for forgiveness. And mistakes."

She'd told Brody everything. She'd shown him her heart and every vulnerability. He knew what Rick had done to her and that she'd been hurt before, and still he'd lied.

She found the last tub of dip. "How can I forgive him?"

"Maybe he's not the one who made the mistake. Or needs forgiving." Karen reached across the center island to tug at Michelle's ponytail. "Think about that, baby sister."

"I didn't do anything wrong."

"Does the Bible teach us to be forgiving?"

"Well, that only goes so far. I mean, I'm not a doormat." She picked at the plastic on the tub of ranch dip. She took great care ripping off the plastic seal.

She had to take her time and do it right because she didn't want to chip her nails.

"Are you crying?"

"No."

"You love him. You really do. It's the real thing." Karen abandoned the bags of chips on the counter and wrapped her arms around Michelle. "Love like that is rare. And it hurts. It challenges us to be bigger and better people than we are. Take my advice and rise to the challenge. Show him what your heart is truly made of. It will work out, I promise it."

How did Karen know? Could she fast-forward through time to see how this was going to end?

But then, Karen did seem to know everything. She had the perfect life. She always made the perfect choices. Michelle couldn't thank God enough for the wonderful blessing of her sisters.

Brody idled the black powerful motorcycle on the shoulder of the road. The West Virginia farm country had changed since he'd been a boy, but the old red barn was still standing. Someone had put on a new roof and painted it white. It looked sharp. Sheep grazed in lush fields.

This was his past. A past he'd refused to think about because it always brought with it grief. Now there were only the happy memories. The field there, where he and his dad once rode the tractor together. And the path between the fences where he'd ridden his horse.

Good memories. He had peace, at last.

With any luck, there would be better memories to make in his future.

He'd sold his town house, had a moving company come for his belongings and now he was heading west. To Montana.

To Michelle.

Would she forgive him? She'd blocked his number, so he couldn't even ring in on her phone. She'd returned his letters. She hadn't answered his captain's call. With the way she was acting, he was probably out of luck.

But he knew she could forgive him. Why? Because he loved her. Fierce and true and forever. Nothing would ever change that love or diminish it. It was a once-in-a-lifetime kind of blessing.

He believed that was the way she loved him. And always would.

He let out his clutch and spun gravel as he pulled onto the two-lane country road that would take him on the journey home.

Not even buying shoes made her feel better. That was a sorry state to be in.

With her cell wedged carefully between her shoulder and ear, Michelle lifted her foot from the gas pedal because she'd crept up a hair over the speed limit on the two-lane country road. "I found some really great boots for when the weather cools down. Yeah, they'll look so great with jeans. I hit an end-of-season sale on sandals and got this kickin' pair of strappy flats."

"Perfect for the singles' night at church," Jenna enthused on the other end of the phone. "I wish I could have gotten off work to go with you. Maybe you'd let me borrow something? I don't have anything to wear."

"Neither do I, but come over after work. We'll get ready together."

"Cool. Later!"

"Later!" Michelle dropped her phone on the seat and blinked at the image in her rearview mirror. A black motorcycle was behind her, getting ready to pass. A man in a black T-shirt and faded denim jeans, his face hidden by his helmet.

Brody! Her heart stopped. No, it couldn't be him. This bike was a different color. It was just wishful thinking. Longing for something that could never be.

It was weird how whenever she thought of him, she ached in the place deep in her heart where she used to feel him so strongly. But the connection between them was severed. What choice did she have?

Okay, she got that he was only doing his job. But he'd captured her heart. He'd made her fall in love with him. If he'd meant it, then why did he leave so easily, as if it had all been part of the plan to gain her family's trust?

Her gaze strayed to the motorcycle lingering behind her. She flicked on her blinker and expected him to pass. But he didn't. He slowed down along with her as she turned into her driveway. He went on by. The bike had a Montana license plate.

It wasn't Brody. He was long gone. After his supervisor had called, there had been no other word from him. Sure, it made her horribly sad. The ache remained deep in her soul, where there was a constant emptiness. An emptiness that no man could ever replace.

She'd thought about what Karen said; not forgiving the one you love is a mistake. But that wasn't the only problem. That wasn't what left her unhappy even after she had new shoes on her feet.

She couldn't stop the heavy disappointment

wrapped around her as she pulled into the carport. No one was around. Her mom was probably over at Gramma's. Her dad was out in the fields, cutting alfalfa. The empty house echoed around her as she ran upstairs to put her new shoes away. If she could find room for them in her closet.

What she needed to do was to force him from her mind. How? She had the rest of the afternoon. Maybe she'd take a long hard horse ride. That would do it. She'd saddle up Keno and take him on one of his favorite trails.

As she tied back her hair into a ponytail, she caught her reflection in the small dresser mirror. She was too pale and had dark circles from lack of sleep.

Jenna was right. What she needed to do was to get out. Do something new. And that's why they were going to the singles' night barbecue tonight, even though they knew every unmarried man there.

She was only going to be moral support for Jenna because Michelle was done with men. Through. Through being used. Lied to. Hurt.

She was just fine on her own. She was happy. She had friends and family. She had her horse. She had two jobs and a little too much credit card debt, but that was her own fault.

She did not need a man to be happy.

The doorbell rang.

Who could it be? It wasn't as if they were expecting guests in the middle of the day when everyone was busy on their farms.

Could it be the deliveryman? She was expecting a catalog order. Had it come already? Michelle bounded down the stairs, going as fast as she could. She couldn't wait to open the box. She'd ordered the cutest little jean jacket and it would look great on Jenna, for the dance tonight—

She flung open the door.

No deliveryman. No delivery truck. No one at all.

But there, perched on the wide rail of the front porch sat a dozen fragile pink rosebuds in a crystal vase. Each bud was perfect, the silken edges struggling to open.

On the rail, beside the vase was a wooden tray from a Scrabble game.

From Brody.

Her legs began to tremble, and she could *feel* him. He was nowhere in sight, but that didn't matter. He was here. She remembered that black motorcycle behind her. That had been Brody. He must have taken the service road instead of turning down the driveway.

He was here? She couldn't wait to see him; she never wanted to see him again. What was she going to do?

As if being pulling by an unseen rope, her feet moved her forward toward the porch rail. Toward the flowers and the nine Scrabble tiles that spelled out Forgive Me.

She wanted to. More than anything. Was it the right thing to do?

She could feel his presence like the hot summer air on her skin. He was coming for her. What did she do? How could she believe in him again? She stared as hard as she could at the little wooden tiles. Terror rocked her. She'd never been this afraid. Never had so much to lose.

His boot rang on the bottom step.

Although she vowed not to, she moved toward him. There he was, looking like a dream come true, one boot on the bottom step, and on his knee held with both hands was a second tray. The tiles spelled Marry Me.

Her bottom lip started to shake. No, it was impossible. He'd left so easily. He'd been playing a part. His wonderful words, his solid promises, his die-for-her love was a fabrication. Right?

"You're crying." He set the tray on the rail and moved toward her.

Could she help it? She was in his arms, letting him hold her, breathing in his comfort like air. She felt as if her heart was breaking all over again.

His hands cupped the sides of her face with great tenderness. With everlasting love. She could feel it; the places in his heart matched hers.

But how could she believe? How could she trust that this was real? That he was what he said?

"Because I love you," he answered her thoughts as if he'd heard them. The pads of his thumbs brushed away the tears on her cheeks. "I left like you wanted, and my love didn't die. It grew stronger. I told you it would.''

So did my love for you. She was too overwhelmed to speak. This couldn't be real. He was a dream, her dream, and dreams ended and then a girl woke up to reality.

"My dear Michelle." He kissed her brow. "I am a man who will love you with everything I am, heart and soul, for the rest of my life.''

Great silver tears filled her big eyes and spilled down her cheeks.

His dear, dear Michelle. He'd traveled a long way to find her. He was in her arms. He was home.

All he had to do was make her believe. "You are the only real thing in my life. You are what matters to me. For the rest of my life, I will protect you. I will provide for you. I will keep you safe and happy and cherished. You are my heart. Marry me. Dreams do come true.''

She pressed a kiss against the pad of his thumb, damp with her tears. "Dreams end.''

"Yes, they do. And that's the good part. This is the real thing.'' He kissed her as gently as dawn, as reverently as a man treated the most important woman on earth. "We get to live the rest of our lives together. All you have to do is say yes.''

"Yes.''

He pulled her into his arms, and she could feel it in the harmony that bound her heart to his, her soul to his. He was right. Their life ahead was going to be better than any dream.

"I love you," she whispered against his lips.

"Not as much as I love you." His kiss was more than a kiss. It was perfection.

Epilogue

"**Y**ou've got paint on your nose." Brody laid the paintbrush on the rim of the can. His wife was looking more beautiful with every day.

Even in a secondhand T-shirt with a big hole in the shoulder, a pair of his old running shorts and speckled with blue paint, she made him brim over with tenderness.

"Hold still." He swiped the paint splatter off the bridge of her nose with the clean edge of his T-shirt. "You're getting more paint on you than on the trim."

"Oh, says the man who looks like he swam in a vat of paint." She wrapped her arms around his neck, not worried about all the dabs of blue still wet on his chest.

"Are you happy?" he asked after a long, passionate kiss.

"Hmm. Delirious."

"We're never going to get this house finished if we keep this up."

"I'm not worried about it." Her favorite place on earth was with her husband. Michelle sighed, contented, and laid her head on his chest. It was impossible to think she could be any happier than this, but she knew this was only the beginning. She knew for a fact their happiness was going to double.

A year had passed since Brody first showed up in her life. They'd had a September wedding in the church where she'd been baptized, with her family surrounding her. They'd lived in the apartment above the garage while Brody helped her dad with the harvest.

Then, after she and Brody had bought the property from her parents, they'd moved into the bungalow where Mick had stayed. Since he was in prison for a few more years, it wasn't likely he would need it.

Did she tell him now, before everybody came? Or did she wait until they were alone, the day spent, and ready to go to bed?

"What are you smiling about?" He brushed his hand down her hair with endless affection.

"I can't keep this secret any longer!" It was killing her. She thought she'd cook a nice dinner, have a romantic evening with him and then surprise him with the news.

But did she do that? No!

His eyes widened. His mouth twisted into a big

smile and then he lifted her up with both hands. "You're pregnant, aren't you?"

"Yes!" She was laughing, wrapping her arms around his neck as he started whooping with joy.

"Hey, you two, keep it down, would you?" Kendra swung down from her gelding. She'd ridden over today.

Behind her Zach and Karen pulled into the driveway in their SUV. Soon Kirby and Sam would follow. Now that they had little Michael, they always ran a few minutes late.

"It's terrible, all this love in the air." Kendra winked as she untied her saddle pack. "I brought snacks."

"We brought hamburger makings," Karen added as she lifted Allie from her car seat.

Allie was clapping her hands together and singing, "Down! Down!"

Zach grabbed his tool bag. "We're here to help install those windows. C'mon, let's get started, if you can pull yourself away from your wife."

Brody pressed his forehead to hers. Michelle knew the bond between them was a precious gift. And it was only going to get better.

"I'll deal with you later," he promised.

"I hope so."

Sam and Kirby were pulling up, everyone was calling out their greetings, but it was only background noise as Michelle watched her husband amble off with Zach, talking windows and something about miter saws.

Dreams came true. Michelle knew that now. Prayers were answered. The gift of life was an amazing one, she thought, as she held out her hands to her niece as Allie came running.

A shiver skidded across the back of her neck. She turned, knowing Brody was watching her. She felt his happiness because it was hers, too. This was the good stuff in life, she had no doubt, as he whispered, "I love you."

As she loved him, heart and soul.

*   *   *   *   *

Dear Reader,

Thank you for choosing *Heart and Soul*. I am so excited to finally tell Michelle's story. I've been fond of her ever since she first appeared in my second Love Inspired story, *His Hometown Girl* (LI #180), where she was Karen's little sister. Michelle was so kind and good and waiting faithfully for the love of her life to come along. And he does, in the form of Gabe Brody, FBI, a man who is more than he seems and her answered prayer. I hope you enjoyed reading herstory as much as I did writing it.

I wish you and your loved ones peace and grace.

Jillian Hart

ALMOST HEAVEN

Love never gives up, never loses faith, is always
hopeful, and endures through every circumstance.
—*1 Corinthians* 13:7

Chapter One

It had been a long, hot day. Exhaustion dulled the edges of Kendra's vision, but the familiar sight of her hometown fortified her, as it always did. The green of a well-kept park. The neat line of railroad tracks on one side of the main street and the tidy row of old-fashioned buildings on the other. The cheerful awnings of businesses. The friendly neon sign of her family's coffee shop still burned a bright blue and green in the front window.

She glanced at the clock on the dashboard—thirty-four minutes past four. Maybe she'd stop and beg for food and drink so she wouldn't have to find something in her practically empty cupboards at home. There was probably a box of her beloved macaroni and cheese, but she lacked the energy and the will to make it.

The brief blast of a siren startled her and she

glanced in her side-view mirror. Sure enough, there was a patrol car behind her. Was she speeding? No, the speedometer's needle was a hair past twenty. If anything she was going too slow.

Maybe the sheriff needed to go around her. Well, she was towing a full four-horse trailer. There was no oncoming traffic. Couldn't he just pass her?

No, he stayed stubbornly behind her, not looking as if he intended to pass. That must mean he wanted her.

What did she do? Too many cars were parked along the street, so she signaled and crossed the yellow lines to the other side of the road. She hoped that wasn't illegal or anything, but it wasn't as if she had a choice.

The patrol car followed her over, lights flashing. Brace yourself, Kendra, here he comes.

The town sheriff stalked toward her. Gun on one hip, his powerful arms held to his sides, he walked with an athlete's strength and confidence.

Cameron Durango. One of the last men she wanted to be alone with in the universe. Had he always looked this good in his uniform? Why hadn't she noticed that before?

She was staring at him! And he was likely to notice that. What was wrong with her? She'd given up putting her faith in men a long time ago. It was a done deal, signed, sealed and delivered. A life decision she'd made, and that was that.

The *last* thing she should be noticing was how

striking Cameron looked in his uniform. Get a grip, Kendra. He's the sheriff. Nothing more. Nothing less. He arrests people. He pulls over perfectly innocent drivers for no reason at all.

His boots crunched in the gravel beside her pickup.

Don't look at him. "I wasn't speeding."

"Hey, Kendra." He whipped off his hat and the breeze ruffled the dark ends of his military short hair. "How are you doing this fine summer's day?"

"Hot."

"Yeah? A fine rig like this ought to have air-conditioning standard, right?"

"Sure, but I'm pulling a full load. I don't want to overheat the engine."

"I understand. I'd baby a new truck if I had one. You got this, what, a month ago?"

She stared straight ahead, not wanting to answer. Okay, she wasn't rude by nature and she felt lame acting that way. But Cameron Durango knew something about her that nobody else did, not even her sisters.

It didn't matter how fine he looked or how friendly he seemed, he reminded her of things best left forgotten.

Couldn't he just go?

"Yeah," she finally said. "That's why I haven't been driving around the truck I used to have, the one that kept breaking down on me."

"Right." Maybe he got the hint, because he paused, as if debating what to do next. Did he leave?

No. He rested his forearms on the door of her truck. "Bet you're wondering what you did wrong to get me on your tail?"

"No. I wasn't speeding." Maybe if she was difficult, he'd leave her alone. Ticket her or whatever he was going to do and be on his way. So she wouldn't have to remember.

"I was sitting in the shade in my air-conditioning, tucked behind the Town Welcomes You sign, hoping to catch a hoard of speeding tourists and boost the town's income, when you meander along, driving responsibly and under the limit."

"You admit it."

"I noticed you were about to lose a tire on your trailer and decided to leave my shady spot behind to come warn you."

Was he trying to be friendly? And it bugged her because she didn't want to like him. It would be way easier if he was going to unjustly ticket her, instead of help her.

She didn't need his or any man's assistance. "I've got doubles."

"Still, you're carrying a heavy load."

"I checked all the tires before I left the auction." He was right, and she realized the same thing herself, but was she going to tell him that? No. "Which tire?"

"Back right. Wouldn't want you to have a blowout or anything. You could get hurt."

He had kind eyes, dark and deep, and a rugged face. Not classically handsome but chiseled as if made from granite. He had a straight blade of a nose, an uncompromising mouth and a square jaw that gave him an air of integrity.

If he were mean, it would have been much easier not to like him. But he wasn't. The worst thing about Cameron Durango was that he was a decent guy. He may carry a gun on his hip and look powerful enough to take down a two-hundred-pound criminal with a body blow, but he had a good heart.

Not that you could tell it from the outside.

Don't think about that night. Cold snaked through her veins, where her heart used to be. If there had been anything redeeming about that horrible night when everything changed for her, it was Cameron's kindness. He'd been truly kind, when she'd neither wanted it nor needed it.

Remembering, she couldn't meet his gaze. Staring hard at the steering wheel, she ran her fingertip around the bottom of the rim. Since that night she hadn't wanted to be alone with any man. Especially Cameron.

"I'll get that changed. Thanks for letting me know. It was decent of you."

"I try to be decent when I can. Especially to a pretty lady like you."

The way he said it wasn't flirtatious or anything, but he *was* sounding friendly. It made her start to shake.

She really wanted him to go. "Thanks again."

But he didn't leave. "Let me guess. You were at

the sale today. The Bureau of Land Management's auction.''

Was he trying to make small talk? It was probably a slow day for him. Hardly anyone was out and about in this heat, but still. She didn't know Cameron well and that's the way she wanted it. Could she be outright rude and tell him so? No.

''I saw the flier—it came to the office. You got wild mustangs back there?''

''Yes.''

She kept staring at her steering wheel. Icy sweat broke out on her palms. This was the way it was whenever she was alone with any man near her age.

Would it always be this way? Prayer had helped her; at least she didn't shake so hard that he might notice.

''Wow. Mind if I take a peek at them?''

Oh, so he was interested in the horses. Kendra relaxed a little but the quaking didn't stop. ''Sure. Just be careful. They're not used to people yet.''

''I'll just look.'' His grin was in his voice.

Kendra's gaze flashed to the side mirror where he was ambling away, his boots striking the dirt at the side of the road with a muffled rhythm.

With his spine straight and shoulders squared, he looked invincible. Undefeatable. Like everything honest and good and all-American. Just as he'd been for her, a calm strength when the world was smashing apart around her.

Get a grip, Kendra. That night was a long time ago.

It isn't worth thinking about. Jerrod was gone and a part of the past. Look forward, not back.

Cameron crunched through the gravel as he returned. "Those are some fine-looking animals you got."

"Thanks." She appreciated Cameron's help, but now she knew about the tire. She would fix it and be on her way—once he was on his. "I don't want to hold you up. I know you have speeders to catch and tickets to write."

"Are you trying to get rid of me?"

Yes. "Here comes a car right now. You might need to check your radar. Could be income for the town."

He peered in the direction of the luxury sedan creeping down the main street. "Mrs. Greenley? Nah, she's driving under the limit, like she always does. I've clocked her for the better part of the six years I've worked in this town and never caught her speeding once. The town is safe from rampaging, careless drivers for a few more seconds, it looks like."

"You can never be too sure. You go back to your speed trap and I'll take care of the tire."

"Afraid I can't let you do that, Kendra." Cameron planted his hands on his hips, emphasizing the power in his arms and the gun on his hip. "This is my jurisdiction, ma'am, and I believe there's an ordinance that states I must aid stranded motorists in my town or suffer serious consequences."

Her left eyebrow shot up. "You're kidding."

"Would I do that?" Absolutely. There wasn't any

such ordinance, but he wasn't about to tell her that? "If I don't make sure your vehicle's safe to drive in this town, I'd be breaking my own laws."

"What laws?"

"The ones that say I'd have to write myself a ticket."

"Go ahead. I don't mind."

"*I* would." He had her, he knew it by the twinkle in her pretty eyes. "Might even have to throw myself in jail and that's not how I want to spend my day."

"So, why would I care? I'm perfectly capable of changing the tire."

"Yeah, but I have a flawless record. Not a single infraction to date. You wouldn't want my reputation besmirched, would you?"

"Sure I would."

Humor tugged at the corners of her soft, lush mouth. Cam felt some pride about that. Kendra McKaslin might look cool and unapproachable, but she seemed like a real nice lady.

He'd been trying to approach her for the last few months, but he had a lot of questions about horses. He didn't know where to start. He didn't want to look like a dummy. After all, a man had his pride.

But Kendra didn't strike him as someone who'd made anyone feel dumb. She seemed as sweet as spring, with her long blond hair shimmering down her back like liquid gold in the sunlight. She'd grown up in one of the wealthier families in their humble valley, but was she snooty?

No. Down to earth, filled with common sense, Kendra was country-girl goodness soul-deep. He could *feel* it. He'd watched her kindness to her horses every time she'd ridden one of them into town on an errand to the store or to visit her family's coffee shop.

She appeared to be real good with the animals. Everyone said she was the best in the area when it came to horsemanship. But he hadn't gotten up his courage to talk to her.

Now was his chance. "I know you're an independent kind of woman. You're more than capable of changing that tire on your own."

"So why are you still standing here?" The hint of her smile grew into a real one.

"I've got an election coming up. What would folks think if they see you stranded here in obvious need of help—"

"Stranded? I don't think so!"

"Still, they'll watch me drive off and leave you behind and draw their own conclusions. All folks will see is that their elected official abandoned a woman stuck along the side of the road, slacking off on his duties."

"Like anyone would think you were a slacker."

"I can't risk it. Folks might vote for my opponent come September. I'd lose my job. Won't be able to pay my bills. You don't want to be responsible for that, do you?"

"Sure." There were more sparkles in her pretty blue eyes.

She had a quiet kind of beauty, one that wasn't only skin-deep.

His chest gave a strange hitch in the vicinity of his heart as he opened the truck's door for her. That was odd, considering how he hadn't felt much beside grief since Deb's death. "Your sister's sign is still on in the window. Why don't you go in, say hello and get something cool to drink? Give me twenty minutes and I'll have this taken care of."

"That's not right. It's my trailer."

"Yeah, well, it's a slow day. I don't see a lot of wild speeders or crime sprees on Thursday afternoons. It's okay to let me do this, Kendra."

He could see the argument coming. He'd learned to read people during his fifteen years wearing a badge. He saw a woman used to doing things herself. "If it bothers your conscience, then you can bring a batch of cookies or something by the station. My deputy has a sweet tooth you wouldn't believe."

She swept down from the seat with an easy grace that she didn't seem aware of.

He was. It sure threw him for a loop.

Today she looked summery and girl-next-door fresh in a white tank top, a pair of jean shorts and slip-on tennis shoes. Her blond hair, streaked by time in the sun, was tied back in a long ponytail. She slipped her sunglasses from the top of her head onto her nose and circled around the rig to look at the damage.

"I think my spare went flat." She said it wearily,

more to herself than to him. Probably expecting some kind of reprimand.

Why would he do that? Didn't a woman who worked hard to make her own living deserve a break? He sure thought so. "Zach's at his garage. I'll take the tire over for him to patch."

"He's my brother-in-law, and I can do it."

"Toll House, no walnuts. I have a soft spot for butterscotch chips.

He left her standing there, watching him with a slack jaw as he yanked the jack from his cruiser's trunk. "I'm helping you, no matter what. Just accept it."

"I should help you."

"Why? It would make me look bad. I've got my public image to think about. Voters care about that kind of thing."

He didn't care about his image, he worked hard to do the right thing and he was proud of his record. He had time, and in helping her maybe he'd find a way to approach her. Ask her professional opinion. "I'm not taking no for an answer. Your only option is to let me do my job."

She studied him and the jack he was carrying and the nearly flat tire. "Fine. Thank you. The horses—"

"Will be fine. I've done this before."

"Okay."

She didn't sound happy, but Cameron bet that she'd let him do it. He wasn't about to budge, he'd been waiting for this chance forever, that's what it felt like. If he had a choice, then he'd want her to stay and watch so they could talk while he worked.

He knew her well enough to know she wouldn't hang around. She kept her distance from men, not just him, and with good reason.

He felt her sadness every time he was around her. Now maybe he was imagining it, because he'd been there to arrest Jerrod Melcher, and he saw how bad she'd been hurt. That was likely to make any woman wary about men for a long time.

It was understandable.

As he watched her cross the road, jaywalking, heading straight to her family's coffee shop, a streak of pain jabbed through his heart. A widower was used to feeling a certain amount of pain down deep, but this was something different. Something that felt a lot like longing.

One thing was for sure. When Kendra looked at him, she didn't feel any positive emotion. Not a chance. When she looked at him she remembered that night. He could feel that, too.

Perhaps he should just leave her alone. Ask Sally at the Long Horn Stables for help instead.

Frustrated, he got to work.

It was *her* trailer, she ought to be dealing with it. But that stubborn sheriff had refused to leave, so what was she going to do? Stand there and make small talk? She didn't need his help and she was getting it anyway. It ate at her as the bell over the coffee shop's door jangled.

The welcome breeze from the air-conditioning skimmed over her, but it didn't cool her anger. Men were bossy, every one of them. Who did the sheriff think he was that he could just do what he wanted to her trailer?

Face it, you appreciate that he's helping.

Sure, but it still bugged her. She was hot, exhausted, and dealing with a flat tire in over hundred-degree weather would have put her over the edge. Well, at least close to it.

Because of Cameron, she was able to rest for a few minutes instead of dealing with one more disaster in a doom-filled day. She didn't want to be grateful to him. But she was.

See why it was a good idea to stay far away from men? Even the nice ones?

"Kendra? You look too hot, are you all right?" Gramma sat at the far end of the otherwise empty room, behind one of the cloth-covered tables. Ignoring her spread of papers and her open laptop, she examined Kendra over the lines in her bifocals. "Something *is* wrong. Why are you back so soon?"

"I'm fine and it's past closing time." Kendra flicked off the neon sign and turned the Open sign in the window to Closed. "How long have you been in here slaving over the bookkeeping?"

"Goodness, let me see." She checked her gold wristwatch. "For much longer than I thought!"

"You lose track of time when you're doing the books. I do the same thing."

"I suppose so!" Gramma took off her glasses and wiped them on the corner hem of her stylish summer blouse. "I've lost two dollars and seventy cents I can't find anywhere. I'd just finish the deposit and say, forget it. But it'll be all I think about when I get home. Come, dear, sit down. You look as though you've got too much sun."

"No need to fuss, I'm fine. I'm going to raid the kitchen and pray there are some leftovers in the fridge. I'm too beat to cook when I get home."

"I knew it. You work too hard, sweetie. You can't work every minute of every day."

"I take a few minutes off now and then."

"Don't sass me, young lady. You've been skipping meals."

"Not intentionally."

Kendra ducked into the kitchen to avoid the lecture. She knew what was coming when Gramma got started. She loved her grandmother within an inch of her life, but how Gramma fussed! Kendra yanked open the industrial refrigerator and studied the contents. Jackpot!

Gramma's sandals tapped on the floor, announcing her approach to the kitchen.

"I can do it myself." Kendra pulled a bowl of chicken salad from the top shelf. "Do you want me to make you a sandwich, too?"

"Me? You're the one needing to eat. Give me that. Where's the mayonnaise?"

"I said I'd do it and I meant it." Kendra wrapped her grandmother into a hug and breathed in the honeysuckle sweetness of her perfume. "You've had a long day, and you don't need to make it longer by doing one single thing for me. You work too much."

"I've got good help. The girls I've hired this summer have been a real blessing. There's the macaroni salad you like in the bottom shelf. No, let me get it."

Kendra snatched the big stainless-steel bowl from the shelf. "Out. Go back to your table. Shoo!"

"Nice try, but I wrote the book on bossy." Gramma dug through the pantry and came up with a wrapped loaf of homemade bread. "We'll both fix us something to eat while you tell me about your new horses."

"You're a tricky woman, Gramma."

"Thanks, dear, I try. Hand me the serrated knife."

Kendra did as she was asked and found two plates while she was digging through the dishwasher. "I won the bid for the prettiest mustangs I've gotten yet. One is as wild and mean as a bull, but the others have potential."

"You bought a mean horse?" Gramma's disapproval wreathed her soft, lovely face, as she cut thick slices of wheat-nut bread. "Is that safe?"

"He's a stallion."

"I don't like the sound of that! Not at all. Boarding

and training horses is one thing. But a stallion? How will you handle him? And he's wild, to boot!''

"I have a little tiny eensy-beensy bit of experience with horses, remember?" Kendra twisted open the jar of mayo. "I've been riding since before I could walk."

"I didn't approve of that, either, the way your father would put you and your sisters on the backs of horses when you were nothing but toddlers!" Gramma's eyes twinkled, though. "He must be a good-looking horse, if you bought him."

"He's a beauty. Bright chestnut coat. Perfect white socks. A long black mane and tail. And his lines... he's got some Arabian in him." Kendra sighed. "Of course, he gives new meaning to the word *wild*. I'm sure I can tame him, so don't start worrying. I haven't been killed by a horse yet."

"Heavens, I should hope not! You *do* have a way with them. I don't doubt that." Gramma bit her lip as she layered meat mixture and cheese on a slice of bread. As if she were thinking better of saying anything more.

Kendra whipped the knife from her grandmother's hand. "You go sit down. I'll finish this up and bring you a cup of iced tea to the table. Go. Away with you."

"You're getting just as bossy as me. I like that." Planting a kiss on Kendra's cheek, she left the kitchen without further complaint.

That wasn't like Gramma at all, but Kendra was

too exhausted to dwell on it. She put away the sandwich makings, grabbed two bottles of iced tea from the case, shouldered through the swinging doors and into the silent shop.

With the wide bank of windows along the end wall, she had a perfect view of Cameron. He was rolling the tire across the street, apparently whistling as he went, looking like a hero in his navy-blue uniform.

"That Durango boy's helpin' you out, I see," Gramma commented as she tapped keys on her computer. "Funny that you'd let a man do something like that for you."

"Don't go reading something into it that's not there."

"Is something there?"

How many times had they discussed this? "I'm not going to get married, you know. Ever. So don't start getting your hopes up. The truth is, I'm so tired I can barely pick up my feet and Cameron offered to help me. He helps with this kind of thing all the time."

"Which kind of thing would that be? A tire low on air? Or helping a very pretty eligible woman?" Gramma's eyes twinkled as if she knew something Kendra didn't.

"If you're going to torture me about this, I'm taking my food and I'm leaving." Kendra said it lightly, but she meant it.

The impenetrable titanium walls around her heart were sealed shut. They were going to stay locked tight. "I'm not interested in Cameron."

"Then why, sweetie, is he fixing that tire for you?"

"Because he's a sheriff and I had a long day in the hot sun and no lunch."

She took a big bite of her sandwich to prove it.

"Fine. All right. I believe you." She held up her hands helplessly. "You can't blame a poor grandmother for hoping."

"Oh, yes I can!"

"Only three of my granddaughters are married and have given me perfect grandchildren. There's no crime in wanting more. Marge's youngest girl married just last year and had a new baby boy last week. That makes for four grandchildren for her. I've got to keep up."

Kendra rolled her eyes, her mouth too full to speak. What was the point? As if Gramma listened anyway. She had her definite opinions and nothing short of laser fire was going to change her mind.

"Cameron is certainly a good man, isn't he? He's so nice and courteous. Everyone raves on about what a fine sheriff he's been."

"Yes, I'm sure he'll be reelected. Now, can we change the subject?"

"Look how handsome he is in his uniform. I have a weakness for men in uniforms myself. The first time I saw your grandfather in his dress blues…it does make a girl feel safe, doesn't it?"

"Stop." Laughter escaped anyway. How could she be mad at her grandmother who so obviously loved the idea of marriage and happily-ever-afters?

But it wasn't for everyone. It even said so in the Bible. God chose different paths for everyone and some women were meant to be married and mothers.

She wasn't. It hurt, but there wasn't anything she could do to change the direction her life had taken.

It wasn't as if she were alone.

Look at the blessings the good Lord had placed in her life. Her grandmother, her parents, her sisters, her friends and her horses. How many people actually got to do what they loved for a living? She'd always wanted her own riding stable, and that's what she had. She wasn't going to complain about her life. Not now. Not ever.

"Oh, where are the books off? This is the most aggravating thing on earth. Who invented bookkeeping, anyway? Whoever he is, he's a very bad man." Gramma's frustration was good-natured as she held up her hand and gave the computer a death-ray glare. "I should just quit, but it'll keep bothering me if I do."

"You're just tired. Let me take a peek." Kendra pulled the ledger so it faced her. "It's probably just a transposition."

"You are simply a wonder, my dear. Thank you."

As she ate, Kendra squinted at the numbers and tried to make her eyes focus. Minutes ticked by as she studied the long row of numbers and paired them against the deposit slip. It had to be a coincidence that she'd chosen a seat that faced the windows, right? She wouldn't pick this spot on purpose because she had a perfect view of Cameron Durango kneeling in the hot sun, working alongside Zach, her brother-in-law, who must have come over to help.

He may be handsome and kind and dependable, sure, but the steel doors around her heart stayed locked.

"Where are the checks?" Kendra tore her gaze from the window and noticed her grandmother's eyes were sparkling, as if she'd noticed where Kendra's gaze kept straying. "Oh, I get it. You think I'm interested in the sheriff."

"Oh, no. Of course not." She was the perfect face of innocent grandmotherly denial. "I was just thinking what a blessing it is that God sends us what we need when we need it most."

"And that cryptic comment means…"

"Oh, nothing about Cameron coming to help you when you needed it, of course. Heavens, no! I was referring to you walking through the door when I was ready to give up in frustration. The checks are here, in the bank bag."

Kendra waited while her grandmother slid the small dark bag across the table. Liar. Whether Gramma admitted it or not, *she* wasn't fooled one bit.

Why argue about it? There was no point. Her grandmother would come to understand in time and to accept Kendra's choices in life.

Cameron Durango, no matter how striking and protective and capable he looked in his uniform, would never be one of her choices.

Why did that make her sad? She decided her barricades were weakening, probably because she was still so tired and hungry.

See? A girl needed to keep up her strength so she wasn't susceptible to random, pointless emotions. It *was* pointless to feel sad about what could never be made right.

She bit into the second half of her sandwich and went to work comparing the thick pile of checks against the deposit slip.

Chapter Two

"Here's your problem, Gramma. It's right here. You've transposed a check amount on the deposit slip." Kendra grabbed the nearby pen and made the corrections. "There. That should do it."

"Wonderful! My dear, what would I have done without you?"

"You'd have found it without my help. I—"

The bell above the door jingled.

Cameron. She didn't need to turn around to know it was him. She *felt* his presence as surely as the current of August heat radiating through the opened door.

Why was she so aware of this man she hardly knew, as if he'd reached out and laid his hand on her arm? It was odd. She'd never felt this before with him or with anyone.

The door clicked shut, and he stood in the direct

blast of the air-conditioning vent. Hat off, eyes closed, his head tilted back in appreciation. He seemed to be enjoying the icy draft as it ruffled his short, dark hair.

"That sure cooled me down." He clutched his hat in his big, capable hands. There was a streak of grease across the backs of his broad knuckles. "Good afternoon, Helen."

"Sheriff." Gramma's pleasure warmed her voice. "It's good to see you. Come in and cool down. Kendra will get you something to drink."

"Oh, I will?"

Leave it to her grandmother to try to matchmake. As if it would do any good. And poor Cameron. He was struggling to be elected, and he had to be *desperate* if he wanted to change her tire in this heat. He shouldn't have to keel over from heat stroke because of it.

The chair groaned in the joints as she stood, although it could have been her knees, but she didn't want to think about the creaks in her joints since she'd turned thirty. Her tennies squeaked on the clean floor as she put as much distance between her and Cameron as she could.

"Iced tea or soda?"

"One of those flavored teas would do just fine." Cameron followed her, as if he wasn't about to let her escape until he had her vote. Surely that's what this was all about.

She wasn't so sure when she turned around, with the cool metal handle in hand, and didn't notice the icy draft from the refrigeration unit. He was behind her, and this time she didn't tremble. She fizzed, like those carbonated bubbles in a glass of cola. She felt bubbly down deep in her soul.

"Lemon-flavored, if you've got it." His voice came warm, deep and as inviting as ever.

The bubbles inside her fizzed upward and she felt lighter than air. As if her soul turned upside down and wasn't sad anymore. How wrong was that? Get a grip, girl.

She handed him the squat bottle. "Anything else?"

"This is all I need." He didn't move away as he covered the mouth of the bottle with his wide palm and twisted the cap. "Zach lent a hand, too, so we did double-time getting it done. You're all set."

"Thanks, Sheriff."

"Cameron. I've loosened your lug nuts, I think we ought to be on a first-name basis."

"Aren't you funny?"

"I try to be. I get that way when I'm sugar-deprived."

"I can take a hint. You want more of a reward for a job well done? My vote isn't enough."

"I could use a snack."

Was it her imagination, or was he trying to be charming? "Does the town council know what you're up to?"

"Why? I'm doing nothing wrong. Every cop has the civil right to doughnuts. Or those amazing choc-olate cookies your grandmother makes if you happen to have any lying around taking up too much space on your shelves.''

He was definitely trying to be nice. It was hard to shoot down a man complimenting Gramma's baking. Maybe that was one way to win elections. What did she know about politics?

''It's your lucky day.'' Kendra spied two chocolate cookies left over from the day's sales, looking lonely on the pastry shelf below the hand-off counter. ''Could you do us a favor and take them off our hands?''

''I reckon I could try. Helping the lovely ladies of this town is my beholden duty.''

He sure *must* want to be reelected, since he was trying so hard. As if he had any real competition anyway. From what everyone said, he'd been one of the best sheriffs the town had ever had. She grabbed the two cookies with a slice of waxed paper and handed them over.

He had a nice smile. Not flashy or too wide, but honest and easy. Sincere. ''My stomach thanks you. Helen, every time I see you zipping around in that little red convertible of yours, I think I've got to get me one of those.''

''Nah, you're too stodgy, young man.'' Gramma teased as she zipped up the bank's deposit bag. ''You're better off in that sensible SUV you drive.''

''You're making me sound middle-aged, Helen. I don't appreciate that.''

''It's not my fault you're stuffy.'' Laughing,

Gramma slipped the laptop into her shoulder bag and, clutching the deposit, she headed for the door. Much faster than usual.

"Gramma, where are you off to in such a hurry?"

"The bank."

"It's already closed."

As if she'd temporarily gone deaf, Gramma didn't answer, just smiled sweetly as she backed through the doorway. "You keep up the good work, young man. It's reassuring to see a man who knows responsibility."

Her grandmother tossed Kendra a knowing wink before snapping the door shut with a final jangle of the bell. That matchmaker!

"What was that about?" Cameron looked puzzled, which proved he couldn't be the best detective.

"It wasn't obvious? My other sisters are married off and providing her with grandchildren, so she's trying to find me a husband, I guess. Sorry about that." Kendra rolled her eyes as she grabbed her half-full bottle from the table.

"Hey, I understand. My grandmother is the same way. She asked me for years every time I saw her, which was every Sunday for church, why I couldn't find a nice girl and settle down." He ambled toward the door, talking conversationally.

The good-natured banter lifted a weight from her shoulders. Cameron was no threat. He was simply making conversation. He'd treated Gramma the same exact way.

More at ease, she followed him and dug in her shorts pocket for her keys. "So, how did you handle your grandmother?"

"I informed her that if I could find a nice girl, then I would marry her. The problem is finding a woman who's interested in *me.*"

"Sure, I can see why that's a problem." Dependable man, handsome and fit and went out of his way to help others. She locked up and tested the lock— sometimes it was tricky.

"Once she saw it from a prospective bride's viewpoint, she stopped bothering me. She wouldn't want to inflict any nice girl with a husband like me."

"There's more to life than having a ring on your hand, that's for sure."

Was it a lie if you wanted to mean what you said, even if it wasn't the truth? Kendra wondered as she loped down the steps and crossed the street.

"Sure," he agreed, keeping stride with her.

Was it marriage she was against, or the fear of trusting a man that much?

They'd reached his cruiser. "You should be safe to drive home."

"Thanks again, Cameron. You have a good evening." She strode around the back of the trailer, jingling her keys in the palm of her hand as she went, blond hair blowing in a long silken ponytail behind her.

Cameron bit into a cookie as he waited by his cruiser to make sure she got on her way all right.

Chocolate broke apart in his mouth, as rich as cake and made richer with sweet chunks of milk chocolate.

It *almost* soothed away his disappointment as Kendra's truck engine rolled over with an easy hum. Taillights winked on and the right blinkers flashed. She eased out into the empty street leaving only tire marks and a hint of dust in the air.

That didn't bode too well, man. She was sure quick to get rid of him. Not that he'd come across as an intelligent future customer. No, he'd yakked on about his re-election when what he should have done was ask her about the boarding fees at her stable.

Seeking refuge inside the car, he started the engine and flicked the air-conditioning on high. Not even the second chocolate cookie made him feel better.

Maybe some things weren't meant to be. And if they were, then wouldn't the Lord present him with another chance?

He was upset, and it wasn't only about the questions he *didn't* ask Kendra. He'd fibbed when she'd asked how he'd handled his grandmother's desire for him to marry. His nana was a fine woman, a real lady, and she worried about him being alone.

The truth was, he'd lost his heart when he buried his wife. He'd lived in darkness ever since her passing. His grieving was done, but the loneliness remained.

He'd loved being married. If he could find a woman that filled him up like sunlight, that made him alive again, well, wouldn't that be something? Did true love happen twice in a lifetime?

He'd leave that answer up to the Lord. In the meantime, his workday was done. There was nothing else to do but go home. He would face the lonely house and the silent kitchen as he did every night and make a tuna-fish sandwich for supper while he listened to the world news.

Alone.

Alone. *Finally.* Kendra collapsed on her second-hand couch and let the window unit pummel her with blessed, cold air. Her fat tabby cat meowed a weak protest from the top of the cushion, but his demand for more treats was the last one in a long list.

She'd done everything. The new horses were in the paddock, the stalls in the stables were cleaned, the horses fed and watered, the trailer hosed out. She'd returned messages, paid a few bills and checked on a pregnant mare.

The cat's meow was louder.

"Pounce, can you wait two minutes? Just two? I don't think I can move."

Meow.

"The treats are on the other end table. I can't reach them from here."

Apparently tired of her excuses, the twenty-pound orange tabby leaped off the top of the cushion and onto Kendra's stomach.

"Okay, I'll get the treats." Laughing, she rubbed

the cat's head, as he purred. The shrill ring of the phone had her reaching for the cordless handset tossed in the mess on the coffee table. "This had better be good."

"Ooh, it is!" It was her littlest sister Michelle, trembling with excitement. Not that Michelle was all that little now that she was grown-up and married. "We're all on our way to the hospital. Karen was admitted about thirty minutes ago."

"She's having the baby?" Excitement must have reenergized her, because Kendra found the will to stand up, carrying Pounce as she crossed the room. "Did you need a ride or is your hubby there?"

"Brody's locking up right now... Oops, I gotta go. He's dragging me to the front door." Michelle was laughing. "See you at the hospital!"

Another niece or nephew to welcome into their family! Kendra tossed the phone onto the cushions to worry about later. She was going to be an aunt—again. She had to hurry. She had to drive. She needed caffeine. Good thing she'd made a pitcher of sun tea yesterday.

A swift brush along her ankles reminded her of her primary mission. The cat led the way to the treat bag and his demanding meow left no doubt. He was annoyed with her.

"I know, that phone was more important than you. I'm sorry, buddy." She gave him an extra treat, rubbed his head while he purred gratefully and made the long journey of about seven steps into the small galley kitchen.

Okay, so she hadn't done *all* her chores today. Bypassing the counter of dirty dishes, she rummaged through the back of the cupboard until she found a clean cup, dumped some sugar in for good measure and went in search of her keys.

Where were they? The cat was no help, as he was settling on his cushion in front of the air conditioner and couldn't be bothered with lowly human dilemmas.

"Found 'em!" On the floor beneath her tennies. "Bye, Pounce!"

The cat managed a disdainful frown, which Kendra took to mean he'd miss her.

Twilight was creeping into the long shadows as she started her truck, but that didn't provide any relief from the heat. No. At least she wasn't towing a trailer, so she punched up the air-conditioning. The sinking sun blazed bright orange and magenta in her rear and side-view mirrors, tailing her as she headed to Bozeman.

The sun had set in a lavender hush by the time she pulled into the hospital parking lot, found an available space as close to the front doors as she could manage and climbed out into the coming darkness.

"Kendra, is that you?" A man's voice rumbled behind her.

Her keys tumbled through her fingers and crashed to the pavement at her feet. She recognized his deep, warm baritone instantly. Smooth move, Kendra. "Cameron. What are you doing here?"

"Startling you. Here, let me." He knelt and retrieved her keys.

It was gentlemanly of him. If he hadn't spoken first, she might not have realized it was him right off. She was used to seeing him in his navy-blue uniform. Tonight he wore a simple T-shirt and jeans, belted at his lean hips, and scuffed boots.

He straightened to his full six feet and held her key ring on the wide palm of his hand. "I've come to your rescue again."

"I guess. If you hadn't come along when you did, I'd have been in a real dilemma, being unable to pick up my own keys."

"See? Glad I could be of service."

"And just what are you doing here anyway? Following me?"

"You'd have noticed in your rearview if I had. Nope, my pager went off halfway through my supper. Big wreck on the highway."

She'd taken the back road to Bozeman, not the highway. "Was anyone hurt?"

"A tire blew out, and the driver was injured. It was the father of a family on their summer vacation."

"Will he be all right?"

"Broke his leg. He'll be spending the night in the hospital, so I told him I'd make sure his wife and kids get settled into a hotel room. During tourist season, you don't know the strings I had to pull for that one."

"That was decent of you."

"Yeah? Well, I try not to be such a bad guy, considering I wear a badge and give people tickets."

"I've heard you cops have unfair quotas to fill."

"Pressure of being a cop." His smile broke wide, showing a row of straight even white teeth and a hint of a dimple. "Why do I have the pleasure of running into you on this fine evening?"

"I'm about to become an aunt again."

"Congratulations." He fell in step beside her. "That's hard work, becoming an aunt."

"Yeah, I have it much harder than Karen. I have to shop in the gift store. I have to sit and wait in those uncomfortable chairs."

"There must be an unspoken but ironclad law in hospital administration that states they can only allocate funds for the most uncomfortable chairs on the planet. They would *have* to buy them on purpose. There's no way they could find those chairs by chance."

"There's an administrator somewhere in this building who has better job security because of it."

The lobby was quiet this time of evening. To Kendra's surprise Cameron stayed by her side as they wound their way to the elevators. He punched the Up button.

An uncomfortable silence stretched between them while they both watched the lit numbers move up and not down in their direction.

What did she say now? She was horrible at making small talk.

A janitor rolled his cart into sight and ambled to the far corner of the lobby. He began washing windows.

Cameron broke the silence. "Did you get your horses all tucked in for the night?"

"Yep."

"That had to be tough. They can't be used to being cooped up in a trailer."

"No, but I've worked with a lot of horses over the years. I sweet-talked them."

Cam could see it in his mind as the doors parted and he followed Kendra inside the elevator. Her gentle words and gentle hands, her quiet ways that told those frightened animals only good things were going to happen to them while they were in her care.

See? He'd asked the Lord for another chance and this was it. He had Kendra alone. Trapped, as it were, in the elevator with him. Folks probably asked her advice all the time.

So just do it. He punched the floor button and leaned against the wall. The car zipped upward, reminding him he had only so much time. "Say, how much does it cost if someone wanted to board a horse at your place?"

Her pretty eyes widened. Had he surprised her that much? She unzipped her good-size purse and started digging through the contents. "It depends. I think I have a price list in here. There are different rates depending on the level of care you want and size stall, feeding plans, training and exercising, that kind of thing.''

Her hair was unbound, and it was full of light, falling to cover her face as she rummaged past a worn leather wallet and a glasses case. He took his time looking his fill, while she was busy and wouldn't notice him gawking at her.

She was prettiest this close, he decided. He could see the scatter of light freckles across her nose and cheeks, probably brought out by the summer sun, on skin golden brown and as smooth as satin.

''Here it is.''

He jerked his gaze to the floor at her scuffed white sneakers, as if he hadn't been looking anywhere else.

The rattle of paper drew his attention. He straightened up, all business. It was hard holding back his emotions, but he was a disciplined man with a plan. He admired the cut of her hands, slender and suntanned, callused from her work, with neat short nails painted a shimmering pink.

It dawned on him that she was waiting for him to take the neat brochure. ''Uh, thanks.''

''I didn't know you had a horse.''

He opened the trifolded lavender paper and stared at numbers that made no sense. His brain couldn't seem to work right. He couldn't believe what he was about to do. Don't back out now, man.

He cleared the nerves from his throat before he spoke. ''I don't. Yet.''

Now there was a dazzling show of his mastery of the language.

She didn't seem to notice. If she did, then she managed to keep her pity for his sorry conversational skills to a minimum. Her voice was as warm as her smile. "You can ask me if you have any questions."

"Or I could just pull you over the next time you drive through town."

"Aren't you funny? Abusing your power as an authority figure." She teased him in return—she couldn't help it—as the doors opened to the maternity wing. "Have a good night, Cameron."

"You, too. Congratulations on becoming an aunt again."

He was gone; the doors slid shut before she could answer, leaving her alone. The chug and chink of the elevators echoed in the quiet. She turned around, eyes down because she knew what was ahead of her.

The viewing window of the nursery where newborns slept tucked tight in their blankets and beds, their dear button faces either relaxed in slumber or screwed up in misery as they cried. A nurse was lifting one tiny unhappy baby into her arms as Kendra passed by.

Don't look. Keep moving.

Her feet refused to work, leaving her trapped in front of the window. It hurt to look. It hurt not to look. She admired the tiny babies, their perfectly formed miniature hands, their sweet faces, and envied their lucky parents.

How was it possible to feel happy *and* sad at the same moment? Happy for the precious new babies and sad because she would never have one of her own.

How could she? She wasn't ever going to date. Never going to marry. Never trust a man that much.

There would be no babies for her.

The grief struck her as it always did like a boxer's blow to her sternum. It was her choice, her decision. She couldn't complain. She wouldn't feel sorry for herself, but when would this consuming longing end?

She turned away before the ache within her could crescendo. Before regret and loss could swallow her whole.

Her sisters were waiting beyond those imposing double doors. Why were her feet dragging? What was holding her back?

It was hard to face how different her life was, from what she'd always thought it would be. That's what. She'd wanted to be a wife and a mother. A horsewoman, yes, but, oh, to be truly and deeply loved by a good man. To have her own children to love and nurture. What could be more important than that?

Don't think about what might have been. She closed her eyes, hoped the Lord would help her find the strength to face her family behind those doors without feeling sorrow over the what-ifs in her life. As hard as it was to see what she might have had, she was truly happy for her sisters and their families. To the depth of her soul.

It wasn't as if she was alone. She was an aunt; she would always have children in her life. She *would* count the wonderful blessings the Lord had given her.

Not dwell on the ones missing.

She squared her shoulders, forced every piece of grief from her heart. She was ready. Behind that door were her sisters and their husbands and their children. Her warm extended family she loved with all her being.

She refused to feel sad, not tonight. Not when there was so much to celebrate. So much to be grateful for.

Cameron couldn't stop thinking about the brochure he'd folded and tucked into his shirt pocket. His mind was half on it all during the time he made sure Mr. Anderson had what he needed for the night. Those prices were reasonable. Better than what he'd expected.

I can do this. Excitement zoomed through him as he gave Anderson the number of the hotel his family was staying at. Optimism gave him extra zing as he punched the elevator call button and waited for an empty car in the quiet hush of the corridor.

Money had been tight for a long time, what with Debra's medical costs and funeral expenses, and selling their house, he'd had to come up with the cash to pay for the closing. He'd worried that buying a horse might be a much more expensive proposition than he could afford, now that his finances were evening out.

The elevator doors opened, the empty car waiting

to take him downstairs. He hit the Lobby button and pulled out the brochure as the elevator descended, clicking off the floors.

It had been a long, hard road taking care of Deb, not as hard as the road she walked with her illness. It nearly killed him having to say goodbye to her. Faith saw him through that tough time and after. He'd only been existing, not living. How did a man live with only half of a heart?

Memories tugged him back in time, when he and Deb were newlyweds. Their budget was tight. It had to be. She was finishing up her legal-assistant course at the technical college while he was hoofing it through the academy. Part-time jobs kept them in a small one-bedroom apartment not far from the campus in Bozeman. They had to work to make ends meet, but Deb had made it fun. She was so easy to laugh with. They laughed all the time.

He missed that. He missed the dreams they would talk about over doing the dishes by hand in the cramped kitchen. Deb wanted a sprawling house just out of town, so she could see trees instead of neighbors.

He'd wanted enough land to graze a horse or two on. She'd liked that idea, and wove more dreams of how it would be when times were better, riding their horses in their fields. What a great life they were going to have. Together.

Grief weighed down his soul.

The elevator inched to a halt and the doors whispered open. The outside world beyond the long wall of lobby windows was dark, and he hated the thought of going out in it.

She'd been gone four years, and the pain of heading home to an empty house still ate at him.

Is that going to change anytime soon, Lord?

Then he saw Kendra through a glass partition in the far wall. The overhead light haloed her golden hair and caressed her creamy complexion. She wore a simple T-shirt and her denim shorts, nothing pretty or fancy or extraordinary, and she looked so lovely.

He supposed it was loneliness that made him look. He missed a woman's presence in his life. The softness and gentleness, the little bottles all over the bathroom counter... He missed all of it.

It was a puzzle, because he'd seen plenty of women over the years. Not one of them made him feel as if the world had simply melted away until there was only her.

She didn't know he was watching as she leaned against the counter, turning to talk to her sister. She sparkled, laughing, tilting back her head to study the array of cheerful balloons floating just out of reach.

He couldn't say why that was, but as he strolled through the automatic doors and out into the parking lot, the night didn't seem as bleak or as lonely as it had been before.

Chapter Three

Squinting against the bold afternoon sun blinding her through the windshield, Kendra set the emergency brake. Okay, how was she going to do this? The cookies were in the back seat, all ready to go, but her sister was in the passenger seat beside her. Michelle was bound to notice what was going on.

If only she'd had more time! The day following Anna's birth had been jam-packed with errands and work and visits to the hospital. Mom and baby were coming home this evening, and there was a lot of work still to be done.

She'd been lucky to get the cookies baked. By the time she might get the chance to deliver them again all by herself, they would be beyond stale and as hard as bricks.

Please don't make a big deal over this, she silently begged Michelle, who was rummaging through her purse looking for her lipstick. Good, she was distracted. "You wait right here where it's cool. Don't move a muscle. I'll be just a second."

"Wait! Where are you going? I thought those cookies were for us." Michelle's hand, holding the found lipstick, rested on the small round bowl of her pregnant belly. "They're not for us?"

"Nope."

"I need cookies."

"Don't worry. I saved a small plate for you."

"But—"

Oh, no, here came the questions! Kendra slammed the door shut before Michelle could get out one more word. Not that she'd succeeded in keeping her mission secret. No, if anything, she was simply delaying an explanation.

Michelle was bound to notice what was going on, since she had a perfect view of the office's front door. She would be pelted with questions on her return as to why she was leaving cookies for the town's handsome and available sheriff.

Would Michelle believe the truth? Of course not! The truth was too boring. Her lovely sister would see romantic intent in a simple offering of thanks. Kendra would never hear the end of it.

This is what she got for doing the right thing. She heard the buzz of the window being lowered the instant she set foot on the sidewalk.

"Ooh, you've got a crush on that new deputy, don't you?" Michelle sparkled with complete delight.

"Sis, you've got great taste. What's his name? Frank? I *knew* it. I knew the right man for you would come along if we prayed hard enough."

See? *This* was exactly the type of thing she was trying to avoid. "I don't have a crush on anyone."

"Sure. I understand. You're doing your civic duty. Thanking the eligible bachelor who protects our town."

"It's not like that."

"Yep, sure, like I understand totally." Michelle feigned absolute empathy, but there was no mistaking that look on her face. "I'm glad for you, Kendra. You deserve a fine man."

Kendra opened her mouth to argue, but what would she say? Denial would only make it look like the truth. She loved Michelle for her kind words, but Michelle didn't know what had happened that night when everything changed.

There'd be no man for her. It was that simple. Kendra had been in love once and it had hurt worse than anything she'd ever known. She'd spent the last half-dozen years picking up the pieces of her life.

She would never give another man that much power over her. She would never trust a man that much. No matter what.

So Michelle could hope all she liked. She could think whatever she wanted. It would not change the facts.

The window buzzed upward, and Kendra could feel Michelle's elation. Now her entire family was going

to hear about this. Yep, she definitely should have
delivered the cookies later in the week, stale or not.

There was Cameron's cruiser, parked neatly against
the curb, polished and spotless.

And why was she noticing it? Didn't she have
enough on her mind with the thousand things she had
to do next? She needed to clean Karen's house, catch
her up on her laundry and do a thorough grocery shop
so her pantry would be well stocked. Then she needed
to figure out what was she going to cook tonight for
dinner for her entire family. *That's* what she ought to
be thinking about.

Not noticing that she had a perfect view of Cameron's desk through the generous front window. And
her stomach should certainly *not* be doing little
quakes, as if butterflies were trapped there.

Why was she feeling this way? There was nothing
to be anxious about. She intended to say hello, leave
the plate on his desk and walk back out. Nothing personal about it. There was nothing personal between
them.

Thank the good Lord that's the way Cameron felt
about her, too. It wasn't as if he thought, as Michelle
did, that romance could be blossoming.

Before she could reach for the tarnished brass knob,
the door swung open. Cameron, looking fine in his
navy-blue uniform, took a step back.

His smile was dazzling. "Come in. I never turn
away a woman bringing baked goods."

"It's bad form to turn away free food," a second man's voice commented from inside the office.

Kendra pushed her sunglasses off her nose and up over her forehead, and the shadows became a burly uniformed man sitting behind a desk in the corner, but she hardly noticed him. Cameron drew her attention as the surprise on his face turned to appreciation.

Appreciation for the cookies, no doubt. She handed him the covered paper plate. "I made a batch with butterscotch chip *and* my gramma's famous chocolate-chocolate chips."

"I don't think there are enough words to thank you." Cameron took the plate eagerly and ripped off the foil. "Frank, you've got to try these chocolate cookies. They sell them over at the coffee shop."

"Try them? Already have. I'm addicted to them."

"Your grandmother could charge ten bucks for a single cookie and folks would still buy two." Cameron snatched a cookie and took a bite.

"Ma'am, we sure do appreciate this." The deputy chose a chocolate cookie from the plate. "I'll just leave you two alone. I've got a report to file, uh, in the back room."

There was no back room. Cameron appreciated Frank's efforts, though, as the deputy disappeared into the storage closet, where they kept their coats and their spare office supplies.

That Frank was quick on the uptake. He saw right off that Kendra was the kind of woman a man wanted to be alone with instead of making small talk while other people watched.

"I hear your sister had her baby. A girl." Cameron held the plate out, offering her a cookie.

Kendra shook her head, declining the offer. "I have another beautiful niece. I'm pretty lucky, being an aunt. It's much better than being a parent, because I get all the snuggles and fun and I get to buy presents, but I don't have the sleepless nights and all the work that goes with it."

"Sounds like a good deal." Cameron wondered at the false brightness he saw on Kendra's face. A face that had small crinkles in the corners of her eyes, marks of character that he found attractive. Hers was not a face of sleek, artificial beauty, and a light within him flickered to life. "I'm glad to know Karen and her new baby are fine. Your other sister is expecting soon, isn't she?"

"Yes, in a few months. We have a lot of blessings to be thankful for in my family. And speaking of blessings, thank you again for help with the tire." Her sincerity shone soul-deep. "If these cookies aren't enough, I can bring by another batch sometime."

"This is more than enough." He'd never tasted a more delicious cookie. He'd never seen a more beautiful woman. There was so much to respect about Kendra, he didn't know where to begin, but if he made a list of all her attributes, it would be a long one.

She was certainly showing good manners in thanking him for helping her. After all, he'd told her he wouldn't be averse to receiving baked goods if she wanted to repay him, but she'd actually come. That said a lot about her.

He'd definitely go with her stables, if he decided he could afford a horse. That was a big question he needed an answer to if he was going to go any further with this notion of his.

"You have a good day, now." She was backing toward the door.

There was no time like the present while he had her here, even if she was halfway out the door. "Say, Kendra."

She hesitated, one hand on her black-rimmed sunglasses perched on the top of her head. She crooked one eyebrow in question.

He didn't wait for her to speak—or to escape. "I want to board my horse out at your place. Except there's one small catch."

"What's that?"

"I don't have a horse."

"Right. I remember you told me." A hint of a smile played along her soft mouth. "How are you going to board a horse you don't have at my place?"

"That's where you come in. I thought with your extensive horse knowledge combined with the fact that you don't want to lose my business to your competition—"

"Isn't that like extortion or something?"

"Sure, but I'm the law and I don't mind a little extortion if it gets me what I need."

Kendra couldn't help it. He made her laugh. Who knew the serious and capable town sheriff had a sense of humor? "I guess when the criminals are in charge, what's a poor business owner to do? How can I help?"

"I've looked in the classifieds and there seem to be plenty of horses for sale, but I don't know where to start. I don't know a thing about them. What's the difference between a quarter horse and a paint? Which is better? The prices seem to range from a hundred bucks to tens of thousands of dollars. I'm lost. I need help."

"I guess I'd better lend a hand, if I want to get your business."

"I knew you'd see things my way. I'd hate to have to tail you through town and ticket you under false pretenses until you cooperate."

"That would be a real bother."

So *that's* why he'd been acting friendlier than usual. He'd been too embarrassed to ask outright for help. Men were so funny. All ego and pride.

She wouldn't mind helping him at all, even if he didn't want to board at her stable. In this world, horse people had to help each other out.

"Why don't you come out to the stables this weekend sometime? Give me a call first, and I'll show you around the place and introduce you to different types of horses. We'll see what you like, and then you'll be able to figure out what you need. Then you can get an idea of cost.''

"Sounds great. I'll do that.''

"Good. You *do* know how to ride, don't you?''

"Uh, well, no. I've given it a lot of thought, and I've always wanted to ride.''

"You're going to love it, don't worry. You're about to take the first step on a great adventure." She lit up, the way she'd been in the hospital's gift shop, all gentle radiance and happiness. "There is nothing like owning a horse. You'll see.''

The first step on a great adventure, huh?

He closed the door and watched while she strolled toward her pickup parked neatly and legally along the curb. She was like sunshine and he felt that way whenever he looked at her. As if she brought light to the dark corners of his life. Warmth to the cold and lonely places.

Stunned, he didn't move a muscle. Just stood watching Kendra's green pickup pull out into the street, blinker flashing. What was that he just experienced? He didn't know, but he *thought* he liked it.

The hinges squealed as the closet door opened. "Is the coast clear?''

Cameron winced. He'd forgotten about Frank hiding out in the closet. "Sure, man. Come on out. She's gone.''

"With your heart, by the looks of it." Frank stole another cookie. "She sure can bake. That's a decent trait in a woman. If you can trust one of them enough to marry."

"Marry her? Whoa. I helped her with a trailer tire."

"Whatever. I'm not gonna argue with you. But a woman like that, she's what? She's got to be over thirty. She's got that riding stable east of town, doesn't she?"

"I heard something like that."

"Careful, man. She's the kind that'll break your heart. Believe me. She's not looking for a husband. She's not the soft, gentle kind of female that needs a man."

"Oh, yes she is." Cameron knew something about Kendra that Frank didn't. What no one else in this town knew.

He well remembered the night when lightning had split the old willow tree in the town park. The fire department had been fighting to contain the blaze that was threatening the entire downtown. Power had been out all the way to Bozeman.

It was also the night he'd responded to a 911 call to a house near the railroad tracks in town.

He'd never forgotten that night. He suspected Kendra hadn't, either.

"It's about time you started dating again."

"Hi to you, too, Gramma." Kendra carefully laid her fragile, newborn niece down in her pretty well-appointed crib. "I'm not dating again."

"Then you're *thinking* about dating." Gramma eased to a stop at the railing.

"Not even thinking about it."

"Well, you *should* be. It's time, my dear. It's taken you a long while getting over Jerrod. You really must have loved him."

Kendra's throat ached at the sympathy in her grandmother's words. At the caring concern that had been there forever, it seemed. Her gramma had always been there to help her whenever she needed it. Except for that one time. That one horrifying time.

She shivered, forcing the truth away. "Can we please talk about something else?"

Unfortunately, her gramma refused to back down. I've gotten to know him when he comes in for early-morning coffee. He likes three straight shots to start his day."

"I'm not interested in the new deputy. Michelle's exaggerating." How many times would she have to say that in the next hour?

"Then it's as I thought. The *sheriff*. Cameron Durango is as good as gold, if you ask my opinion. Sad it is, that he's a widower at his age. Not many know how hard he had it, taking care of his wife when she was ill. Cancer is a hard enemy."

"I didn't know you knew Cameron so well." Kendra didn't know that about his wife.

She hadn't even known he'd been married. She could hardly keep up with her busy life. But it struck her hard, realizing that he was alone. He'd already lost everything that could matter, and he wasn't much older than she was.

"How long ago was that? I would have remembered the funeral."

"His wife wasn't a member of our church."

That explained it. No wonder Cameron was looking for new activities to fill his leisure hours. A horse, what an excellent idea. Horses were more than pets, they were amazing, compassionate creatures. Most of her best friends had been horses.

Maybe Cameron could find the same kind of comfort she'd found.

"Michelle misunderstood. Cameron is interested in boarding a horse with me. That's all."

"Is he? I'm glad he's starting to live his life again. It takes time, getting over that kind of grief. I know you'll be good to him."

"As I am to all my clients." She hoped Gramma would get the hint.

"I know, dear, but a grandmother has to hope. Cameron would make a fine husband."

Kendra rolled her eyes. "You would have said the same about the deputy. Or anyone else, for that matter. You just want me to be married, like a good woman should be."

"That's right. While I believe a woman ought to wait for true love to come along, I know you would be happier with a husband of your own. With babies of your own."

Her own baby. Kendra ached in her soul, for that's

how deep the yearning went—and how deep the wound.

Not that she could let anyone know. Not even Gramma. She swallowed hard, burying her pain. "You're one to talk. You are a businesswoman. You said buying half of Karen's business was one of the best things you ever did."

"Yes, but I've been married. I've raised my family. There is a season for everything." Gramma brushed her hand over baby Anna's tuft of downy golden hair. "Hello, sweetheart. You are amazing, yes you are."

They stood together, side by side, gazing into the crib where the baby blinked up at them, drifting off to sleep.

"So soft." Love vibrated in her grandmother's voice. "There's nothing like a newborn life."

"Nothing so precious," Kendra agreed.

"There is one thing as precious. Love between a wife and her husband."

"You had to go and ruin the moment, didn't you?"

"I'm just getting my shots in while I can, dear. If you are lucky enough that true love finds you, my beautiful granddaughter, I hope you stop working at your business long enough to grab hold of what matters."

The wisdom in her grandmother's words left her shaky. Kendra didn't doubt the wisdom. True love *could* exist.

But to her? Never. It was a fact. "Are we done talking about this now?"

"I suppose." Gramma fell silent.

It was reassuring, watching over little Anna while she slept. She scrunched up her tiny rosebud mouth, looking even more adorable in her relaxed, peaceful slumber.

Faint noises from downstairs drifted along the hallway, Dad's low voice and Mom's gentle alto answering him. The *clank* of the oven door closing. The *clink* of silverware as someone was setting the table. The delicious aroma of the casserole Kendra had put in the oven. Mom must have taken it out to cool.

The sounds of family.

She did not take lightly this blessing the good Lord had given her. She had a big, loving extended family. She was thankful for them down to the depths of her soul.

There is one thing as precious. Love between a wife and her husband. Not for me, she told herself. Not ever.

Her life was enough. It *was*. She would not let her grandmother's kindly-meant words hurt.

"Isn't little Anna something?" Gramma sighed. "She looks like you did, you know. That little button nose. That round darling face. That's what your little girl will look like one day."

"Don't, Gramma." Gasping on pain, Kendra spun away, heading for the door.

"Honey, are you all right?"

"Sure."

It was only a half fib. She *intended* to be fine.

Tucking away the raw hurt, she kept on going. Gramma needed time alone with her new great-granddaughter, and there was the supper to see to. Kendra was the self-appointed cook for the night, and she wasn't about to let someone else take over.

That's the reason she told herself for hurrying from the room. It wasn't because of the tears in her eyes. Of the sadness that haunted her through the days and into the nights of her solitary life.

Her cell buzzed in her back pocket. She wasn't in the mood for personal calls, but she withdrew the small handset and glanced at the screen. With her business, she was always on call, emergencies happened.

She saw with relief that it wasn't Colleen calling her from the riding stable. No, the name on the screen was Cameron Durango's.

She almost sent the call onto her voice mail, but she remembered what Gramma had told her. His wife had died. How difficult that had to be, to lose so much.

That's why he was calling. Why he'd helped her with the tire and took the time to talk to her in the hospital. He was looking to make a new life. To fill his empty time with new activities.

How could she *not* help him? She might never know the depth of what he'd lost when he buried his wife, but she understood heartache. She understood what a future with no love and no marriage looked like.

She answered the call. "Hi, Cameron. You must be pretty anxious to buy a horse."

"I guess I am." He had a good-hearted voice, kind and resonant. "You said to give you a jingle. That maybe you could find time for me to come over. Take a look around."

"I'd be happy to help you out. I'll be working all morning tomorrow, but I should have a little free time after noon."

"How about one? Will that work?"

"One o'clock sounds fine. You know how to find me?"

"Wouldn't be much of a sheriff if I didn't."

"Good." The cool, polite tones had vanished from her alto voice, and she sounded friendly enough.

Cameron took that as an excellent sign. "I'll be there. I sure appreciate this, Kendra."

"No problem. Take care."

"You, too."

He hung up the phone, the silence of his small kitchen echoing around him. It had been a long time since he'd let hope into his heart.

How good it felt.

Chapter Four

Kendra sliced open the fifty-pound grain sack with her grandfather's Swiss Army knife, folded the blade away and tucked it safely into her jeans pocket. Sweat gathered along her forehead and trickled into her eyes.

She blinked against the sting, swiped her forehead with the back of her forearm and hefted the awkward sack onto her shoulder.

Was she thinking about her next riding class? Worrying about Willow's overdue foal? Hoping no riders took off on the out-of-bounds trail and ran into a hungry wolf or mountain lion?

No, of course not. What was she thinking about?

Cameron. Ever since she took an early lunch break and remembered he'd be showing up in a few hours.

Ever since she had checked her watch every few minutes, as if she was worried about missing him.

How crazy was that? Cameron was a grown man. He was perfectly capable of finding her. It wasn't as if she were hiding in the woods. She was in plain sight from the paddocks. Since it was a busy Saturday with tons of people around, he'd have plenty of people to ask where to find her. That is, if he even showed up.

Stop worrying about him. She braced her feet, bent her knees and tipped the gunnysack forward. The ping and rush of falling grain sliding into the fifty-gallon drum echoed in the feed room, providing a welcome distraction. The sweet-scented dust sprinkled everywhere.

Was it one o'clock yet? Or a few minutes after? And what was with her that she kept wondering about him? It was what Gramma had said about him. It had touched her heart and taken root. *He's starting to live his life again. It takes time getting over that kind of grief.*

Sympathy welled up within her. He'd lost a wife to cancer, when they'd both been so young. It reminded her that tragedy happened to everyone, even the faithful. As much as she'd been hurt, other people had lost more. Been hurt worse.

She patted the last of the grain from the sack, grabbed the end corners and shook. Stragglers tumbled into the dusty heap and she coughed, breathing in the molasses-flavored dust.

She saw his polished black boots first at the edge of her vision as he hesitated just inside the doorway.

His boots were unfamiliar to her, black and expensive but not tooled, and not a traditional riding boot.

That must be the reason she knew it was Cameron before she swept her gaze up the rock-solid length of his jeans, ignoring the holstered gun and pager at his belt, along the flat hard ridge of his abdomen and chest to the stony square of his jaw.

He wore a gray T-shirt, and reflective wraparound sunglasses hid his eyes. "You are one hard woman to find."

"I'm not hiding. Just working. There were plenty of people to ask where I was. Didn't anyone help you?"

"Didn't ask."

Ah, typical man. She should have known. Real men never ask for directions. No wonder she'd been worried about him finding her. She must have a sense about him, and how weird was that?

She tossed the empty gunnysack onto the pile in the corner.

"I'm glad to see you were brave enough to come."

"I'm no coward. Why, did you think I was?"

A coward? No one in their right mind would think that. Anyone who looked at him would think he was the bravest man ever. He emanated strength and heart. "A lot of folks call, but once they get out here and see how big horses are up close and personal, they miraculously change their minds."

"I may be a lot of things, but I'm no coward and I'm dumb enough to be proud of it."

"An honest man. I like that."

"Since I'm being honest, I guess I'd better admit that I haven't seen any horses up close yet. My courage has yet to be tested."

"Why put it off? Come with me." She fastened the lid, locking it against field mice, and swung her Stetson from the hook on the wall. "I hope you came prepared."

"To ride?" The cords in his neck tensed. He stood rooted to the floor as she slid past him into the main breezeway.

"You look a little nervous, Officer."

"Me? Nervous? Nope." He squared his wide shoulders, like a soldier preparing for battle. "I face danger every day. Armed felons and criminals and gunfire. I'm not scared of a horse."

"I like your attitude," she replied over her shoulder as she led the way through the main stable.

"What attitude?"

"Confidence. You're going to need it."

His gait fell in stride with hers, easygoing but with a hint of tension. "Why do you say it like that? Like I've got something to fear and you're not gonna tell me what it is."

"Don't worry about it. There's nothing to fear. Really." She liked the crook of humor gathered in the corner of his mouth.

It wasn't fair to tease a little nervous, first-time rider, but Cameron looked so big and strong, like a man who couldn't ever be scared of anything, she couldn't resist. "You aren't afraid of hitting the ground hard, are you?"

"Who, me? No. Thanks to you, I'm so relaxed about this."

"I'm glad I could help." Biting her bottom lip to keep from laughing out loud—how long had it been since a man had made her laugh?—she stopped at the head of the aisle, where a long row of stalls marched through the bright sunlight from the skylights overhead to the far side of the stable.

A few horses came to look, peering over their gates, some nickering, some scenting in the direction of the stranger. Most of the stalls were empty. The scrape of a pitchfork in the distant corner accompanied the familiar scents of fresh alfalfa and straw.

"Sure is a nice operation you got here." Jamming his hands in his pockets, he took his time looking around. "Clean. Nice. Who did the construction, one of the outfits in town?"

"No. Me and my cousin Ben did. My dad helped out when he could."

She looked with pride at the building she'd put together with her own two hands. She'd had help, but she'd checked books out of the library and studied, and her neighbor, Mr. Brisbane, was a retired carpenter who liked giving her advice.

"*You* did this? A woman of many talents. I'm impressed."

"Not going to censure me?" Kendra relaxed as the corner of his hard, lined, masculine mouth cinched up in a grin. "I got a lot of that when I bought this place."

"I remember this used to be an old homestead. Weren't the outbuildings falling down in the fields? You really turned this place around."

"Thanks." Pride shone like a soft new light.

She'd worked hard, he realized. Sacrificed a lot of her time, her energy and her courage to build this place with her own hands. Not what a lot of women her age did. No, they were falling in love and planning weddings and enjoying all that a marriage brought. A home, maybe a new car or two, babies to welcome into the world and raise.

He hadn't known she'd literally built this place. It had to have been about the time Deb was diagnosed and his world fell apart. He hadn't noticed much in the way of anything after that. Woodenly doing his job to the best of his ability and hurrying home to her, to all that mattered to him.

Sadness crept into his heart, for Deb. For Kendra. That had to be around the time he'd handcuffed Jerrod. "Folks didn't criticize you for doing all this, did they? This is an incredible job."

"Thanks." She shrugged, turning away from him as if to hide her true emotions.

All he saw was Kendra, as she always looked, hair tied back neatly, shimmering in the sunlight, casual but looking impeccable in faded jeans and a shirt, scuffed riding boots and a leather belt cinched at her slim waist. A small gold cross glinted in the hollow between her collarbones.

Had she put all her heartache into this place? Working hard to forget, moving so far out of town for peace, for distance from anyone who could hurt her?

He knew something about heartbreak.

He could see the spread through the wide double doorway at the head of the stable. Perfect rail fencing, groomed paddocks, mellow green meadows, covered arenas, two other new stable buildings and the hint of the original brick cottage nestled behind two ancient maples.

A massive change from what this place used to look like—a forgotten, falling-down homestead that had sat unused, except for the grazing cattle and growing hay.

He'd always assumed she'd had the place rebuilt. She came from one of the area's wealthier families. She could probably pull together a loan for that kind of an investment. But to have done this herself?

He was real glad he'd chosen to go with her stable.

She ambled away from him. Her gait wasn't jaunty, but not slow, either. A graceful, quiet way she moved. Unconscious of her country-girl beauty. Looking so wholesome and good-hearted, she made him notice.

What are you trying to tell me, Lord? Puzzled, Cameron followed after the lovely lady who was affecting him.

"Come take a look," she invited, pausing in front of a stall with a horse in it.

The big animal made a low sound in its throat, nosing over the low gate to press its muzzle into Kendra's waiting hand. Nuzzling against her palm, sighing at the wonder of Kendra's caring touch. The horse closed its eyes in obvious bliss.

"This is one of my best friends, Willow." Kendra leaned her forehead against the horse's, their affection for one another clear.

As warm as sunlight and twice as dazzling, the woman before him changed. Her defenses falling, she looked better, brighter.

That horse looked awful big. Kendra was right. He also saw the bond between woman and horse. Friendship.

Yep. He could use some of that.

"Oh! Stop that, Sprite!" Kendra's reprimand was sprinkled with merriment as she whisked her ponytail out of another horse's mouth. "Stop being jealous."

"Your horse, too?" He'd seen her on one that looked sort of like that when she rode to town. From the shadows in the neighboring stall, he couldn't get a real good take on the color of the horse, except it was dark.

"Yeah. This is my barrel horse. We took first in the state last year, but I'm not competing anymore."

"I read about that in the local paper. Hometown girl does good."

She rolled her eyes. "Not so good. It's really the

horse.'' She didn't know how to say it, but she was blessed to have these horse friends in her life.

''So, are these all your animals?'' He gazed down the aisle at the other animals holding out for attention.

''Not the rest in this aisle. This is my best rental stable. Nice big box stalls with attached corrals for them to stretch their legs during the day.''

''Looks like you've got a lot of space available.''

''No, it's Saturday. Our busiest of the week. Kids come in to spend the day with their horses.''

''Just kids?''

''Mostly, but about a third of my clients are adults. Lots of country girls like me, who grew up on a little land with room enough for a horse. They have to work in Bozeman where the jobs are and can't pasture a horse in a subdivision, so they board here. It's a good compromise.''

''Looks like you do a good business.''

''It's what I love.'' And what she knew. Horses were her life. She gave Sprite a snuggle before leading the way down the mostly empty aisle.

''Meet Jingles. She's an American quarter horse—'' Kendra giggled as the horse lipped her cheek. She pulled a roll of spearmint candies out of her pocket and slipped the horse two.

Cameron watched in amazement as the horse crunched the hard candy into pieces. ''She can eat that? It won't make her sick?''

''Jingles has a sweet tooth, just like her owner.'' Kendra stroked the mare's golden neck. ''She's a great horse. The breed is smart, loyal and fast, has great endurance and good tempers. Can't be beat for saddle riding.''

''I saw a few ads for quarter horses in the paper. Sure is different seeing them up close. I remember they were pricey.''

''They can be.'' Kendra remembered how her parents had scrimped and saved to help her buy Jingles for her fourteenth birthday. She'd taken Jingles all the way to the state competitions and won, five years running, but it had been a sacrifice for her family, she remembered.

Cameron was looking for a new hobby to fill his leisure time, not a financial drain. And the look in his dark, steady gaze when he looked at the horses was nothing short of longing. He wanted this new life so badly, she could feel it.

He'd be awesome with a horse. It was easy to see. He had the right character—even tempered, level-headed and kind.

He had a lot to offer a horse. And the companionship a horse could give him, why, it would help ease the lonely hours he had to be facing.

She so wanted to find the right match for him. ''I promise we'll find something affordable. Have you figured out what you can spend?''

He shrugged. ''I'm flexible. I just don't want to buy something fancy when I'm more of a sensible sedan sort of guy.''

''No, not you.''

"Okay, a four-wheel drive, independent-suspension kind of man, but don't tell anyone. That would blow my shot at winning the election."

"I can keep that secret...for a price."

"Just add it to the tab I'm about to charge up."

He had a nice laugh, warm and deep like summer thunder over a mountain valley. Was it her imagination, or was she relaxing around him? She wasn't shaking and she'd forgotten to be wary.

What was that all about? She hadn't felt this safe being alone with a man who wasn't a member of her family for years. She spun on her heel and led the way through the blast of an industrial air-conditioning unit.

"C'mon back to my office," she called over her shoulder when he didn't follow her. "I've got price lists on everything you can expect to spend, from vet bills to the kind of tack you're going to need and what it will probably cost."

"Wow. That sure saves me a lot of research."

"It's good to know what you're getting into. I've made up brochures on everything you need to think about. If you're really going to do this, it's a bigger commitment than most people expect."

"The worthwhile relationships always are."

Was it her imagination, or did he sound as if he was hurting? It made her remember Gramma's words. Cancer is a hard enemy, she'd said. Was Cameron thinking about the wife he'd lost? It sounded as if he had been devoted to her, had cared for her through her illness.

What did they say about him? That he was a rare and devoted man. She ached for his loss.

It was a good thing he'd gotten up the courage to ask her about finding a horse. She *so* wanted to help him. She shouldered through her door, ignored the pile of paperwork heaped on her secondhand desk and flipped through a drawer for the right brochures. "I'll give you my rental rates for the different horses. Rent—if you want to start riding lessons before we find your perfect mount."

"Wow." He bent to study the brochure, giving her a perfect view of a cowlick at the crown of his head.

Her stomach fluttered, and she knew it was that sense of rightness, when everything fell into place. She liked to think the work she did with her stable made a difference, however small in the world, for the people and children who came here.

By the look of hope on Cameron's face, lined by sun and hardship, she knew he would find happy hours ahead and the companionship he'd been needing.

He refolded the brochure and stuck it in his back jeans pocket. "I'm real sure about this. I've been giving it a lot of thought for some time."

"Good. When do you want to get started?"

"I've got time now." All of it lonely, so much of it that it hurt to think about too much. He pulled a quarter-folded section of newspaper from his back pocket and studied it. "I've circled a few ads that look good. What do you think?"

She bent close, taking the page he offered. The newsprint rattled as she studied it. Cameron dared to edge close enough to peer over her shoulder. He'd never stood so close to her before, and it was like being touched by spring. She smelled sweet like flowers.

She'd sure make a nice wife. Where did that thought come from? The realization filled him, steady like winter rain, when he ought to be paying attention to what she was saying. Her mouth was moving, he could hear the gentle alto of her words, but he couldn't focus.

His pulse drummed in his ears and seconds stretched long, the way they did when he was on the job, his Smith & Wesson drawn, adrenaline pumping and senses heightened.

There might not be a perp pulling a gun on him, but as he felt the silken graze of Kendra's hair against his jaw, he knew this moment was as pivotal.

Kendra must have realized stray strands of her hair had escaped her ponytail. Her hand brushed those wisps into place behind her dainty ear, where a small diamond winked on her earlobe.

She liked jewelry, he realized, something he'd never noticed before. The necklace, the tasteful set of pierced earrings and a small ruby ring on her right hand.

"I know this person, and no, this isn't a good deal.

Basically, she's wanting what a luxury sedan would bring in when what she really has is a base-model economy car."

"I like a woman who uses terms I can understand."

He was rewarded with her gentle smile. "This one's a student of mine. Her mare is a nice midsize car at a reasonable market price. She's one aisle over, if you want to go take a look at her."

"I'm here. Might as well." He tried to sound casual, as if it was no big deal.

No, this was *huge*. It had been tough coming to the place in his life where he'd finished grieving, hard to let go and accept that he still had a life. And that Deb, the angel she surely was, would want him to live and not just put one foot in front of the other, sleepwalking through life.

Life was a finite gift. He'd learned how important it was to spend this time on earth wisely, with love and purpose. That was why he was here now, following Kendra through the stable and into the bright light of day.

This was one thing of about a million that she loved about her work. Helping bring a deserving horse and rider together. And in Cameron's case, it felt like a personal mission as she arrowed through the sunny grounds, waving to kids on their horses calling out her name.

"Are those kids you found horses for?"

"No, kids I taught to ride."

"Cool." His boots crunched in the gravel next to her. "Do you teach all the riding classes?"

"About half of them."

No matter how fast she walked, he stayed right there at her side. This was business, and showing Cameron around was no different than the hundreds of other times she'd done this with other potential boarders.

Why was she more aware of the sound of his gait, confident and strong and slightly uneven? Had he been wounded in the line of duty? He might be casually dressed in a T-shirt and jeans instead of his navy-blue uniform, but there was no way on this earth she could forget he was a sheriff.

She turned cold inside and refused to let the next thoughts come. Or the memories of a time she needed to forget and never think of again.

Could a person bury memories forever? She was going to give it her best shot. What mattered was this life she'd built, the kids practicing their riding skills in the different arenas or paddocks. The giggling girls in groups of two or three that rode off on the manicured trails.

This was her life. Think about that, Kendra.

"This is the riding arena." The covered, open-air area was fenced with riser seating on the far side. "We do our Western training and competitions here."

"I see the barrels." He squinted, gesturing to

where a white mare dug into a tight corner around the final barrel, kicking up dust on her ride home. "Is that the horse?"

"That's her. She's a pleasure to ride."

"She looks too fancy for me."

"She's well priced, but she's trained for competition." How could she be so dense? "I never asked what type of riding you wanted to do."

"The sheriff over at Moose Creek is a good friend of mine. He's a horseman and takes his mount out in the mountains to hunt and fish. Says there's nothing like riding trails to get away from it all."

"He's right. That's what you'd like? A horse to trail ride with?"

"I used to head out into the mountains all the time. Hiking, skiing, fishing, hunting, camping. Then Deb got sick and everything changed."

Life could be so unfair sometimes. Kendra didn't have to ask if he'd had a happy marriage. It was in his voice, on his face, in his stance.

"Hey, Kendra." Susan, the rider on the white mare, headed over. "I noticed you two checking out my horse. Are you thinking about buying?"

"He's just starting to look." Kendra leaned her forearms on the top rail of the board fence, glad to see one of her oldest friends. "You know Cameron, right?"

"Sure." Susan gave Cameron her best smile. "Not here to give any of us a ticket, are you, Sheriff?"

''Nope. Off duty today.'' He offered his hand to the horse and let the mare scent his palm.

There was something about the man's hands. Something rare and striking. They were strong and square with broad palms and long, thick-knuckled fingers. His skin was bronzed by a summer spent out of doors and dusted with a trace of dark hair. Hands that looked brawny enough to break bones.

His tenderness was unexpected as he stroked the mare's velvety nose. The mare responded with a friendly nicker deep in her throat. Kendra watched, astonished, as before her eyes Cameron's tough-guy shield fell away, the only face of this man she'd ever seen.

Standing before her, graced by the vivid sun, the real Cameron Durango was revealed. His integrity of steel. His caring nature. His excruciating loneliness.

As the lucky mare nickered again, nudging his hand for more attention, Kendra realized she wasn't afraid around him, not any longer.

She felt safe with him, because look at him. He was a truly good man. Hard lines cut into the corners of his eyes and around his mouth. Put there by hardship and worry and sadness. By grief she couldn't begin to compare hers with.

How could she not like him? He was lonely, and she knew something about that. She'd do her very best to find him the right horse. The friend he was looking to make.

He looked over his glasses at the woman in the saddle. "Why are you selling her?"

"Financial problems."

What was her name? Susan? She'd been a few years behind him in school—and sure looked sad about having to sell her horse.

He supposed it was easy to become attached. It was just as well he didn't want such a...a *woman's* horse. "She's way too fancy for the likes of me."

Susan looked relieved. "Kendra, I'll stable her myself."

"No problem." Kendra shrugged, waving off some unspoken concern with one slim hand.

She obviously ran a healthy business here. The girls clinging to the backs of their big horses ringed the arena, taking turns at the barrels or, in the corner, waiting for the comments of a woman instructor.

It was clear that Kendra was a good businesswoman, but she wasn't ruthless. He hadn't thought she was, or he wouldn't be standing here, but it was reassuring to see.

"If you want to wait a few minutes until Colleen is done with her class..." Kendra said without looking at him, taking great interest in how the class across the way was going. "It's too bad I have a class in a few minutes, or I'd personally stay to show you some of our trails."

What? "You're sending me out in the mountains with a stranger?"

"Don't worry, Colleen has all her shots."

He liked a woman with a sense of humor. "I'm glad to know that, but my big worry is you. You don't invite greenhorns like me out here, do you, and play practical jokes on them?"

"It's tempting, but I won't put you on the back of a wild horse and abandon you."

"Whew. I was worried."

"You look it. You have a suspicious nature, Sheriff."

"Just because I'm suspicious doesn't mean they aren't after me."

"That's paranoid, not suspicious."

"I knew that didn't sound right. Say, how long are your classes? I don't mind hanging around until you're done. I've got nothing else to do."

Kendra waved at the instructor from the class in the far corner that was disbanding.

Maybe he ought to be insulted Kendra was trying hard to get rid of him. She was probably busy, and he *had* taken up a chunk of her time. Why did he feel disappointed at the idea of her leaving him?

At first he barely noticed the brunette approaching on horseback. She drew her horse to a stop, studied them both and couldn't hide the big grin on her face. "Whew, what brings you out here, Sheriff? It's nothing serious, right?"

Kendra spoke up. "Cameron here is thinking about buying a horse and boarding here."

"Well, don't let me get in the way of business." The instructor tossed Kendra a secret look. "I don't mind taking the last class of the day for you. I could use the extra hours if you want to take the sheriff into the hills.''

As if mulling it over, Kendra blew out a breath, ruffling her wispy bangs. ''Fine by me. That is, if the sheriff can stand more of my company.''

''I've suffered through worse.''

''Me, too.'' Trouble twinkled in her eyes. ''That only leaves one question, cowboy. Are you ready to ride?''

''Sure thing. I'm up for the challenge.''

Her smile was like heavenly light, warming him to the soul, as she spun away on the heel of her scuffed riding boots, calling out to someone just out of sight in the stable. Why did it feel as if she were taking his heart with her?

Chapter Five

Kendra gave the cinch a hard tug and tightened the buckle a notch. She always did her best not to be alone with any of the men who'd come her way, in a business sense. She'd gotten very practiced at it, but apparently not practiced enough because she was alone with Cameron.

Well, not *alone,* exactly, considering there were about fifty people around within calling distance. But soon they would be.

This is business, she reminded herself firmly. She was safe with Cameron. Not only that, but it felt like divine intervention, somehow. As if she was the one who could best help him find the right horse and a new, rewarding hobby to fill his time.

The horses in her life had certainly made hers fulfilling.

The old gelding she was saddling waited patiently

as she gave the cinch a final tug. One of the first horses she'd gotten for her ranch and her best beginner-class horse.

"You're a good gentleman, Palouse." Kendra patted the gray roan, his dappled coat and his white mane a throwback to his wild mustang heritage, and let him nuzzle her gloved hand affectionately. She slipped him a peppermint.

"I see you're a tough master." Cameron ambled close, planted his fists. "Do the animal-control people know about you?"

"They sure do. I'm on the top of their list to bring recovered horses to."

"Suppose I should have guessed that before I tried to tease. Horses must be abused, like any animal can be."

Or person, Kendra didn't add. "It certainly isn't the animal's fault. Horses need to trust their owners one hundred percent. They want to trust. They are loving creatures that don't deserve harsh treatment. I've rehabilitated about a dozen horses. Palouse was one of them."

"You'd never know it. He's as calm as could be. You must have done wonders with him."

"He's the wonder. You wait until you get to know more horses, then you'll know what I'm talking about. They are special blessings, and to share trust and love with them is a privilege."

There was no mistaking the big gelding's trust in her as he watched her with an adoring gaze.

That said a lot about the woman, in Cam's opinion. Professionally and personally.

"I've got Palouse saddled. How about you, are you ready to go?" She gathered the long leather straps of the reins.

As if he knew what to do with those. "Are you sure he'll go easy on me?"

"He's one of the gentlest horses I know. Six-year-olds learn to ride on him."

"I'm well past six, so I reckon I can handle him."

"That's the attitude I like to hear. Just put your foot in this stirrup and grab the saddle horn. Give a little hop and lift up into the saddle. Like this."

She demonstrated, rising up so she stood straight in the stirrup, her weight balanced on her one foot as if she were born to do it. "Ease your leg over his back, careful not to scrape him with your boot and settle into the seat. Don't let your weight drop, just lower your fanny into the saddle."

"I can do that. I've watched enough westerns, I ought to be able to ride by osmosis."

"Fine, then mount up, could you?"

"Sure thing, little lady."

Kendra held the stirrup steady when he had trouble catching it with the toe of his boot. Just as she'd do for any new student taking his first ride.

Why did she feel different? It was as if something was buzzing around her, like the charge in the air before a thunderstorm.

But the skies were clear to the west and to the south, where summer storms often started.

It was Cameron. He seemed to take up all the empty space around her, although it made no sense. She could smell the clean woodsy scent of him and hear the creak of leather as he stepped into the stirrup. Muscles corded beneath his sun-bronzed forearms as he rose into the saddle, casting his shadow over her.

How could she not be aware of him? Of his power? Of his striking male presence? She didn't want to trust any man again, but that didn't mean she was immune to a good man's appeal. It only proved she should have paid Colleen to take Cameron around instead of taking over the class.

Why hadn't she? It didn't make any sense. What was the difference if Colleen was paid for an extra hour on the trail or in the arena? Why hadn't Kendra thought of that at the time?

Because there was obviously something wrong with her brain whenever the handsome sheriff was around, that's why. As if her synapses misfired. How else could she explain it? First, she let him repair her trailer tire—*not* what she'd let any man other than her brother-in-law do. Now she was riding out with Cameron.

Hadn't she learned enough lessons from Jerrod?

Yes. She might be *aware* of Cameron but that didn't mean she was *interested* in him. It was something that could never be. The barricade around her heart was impenetrable and was going to stay that way.

She slipped Jingles a peppermint from her jeans pocket and pressed her forehead to the mare's sun-warmed neck. The comforting scent of horse eased away the worries knotted in Kendra's stomach.

Tension eased from the back of her neck as Jingles cuddled back, leaning against Kendra's body in unspoken affection. As if the mare was telling her, *You're not alone. I'm here. You can count on me.*

"And you can count on me, friend," Kendra whispered, tracing her hand through the mare's platinum mane. "Let's go for a ride."

Jingles stomped impatiently, and Kendra didn't look at the man watching her as she hiked up into the saddle and reined the mare around. Why did she feel Cameron's presence as tangibly as the heat of the sun on her face?

She demonstrated how to hold the reins in one hand, and leaned over to make sure there was enough slack in the straps he held. "Palouse knows to follow me. Just keep the reins at the saddle horn, easy like this. Don't jerk them and don't kick him."

"So basically I just sit here."

"Yep. Palouse knows what he's doing, so you can just enjoy your first ride. Just trust him and enjoy the view."

"I thought horses could be unpredictable."

"They can be, but Palouse is eighteen. That's pretty old for a horse. This graybeard's seen just about everything, and he knows his job. He takes it seriously. He'll take good care of you, if you're kind to him. That's the way it works best in the horse world.''

"Know what? The ground *does* look a long way down from up here.''

"And it's hard when you hit.''

"You're teasing me, right?''

"Sure. Yep. Just teasing you.''

She took off ahead of him, and the big horse lumbered into motion beneath him, scaring him near to death because it just didn't feel right. He was going to tip out of the saddle. He had some real concerns, the ground *did* look like it was uncomfortable to land on.

And was he thinking about falling to his death? No, he was watching Kendra. He was noticing the sparkling warmth within her.

The horse beneath him picked up speed as they strolled through the stable yard, his gait an unsettling rocking and swaying that was likely to make Cam seasick. Either that, or he was going to lose his balance and fall like a klutz into the gravel.

He was an athletic man and an outdoorsman, and he liked every outdoor activity he'd ever tried. Except this. This was *not* like pedaling a bike or zipping down a hillside on a motorcycle. He wasn't in control, and he didn't know if he liked it.

You've got two choices, man. Abandon your plan, or go ahead with it.

Maybe he would learn to love riding horses. Although that probability was growing smaller as time passed. The seasick feeling was getting worse with the way the horse was rocking forward and back, and Cam was sitting up on top like a tiny boat on a rolling ocean. Yep, that's what this reminded him of. The ground swayed beneath him.

People called this fun?

His stomach clenched like a fist. He wasn't going to get sick, right? In front of Kendra? *That* would be real attractive. She'd certainly never look at him again in the same light.

If it's not too much trouble, Lord, please get me through this. I'll tough it out, I promise. Just a little help would be appreciated.

"This is why I had to have this property." Kendra's soft alto, as gentle as spring rain, caught his attention. Made him look up and notice that the golden fields of her horse ranch had fallen behind them and they'd crossed into the tree line.

They were surrounded by sparse lodgepole pine, cedar and fir. The evergreens clung to the stubborn earth with tenacious roots, their branches spread wide to catch the sun. The trees were scattered, casting shadows across the open ground between them.

He forgot to feel sick taking in the awesome beauty of the rising foothills, the towering amethyst peaks of the Bridger Range ahead and the true blue of the Montana sky above. But such beauty seemed fleeting when Kendra pulled back her sleek golden mare so they were side by side.

Her Stetson cut a jaunty angle to block the sun's glare. She studied him from under the gray brim. "Don't you love this?"

"What's not to love?" He could learn to like feeling seasick.

She apparently wasn't fooled as she squinted, studying him. Did he look as green as he felt?

"Do you want to head back?"

That would mean his time would be over. That was *not* what he wanted. No way.

He would stick it out, whether he survived it or not. "I'm likin' this well enough."

"I think you're lying." Her eyes twinkled.

"Yeah, but I *will* like this. Once I get the hang of it. It's kind of like riding a canoe upside down in an ocean."

"At least there's no storm swells."

"True. No hurricanes."

"No waterspouts, whirlpools or tidal waves. See? Riding is pretty tame compared to other sports."

"Like what sports? High-altitude parachuting? Free rock climbing?" He gave thanks they'd come to a swaying stop. "You ought to smile more often, Miss McKaslin."

"I smile all the time."

"You smile about as often as I do."

Cameron had a whole lot more to be sad about, in her opinion, than she ever would. No, the Lord had been generous with all His blessings in her life. But Cameron…

She shut off the image of him taking care of an ill woman, bringing her meals, tucking the blankets beneath her chin and reading to her in the soft glow of a small lamp. She knew he'd cared for his wife like that, because she'd seen the tenderness in him when he'd patted Palouse's neck. The goodness shone in him like the sun, radiant and unmistakable and genuine.

Time for a subject change. The more of a hero she made Cameron Durango, the harder it was going to be to keep her shields up full force.

Business. This is about business, Kendra. Stop forgetting that! She nosed Jingles into motion along the groomed trail, between the sweep of fir boughs and the call of a red-tailed hawk overhead.

"We offer over forty acres of riding trails on-site, and national forest borders one side of my property. There are miles of old logging-road trails, although it's not the best time of year to go wandering up into the mountains alone."

"I suppose that's what those ropes across the trail ahead would mean."

"Exactly, but we'll ride around them. I think we're both experienced enough to handle any wilderness situation."

"I'm armed, if that helps."

"Am I that dangerous, Sheriff?"

"Maybe," he quipped. "No, I'm the only sheriff in these parts. When I'm off duty, I'm still on call."

"You want to keep going?" Her question was gently spoken, but it was a challenge.

He couldn't resist a good challenge. "You lead the way. I'll follow."

"Here's a hint. Don't look down, okay? You'll do a lot better. C'mon. I promise, you'll like what you see if you just stick with it."

He already did. She balanced ahead of him on that golden horse of hers, riding into the long rays of light arrowing through the trees, her blond hair whipping behind her.

The horse lurched forward beneath him. Cameron swallowed. Don't look down? Then he'd keep his gaze on her. Fir boughs brushed his knees and his elbows as he followed her. He wouldn't think about the narrow path the horse was now following, or that it fell away into nothing, except for the sturdy split-rail guard that stood between him and the hereafter.

"You let kids ride on this?"

"Trail safety is part of the lessons they take. You aren't afraid of heights, are you, Sheriff?"

"No. Heights don't bug me. Falling hard and breaking a few bones does."

"It isn't a far drop, and the trail is as wide as a road. Horses are surefooted. You're perfectly safe. What do you think of the view?"

He'd forgotten to look around him. He'd been so busy watching her. Watching the graceful arch of her neck, the delicate cut of her shoulders. The hint of her shoulder blades against the soft white knit shirt she wore.

The golden shimmer of her hair, caught back in a white scrunch thing at the base of her neck, shivered over her shoulder as she glanced back at him.

"When I first viewed this property, I was disappointed. The outbuildings were so run-down, useless, and the house hadn't been lived in for twenty years. But the moment Jingles and I set out here up this trail, I knew I'd come home. Look."

They curved around a granite outcropping and the rough amethyst peaks of the Bridger Range speared into a sky close enough to touch. The rugged foothills of meadows and trees spread out around them, climbing upward, as if in reverence to the mountains.

"God's handiwork sure is something." It was all he could think of to say.

"Exactly. Forty acres of this is mine. Mostly wilderness except for the manicured trails. I know, because I made those trails myself."

He shouldn't have been surprised, not after she'd admitted to learning better than adequate carpenter skills. "When did you buy this property?"

"About six years ago."

That explained it. Right after he'd rescued her that day. Right after he'd driven her to the hospital. Sorrow for her banded his chest like a vise.

Had she put all her heartbreak and all her broken

dreams into this place? "Must have been difficult clearing these paths."

"It took me most of four months working every afternoon until dusk. I got pretty good with an ax, a saw and a shovel."

"You did all the railing, too?"

"Until my blisters had blisters."

Forty acres of trails? It had to have taken the better part of a year. How could someone so small and delicate work that hard?

Heartbreak. He knew, because that's how it had been after Deb passed. He'd worked long hours taking up the slack of being a single officer in a growing district, until the city had hired a deputy. He hadn't realized how much he'd stayed at the office, doing paperwork well into the evening until Frank had shown up to help out.

Only then had Cam been aware of the aching emptiness in his life.

Yeah, he knew what Kendra was talking about. He took in the rustic trails, groomed so they blended well with the environment, and the carefully constructed wooden rails that marked the edges of the trails. Solidly made.

This is where Kendra had put all her broken dreams.

It took a lot of guts to put your life back together. He admired her more as the horse moved beneath him, obediently following Kendra.

This isn't so bad, he realized. There was a sort of

rhythm to the horse's gait, and he was starting to get the knack of this riding thing. At least he didn't feel seasick anymore.

He breathed deep, taking in the beauty of the day. A strange weightless feeling expanded in his chest. Something he hadn't felt in more years than he could count—happiness.

He wanted to remember this forever. How the clean mountain air smelled like summer and sage and pine needles. The rustle of the wind in the bear grass. The faint *thunk* of hooves on the hard-packed earth. The creak of the leather saddle beneath him. The sense of rightness—as if heaven were smiling down on them in approval.

"Look, there's a fawn. He's still got his spots." Kendra whispered, her horse stopping in the middle of the trail. "Do you see him?"

Branches swayed peacefully to his left. If he squinted, Cam could make out the faint outline of a doe frozen in the underbrush, ears alert, soft eyes unblinking, tensed as if ready to flee. At her side was a fragile, knobby-kneed fawn.

They were within throwing distance. Too close for a wild animal's comfort, surely, but instead of streaking off and taking her baby with her, the doe blinked, watching Kendra.

"You must ride up here a lot." He pitched his voice low, to keep from scaring off the deer. "She's used to you."

"Sure she is. Wildlife comes down into the foothills to feed this time of year, when the mountains get so dry. After I bed the horses for the night, I go out and leave some hay and grain in the feed troughs for them. She's probably one of the deer that waits for me every evening. When they know you're not hunting them but bringing them grain, they get pretty bold.''

''Do they come right up to you?''

''Within a few feet.''

If he were a deer, he'd come up to her, too. Her gentle voice and radiant kindness were unmistakable. He had no problem picturing her feeding the wildlife. Not as many landowners in these parts would be so generous. Wild animals were seen as nuisances, mostly. And often dangerous.

As delicate and willowy as Kendra looked, she had confidence, too. She was capable. She knew how to take care of herself in the backcountry. He guessed the small pack tied to the side of her saddle, hardly noticeable, held necessities like a hand radio, knives, snakebite kit and maybe a small handgun. It looked just the right size for all that.

''I get mostly deer, elk and a few moose. The deer are the most frequent. They show up every evening and lay around the house on my lawn to sleep. I had to put up ten-foot lattice all around my rose garden to keep them out.''

''I take it they eat roses?''

''Oh, do they. The first summer I was here, they ate my tea roses down to the stems. Let's leave mama and baby. I saw some moose up here just yesterday. Maybe we can spot them again.''

''Suppose you see more dangerous critters up here, too.''

''Sometimes.''

The path had turned steep and rocky, but Kendra didn't seem worried as her surefooted mare curved around the steep hillside toward mountains so close, he had to tip his head back to see their granite faces.

''Sometimes? That doesn't sound reassuring.''

''I've come across everything from rattlers to bears.''

''And lived to tell the tale, huh?'' He hadn't guessed she'd like the backcountry, too. A lot of women preferred shopping malls to spending a day where wolves and bears hunted.

''Mostly I mind my own business, they mind theirs. But that's why I keep the riders down below the tree line this time of year. So they're safe.''

They'd risen so high and fast up the slope, he couldn't see her ranch below, just the far edge of the extensive valley stretching out behind him in gold and green.

''Want to head back?''

She'd noticed where he was looking. ''Back? No, I was just taking in the view. You can see the Rockies from here. And the Tobacco Roots.''

''Can you imagine when all this was wilderness, before the settlers came from the East in their wagons?''

"It had to look like this. Except *wilder*." Lewis and Clark had come this way in their canoe and crossed on foot the rest of the way, over the Great Divide. "Clark wrote of seeing nothing but giant herds of elk and deer and buffalo for miles."

"It's amazing to think that it's still the same wilderness, isn't it? Without the giant herds."

"That what I love about heading up into the backcountry. It's finding that part of Montana that's wild. The way it was a hundred years ago."

"Exactly."

How weird that he felt that, too. Kendra didn't know how to explain it, just that she was aware of the past that had come before her, in the hunting pair of eagles overhead and the peaceful deer resting in the undergrowth or the quiet reverence of an old-growth pine grove that had clung to the side of the mountains when natives hunted and cared for their families and each other.

God's handiwork was timeless.

They rode in companionable silence for a long while, until the sun touched the tops of the trees, making long shadows in the bunches of wildflowers and bear grass.

When she heard the faint rush and gurgle of running water, she guided Jingles off the beaten path and through the shade of Douglas fir. Creek water trickled over smooth, round rocks, so clear and clean it sparkled like diamonds in the sunlight.

"My favorite picnic spot. Just Jingles and I know about it."

"Not anymore."

"I guess I can share this place with you, since you understand." She let the reins slide through her fingers, giving her mare enough slack to sip from the fresh cool water.

Palouse came to a rocking stop and did the same.

Wow. This was going better than he'd ever thought. He leaned on the wide shelf below the saddle horn, the way he'd seen his heroes Clint and John do.

What should he say now? No witty banter came to mind. Think, man. He felt itchy. Antsy. Why?

"Look, fresh tracks." Kendra swung nimbly out of the saddle.

Okay, that was why. Were they in danger? "I don't think that's a good idea, getting down like that." They were cougar prints. He could see them plain as day at the edge of the creek, beginning to fill in with water. "The cat was just here."

"Still is." Kneeling, Kendra nodded toward the way they'd come. Calm, quiet, not moving.

That was good. Never a smart idea to act like panicked prey in the backcountry. He eased down slow, glad for the locked and loaded Smith & Wesson on his hip.

"I've never had one threaten me. Mostly they keep their distance. Look, there she is. Under the fir branch there against the bank, crouched low. Oh, she's pretty."

Cam couldn't spot the animal from where he was, and he didn't like that. The back of his neck prickled. He liked to keep an eye on his enemies, assuming the mountain lion was looking for an early supper.

Then he saw it, a second before the low fir boughs shivered. He had his gun in his hand and was on his feet in front of Kendra, ready to protect her with his life.

The golden brown blur slipped soundlessly away over the carpet of the forest. The branches shivered, and the next instant there was no trace of the predator. Adrenaline kicked in, thrumming through him until he could hardly breathe.

He'd been so rattled, so fierce with the need to protect her, that he wasn't thinking straight. He was a tracker. He could see plain as day the cougar hadn't been hunting. Now he felt like a fool and reholstered his revolver.

"Awesome." Unaware, Kendra rose gracefully and handed him a small bottle of water from her small nylon saddle pack and kept one for her.

"You were going to protect me." She sounded amazed as she removed the plastic lid with a supple twist of her wrist and took a long pull.

"You? No, I was worried about *me*. I didn't want to be that cougar's early supper."

"You have a real protective vibe going, don't you, Sheriff?"

Did he look as embarrassed as he felt? "Part of my job. Habit."

"Habit? Like how you serve and protect?"

"Hey, don't go thinking I'm noble or something, because I'm not." How was he going to talk his way out of this one?

"Oh?" She crooked one eyebrow, not fooled.

"I was protecting my best interests. You know the buddy rule?"

"Sure. Don't go into the woods alone, so you have someone to help if you need it."

"Sure, but there's more to it than that. I always make sure I go with a slower runner, that way if a bear or a cougar takes after us, you'd be the first one they'd catch and I'd be just fine."

"That's a fine plan, but guess what? How do you know that I'm a slower runner than you are? That's why *I* wanted to take you out here instead of Colleen. She's a really slow runner, and I'd hate to lose another employee. They take time to train. You, on the other hand, what's another boarder? They're a dime a dozen."

"You'd let a bear eat me, huh?"

"Absolutely. About as easily as you'd let a bear attack me."

She couldn't remember when she'd laughed with a man like this since Jerrod. It just went to show what a decent man Cameron was. He'd jumped to protect her, physically put himself in harm's way for her sake. Without a thought. He just did it.

Just as he'd done before.

The laughter inside her vanished.

She retrieved her reins, fighting to keep from remembering that night. The scent of cooled sausage-and-olive pizza sitting on the kitchen table. The rhythm of rain beating the aluminum siding. Thunder crashing overhead as if the night were breaking apart around her. Cameron pounding at the door, the flash of red-and-blue strobes cutting through the closed slats of the plastic window blinds—

"Are we heading back?" He sounded disappointed.

She gathered her reins, keeping her back to him so he couldn't see her shivering or the goose bumps on her arms, even as the bold sun scorched her skin.

He mounted up clumsily, but good for a second attempt. "Know what I think?"

Kendra found herself in the saddle, reins gathered, turning Jingles away from the creek and toward the trail. Toward home. She wanted to go home.

"I like this. It's peaceful. It's closer to being like hiking than I thought it would be. Not as near to the ground."

She nodded, acknowledging his attempt at humor.

"It's peaceful. Closer to nature, something you don't get on a motorbike or four-wheeling."

A tip of a pine bough brushed against her cheek, startling her. Reminding her where she was. She was here, safe, the memories were gone, tucked safely away behind the shields protecting her heart. Leaving a growing emptiness.

An emptiness that had swallowed all the warmth

and laughter she'd felt with Cameron. That left her feeling alone, as she was meant to be.

She stayed several yards ahead of Cameron on the return trip through the tree line and along the well-used path until the fields and the paddocks and the buildings came into sight.

the back porch she'd tell Gramma. That's all for now. Being alone, she was meant to be.

She sat and stared a while longer. A Chinook on the wind whispered through the tree tops and along the eaves, still humming those ancient melodies that the moments fade into song.

Chapter Six

Kendra couldn't resist standing at her new niece's crib for a few more moments, gazing down on the sleeping infant, so sweet and precious and new. Love shone like the sun inside her heart. Gramma's words came to mind. *That's what your little girl will look like one day.*

No way, Gramma. Kendra brushed her hand over the infant's downy head, her fine hair already thicker and curlier than when she'd been born. She was a McKaslin, all right, with the gold locks.

"You look like your mom, not me," she told the baby, who sighed in her sleep, pressing into Kendra's touch.

Oh, I'm going to spoil you rotten, little girl. It was an aunt's privilege, after all. She thought of all the birthday presents to buy, all the fun outings ahead, finding her first pony and teaching her to ride. Buying her riding boots and her first cowboy hat. So much to look forward to.

She felt a tug on the hem of her denim shorts.

"Auntie Kendwa?" A big girl, two and a half years old, Allie stretched out both adorably chubby hands. "Up!"

"Hey, princess." Kendra settled her niece against her hip, heading for the door. "Are you up from your nap already?"

"Mine!" Allie pointed to the baby in the crib.

"That's right. She's your little sister. Isn't she nice?"

Allie nodded, her silken gold hair as soft as silk against Kendra's jaw. She smelled of baby shampoo and the laundry detergent Karen used and that sweet little-girl scent that was everything good. "Allie want cookie."

"Are you a hungry girl?"

A very serious nod. "Hungwy."

"Then we'd better go downstairs and check out the cookie jar. There just might be chocolate cookies."

"Yum."

Thoroughly charmed, Kendra started down the stairs and onto the main floor, careful to be quiet as she circled past the living room, where Karen was stretched out napping on the couch. She didn't stir.

"Cookie! Cookie!" Allie clapped her hands together, steepling her little fingers when she saw the jar had been refilled, thanks to a late-night baking.

"You can have two." Kendra handed one to the girl, who took a big bite and chewed happily.

She slipped Allie into her high chair, buckled her up and locked the tray in place. She left the second cookie within reach while she searched through the cupboard for a cup. When she turned around, Allie had a cookie in each hand, both missing a big bite out of the tops of them.

Too cute. Kendra felt her self-protective armor settle back in place. This is *not* what it would be like if she had a family of her own—she wasn't going to think like that. She wasn't ever going to go there. To start picturing in her mind what it would be like if she could find a man to trust.

A man like Cameron. The thought breezed into her mind so fast and stealthily, she couldn't stop it. And where had that come from? She was *far* from interested in the local sheriff. Really. She was fine all by herself. Just fine.

A light tap on the screen door had Allie squealing. "Gwamma! Gwamma!"

"Yes, it's me, little darling." Gramma slipped into the kitchen, carrying an insulated casserole dish and a rolled grocery bag on top, which she set on the edge of the kitchen island. "I brought dinner for you girls. I know, you were going to handle it, but you've been doing so much lately, I couldn't help wanting to pitch in."

"Thank you, Gramma." Kendra kissed her grandmother's soft cheek, as delicate as paper. "You look snazzy. Where are you off to with your boyfriend?"

"Imagine, a boyfriend at my age." Gramma sparkled with happiness as she pulled a small stuffed tiger from her purse, heading straight for the high chair and the little girl who was clapping in glee. "Look what Gramma got you."

"A kitty!" Chocolate ringed Allie's mouth and crumbs rained from her fingers as she reached out to claim her new toy.

"There's a concert over at the university," Gramma explained while Kendra poured Allie's milk. "Selections from Chopin. You know how I love classical music. Willard is spoiling me."

"I knew I liked that man." Kendra was glad to see that her grandmother, after being a widow for so long, had found someone who made her happy.

Please, help him to continue, she prayed. She worried about her gramma, who was so trusting. Sometimes it wasn't easy to see what lurked hidden inside a person—a man.

Isn't that how she'd felt about Jerrod? He'd been a truly wonderful boyfriend at first. And then—

Her stomach turned to ice and her hand shook. The spill-proof lid skidded through her fingers and milk sloshed over the rim.

"I'm glad you're taking your time getting to know Willard." She grabbed a paper towel to wipe up the mess. "It's good to go slow."

"I'm enjoying every moment. It's shameful how

he spoils me. I tell him so, too, but do you know what he says? Get used to it, Helen. Goodness. He's all but swept me off my feet.''

''It's good to keep your feet on the ground.''

''That's sensible advice from a woman who has never truly been in love.'' Gramma took the lid and snapped it into place. ''True love is worth the flight and the fall. It's the journey that matters, dear. What choices we make, to love and to live, especially after we get hurt. Love is never a mistake. Remember that.''

Yes, it is. What else could Jerrod have been but a mistake? Maybe she'd been blind, but Jerrod had seemed kind and gallant at first. With everything she was and everything she had in her soul to give, she'd *wanted* to fall in love.

And she had. She'd been wrong. She'd made one huge glaring mistake, just one.

Nothing would ever be the same again. Nothing would ever be right.

''Great-Gramma loves you, darling.''

Kendra watched as her grandmother kissed the top of Allie's golden head, all curls and silk.

''I think it's great you're helping the sheriff out.'' Gramma flashed Kendra a knowing look. ''He told me all about it when he came in for coffee this morning. Said how you were helping him find the right horse.''

''It is my job.''

''Exactly.'' Sparkling, full of hope, Gramma

headed to the door in a swirl of color and beauty. "I'm so pleased you do your job well. Keep up the good work."

Really. Kendra rolled her eyes. "You could mind your own business."

"What fun would that be? Oh, hi, girls. I'm on my way out. Michelle, you're glowing. Kirby, you look pale. Are you getting enough sleep?"

"I had a late call last night," replied Kirby, the nurse, as she held the door. "Have a good time, Gramma."

"Yeah, and behave!" Michelle called out, teasing. "I'm not sure about that grandmother of ours. Out until all hours of the evening with that boyfriend of hers."

"The literature professor." Kirby, a year younger than Kendra, set the board game and the foil-covered cake pan on the table. "Are you ready for game night? I made chocolate cake."

"Is that taco cheese-and-macaroni casserole I smell?" Michelle followed her nose to the counter. "Ooh, and Gramma's homemade rolls. We're eatin' good tonight, but not as good as little Allie."

"Hello, cutie pie." Kirby freed their niece from the high chair. "Where's your mommy?"

"Sleeping," Kendra supplied while she preheated the oven. "You guys watch Allie for me, and I'll get supper on for us."

"My pleasure." Kirby spirited their niece away.

Leaving Michelle to lean against the counter and

gloat. "Do you know what I heard? That you spent yesterday afternoon with a certain handsome lawman. One that was the recipient of your baked goods the other day."

"You mean Frank, the deputy?"

Michelle scowled playfully, because there was an abiding love between them. "Cameron is a good man. Good in the way that matters. The kind of man that stands tall and loves deep. Way to go, sis."

"I'm not seeing the sheriff."

"Face it. You literally *saw* him. You were alone with him. I'd call that a date."

Her stomach turned into a cold, hard ball. "You're making something out of nothing. It's business. He wants to buy a horse. I'm going to help him. I do that. I own a riding stable, remember?"

"Yeah, but it doesn't have to be *all* business." Michelle grabbed the board game and began unboxing the set. The clatter of tokens and the spill of hotels filled the silence between them.

Kendra took the lettuce from the refrigerator and tore open the plastic wrap. Why were her hands trembling again? It's just business, she wanted to say one more time convincingly, but to who? To Michelle? Or herself?

Cameron is a good man. Good in the way that matters. How did Michelle know? And were there any good, decent men left out there? The kind that never hurt, that always stayed? How would she know when she found one?

Or would she make the same mistake?

As if in answer, her arm ached, the pins and plates that had held her bones together gone now, but the memory remained.

As deep as those scars had gone, there were others that had cut more deeply. Those scars hurt, too.

It was amazing the difference a new interest could make in a man's life. Cameron had slept like the dead, something he hadn't done in more years than he could count.

Rested, it was that much easier to face work on a Monday morning, whistling while he strolled around the echoing office making coffee and punching out reports.

Frank happened by a few minutes before eight o'clock, keys jingling, looking dog tired. "What's with you? I could toss you in the holding cell. There ought to be some ordinance against being happy before coffee."

"I've already had mine. It's hot." He gestured toward the low filing cabinet where the coffeemaker sat, light on, coffee steaming.

Frank frowned and he grabbed a mug with a clink and poured. "It's got to be that woman. If you're dating her, then does that mean we'll be getting more cookies?"

"You can hope, but I'm not dating her."

Frank swiped one of the last two from the plate by the sugar packets. "Want the last one?"

"Already helped myself." Cameron stapled the last report and checked his e-mail. Nothing much, just a reminder for this month's council meeting from the mayor's secretary.

"Hmm, these sure are good." Frank chewed as he headed toward the door. "Did you score another date with her for this weekend?"

"I told you. I didn't have a first date with her."

"That's your story. I don't think you're telling me the truth, man."

"That's none of your business."

"Sure it is, if cookies are involved."

"We didn't have a date, but I did spend time with the lovely lady over the weekend."

"You mean a woman that fine actually deigned to speak to a guy like you?"

"A few words. I'm thinking there'll be more if I board a horse at her place."

"Wait. Hold it. What horse?"

The phone at his elbow rang, the first line lit up bright red. He grabbed the receiver, since Frank was taking his last bite of the cookies.

"Hello, Sheriff," said the sweetest voice ever.

"*Kendra.*" Did he sound way too unprofessional or what? He cleared his throat and tried to sound more dignified. "What can I do for you on this fine morning?"

"I've got some good news for you."

"I like the sound of that. Frank and I polished off

the last of your cookies, crumbs and all. Thank you. Haven't had better cookies."

"I'm glad you liked them."

Was it his imagination, or did she sound glad to talk to him?

"I may have found the perfect horse for you."

"Worked on that mighty fast, did you?"

"That's my job. I put out a few feelers, and guess what? I just got off the phone with a former client. I taught his kids to ride, and they're a very fine family of horse lovers. They have a gelding they're interested in selling, but only to someone who will be good to him. He's a registered quarter horse, but they are willing to budge on the price quite a bit. They'd rather he went to a good home."

Nerves coiled in the pit of his stomach. This was a big step. He was ready for it, but... "I don't want to make a mistake. Is he a good horse?"

"I trained him."

That said something. "Would *you* buy him, if you were me?"

"Absolutely. Warrior is a good-hearted animal. Plus, he's trained for the backwoods. The father and son are outdoorsmen, like yourself. The son's going off to college, and they don't want to sell, but they don't want the horse to be lonely, either. Would you like to look at him?"

"Would you come with me?"

"Sure. Let me check my schedule." He could hear

Kendra flicking through her paperwork, all business. "I could do it this evening."

"So can I. Want me to ride out and pick you up?" A man could always hope.

"Oh, no, that's going well out of your way."

"You're going out of yours to help me. The least I can do is provide the transportation."

"Don't worry about it. I do this all the time."

"As long as you're sure."

"Absolutely." Kendra couldn't believe what a nice guy Cameron was. She thought about what her sister had said. *The kind of man that stands tall and loves deep.*

Michelle was happily married. Maybe she knew the measure of a man when she looked at him. Kendra couldn't argue that Michelle was right.

Only the Lord knew how protective he'd been to her the night her life was in danger. How tall he'd stood. How strong.

How kind he'd been in the face of devastation and broken faith.

But if she ever trusted a man again, it would not be one who carried a gun on his hip. Not a man who stood strong against violence and won. The constant reminder of what she'd endured would just be too painful.

She squeezed her eyes shut, forcing away the image of Cameron on that cold, rainy October night taking Jerrod down. Fear took hold of her stomach.

Don't remember.

She cleared her throat. Business. That's what she had to focus on. And the fact that the Lord would not have led Cameron across her path once more if there wasn't a greater purpose. She'd received the sheriff's help; it was her chance to help him in return.

It felt right. Maybe it would help her find a way to forget and forgive. To bury that horrible time forever.

She forced cheer into her voice. "Do you know the Thornton's ranch? I'll meet you there at seven?"

"I'll be there. How do we do this? Do I need to bring my checkbook or anything?"

"You can, but you don't have to make a decision today. It's good to meet the horse and see if your personalities mesh, if he's what you want in a friend. A lot of folks look at a dozen or more horses before they find the right one."

"How do you know when you do?"

"You just *know*. You feel it in your heart. Do you know what I mean?"

Boy, did he. He had to wonder what he was feeling inside at this moment.

As he said goodbye and replaced the phone in the cradle, he realized he wasn't alone in the office. Frank was sitting across the room at his desk, staring right at him, one eyebrow raised—whether in disdain or approval, it was hard to tell.

I get to look at a horse tonight. It was all he could do to hold back his excitement. It made him want to get up and do a happy dance right in the middle of the street, but he restrained himself.

He settled for a second cup of coffee instead. Life was looking up. For the first time in a long while, he was glad to be alive.

As she kicked up a cloud of dust behind her pickup, barreling down the country road to the Thornton ranch, it hit her. Should she be speeding when she knew a sheriff was around? Not that she was speeding badly, just pushing the needle a little over the legal limit. She was running late.

Better late than a lawbreaker. Or having to pay for a ticket. She eased her foot off the gas and not a moment too soon. There was a gray patrol cruiser. Was it Cameron?

No, she realized as she moved over on the narrow road to give the oncoming car plenty of room. It was the new deputy. He had his window down and saluted her as they both slowed.

"Going a little fast, weren't you?" Easygoing and polite, the deputy flashed a grin at her.

"Yeah." It hurt to admit it. "I'm late meeting your boss."

"It's awful generous of you to help him out like this. He seems to really want a horse."

Was it her imagination, or did the deputy seem sarcastic? Not mean sarcastic, but as if he knew something she didn't. Oh, wait, she knew what he thought. He thought she had a crush on Cameron, too.

Her face grew hot. Really! Bake cookies as a thank-you, as a good gesture, and look what happens.

She was really starting to regret making those cookies.

It had been all her sisters could talk about last night, when they were *supposed* to be having a sisters night, talking about what really mattered. Not about her ridiculous, nonexistent *thing* for poor Cameron. He had enough on his plate grieving his wife and trying to get on with his life.

"Just doing my job." She shrugged, knowing it was a lame answer, but it was the truth.

"And I'm doing mine. Would you mind handing over your license and registration?"

"Not going to let me get away with it, are you?" Resigned, Kendra grabbed the registration from behind the visor and rummaged through her purse for her ID. She handed it through the window. "I couldn't have been going more than three, four miles over the limit. I know, because I was afraid Cameron was going to catch me."

Frank studied her license. "You got a birthday coming up."

"In a few weeks."

"Well, I suppose it would only be decent of me, since I'm that kind of guy, to let this slide once." Was that a hint of trouble sparkling in Frank's eyes, as he held out her license?

"You are? Oh, that's great. Thank you."

"Wait. You didn't let me finish. You know how it goes. I do something for you, you do something for me. Chocolate-chip cookies. Lots of them." He saluted her as he drove away.

More cookies? She was going to have to bake more cookies? She would rather have had the ticket!

Cameron was waiting for her in his SUV when she pulled up. There was no way she was going to explain why she was late. She'd just drop the cookies off sometime when he was out on patrol. It couldn't be too hard to figure out, since he parked along the curb whenever he was in the office, right?

"I was beginning to think you'd stood me up for a better-looking guy." He adjusted his Stetson. "Have any trouble?"

"I'm always into trouble, you must know that by now."

"Yeah, I pegged you for trouble the day I moved back to this town. Riding horses. Building your own business. Sad you have no sense of responsibility."

"You're in a good mood. You're excited about this. You should be. Getting your first horse will bring about a wonderful change in your life. I promise you."

"I'll hold you to that." He looked changed from the quiet, stoic officer she'd seen around town for years.

This evening, as the sun sank low in the sky, he seemed more alive.

This was what she loved. Walking along a newly painted fence line with the scent of horse on the breeze. Seeing three saddle horses, two geldings and a mare she trained, grazing in the shade near the creek. The crunch of gravel beneath her riding boots. The anticipation of seeing Warrior again, and the Thorntons, who were good people.

"Sure is nice of you going to all this trouble for me."

"Stop thanking me. I love horses, and I hope you will, too."

"Been looking forward to this all day." He slowed to match his pace with hers. "The owners are negotiable?"

"I spoke to them again just before I left." She gestured toward the stable, bypassing the house, as if she'd been here many times before. "Mr. Thornton is more concerned with their horse finding a good home rather than what money they get for him. There he is. The black one in the paddock."

"The all-black one?" He looked like a show horse, all gleam and polish and fine bold lines. Cam might know next to nothing about horses, but he could see this was a quality animal. "That one looks too fancy for what I need."

"He's a trained trail horse, for all terrain and all seasons. He can pack, hunt, jump, lead and rope."

"Sounds like what I'm looking for. Hi, fella." He held out his palm.

The big animal studied him with intelligent eyes. He was huge, the biggest horse Cam had seen yet. The animal's big velvet nostrils flared as the gelding sniffed his hand, then nickered low in his throat.

Could he handle him? Cam wondered.

As if in answer, the horse nosed him. A spark of affection flashed to life in Cam's chest, like a flint striking kindling. What a fine horse he was.

"Hi there, Evan!" Kendra waved in a rider trotting into sight from the hillside trails. "Your horse is lookin' good."

"The work you did with her sure helped her gait. Hi, Cameron." Evan swung down from the saddle.

"Howdy." He knew Evan well enough, he'd been years older in school. He was without a wife these days. Is that why Cameron felt protective? Or was it jealous?

That realization made him uneasy. Jealous? He didn't like to think he could let that undesirable emotion into his heart. But he couldn't deny a certain fierce urge to make sure Evan kept his distance from Kendra.

Kendra didn't seem to notice as she stroked her sensitive fingertips down Warrior's neck and spoke to Evan Thornton as if they were old friends. "Is Kevin glad to be heading off to his second year of college?"

Evan's affirmative answer sounded somewhere in the distance. All Cameron saw was Kendra. The world around him had disappeared; there was only her. The soft spring scent of flowers, the feel of her, as if it wasn't just his heart reacting, but his soul was aware of hers.

How was it he could feel her spirit? Strange, the power of it. He didn't understand what was happening. Only that he'd never seen such beauty in his life—and he wasn't referring to the glitzy, primp-in-front-of-the-mirror kind. Hers was a beauty that lasted. It shone from the inside and made the lovely woman she was all the more breathtaking.

Dressed in a plain gray T-shirt, ordinary faded jeans and scuffed riding boots, she was extraordinary. His chest ached with the wonder of it.

"He likes you." Kendra smiled and it was like the first day of spring after a long and bleak winter. "Evan, can we take Warrior for a ride?"

"Sure thing. His saddle's in the tack room in the barn. Want me to do the honors?"

"I can handle it. What do you think, Cameron?"

The poor man looked love struck. "I'd like to, but the truth is, I think he's way too fine for the likes of me."

"I think he's perfect for you." Who would have thought that the strong and practical town sheriff would fall head over heels for a horse? She couldn't be happier for him. "You like the mountains, and he does, too."

The gelding nudged him, nearly knocking him off his feet. "Whoa, fella. Take it easy on me."

"See? He feels the same. Maybe he can sense you two are kindred spirits. He's been lonely for the whole year Evan's son has been away at college. He wants someone who likes to ride high up into the backcountry and camp and fish and hunt."

"I can't ride worth squat. You know I just sat on

that horse of yours, Palouse. I imagine Warrior is used to a skilled rider. Someone who knows how to handle him.''

''So, you'll take lessons. I'll teach you to ride him. You can stop off in the evenings after work to spend time with him. Get to know him. Develop a bond and trust between you.''

Exactly. If God answers prayers and can look straight into a man's heart to see the goodness through all the bad, then the Lord would see how much he wanted this.

The Lord might see, too, how Cameron was thinking about more than the horse.

''You've got a deal, Kendra McKaslin. You teach me to ride him, and I'll buy him.''

''Oh, what a lucky horse you are, Warrior.'' Kendra shone with all the beauty of a summer's sunset.

Words died in his throat. No, he was the lucky one. Cameron said nothing more. He didn't have to. He felt as light as air, as Kendra smiled, just for him, like a gift from above.

Chapter Seven

Okay, here goes nothing. Kendra clutched the paper plate stacked high with cookies and marched straight to the front door. A banner advertising the upcoming Harvest Days festival flapped overhead as she hurried past the antique shop and into the sheriff's air-conditioned office.

"You remembered." Frank rose from behind his paper-piled desk, but he looked uncomfortable instead of glad to see more cookies. "Cam isn't in. He stepped out for a few minutes. Ran out to grab us both a couple drinks from your sister's coffee shop."

"Too bad there isn't a doughnut shop in town." Kendra quipped so she didn't have to comment on Cameron's being absent, because she'd timed it that way. She'd spotted his cruiser pulling away from the curb from the Feed and Grain store, where she was putting in her monthly order.

But if he went to the coffee shop, that was like four blocks away. In this heat, it made sense he would drive, but that meant it was a short trip. He'd be back any second!

"Hope this fulfills the requirement, Deputy." She slipped the covered plate on the edge of his desk. "Thanks again for looking past my indiscretion. I have been very careful with my speed every since."

"I'm glad to hear it. Mmm." He bit into a cookie like a hungry kid.

She took advantage of his chewing to head straight for the door. "Have a great afternoon!" she called, and she was free. Safely on the sidewalk, escaping before Cameron—

"Where's the fire?" a friendly baritone rumbled as two big hands caught her elbows, stopping her before she ran full speed into him.

Cameron. Her heart stopped. Already he'd released her, but the imprint of his fingers banding her arms remained. Her mouth opened, but she couldn't think of anything to say.

"Hey, did Evan Thornton get a hold of you? He said he'd trailer my new horse over to your place sometime late this afternoon. I figured I'd pop on over to your place to see him."

There was something wrong with her mind. It wasn't working right. It was as if her neurotransmitters had forgotten how to fire. All she could do was stare up at the man towering over her, looking dashing in the well-fitted uniform.

"I'm taking your advice. I'm going to go slow, spend time with Warrior. Let him see I'm the best friend he's ever gonna have."

"F-fine." There, at least her tongue was starting to work, although she sounded lame and half-dazed.

Had he always had such an amazing smile? Kendra couldn't seem to remember but her feet were carrying her down the sidewalk. Cameron watched after her, as if he were making sure she wasn't likely to plow into someone else head-on.

"I'll see you tonight, then," he called the length of the sidewalk. "Is there anytime you consider too late to stay? You must close up shop sometime."

"Uh, until dark?"

She didn't sound too sure of her answer. Cameron figured not too many folks stayed out with their horses late into the evening. Well, wasn't that nice? He was interested in her. He'd be able to spend more time with her.

A hard band of fear tightened around his chest. Was that really a good idea? Was he ready to start caring about another woman? He didn't know if he could ever risk his heart again. He wouldn't trade a second of his time with Debra. He'd loved her deeply. Losing her had been the toughest thing that ever happened to him. He couldn't go through that again.

"Where's the iced tea?" Frank asked from behind his computer monitor.

"Closed. They're cutting back hours, I guess."

"I'd be mad, but guess what? I wrangled more

cookies out of your girlfriend.'' With a sly grin, Frank bit into a chocolate cookie.

"She's not my girlfriend." Cam helped himself. The plate was stacked high—had to be two-dozen cookies. "Way to go. How did you finagle this?"

"I was just out patrolling. Doing my job like a good deputy. I couldn't help it that she was going twenty-six in a twenty-five zone. I *had* to reprimand her."

"You had no choice."

"Exactly. Know what else I found out? Her birth date. It's coming up, too. Thought you might want to know."

"Why? I'm not exactly a member of her inner circle."

"But my guess is that you might want an invitation to the party. If you can't admit it to yourself yet, then fine. Denial is as good of a way to cope as any." Frank hit a key and the shared printer came to life, spitting and sputtering in the corner.

"I thought you didn't approve of her."

"It's not my call. But admit it. You like the woman." He scribbled something on a memo pad.

"Sure, I like her. Who doesn't like her?" She was friendly and beautiful and helpful. What wasn't to like?

Cam knew perfectly well that wasn't the kind of *like* Frank was talking about. He meant romantic interest. That was exactly what Cam was wondering, too.

* * *

It hadn't been the best day. Kendra left the cordless phone on the desk. It *looked* as though she had enough of a crew to cut hay, although she couldn't be sure.

She wasn't offering top dollar—she was meeting a good field wage, but she didn't have the capital right now to compete with her neighbors for the limited amount of teenagers and part-time field-workers in the valley.

She couldn't blame the workers for wanting to make the most pay they could, but if she heard one more, "I'll come in the morning if Mr. Brisbane's crew is already full," she was going to, well, do the entire haying herself.

"You look beat," Colleen commented from where she was upending a grain bucket into a stall trough. "Did you need help making any calls? I don't mind playing the tough guy."

"Thanks, I may take you up on that tomorrow. I have ten delinquent accounts and they keep avoiding me. I've left messages, I keep trying to hunt them down in the arena. Nothing." Kendra didn't add that she could really use that money. Things were tight—but then, they were always tight. Just a part of being an upstart business, that was all.

"If you want to show me the list, I can help you hunt them down in person." Colleen swiped the sweat from her forehead.

Colleen was a hard worker, and one day she wanted to open a stable of her own. It would be good to teach her more of the business side of things. "Meet me in my office first thing tomorrow."

"Awesome." Colleen flashed a grateful smile before refilling the ten-gallon bucket. "Oh, I forgot. The sheriff's new horse came in while you were out in the fields. I got Warrior settled in a nice corner box stall like you asked."

"You are wonderful, Colleen. Thanks." Kendra took a step, saw Trisha Corey, fresh off work, head down the aisle toward her horse's stall. Seeing the woman reminded her that Cameron would be coming by soon, as he'd promised. "Can you do me a favor?"

"Name it."

"Could you show the sheriff to his horse when he gets here? Answer his questions, that kind of thing? I haven't really gone over a lot of things with him yet." Oh, and the contract. She had to get his contract printed out.

Her stomach rumbled. She had skipped lunch again. Maybe she'd print off the paperwork while she cooked something quick to eat. Oh, and she had to balance the checkbook so she knew if she could make a payment to the feed store.

She mentally added that to her list as she swept down the main aisle toward the back exit. The long diaphanous rays of the evening sun streamed through the double doors like a path at her feet.

She noticed Cameron's dark blue SUV ambling

down her graveled driveway. True to his word, he'd come to spend time with his horse.

It was the hand of Providence that brought the right horse in his direction, and she was glad for him. As she followed the rail paddock toward her little cottage tucked on the rising knoll of the property, she had a perfect view as he parked, climbed out, adjusted his Stetson and glanced her way. His hand shot up in the air in a manly wave.

For one fleeting second, a tide of joy lifted her up. Happiness? No, she *couldn't* be happy to see him. What sense did that make? She was glad he'd come for his horse's sake. That was all.

She stopped to check the roses in her backyard garden, grabbed the shears and snipped off a few fragrant yellow blossoms on her way in. Her cat was a huge marmalade lump on the couch cushion in front of the air conditioner. He opened one eye a slit, appraised her mildly, then let his eye droop.

"Good to see you, too, handsome. Don't get up or anything." She snagged a bud vase from the shelf over the refrigerator and filled it with lukewarm water. She heard the thud as he jumped down from his perch.

He wove his way around her ankles, mewing pointedly.

"I know. I'm sorry. I'm late." Where did she put the can opener? "You know what I need? Two can openers, so when I lose one, I can still open—"

She felt a change in the air, like a charge of anticipation before a thunderstorm. It trickled across her skin like a temperate breeze. It filled her senses like the sharp, heavy smell of ozone that accompanied thunder.

Cameron. She *felt* him. She saw him without turning around, striding with that easy gait of his, relaxed because he'd changed out of his uniform and was wearing those worn-comfortable jeans and a plain T-shirt that made him look like a hero out of a western.

Every cell of her being focused on the tap of boots against the wooden porch.

"Do you always do that?" His baritone shivered over her.

"Do what?" She couldn't think again. "Lose my can opener?"

"Talk to your cat. As fine as he is, he can't talk back."

"No, but he makes faces like a teenager, so I figure there has to be some cognitive function behind the sneer. See? He lifted his lip at me."

"I've never had a cat. Call me a dog person. Well, a horse person now." He was wearing a grin that showed off two dimples to perfection.

She placed the vase and delicate roses on the breakfast bar, where she intended to eat her supper, whatever it might be. But first, she'd deal with Cameron. "Have you seen Warrior yet?"

"Gave him a pat on the way by. The gal that works for you, Colleen, was real helpful, but I told her I needed to see you."

She hadn't realized he was holding one hand behind his back until he produced a small present, wrapped in black-and-gray-striped paper with a bow taped to the center. "A gift? But why?"

"To thank you. You went out of your way for me, helped me, and I sure appreciated it." He set the offering on the edge of her kitchen table.

What a nice, thoughtful man he is. Clearly, wrapped in the plain paper, it was nothing romantic or inappropriate. And how could she say no? "I truly don't need a gift."

"It's good manners. Besides, after baking us another round of cookies, I figure it's a fair trade. Butter and sugar costs money." He winked, so she knew he was using humor to lower her defenses, to make it all right. "Go ahead and open it."

She eyed him suspiciously for a moment, and panic knotted behind her sternum. A gift. That wasn't appropriate at all, was it? Should she give it back? "This is too much."

"You don't know how much I was sweatin' all this stuff. What horse? What kind of horse? Would I pay too much? Or get a lemon? Would I even like riding? It's been bugging me for months, and you come along and make it so easy. Thank you."

The corners of her soft mouth quirked as she plucked the bow off the package. It was all he could do to stand still while she pulled carefully at the layer of wrapping tape he'd used on both ends.

"This package is hard to break into." She studied

him through her thick lashes as she reached into a drawer and pulled out a small pair of sharp scissors.

He knew what she was doing. She was watching for any hint of romantic intentions. That's why he'd used black paper, which was about as far away from romantic paper as a guy could get, he figured. And why he purposefully tried to act indifferent, even if his pulse was thudding so hard in his chest he swore she could see it against his shirt. All this was telling him Frank might be right. He might *like* Kendra. More than he wanted to admit.

"Oh, Cameron. Thank you." The loose strands of gold that had escaped her ponytail throughout her long day's work framed her face in soft waves. True pleasure drew color into her cheeks. Her eyes sparkled as she pulled the DVD case from the wrapping paper. It was one of her favorite westerns.

"Do you have it already?"

"No. I've been renting instead of working on my movie collection." She gestured to the other side of the room where a small TV sat on what looked like a newly varnished antique trunk. On top of it sat an economy-model DVD player and a set of rabbit ears.

"A collection, huh? That sounds impressive."

"Yeah, doesn't it?" She crossed in front of a small coffee table and a covered, overstuffed couch to set the DVD case next to the TV. "Now I have, wow, one movie. It's a *very* selective collection."

"You have good taste." He didn't have to wonder to see how tight Kendra's budget had to be. She'd made those curtains herself, he figured, since his Deb had sewn and he recognized the touches no discount-store-bought item could provide.

The furniture was all secondhand and probably older than either one of them, but it was dusted and polished, refinished and cozy. The cottage was small and feminine—there were ruffles and lace, not a lot of it, but even a small amount was too much for a tough guy like him. It made the back of his neck itch.

He felt like a bull penned in a field of daisies in this small feminine home next to this petite, feminine woman. For all the hard physical labor she must have to do to earn her living, she was really a wisp of a thing, all long limbs and quiet elegance.

Tenderness flickered to life in his chest and glowed like a candle's soft radiance. *Lord, are you trying to tell me something?* "I'd best let you get to your supper. What are you making?"

"I'm clueless. I haven't browsed through my cupboards yet."

"I don't imagine you have a lot of time for cooking."

"I manage, since the other option is starving to death."

"It's hard to cook for just one person. If I whip up something like lasagna on the weekend, then I wind up eating it all week."

"You could freeze portions in those little freezer bags. The kind that lock out freezer burn. That's what

I do. Except then I run out of time to cook or shop, especially this time of year.''

She yanked open the secondhand appliance—it had to be a good thirty years old, since it was the shade of yellow popular in the seventies. ''See? That's what I do with my hamburger. Make them ahead and freeze them.''

''That's a smart idea. I ought to try that.'' He would—except that he wound up making a sandwich more often than not. He'd never gotten used to the quiet of the kitchen in the evening. He and Deb always used to cook together. ''Well, I guess I'll head back to the stable.''

''Want to stay? I have extra patties I could defrost.'' Now why did she ask that?

Because it made the loneliness that lined his face vanish. ''They wouldn't be too much trouble?''

''Not if you want to start the barbecue for me.'' After all, his gift had her feeling guilty.

''I'm a pro when it comes to barbecuing.'' There was no mistaking the ridge of muscle that flexed and stretched his white T-shirt. No mistaking the power of the gun holstered at his hip. ''Matches?''

''In the top drawer closest to you.''

The sheriff's step was light, his grin cheerful. She liked him this way—steady and as dependable as the Bridger Mountains, but buoyant, too. Maybe it was because he was stepping out of the last stages of his grief.

Her door squeaked shut. A sharp, punctuated

"Meow!" had her looking down at the cat still glaring with disapproval.

"Be nice," she told him with a laugh. "He's not staying. He's just passing through."

Pounce did not seem reassured, even after she forked his favorite salmon cat food into his food dish and broke it up into small chunks for him.

She'd never ever had a man in her house before, aside from her dad and brothers-in-law. Cameron's presence was tangible, although he was on the deck out of sight. She felt the masculine power of his being. It shrank the already too small kitchen, it filled her tiny house and made her feel vulnerable.

The grill's lid squeaked as he lifted it. She heard the strike of a match, smelled the flare of sulfur and the burn of residue from the grill. The scrape as he cleaned the metal rack. The *clink* of the lid lowering into place.

He was a big man. He filled the door frame as he strolled inside, replaced the box of matches and planted his hands on the edge of the counter. "Anything else you need done?"

"Nope." She hit a button and the microwave began humming. She'd acted on impulse. When was acting on impulse the *best* idea? Never!

"Better make use of me while I'm here. I'm pretty good at making a salad."

"Define salad for me. My experience with men is that they avoid vegetables as if they're poison."

"Not true. Throw bacon on it, and I'll eat it. Even a heap of lettuce leaves."

"Just what I thought. I'm not about to trust you with the single most important part of the meal."

"The meat?"

She rolled her eyes. "Lettuce from my garden. Fresh carrots straight from the garden. I'm going out to pick a tomato."

"I can do it."

"I'm sure you can." She had images of her father bumbling around her mom's garden before he was banned for life.

"You don't think I know what I'm doing?"

"What man does?" In a flash, she'd taken a plastic bag from the second drawer and was out the door. "Do you have to follow me?"

"I've got to prove myself. I can't have you thinking I'm a failure when it comes to picking vegetables. My reputation is at stake. I've got the election to think about."

"Aren't you running uncontested?"

"Sure, but there's always the write-in option. I can't have a surprise last-minute candidate stealing my job." He knelt down beside her in the soft earth. "How many carrots do you need?"

"Sixty. Maybe seventy." She brushed away the loose dirt from a carrot's base, the feathery leaves tickling her forearm as she grasped and pulled.

He was scowling at her. "I'm going to pretend I didn't hear that." He twisted a plump red tomato off its rambling vine. "Is it just me, or do you treat all your boarders like this?"

"Boarders aren't allowed in my yard."

"Guess I'm just special."

"Nope. I haven't given you the printout with all the rules on it yet."

"I'm breaking some kind of law being up here?"

She shook loose dirt off the carrot and plunked it into the sack. "I suppose there's exceptions to every rule, Officer, but as you know, that comes with a price. I guess you owe *me* a plate of cookies."

"You play tough but fair."

"I'm only kidding. You don't owe me any cookies. My house and yard are off-limits. I'm hardly ever here. I'm almost always down at the stable or riding most of the day, but when I'm here I just want a few quiet minutes."

"I know how that is, since I'm always on call." He added a tomato to her bag. "It's not so bad. Frank and I split weekend duties. You know, patrolling the roads, keeping an eye out for mischief, making sure no one's driving drunk, as far as we can tell."

"I never gave it much thought." She plucked a fat, sweet cuke from the vine and, taking the bag with her, rose to check the tassels on the corn. "You must have to give up a lot of evenings."

"It's an honor, serving the people of this fine town." He didn't know how else to say it. It sounded hokey, and he was embarrassed, but he was proud, too. Proud of the difference he made in people's lives every day.

"Even if it's just lending a hand with a trailer tire, or making sure a mother with two little kids isn't stuck in bad weather when her car breaks down. There isn't a lot of crime in these parts, but I'm there if anyone needs me."

Would Kendra understand? She had to know, more than most, what he was prepared to do to serve and protect. He dug his thumb into gold tassels and smiled at the bright yellow husks beneath. "How many do you want?"

"You pick what you can eat."

"Got any real butter to go along with this? I can eat a lot."

"Real butter. I just might let you use the salt and pepper, too."

"Pepper? Uh." He winked at her as he snapped off two ears of corn, followed by two more. "How many are you picking? Five, no, six. You can eat that much corn? A little skinny thing like you?"

"Half of this is for Colleen. I'm going to give her a jingle and ask her to join us."

"Don't trust me enough to be alone with me, is that it?" His heart drummed as if he'd run his usual seven daily miles all uphill. He was teasing, but he wasn't.

Something crossed over Kendra's face, a shade of emotion that made her eyes darken. "We're not alone, Officer."

As if in answer, her big plump cat curled around his ankles. A horse's nicker lifted on the wind. There, looking at him with a stare of unveiled assessment were two horses, the ones he recognized from the stable that one day, and the pretty golden mare she'd ridden on the trail.

She kept her animals in the paddock closest to her house, did she? They were watching his every move with great interest as he trailed Kendra over to the board fence.

"I'll leave you to do this. Just toss the husks over the fence and let them duke it out." Kendra rolled the corn ears gently to the ground. "I'll go start the salad, check the meat and give Colleen a call."

"Sure thing." Here he'd been hoping this would be a supper for two. The least Kendra could do was to stay and husk the corn with him, so he could watch her sparkle in the sun and try to charm a few more smiles out of her.

She tapped away down the flagstone path, wound through the pleasant tangle of bright roses flowering every which way and color, then disappeared into the house.

Without her, it seemed as if the daylight had dimmed. He waited for a glimpse of her while he husked corn. The horses jockeyed closer, stretching their necks eagerly over the top rail.

He caught sight of Kendra at her kitchen window, washing vegetables while she chatted with the phone tucked between her shoulder and her cheek.

Disappointed wasn't the word he would use to describe the rake of pain in his heart. It was much worse.

Night wrung the last of twilight from the sky. The last traces of magenta and purple brushed the underbellies of nimbus clouds and then retreated into darkness.

Kendra tapped a few numbers on the keyboard and double-checked them on the screen to the numbers scribbled in her green columned ledger. She was halfway through her accounts receivable posting, and her eyelids kept drooping.

A yawn nearly split her in two. She hit Save and left the cursor blinking. Steam from her cup of vanilla red tea invited her to take another sweet, spicy sip. Over the top of the rim she could see the twin beams of headlights pulling out of the gravel parking area down below.

Colleen's pickup, it looked like, ambled a few yards and then hesitated. Was a horse out? Kendra wondered and just as quickly realized a SUV's dome light flashed on. She recognized the faint profile—Cameron.

Colleen and Cameron were talking. During supper at her small table, Cameron had regaled them with funny tales about his last fishing expedition and the last time he'd been shopping in the mall, how he got lost in a department store he couldn't get out of. He'd had them laughing too hard to eat.

Had he been trying to charm Colleen? Maybe so. Kendra took another sip and watched as the pickup rolled ahead, lumbering down the roll and bends of the driveway and out of sight.

Cameron's dome light died. The lights flared on and he drove away into the darkness.

Why did it seem as if something were tugging at her soul? She couldn't describe the sensation, her protective shields were up and fully functional so she couldn't feel what was behind those steel walls.

Cameron was a widower. Colleen was alone, too. Maybe it was Providence that had a hand in their coming together. Cameron would be coming often to visit his horse, to take lessons and to ride the trails when he was more accomplished.

Maybe she could make sure that Cameron wound up in Colleen's classes. Who knew where that would lead? Maybe the two of them would find they had a lot in common. Maybe they'd begin dating. Fall in love.

Wouldn't that be great for them? Why did that make her ache, when she'd vowed not to feel anything at all?

The hum of the computer fan in its casing sounded noisy. As loud as the window unit in the other room. She set her cup onto the ceramic coaster with a clink that sounded as jarring as a gunshot.

The quiet echoed around her. The emptiness inside her echoed, too. She was tired, that was all. Some nights the solitary life she'd chosen weighed on her heavily.

But it was a safe life, she reminded herself as she gathered the daily checks together, stamped the back of them and tucked them into an envelope for tomorrow's deposit.

Shadows moved in the gathering darkness outside. Her horses came to check on her before bedtime, crowding together to try to get a look at her through the window. Three horses and the shorter, limping gait of her old pony. Their silhouettes pushed at the rail fence. A sharp neigh was a welcoming sound in the stillness.

"I'm coming, Honeybear." She left her tea and computer, squeezed along the narrow space between her bed and the wall, for the room was small, to the doorway.

Pounce opened his eyes a slit to follow her progress through the living room to the back door. She grabbed a handful of candies on the way out, the heat of the summer's evening a shock on her skin as she loped out to meet her best friends.

Her sweet gray-and-white pony, the one she'd learned to ride on, as had all of her sisters, crowded the fence. They'd always had a close bond. She gave him a peppermint first, the poor old guy, and he nudged her hand in affectionate thanks.

Jingles snorted, shaking her head as if she was in command, demanding a candy next.

"Oh, you think you're all that, don't you?" The

quarter horse knew she was, and Kendra wasn't going to argue with her. She doled out the candy, ran her fingers through Jingles's mane and through Honeybear's forelock before giving Sprite the last mint.

Deer were daring to make their way through the field grasses, cautiously moving with the darkness. The sounds of night coming—the hoot of an owl, the sharp, high cry of a distant coyote, the whoosh of a horse exhaling as it settled down in its stall for the night drifted on the warm, temperate breezes, buoying her spirits.

This was her life. It wasn't the one she'd always thought she would have. She could almost hear the echoes of that life—the warm rumble of a good man's voice in the kitchen behind her, the distant laughter of happy children—but then the memories weighed down her heart.

Her life was a good one, and she was thankful for the peace of the evening. Maybe she'd head down to the barn and check on Willow. Make sure everything was settled for the night.

Night chased the last of the shadows from the earth. Kendra climbed through the fence, greeting her friends, and they accompanied her through the darkness, following the worn dirt path by feel and by memory. She didn't mind the coming night or the darkness surrounding her, for it made the stars shine all the brighter.

Chapter Eight

Cameron's evenings fell into a rhythm. After his workday was done, and barring any emergencies or calls, he'd head home for a quick bite and a faster shower before driving all the way out to Kendra's ranch.

Once on his trip out, he caught sight of her in the seat of the cutter, riding the ten-year-old machine in the golden fields that paralleled her mile-long driveway. He waved, but she couldn't have seen him with the sun's glare in her eyes.

When he'd asked the helpful Colleen if Kendra was avoiding him or something, she'd only said it was a busy time of year, with haying the hundred acres— of her own hay fields plus those she leased every summer.

Sure, he could see that. But did she work all the time? He tried dropping by to slip Warrior a treat early before he started his morning patrols, but Kendra was already in the fields, or so the teenager cleaning stalls told him.

The one evening he did spot her, it was late and she was out in the far field, nothing more than a willowy slip in the distance. She stood still with a hand outstretched to a magnificent red horse who looked ready to charge her instead of accept whatever treat she held flat on her palm.

After he'd said hello to Warrior—the horse had been awful glad to see him—he bided his time figuring Kendra would have to come in when the night wrung the twilight from the sky. But no, she'd untethered her golden horse from the fence and rode off bareback into the hills.

He waited another hour, long after the last employee had finished with her chores. No Kendra. He'd given up, wearing his loneliness like a too big coat on a hot day.

He was forced to deal with Colleen, Kendra's second in command, when it came to decisions about Warrior's care. He signed a contract and wrote a check to McKaslin's Riding Stable and studied the class schedule. A new session of beginners' lessons started soon and it was something to consider. Colleen offered him private lessons, since the group lessons were mostly little girls on their first horses or ponies.

When he asked when Kendra would be available to give private lessons, he was flat-out stonewalled.

"Oh, not until sometime after haying season. It's a busy time of year, and you don't want to put off learning to ride Warrior, right? These are the last sessions before school starts."

Even thinking about it now, in the quiet of his patrol car, annoyed him. He knew Kendra was busy, but twice he'd spotted her in the stable when he'd pulled into the driveway. By the time he'd parked, she was gone. He'd respected her rules and hadn't ventured up to knock on her back door again. He knew she wasn't there anyway.

When he'd checked the schedule, Kendra was listed as the teacher for several advanced classes, things like barrel racing and Western show. There was one beginners' class she offered two afternoons a week.

Avoiding him? Yep. He'd wager money on it and he wasn't a betting man. Did she feel the same way he did? That there was an attraction between them? Something with potential, and maybe she wasn't interested in pursuing it?

Don't read too much into that, man. She's busy running her business. He didn't know if he wanted to risk his heart again and go through the pain of loving in a world with no guarantees. And yet the time with Debra had been worth all the pain and more.

He wasn't a waiting man. Not anymore. Life was a precious gift and he couldn't waste it, walking through life, filling his days with loneliness. Did that mean he was ready to love again? Maybe he ought to find out.

He'd thought maybe Saturday would be a good day, and even traded the workday with Frank. But there had been a sort of competition and show put on by Kendra and her employees.

Every time he saw her, she was judging a string of nervous-looking kids dressed in tooled Western wear perched atop glistening horses being put through paces and moves and inspections.

Maybe he'd sit with the rest of the spectators on the risers on the far side of the covered arena where it was shaded. He even deposited two quarters for a soda into a vending machine near the stands. The bubbling cola slid down his throat like ice, cooling him on what had to be the hottest day of the year.

Kendra was handing out ribbons for the winning riders. He noticed she had ribbons for every one of the grade-school-age kids.

Cam took his time circling around; the stable yard was jam-packed today.

He had all day off, thanks to his deal with Frank. His pager was off, his gun was locked in the closet at home and he was a free man. Free to wait Kendra out, even if it took until midnight to get her alone.

The tinder-dry grasses crackled beneath his boots as he headed for the shade. He noticed a cigarette butt someone had left smoldering behind the seating, despite the No Smoking At Any Time signs posted, and crushed it with his heel.

"Hi, Cameron," Cheryl Pittman called out.

They'd gone to school together. She'd married, had kids and put her minivan in a ditch last year when the winter winds had frozen the rain on the road. He'd driven her and her kids home that day.

He nodded a polite greeting. "Howdy, Cheryl. Is your oldest competing in the show today?"

"She sure is! Caitlin's already won two blue ribbons. It sure is a nice setup Kendra has here, don't you think? Great for the kids. I hear you bought yourself that fine hunter the Thorntons had up for sale."

"Guilty. Hope you have a good day, Cheryl." He tipped his hat, moving on, studying the families that had gathered to watch their kids compete.

It didn't take much to see how his future *could* be with Kendra. Kendra's life was her family and her horses, anyone with an eye could see that.

Sundays would be enjoyed with her family, the sisters taking turns hosting the meal and spending the evening together.

The rest of the weekends and evenings would be spent in the stable. He had no problem with that, once he figured out how to be halfway as good a horseman so that he could keep up with her.

He watched a pair of little girls, probably second- or third-graders, ride by on their horses, giggling and looking as wholesome and as happy as children ought to be.

This would be a great place to raise kids. The thought stuck with him as he climbed the bleachers, nodded hello to everyone who said hi. He'd grown up in this town. Add that to being the local law, and he knew just about everyone.

He found a lonely stretch of bench and settled down to keep an eye on Miss McKaslin.

All his senses were filled by the slender woman looking at home in a sleeveless cotton top, faded jeans and black leather boots. Her hair was pulled back into a soft ponytail that swung with her easy, graceful stride.

Cameron couldn't help noticing the hard ridge of her shoulder blades edging the back of her shirt and the knob of bone at the curve of her elbow. She was spare, not a lot to her for all her strength and her self-sufficiency.

Tenderness warmed the center of his chest thinking about how fragile she looked, those fine bones of hers, the lean cords of muscles in her forearms as she unlatched a gate with her narrow, agile fingers.

The tenderness inside him grew. Like the burst of light, suddenly so bright at dawn as the sun broke boldly over the mountain range, that's what it was like. One moment he was sitting in shadows, and the next he was too blinded to see. He was overwhelmed by the intense desire to be the man who would love her for all the days to come. To keep her safe and cherished and happy.

He loved her. Just like that. Like gravity suddenly snaring a hunk of meteorite and yanking it through space.

"Sheriff?" It was one of the stable girls holding a cordless phone. "The, um, deputy's asking for you."

That could only mean one thing. An emergency. He thanked the girl, took the phone and said goodbye to any chance of seeing Kendra—again.

The remnants of smoke hazed the evening sky as Kendra nosed Sprite off the main road through town. It was quiet, the businesses closed, the sidewalk empty, only a few cars parked in front of the few restaurants in town.

The black scorched earth next to the road was visible on this end of the street. Like an ugly scar, it marred the golden crisp fields on the far side of town and into the distance, smoldering. A local fire truck was pulled to the side of the road, the men probably looking for hot spots. The acrid scent lifted and fell with the breeze.

She reined her gelding down the closest alley and spied a familiar SUV idling in line at the drive-in's take-out window. Why was her first thought to turn around and head somewhere else? Wrong. Cameron was a client and an acquaintance.

Earlier today, she had felt his intense gaze when she'd been handing Brianna Pittman her second-place ribbon. She'd known the instant he'd stood from his place on the bleachers and left. She'd felt the change in the air.

There had been nearly fifty people in the stands watching the show. Maybe as many milling around.

Why was she aware of the comings and goings of that one man?

She reined Sprite into place behind his vehicle. She watched the line of his shoulders tense, as if he felt her presence, the way she felt his. Like autumn in the air. Like a change that couldn't be seen or measured, only felt.

He glanced in his rearview mirror. His side window lowered. "Is that legal?"

"What are you going to do, write me another ticket?"

"I could get a few more cookies out of you."

"What? You owe *me* cookies."

"I've been trying to pay you back, but you've been busy, I guess."

She shrugged. What was she going to say to that? She'd been trying to avoid him. She wasn't going to lie about it, but she didn't have to admit it, either. "Move ahead, Officer. You're holding up the line."

His vehicle eased ahead to the posted menu, and she listened to him order two bacon double cheeseburgers, onion rings and a huckleberry shake.

From her perch, she could see Cam's profile perfectly. The striking darkness of his short hair, which was very masculine on his square, chiseled face, and the hint of a day's growth on his jaw.

Why did her fingers itch to touch that stubble?

She couldn't deny the truth any longer. A truck pulled up behind her, brakes faintly squeaking as the sheriff moved on, cornering the building.

A teenager's cheerful voice crackled out of the thirty-year-old speaker. "Welcome to Misty's. Can I take your order?"

"A bacon double cheeseburger, onion rings and a huckleberry shake, please."

"Thank you! That will be three-seventy-three, please."

Kendra pulled the folded dollar bills she'd dug out of her purse and nudged Sprite ahead in line.

Two little girls rode up behind her.

"Hi, Kendra!" Caitlin Pittman said in unison with her best friend Tiffany Corey.

"Hi, you two." Kendra saw her past in a flash, how she used to ride to town with her sisters and best friends so long ago, to order double-dipped cones from the drive-through window.

It was a tradition in this town for little girls who had their own horses to ride.

The sheriff was reaching for his white paper bag of food. He pulled ahead, idling, while Kendra handed over her money in exchange for a bag and a big white cup of her own.

"Plan on riding home with that? Or eating here?"

"It's a mystery and I'm not telling you." She didn't mention they'd ordered the same meal. Lots of people liked bacon double cheeseburgers. Probably half of the town. "What happened? You were watching the show and then you weren't. Was it the fire west of town?"

"Grass fire. Some dolt must have tossed either his

match or his cigarette butt out his window. We got it out before it took out any homes.''

"I'm not surprised." Cameron was a powerful, capable man. He could do anything. "Stopping for a late supper?"

"Yep. I'm too beat from helping out the fire department to try to make something at home. I don't think I'll be heading out to see Warrior tonight."

"I'll give him a little time when I get home, on your behalf."

A little time. That's all he wanted. "You've got dinner and I've got dinner. We're both alone. We might as well eat alone together."

"I've got Sprite. I don't want to leave him outside while I go in."

"Then we can eat right here in the parking lot. How about it?"

"I'm only saying yes because I'm hoping you'll make good on your cookie promises."

"I've got something better than cookies." He pulled forward into a parking space before she could answer. Keep her guessing. Why not?

She swung down, graceful as a dream, and her big gelding followed her, hungrily trying to nip at the food bag. "I guess I can humor one of the men who gave up his Saturday to help put out a wildfire."

"Careful. You're making me sound noble."

"Right. We can't have that." She sat down beside him on the shady grass.

They sat nearly elbow-to-elbow, unpacking their

food in silence. *Think of something brilliant, man. This is your chance to dazzle her.*

Then he noticed her order. It was the same as his. See? It was a sign from above. "Did you get your hay in all right?"

"The barn is packed and ready for winter." She stole a crisp onion ring from the bag. "Every year it's getting harder to find field hands."

"I saw you out on the old cutter. Was it your dad's?"

"That's the great thing about having a farmer for a father. He gave me his old tractor, too."

"So, if you have your hay in, then you don't have any more reasons to avoid me. Do you? Unless you're having another competition next Saturday."

Heat swept up her neck and into her face. Had she been that obvious? She'd been hoping he hadn't noticed! "I *have* been busy." *Trying to avoid you*, she didn't add.

"I'm a good guy. Look, I'm the sheriff. I know things about people in this town, private situations and sadnesses that most folks don't want known. Yours wasn't the only domestic-violence call I've ever answered."

Her hand shook so hard, she put down the milkshake. Sprite nudged the bag, and she handed him an onion ring. His velvet-soft lips nipped it from her hand and he chewed, satisfied.

"I never talk about what happened. Nobody

knows. Nobody but you. I think my sisters suspect what happened, but I've never told them.''

''How did you explain the surgery and the cast?''

''Stable accident. A horse shied and crushed my arm against the wall.'' It had been plausible, but that had been one of the only lies, and the last lie, she'd ever told anyone.

What happened with Jerrod had been horrible. It had made her feel bad through and through. But to have lied to cover it up, that had been so much worse.

''I can't talk about this.'' She went to grab her food, but his big hand covered her arm, stopping her.

His palm was warm and the power and strength of him wasn't frightening. It was comforting.

''We don't have to say another word.'' His voice was velvet. It was steel. It was everything strong and everything kind. ''I want you to know I've filed that night away with all the others and locked the door. I did what I could to help you then, and I will now. As a sheriff. As a man.''

''You sound like a campaign slogan.''

''I'm getting the knack of running for office. I *think* that's a bad thing, but I can't seem to help myself.''

At least that cracked the hold sadness had on her. The sorrow eased from her eyes. ''I have been avoiding you. I shouldn't have tried to pretend that I haven't.''

''I figured out why. It's all right.'' He unwrapped his burger. ''We could be friends, you know.''

''Friends? No, I never mix business with anything

personal.'' She waved at the little girls riding away from the take-out window, each holding a double-scoop, double-dipped cone.

He chuckled. ''Yeah, I notice you never mix business and personal feelings.''

''They're little girls. I like kids.''

''You could treat me like that. I could wave, and you could wave back. I might say hello, and you might say something friendly back. Think that would be okay?'' He waited for her to nod.

But she neither affirmed nor denied as her cell phone rang. He knew it was bad news. It had to be— he could feel it in his gut. He watched her pull the small phone from her back pocket and frown at the screen.

''Colleen?'' She listened for a moment. ''Thanks. I'll be there as soon as I can.''

''Do you need a ride?'' He rose, ready to assist her in any way he could.

''No, my best mare is about to become a mom, so I've got to go. My boy will get me there soon enough.'' There was no mistaking the affection in her voice as she took hold of the gelding's leather bridle.

True love shone in the big horse's brown eyes as he tried to steal another onion ring, and she let him before mounting up with the ease of someone who'd been doing it all her life.

Kendra was a soft touch. As warm and loving a woman as he could ever hope to find. He'd come so close tonight to making this almost a real date. Maybe next time he'd get it right. Hopefully, there would be no emergencies with his work or hers.

A little help, Lord, he prayed, as he handed her the giant-size foam cup—the huckleberry shake, just like his.

There was no mistaking the warmth in her gaze, in her smile—a small sign, but it was enough for him.

"Thanks for the company." She tucked the food bag in the cradle of her lap.

With the milkshake cupped in one hand, the reins in the other, she turned Sprite toward the alley, where she'd come from. She was like rain, soothing and refreshing, on the wind of a needed storm.

He felt the turmoil in his heart, not knowing which way this would fall. He waved and watched her ride between the buildings until she was out of his sight.

He packed up, no sense in eating alone in the parking lot. Probably someone would spot him and come up to him with some problem or another that needed taking care of. And he was off duty tonight. He was dog-tired, he was hopeful and he was defeated all at once.

Alone, he headed the Jeep west toward home. Right before he turned onto the highway he spotted the faint silhouette of woman and horse. Framed by the lavender hue of twilight, she rode into the sunset with her ponytail flying in the breeze.

What hurt in his soul, he couldn't say.

Cameron was in the back of her mind late into the night. The vet stopped by twice to check Willow's progress, and after long hours of walking the mare, Kendra was grateful to settle her horse into a birthing stall.

A little filly was born in the wee hours of the morning and was sleeping curled up beside her mother, her tummy full and as shiny as a new copper penny.

Even as Kendra climbed to her feet, weary, taking away the bucket of warmed mash she'd fixed for the tired new mother, the image of Cameron kept troubling her. She'd felt aware of him, the way a woman is aware of a man she's interested in, as he'd huddled next to her in the drive-in's parking lot.

The past was troubling her. Her fears were troubling her. It was hard not to forget the stalwart sheriff who'd drawn his gun that rainy night long ago and taken the blow that had been meant for her.

What was she going to do about Cameron? No, more honestly, what was she going to do about her reaction to him? Would she always see the past when she looked at him?

She thought she'd buried those memories well and deep. Yet here they were rising to the surface, haunting her on a beautiful August evening when she was safe on her horse, riding as she always did.

All that she had to be grateful for, so why couldn't she concentrate on those things? It was as if the steel walls around her heart had been penetrated.

She would pray harder, that's what she would do.

Ask the good Lord and His angels to help her leave the past where it belonged.

So that when she looked at Cameron now, she would see the helpful lawman who'd changed her trailer's tire, who owned Warrior, who rented stall number one-fifty-three.

Cameron was the man who'd been perceptive enough to see not the woman who'd been rushed to the hospital that long-ago stormy night but the woman she was today.

If he could do it, then so could she.

Dawn had taken command of the sky, coloring the horizon with reverent mauves and lavender tones that made the hush in the moments before dawn fill her up to the brim. Peace surrounded her from all sides— the rolling fields, the sleeping foothills and the mountains holding up the sky, touched with predawn's light.

She couldn't explain the feeling that washed over her like the first bold curve of light breaking over the giant Bridger Range.

With every step she made on the well-worn path between the stables and her tiny house on the knoll, she felt her life change around her and she couldn't say why. It was as if the path ahead of her shifted.

How could that be? It looked the same to her as it always did.

The horses in their paddocks called to her in turn or watched her pass with friendly gazes. Sprite and Honeybear trailed along beside her, the board fence separating them. Jingles was waiting at the corner post, gazing curiously into the backyard, as if something had caught her interest. As if something was different on this beautiful morning.

The imprints from a man's boots didn't frighten her as she followed the stone walk to the porch. He'd tracked through the spray from the automated sprinklers.

On the top step, an orange furry mound was waiting for her, one eye slit to watch her approach.

If there'd been anything wrong, then the cat would have told her. He was far too calm for there to have been a burglary, uncommon in a town where most people didn't lock their doors. No, Pounce's attitude was more disapproving than anything.

The small self-stick note on the white frame of her screen door did surprise her. The writing was bold, straight up and down without a slope and as confident as the man who'd written it. "Kendra, I let myself into your kitchen. But when you see why, I hope you'll forgive me. Best, Cam."

What did that mean? What had he done? Had she forgotten something at the drive-through? Her cell phone? Her keys? She hadn't taken more than that with her.

The instant she opened the door, she breathed in the scent of warm bacon, sausage and eggs. The sharp comforting scent of coffee. Her coffeemaker was on, still brewing.

The preheat buzzer on the oven beeped. Had she just missed him?

It was as if she could sense him in the room. The change in the atmosphere. The faint scent of his woodsy aftershave. She ought to be mad he'd just walked into her house uninvited, but how could she? He hadn't violated her space, that wasn't the way this felt. It felt, as she opened the oven door, like comfort.

How many mornings had she walked through the back door just like this? Exhausted from a long night sitting up with a sick horse, hers or a boarder's, when the owner would not. Or from welcoming a new foal into the world. Or a dozen other disasters or problems that were all part of her life here.

Every time she'd stumbled into this kitchen, half-ill with exhaustion to measure out fresh grounds into her coffeemaker, she'd prayed for the same thing. That the strong black brew she was making would give her enough kick to make it through a hard morning of feeding animals and cleaning stalls and training and exercising before she could sneak a nap in one of the empty stalls or in the chair in the corner of her office.

She'd rebuilt this cottage from the foundation up, with her own hands and a ton of advice, because she'd had to—it was the only way to afford her dream. She'd measured and hammered and sanded and painted.

She'd hung the cabinets and laid the countertop. Hunted through garage-sale bargains and every relative's attic and basement for furniture to refinish. She'd lived here for five years, almost six, and this had been her house. Never her home.

Until this morning. It felt comforting. Sheltering. Welcoming. How had Cameron done this?

The plate was heaped with a cheese omelette, glistening sausage links and crisp strips of bacon. A stack of well-buttered toast sat on a second plate. It was from one of the restaurants in town, she knew, because she'd ordered this meal many times while she'd met one sister or another in town for breakfast.

Had a man ever been so thoughtful? Kendra couldn't believe it. That he had gone out of his way like that. He must have heard from Colleen about Willow's long labor. Since classes started today, she assumed Cameron and Colleen had been in communication. Maybe even more.

Good. She would be glad for them. If this was the way Cameron treated his friends, then how much more wonderfully would he treat a wife? Colleen had had a lot of hard knocks in her life. She deserved a good, decent man to cherish her.

A warm silken glide around her ankles reminded her that she wasn't alone. She had her cat demanding she feed him, and feed him now, thank-you-very-much. Her beloved horses were at the gate, less than five feet from her kitchen window. Like good old-time friends watching her through the grass, waiting for her to come be with them.

After she fed the cat, she'd take three apples with

her plates of food and her cup of coffee and eat on the picnic table out back. With her friends.

She wasn't alone, see what a good life she had? And if so much was missing, the presence of a man in her kitchen, the ring of children playing in the next room, then she refused to dwell on it.

She tucked that longing away with the emptiness where her heart used to be.

Life was what you made of it, right? Her old defenses fell back into place, and her loneliness vanished when she stepped out into the brand-new light of day. She let the sun wash over her as gently as grace.

Her old pony nickered a greeting, the horses already shoving at each other, impatient for their expected apples.

Cameron enjoyed his second cup of coffee as the sun climbed out from behind the granite mountains to cast light and shadow across the roll and draw of the golden valley. If he followed the trail where the sapphire river cut into the valley to the emerald foothills, he'd face the direction where Kendra lived.

Had she found the meal he'd left warming? Was she pleased? Did she understand what he meant by it?

He sipped in the richness of his coffee and leaned against the door of his cruiser. Maybe the mornings he spent alone were numbered.

Feeling as light as those clouds skimming the blue of the sky, he whispered a prayer of hope.

Chapter Nine

"I've got a lesson starting in a few minutes." Kendra left the pitcher of cold sparkling sun tea on the picnic table where her oldest sister and new baby were relaxing.

Allie, a big sister now, played with her baby doll in the shade from the maples and the lilacs. Across the fence, Honeybear was watching the little girl with wistful eyes.

"Hey, Allie." Kendra knelt down beside her niece and held out a carrot freshly pulled from the garden. "Do you want to feed Honeybear?"

Allie stopped the important job of changing her soft-bodied doll to stare at the pony with wide eyes. "No."

"Honeybear likes you. See how he's smiling at you?"

"No."

"Your mommy rode him when she was your age. He loves little girls."

The little girl wasn't convinced. She stood unblinking, watching the pony leaning between the boards in the fence, more interested in having a little girl to adore him than in the carrot Kendra was holding.

"Here, I'll leave this with you." Kendra handed Allie the carrot, which she dropped.

Honeybear looked devastated.

Kendra laughed and ruffled the pony's forelock. "Karen, why don't you convince her? I've got to go."

"Sure, after I'm done feeding Anna." Her sister looked as beautiful as a Madonna, cradling her child, so happy she glowed.

Karen's husband was good to her. Anyone could see that. Through years of marriage and the addition of two children, the love husband and wife shared still seemed to burn with rare luster.

Kendra hurried away and grabbed her hat from the newel-post and headed down the path to the stables before she took that thought one step further.

Ten-year-old Samantha Corey passed her in the aisle, her hair swept back in a French braid. Her cousin Hailey on her black gelding had ridden over from her land just out of town. She greeted both girls, wished them a safe ride and reminded them to stay on the three main trails.

"We're not gonna go out that far," Samantha assured her.

"Yeah, it's too smoky," Hailey added.

The northwestern wind was pulling smoke from the north, where wildfires raged at the border of Glacier National Park. An acrid haze was creeping along the Rockies, hiding their grand peaks from view.

"Everyone is waiting and ready. Lora's with them right now. Oh, there was a last-minute addition and I've got Palouse saddled for you." Pammy Pittman, one of the teenagers she employed as a summertime stable girl, handed over the reins.

"Thanks, kiddo." Kendra took the worn leather straps. "It's just you and me, fella. Is that all right with you?"

The gelding nickered his approval, and Kendra gave him a hug. He'd been the first horse she'd bought for her ranch. He'd been with her from the start and she loved him, this sweet old gentleman who would never be forgotten, not in her stable.

She rode through the arena gate to see five little girls, all grade-school age, sitting in anticipation atop her gentlest stable horses and big, hulking Cameron Durango in jeans and a black T-shirt that read Montana's Finest in fading gray letters.

"Good afternoon, girls. And Sheriff. What are you doing here?"

Cameron flushed as he fidgeted on his saddle. "I'm here to take riding lessons. There's got to be more to this than just sitting here."

The girls giggled.

What was she going to do now? Kendra circled the

riders. The horses swished their tails patiently. They'd done this too many times to count. She checked her clipboard. She spotted his name on the last line scribbled in purple ink—Colleen must have registered him. He hadn't opted to take lessons from Colleen, and Kendra wondered about that.

"All right, kids and Sheriff, Lora is the lady that helped you mount up. She's going to demonstrate for us today. See how she's holding the reins?" She started to teach, her words second nature as she wove between the horses, correcting one girl's death grip on the leather straps.

"Am I doing this right, teach?"

If Cameron could make wisecracks, so could she. "You know you are. Are you going to be my troublemaker, Sheriff?"

"Not me. Watch those girls, though. Wolves in sheep's clothing." The corner of his mouth curved as he tried not to chuckle.

"I know a wolf when I see one, mister." She curled her hands over his wrist, not surprised by the heat of his skin. By the hard feel of muscle, tendon and bone. His nearness moved through her like a wave in an ocean, rippling deep to her soul.

"Don't make a fist of your hands. Relax, let the reins lie between your fingers."

"Like this?"

"Exactly. I thought you were going to take private lessons."

"When I called, your employee answered the

phone and told me that you were all booked up for private lessons.''

"Colleen teaches, too.''

"I wanted to learn from you. They say you're the best.'' If pride swelled in his chest when he said that, at least it didn't show.

"Well, I don't know about that, but if you decide to admit that you're as uncomfortable as you look in a class of kids a third of your age, then you can drop out.''

"I'm not a quitter, ma'am.''

"I'm starting to notice that.'' She cast him a bemused look, moving along to check on the others.

So what, he stood nearly two feet taller than any of his fellow students. He was staying put. Kendra was here. It was that simple.

A little awkwardness and feeling out of place was worth it. It was hard to know what would happen between him and Kendra. He'd lived in the dark for so long. Did he have a chance with her?

As if she could feel his question, Kendra glanced over her shoulder at him.

Yep, she liked him. Her look said, "I'm watching you, Sheriff.''

He remembered the good times, before Debra had been diagnosed. The cozy weekend mornings sharing the newspaper and sipping coffee. The welcoming love when he stepped through the door after a long, hard day. To live in the light of his woman's love.

Of Kendra's love. Was that a possibility? Could he find the strength to go through that again? The risk?

What if he didn't? What would he have then? More mornings spent hurrying from his empty house, letting his job fill his days to cover up his loneliness? Of reading the paper alone before church on Sunday mornings?

"Are you doing all right?" Kendra's gloved hand brushed the back of his wrist, a brief, casual touch. Her smile said, "I'm glad you're here."

The bottom of his heart glowed, and he had his answer.

Was it her imagination, or had the hour flown by? Kendra dismissed her class, waited to make sure each little girl had dismounted from the horses, except for the Redmond girl who had her own pony.

Cameron led his big gelding from the arena, trying to catch her eye as she chatted with one of the student's moms and exchanged a few words with Colleen, who was moving in to teach the next class and took Palouse from her to ride.

Friendship. What could be complicated about that? While he waited on the other side of the white board rails, it was as if her soul turned to him like a flower followed the sun, seeking that undeniable brightness.

She needed to thank him. She was afraid to thank him. Why? They were friends now, right? She could walk up to him and say, *Hey, thanks Cameron. That was nice of you.*

Why did she hold back? Her stomach muscles knotted up and she stayed where she was, enduring a mother's natural worry and reassuring the woman that the right training would make her child safer on the back of a horse. All the while, she felt the tangible weight of his gaze and the warmth of his presence like the sun on her face.

She knew the sound of his gait on the earth. Knew the rhythm of his breathing as he approached her, now that the students and mothers had gone and the new class was in session in the ring.

She had her sister and nieces waiting up at the house, but did she want to see them? No, she'd rather let Cameron's shadow shiver over her. She'd rather anticipate seeing his smile.

"I have to give you credit." She spoke before he could. "You toughed it out like a real trooper."

"I told you that I'm no wimp. I'm looking forward to the next class."

"You have perseverance. I have to admire you for that. You really must want to learn to ride."

"Do you think? Did you see all those eight-year-olds?" He felt as tall as the moon. She admired him. That sure made a man feel good. "I think I was at the top of my class, don't you? I outreached everyone. I'm definitely far a*head* of them."

"Are you trying to make really bad puns? I can't believe this. Mild-mannered, reliable Sheriff Durango has the worst sense of humor in the county."

"Not every man can be perfect."

"Oh, as if any man can come close!"

He loved making her laugh. He stepped closer, breathed in the sweet wildflower scent of her and wondered if her skin was as silken as it looked. "Hey, I resent that. I think I did pretty good for an old man."

"Old? Stop that. In my book, there is no such thing as old. You might want to consider private lessons. I know we can get you on the schedule somewhere."

"With you?"

"Why me?"

"Why not you? Personally, I'm sure Colleen is a nice enough girl, but she's not my type. I don't want to give her the wrong idea." Oh, he wanted to give Kendra the right idea. Now that he was sure of his feelings. Of his future.

"Oh, all right. How can I deny the man who brought me breakfast?"

"You haven't thanked me." He sidled up close, so his elbow brushed hers briefly as he leaned his forearms on the top rail.

"I'm not in the habit of thanking men who break and enter."

"How about if I admit my guilt. I could bribe you to forgive my transgressions. Say another DVD? Maybe a box of popcorn? I could volunteer to help you hold down the couch while you watch the movie."

"You're a noble man."

"Don't I know it. You'll be around at sunset?"

"Show up and find out. Well, my sister's waiting up at the house. I'll see you later."

"Later."

Kendra had said yes. She'd said yes! She liked him. She thought he was funny. She thought he was a man to admire.

A fierce love filled him up until he hurt with it. How could it be so sudden, but there it was, honest and pure and true. Wasn't love a gift from God?

It was what he always believed. All the long nights he couldn't sleep, lonely for Debra, just lonely. All those prayers in the lonesome night, and this was his answer.

He was being given a second chance. At love. At life. *Thank you, Lord. I promise, I won't waste a moment of this gift.*

Emotion wedged tight in his throat as he watched Kendra stroll away, waving her fingers in a dainty goodbye, taking every piece of his heart with her.

Where had the day gone? Kendra emptied the bucket of grain into the feed box in the northern paddock, where she'd built the fence eight feet high to hold the wild horses she rescued. A friend from high school worked in the Bureau of Land Management and called her when there were mustangs in need.

The copper stallion kept his distance. He'd stopped trying to bite her, but he refused to be cordial. He dismissed her as neither dangerous nor useful to him.

He even refused the tasty grain she brought, trying to tempt him into being friends.

The old mare, who bore deep scars across her withers and haunches, claw marks from a cougar, was the bravest of the bunch. What good potential she had. Already sweet-natured and social, she was the one most likely to be gentled. She had a smart, searching gaze.

After she realized the human in their midst brought grain and kind words, the mare waited a few wary yards from the wooden trough.

"Hello, pretty girl." Kendra upended the bucket and the rushing sound of corn and oats tumbling into the wooden feeder frightened all four horses.

The stallion took off at a fast run, neighing at her angrily, circling and tossing his head. The dun mare and foal followed him halfheartedly, not too sure they wanted to leave the grain behind.

The older mare, her black-and-white markings the same as the Indian Ponies that had run wild in this mountain valley and across the plains of Western America, shied a few steps. Scenting good food not to be found in the wild, she waited until Kendra moved a few paces back from the fence before moving cautiously forward to nibble up the sweet grain.

The stallion stayed back, teeth bared but scenting the food. The mare and colt stood indecisive. They'd approach in time. In the meanwhile, the white-tailed deer gathered in the tall grasses at the edge of the paddock, soft brown eyes watchful and ears upright, vigilant but unafraid.

Overhead a hawk circled, calling to its mate, hunting for field mice.

A beautiful evening. Kendra chose a spot, the tinder-dry grasses crackling beneath her riding boots, and sat cross-legged. She could smell autumn in the cooler breeze and in the softening of the blazing sun.

She cracked open her dog-eared paperback and began to read aloud, so the horses would get used to her voice. Used to her presence. See there was no threat.

Hooves thudded on the hard-packed earth behind her. Honeybear's velvety nose tickled the ribbon trim on her shirt. She reached up to stroke the pony's neck.

Sprite and Jingles grazed nearby, the ripping and chomping sounds as comforting as the muted light from the setting sun, as familiar as the sound of her own breathing.

She was surrounded by her best friends. Why did she feel so solitary? The space around her so open? It was a breathtaking evening and she had no one to share it with.

It was oddly comforting how she thought of Cameron every time she felt lonely.

He'd been funny today, so big and tall and out of place in the class of giggling, horse-crazy eight-year-old girls. How that man could make her laugh! Images of how his grin started with the crook in the corner of his mouth and spread across his face. She recalled how he'd teased her…how he'd confessed he wasn't interested in Colleen.

Why did she feel lighter knowing that?

She knew the moment he came into sight on the path between the stables and her house, even though her back was to the cottage. Like an angel's whisper, she heard him. The familiar pad of his gait, how it moved through her like music. She could feel the heavy weight of sadness he always carried. The steely integrity of the man. The zing of joy when he spotted her in the tall golden grass.

When she turned, he stood on the crest of the hill with the garden and cottage framing him, the broad strokes of sunlight cutting around him.

Like a warrior, he stood with shoulders square, both hands on his hips, strong legs planted. The light and shadow played with him, rendering him in silhouette and in the next blink full living color.

When she looked again, it was only Cameron striding toward her in a plain navy Henley and ordinary faded denims. A little of the warrior, of the hero she'd seen, remained, hovering around him like the light.

Her shields dismantled. The emptiness inside her ached like a second-degree burn. Throbbing and stinging and nothing would stop it.

Friends, he'd said. She'd be honored to have a friend like him.

"Isn't this a lovely sight?" His deep baritone rang in harmony with the peaceful night, but the deer took discreet steps backward and melted into the tans and dark golds of the dried grasses and brown earth. "Guess I scared them off."

"The stallion doesn't like you around, either." She watched the stunning animal arch his neck, prancing, snorting as he danced out his challenge. "I haven't named him yet. He's feisty, but he's got a good heart, and he's not terrified of people. My guess is he ran wild next to a farmer's grassland, because he's used to all this. He's curious about me, when I'm not looking."

"He looks ready to take a bite out of me. I sure am glad there's that fence between us."

"And solid, too. I sank the posts myself." Kendra closed her book and stood, sweeping off the bits of dried grass and earth from her jeans.

"Some light reading?"

"Steinbeck's *The Grapes of Wrath.* I always read the classics to the horses."

"They like that better than, say, a good suspense novel? And they tell you this?"

"Yep. Who doesn't enjoy a good story?" The pony tried to grab the book with his teeth, maybe thinking it would taste good. "See?" Laughing, she took the book. "Do you feel up to another lesson tonight?"

"To tell you the truth, my south end's pretty sore from that trotting you made the horses do. The rest of me feels as if I spent time in a blender."

"Well, that's what I was trying to teach you. Posting. You don't just sit like a lump of clay in the saddle. It's work. It's a skill.''

"I've had a tough day, teach. I wouldn't mind a nice slow ride, with no trotting and no work.''

"What happened?''

"Had a call come in to assist the officer in the next town over. Domestic-violence call, hostage situation. It turned out all right, but a tense situation for everyone involved.''

"Oh.'' The light inside her died. How could she be friends with the man who knew her secret? Who had seen with his own eyes her most shameful moment?

Let it go, Kendra. She stood on her faith like the earth at her feet. The Lord would see her through this.

So why had Cameron come into her life? At first she'd thought it was to help him. Now she wasn't so sure.

"I'm glad everyone is safe,'' she said, as if he'd been talking about anything but possible violence, and gave Honeybear a hug. "My sister came by today. We're giving my little niece our pony to learn on.''

"That sounds generous of you.''

"No, Honeybear belongs to the whole family. He's been passed down from my aunt's kids, who learned to ride on him, and then to us girls. We had lots of other horses, of course, but he's always been our favorite. He's the sweetest animal in existence, aren't you, boy?''

The old pony, with gray in his muzzle, leaned lovingly against Kendra's stomach. She rubbed his ears with tender respect.

Cameron's throat closed. He'd never had much of a family life. And with his mom scraping by to keep a roof over their heads, there was never extra money for things like a pony. "Before my wife got sick, we'd talk about what we wanted for our kids. The things we didn't have growing up. Music lessons and a fancy swing set in the backyard, and land enough for a pony or two."

What could she say? Cameron's loss moved through her, more deep and painful than her own. To have loved and have been loved, to have dreamed and dared to see a future like that, only to have it snatched away... She couldn't imagine the depth of his grief. "You lost your whole life."

"That I did." He obliged Honeybear's gentle request for a chin rub. "Some folks might get real angry at God. Debbie was in her twenties and she fought hard and suffered."

He'd buried the memories because they hurt with an agony that was too powerful for words. How hard Deb had struggled, enduring chemotherapy and radiation treatments that nearly broke her. Her faith had never wavered.

His had come close to buckling. And now he was stronger for it. "God did me a favor, giving me those years with her, and I'm grateful for every one of them. Debbie was good and kind and had a beautiful spirit. Loving her was a rare gift.''

A gift? Having to bury a wife didn't sound like a gift. Cameron rubbed his eyes, and in that moment, as the wind gusted and ruffled his short dark hair, she saw deep into the man. With his defenses down and the shadows in his eyes, he was no longer the helpful, friendly, sometimes wisecracking sheriff who protected and served. This man had a tender heart that had loved fiercely. Faithfully. Fully.

Michelle had been right. Cameron was the kind of man who stood tall and loved with his entire soul.

There were men like that? It didn't seem true. It couldn't be possible. Her arm ached, no longer broken, and her soul hurt like spring's first sudden touch. *Lord, don't make me feel this. I want to forget.*

There was no answer on the wind. Nothing changed in the world around her. The season was turning, summer's hold slipping as the dry grasses rustled in the wind and the sun lost its warmth. She shivered, although she wasn't cold.

''Colleen said she'd saddle Warrior for me and leave him inside the back gate. I could sure use a peaceful ride tonight.'' Cameron strode away, his shadow long on the uneven grass.

Me, too. Brittle, feeling like cracked ice ready to shatter apart with any more pressure, Kendra wrapped her arms around Honeybear. Breathed in the wonderful horsy scent of his warm coat. Felt his comfort in the press of his big body against hers.

The pain remained, tamed into a dull, old ache in the middle of her chest. Arthritic and endless.

She'd ride Sprite tonight, bareback. Too tired to bother with a bridle, she hooked her fingers around the blue nylon cheek strap of his halter and led him through the field and into the stinging rays of the sinking sun.

Cameron was glad for the silence. God's hand was in nature's beauty all around him and it was a comfort. The sweet sap of pine, the sharp scent of earth, the trickle of a runoff creek through a mountain meadow where elk drank and birds took flight.

Kendra stayed beside him. That was good. It was bad. Good because her presence soothed him. She was serenity and peace and goodness, and she didn't even know it. But this love he felt for her scared him. It moved through him like a double-edged blade, cutting so deep to his very core that his entire being felt exposed. Down to the bottom of his soul.

He could feel her within him, as if they were somehow connected. Somehow a part of one another. He felt the raw, wounded places within her heart. In her spirit.

He'd loved Debra with all he had in him. Their marriage had been great. They'd laughed all the time, each put the other first, found comfort in taking care of one another. She had been his world, his entire life. When she died, he had, too, in all the ways that mattered.

He'd never thought he could recover from that black, suffocating grief, but the Good Lord had seen him through it every step of the way. Changing him like a season, healing his heart slowly so that he could live and love again. Cameron had no doubt he was made to love this woman now, at this time and forever.

Did it have to be so powerful? He'd never known a love that tugged at him like a lead wind, consumed him like a wildfire, made him feel wide open and exposed. When Kendra breathed, he did. He swore their hearts beat in rhythm. She opened her mouth to speak and he could feel her words before she said them.

The good Lord hadn't led him to merely a new wife, but more. A soul mate.

Did Kendra feel this, too? Cam couldn't tell as he reined Warrior in, proud that he now knew the right term, and dismounted with a creak of leather. He ached from the balls of his feet to the top of his head.

Now he knew why Kendra was in such good shape. It wasn't only because of the barn work she did. Riding took strength and endurance. Whew, he was sore, and he ran three miles every morning.

Kendra moved like the water, sure and easy and weightless, as she dropped the blue strap of the lead. She hadn't even bothered with bridle or saddle, and left her gelding to graze, his halter strap dangling. Did he do the same?

Kendra answered his unspoken question. "Warrior's trail-trained. He knows not to run off. Come, follow me, there's something I want to show you.''

She led the way through the streams of light, the glow from the setting sun casting her in a rose hue, haloing around her. Smoke's haze hid the faces of the granite peaks that were close enough to touch. The meadow was a precipice holding them high, bringing the sky near.

Kendra walked to the edge, ringed by hundreds of wild sunflowers. They brushed her slim ankles, their faces followed the descending sun and looked as if they followed her, too.

When she smiled at him, he took her smaller hand in his.

''You're afraid of heights,'' she guessed. ''It's all right. We're perfectly safe. It's a cliff, but the granite beneath us is thick and solid. It won't give way.''

He nodded, unable to speak past the emotion caught in his throat. She'd misunderstood. Did he tell her? How could he find the right words?

His emotions remained tangled in his throat. The power of her touch, the connection that bound his soul to hers, expanded like the twilight, pulsing as if with a life of its own.

He let the brightening hues of sunset speak for him. Crimson seized control of the sky, luring a bold purple to join her in painting the bellies of the nimbus clouds gathering at the southern horizon. The last light blazed in a fiery liquid-red, and it felt as if the pain of his old life was falling away, the last of his grief and loneliness.

With Kendra's hand tucked warm and solid in his, his life changed. The sun sank beneath the jagged-toothed mountains, taking the golden light with it, leaving only the bold-colored clouds and the coming darkness.

"There's Mars," he opened his mouth to say.

"There's Mars," she whispered.

Like minds, he thought. It's more than that. When she sighed, her emotion moved across his soul like the shadows across the sky. The last colors leached from the thunderclouds, drawing the night with them. She withdrew her hand and he let her go, the connection unbroken.

A part of him moved with her as she stood near the edge of the precipice, a shadow and a voice in the night. "Sunflowers are my favorites. They raise their faces to the dawn every morning and look to the sun as it moves across the sky, never wavering. At day's end they watch patiently as the sun sets, heads bowing in prayer. See?"

His throat ached worse, as if razor blades were lodged there, making it impossible to speak.

"They remain patient, waiting through the darkness to lift their faces in worship come the next day's light. I think faith ought to be like that."

"N-never wavering?"

She wrapped her arms around her middle, but she couldn't keep in all the pain. Being with Cameron made the indestructible titanium shields around her heart fall to pieces as if made of tinfoil.

She didn't want to remember. She didn't want to go back, but it didn't matter. Images overtook her, the smell of pizza cooling in its cardboard take-out box, the linoleum floor hard against her forehead, the grit of dirt on the floor from Jerrod's work boots, his hard lean form towering over her, his anger tainting the air like black, suffocating smoke.

Shaking so hard from pain and fear, shaking harder now. The sting from his slap to her face like a burn on her cheek, her ears ringing. She'd raised her arm to block his next blow, but she was powerless to stop his fear. It was like a wildfire, feeding on itself—

Stop. Stop remembering. She wanted to stomp out the memories like a spark in the grass, killing the fire before it could rage out of control and consume everything she'd carefully rebuilt.

I won't let that happen. The memories kept coming. The nausea gripping her stomach. The shocked seconds before the sharp jabbing pain registered. Lord, help me. Please, I don't want to remember.

She didn't want to forget. She'd trusted the wrong man once. She was doing it again. Cameron moved silently. She felt his approach like the breeze ruffling her ponytail. She tensed a nanosecond before his hand cupped the back of her neck.

The warm solid comfort of his touch ripped like newly sharpened steel through her exposed core. The place in her soul she guarded the most.

I won't trust him. She held on tight to that vow. *I will not. No good can come from it.*

"Love is like that. Never wavering." Cameron's touch against her neck strengthened.

"Not in my experience."

"*True* love. If it's not steadfast, if it's not giving and tender, then it isn't true."

His touch sparkled along her skin like the first stars in the night, like hope in a void.

A hope she would not believe in. She sidestepped, slipping away from his comfort. Remembering the man in uniform who took the blow meant for her. Standing over her, as lightning outside the picture window cast him in shadows, knocking Jerrod to the ground in a single maneuver, gun drawn and gleaming as the lightning flared again—

She screwed her eyes shut, refusing to see any other man in Cameron. He may be tender, he may be true, but he was a man of violence.

The stars shone as she turned her back on the view. Trudging away from Cameron as fast as she could go, she tripped on a fallen limb and slipped across stones in the creek. Whistling for Sprite she reached for the horse, who came to her, a warm comfort she could always trust.

"Time to go home, boy." She kicked up, swung her leg over his haunches and settled on his broad back. Sprite lipped her knee, as if sensing her pain and attempting to reassure her.

She felt Cameron's approach, the buoyant buzz of

his nearness weighed down by the despair that emanated from his soul. She'd hurt him. She hadn't told him it was her memories that made her walk away—not his wounded heart or his belief in true love.

She led the way through the woods and down the hillside where the darkness gathered. Where loneliness pulsed like a broken bone. The coming storm was swift, stealing the last of the stars from the sky. Rain broke from the sky as she dismounted outside the main stable.

"I'll put up Warrior. Go on home." She kept her back to Cameron and pretended to be busy with her horse, so he wouldn't guess her regret as he walked away, lightning outlining him as he strode through the grounds toward his truck.

The rain chilled her. Wet her to the skin. She remained unmoving until the red glow from his vehicle's taillights vanished in the night and the wind.

Chapter Ten

The banner overhead flapped cheerfully in the breeze as Kendra eased the double baby stroller off the curb and onto the people-filled street.

The first day of the town's annual Harvest Days was in full swing. She had Allie and little Michael all to herself, and a whole day to be a doting aunt ahead of her.

She *should* be happy, for spending time with her niece and nephew was one of her most favorite things. The way she'd treated Cameron remained a dark cloud in her heart, the same way the remnants of last night's storm lingered with a dark promise in the eastern sky.

She'd hardly slept last night. It was easier to blame it on the crashing of thunder that kept her from drifting off and the worry of lightning striking the forests on her land and starting a wildfire.

A chunky toy plane crashed to the street, launched from inside the stroller.

"No!" Michael shouted with glee.

Kendra retrieved the toy and tucked it away. "That's a good arm you have, but let's—"

"One day he might pitch for the Mariners," came a chocolate-rich voice from behind her, as familiar to her as her own.

Cameron. Her spirits soared heaven high and plummeted straight to earth. After the way she'd behaved last night, how could she face him? He'd opened up to her and she'd pushed him away. What was she going to say to him?

"Vanilla latte for you." He handed her one of two tall coffees from her family's coffee shop. "Your grandmother told me how to influence you."

"Influence me to do what?"

"To be forgiving." He knelt, making a face at Michael who laughed. Allie frowned at him, clutching her stuffed pony. "I see the company you keep is improving. You two are sure a better choice than the local sheriff."

"I take any opportunity I can to make full use of my aunt privileges."

"Deb and I never got around to starting a family." Cameron sounded wistful, in the way of an old wrong that could never be righted. "About the time we decided to, she was diagnosed. Guess it wasn't meant to be."

"It's a lot to lose, a future with children in it."

"Guess you know something about that. Can't have a family without getting married first."

"Exactly." Preferring to say nothing more on that painful topic, she deposited a handful of fish-shaped crackers on both trays.

Allie chose one carefully and popped the whole thing into her mouth, beaming like the precious angel she was.

Michael smacked his tray with his beefy little fists and cracker crumbs spewed in every direction. His gleeful laugh usually chased all the shadows from Kendra's heart.

Not this time. The yearning was plain and honest on Cameron's face as he pushed a couple of crackers from the edge of Michael's tray to the center for more fist-bashing. He wanted children.

Her arms felt empty, her life desolate. She dug through her purse for her sunglasses, blinking hard to keep the sun's glare from her eyes. She *wasn't* crying.

"Good punch you've got there." Cameron stood with coffee in hand, wearing a brown leather jacket over his usual T-shirt and jeans. He looked like everything decent and dependable and capable in a man. Everything a good husband and father should be.

She had no right to be noticing that.

Just because Cameron was a truly good man, that didn't mean she had to go falling in love with him. She had a willpower of steel.

What about him? Was there a chance he was falling for her?

No way. Impossible.

Then why did her hand tingle with the memory of last night on the mountain? Her palm had fit snugly against his, a perfect match.

He took the stroller from her as if he had every right to possess it. "I'm an only child, so there are no nieces or nephews for me to spoil."

"You think you can borrow mine?"

"Why not? I'm an accomplished driver. This vehicle has four wheels."

If Cameron kept charming her with his humor, she *was* going to love him. Then what would she do? "You must have better things to do on your day off than to hang around with me."

"I'm not hanging around with you. I happen to be buds with Allie and Michael here. Right, guys?"

"Pony!" Allie shouted, spotting a horse and rider at the edge of the crowd.

"Exactly. My sentiments, too, Allie. Are you ready, Michael? Are you both belted in? Does this thing have a fifth speed?"

"Don't give Michael any ideas. He likes to go fast, just like his father." Why was he doing this? Showing up like this with her favorite coffee, taking over, helping out, acting as if last night hadn't happened. As if she hadn't walked away when he was reaching out to her. "I suppose you're out helping everyone with small children?"

"Sure. Thought I'd start with you first. I've got an election to win."

"That's coming up, isn't it? After this weekend?"

"Yep. This Tuesday. That's why I have to make the best impression I can. Thanks for letting me rub shoulders with you and Michael and Allie. Folks are bound to be impressed."

"You're running unopposed."

"Still, I don't want to get too confident. Put-the-cart-before-the-horses kind of thing."

"You have the job and you know it." He looked so *right* pushing the stroller. He would make some lucky woman a fine husband.

But *not* her. Didn't he know that? He wasn't trying to *date* her, was he? "I have to be honest with you. I think you have the wrong impression of me—"

"Stop." His hand, big and rough and warm, settled on her shoulder. There was strength in his touch. Tenderness. "I have the right impression of you, Kendra Nicole McKaslin."

"And you know my middle name because—"

"Frank got a peek at your license, remember? Don't ever trust him. He blabs. Can't keep anything to himself."

"See? That will teach me never to speed, even fudging it by a few miles per hour."

His chuckle warmed her and wore down her resistance.

"Kendra, would you do me a favor?"

She took a sip of coffee, savoring the vanilla flavoring. "What do you need, Sheriff? Trying to get my vote on Tuesday?"

"Nah, I figure I've already swayed you to my side."

"Hmm, maybe I have a write-in candidate I'm supporting."

"The vanilla latte didn't buy your vote? Then I guess I'll have to treat you to a cinnamon roll, too." He halted the stroller in front of the local bakery's booth. "What do you think, kids? Can I bribe you, too?"

"Bribing? You're spoiling them."

"Just following your example." Cameron ordered enough big gooey rolls to go around plus enough napkins to wipe up the kids afterward and dug in his wallet.

"What's the favor?" she asked, watching him toss a five on the counter.

"Stop worrying about my motives. Got it? I thought you and I agreed to be friends."

"We did, but last night—"

"Last night, I took your hand. Sometimes friends do that. They also step in when the other looks lonely."

Lonely. Cameron was lonely. That's why he'd joined her and the kids this morning.

He stuffed his wallet into his back pocket. "Look at all the families here. Go ahead. Look."

"I don't have to."

"I look at them all the time."

Husbands and wives walking side by side, hand in hand, arm in arm or in that companionable closeness that said, We're together. We're in love. We're a team. Children in strollers or carried on hips or trotting ahead yelling, Daddy, Daddy, can I have some cotton candy? *Please?*

Yeah, she knew. Everywhere she looked she saw what she could never have. Everything she wanted.

Did Cameron feel this way, too?

Kendra accepted the iced cinnamon roll he handed her. The carnival music swelled, lifted by the growing wind. Kids racing by, wind chimes for sale jangling in the next booth and the faint smoke from the fireman's barbecue were all background.

Cameron was front and center to her, the big man he was, down on one knee, handing Allie her miniature-size roll and patiently breaking Michael's into bite-size pieces.

"I suppose you can hang with us," she told him, the shadowed places inside her hurting. "As long as I get some kind of favoritism after you're elected. For helping your image."

"Sure thing. I'll treat you to one of those lattes anytime you want."

"Deal." See? They were friends and only friends. Wasn't that what Cameron meant? He was trying to reassure her, and why did that make her feel even worse?

Allie squealed, pointing. She'd spotted a vendor's booth of stuffed animals.

"All right, little lady. Your wish is my command." He steered the stroller in the direction Allie indicated with both hands reaching. "Hi, Phil. I guess we're gonna need that stuffed pinto pony here in front."

"No, put your wallet away. This is my day, and you're not going to spoil it." Kendra had already whipped out a ten-dollar bill from her back pocket. "And the stuffed helicopter for Michael, please."

A meteorite might have fallen from the sky and smacked him right in the middle of the forehead, that's how Cameron felt, affected as she slipped between him and the counter. So close to him, only air separated them.

If she turned a fraction of an inch, he could slant his mouth over hers in a kiss that would change both their lives. Maybe alter the way she looked at him forever.

Lord, please change Kendra's heart. I'm a patient man, but loneliness is killing me. What he wanted was standing right in front of him. He fought to keep from reaching out. How was it possible to love someone fiercely who didn't love you back?

Or was loving her a lost cause?

"What?" She crooked one thin eyebrow, as if puzzled why he was staring at her openmouthed, like a fish out of water. Or a man struck dumb by love. "Did you want a stuffed helicopter, too?"

"Nah, I'll pass, thanks."

"You look more like the adorable teddy-bear type."

"What?"

"Admit it." Laughter lit her up like the corona on

the sun. With her hair down, rippling in the wind, in a worn denim jacket and jeans, she was unaware of her effect on him. She flicked a few more dollars onto the counter.

"No—" he protested, but it was too late. The vendor was already handing over the little brown bear and Kendra's change.

No macho, gun-toting officer of the law would feel comfortable hauling that around the town streets for everyone to see.

Embarrassed, he yanked a five out of his wallet. "Fair play," he told Kendra before she could protest. "That yellow cat way in the back, it's all yours. And you've got to carry the bear."

"Fine, but lunch is my treat," she spoke up, as if he'd agree to that.

"I could be pretty hungry. I might need two fair burgers. Maybe even three."

"Ooh, and we'll get a big tub of onion rings to share," she agreed, accepting the soft-bodied, striped orange cat. "Thank you, Cameron. For everything."

"My pleasure. This is the best time I've had at a shindig like this in years. Since Deb passed." His throat ached and he turned away, because he was a real man, and real men didn't get sentimental in the middle of a crowd. "I ought to be thanking you."

"Oh, Cameron." As if she could peek into his soul, her eyes filled with a beauty he'd never seen. He could see her soul, too, aching for him. "I'm glad you muscled your way in and stole the kids from me.''

''I didn't steal them. I just, uh, took charge. I'm sheriff. The town pays me to do that.''

''Sure.'' As if she didn't believe him for an instant, her hand settled on the back of his right wrist. She squeezed gently, comfort flowing from her heart and into his.

Like a new star bursting to life in a night sky, that's how he felt. As if he'd taken his very first breath, opened his eyes for the first time. A new man, he didn't dare to move as the light, quick brush of her fingers ended and she moved away.

''You can hang with me and the gang for as long as you want. But I warn you, Michael shrieks. Allie cries. Oh—'' Laughing, she knelt to break up a fist-fight inside the stroller. A good-natured fight, since no real harm was done.

Cameron knew he was grinning like a fool, but he couldn't help it. Was his cause lost? Hardly. He *was* on the right path. He just had to keep going steady and slow. Show her he was the one man she could trust above all others.

It was his intention to show her that the greatest strength in this world was a man's tenderness.

''Where to next, lovely lady?'' he asked, taking charge of the stroller. ''Wind chimes or stained glass?''

''Ooh, I have a weakness for stained glass.''

''Then follow me.'' Cameron led the way through

the stream of people heading in the opposite direction to the row of booths on the other side of the park. "Look, there's something for you right there."

"The horses." Beautiful mustangs, painstakingly created in colorful glass, dashed along the circumference of a delicate vase. The green Montana prairie rolled beneath their hooves and the brilliant sapphire sky watched over them.

I have to have this. Kendra reached for the fragile piece and plainly saw the one hundred and twenty dollar price tag spinning in the breeze. It was exactly eighty more dollars than she had in her purse.

"It was made for you," Cameron mumbled in her ear, one hand on the stroller, the other fingering the price tag. "Are you going to get it?"

I wish. "Not in my budget. But maybe there's something that is." Beautiful colors sparkled in the sunlight, garnering her attention. She could get something small, maybe something to glitter in her kitchen window. "There, I'll take the hummingbird."

"Not the vase?"

"The hummingbird," Kendra handed over her twenty, complimented the artist on her exquisite work and waited while her blue-and-emerald hummingbird was wrapped in tissue paper. "The parade should be starting soon. Did you want to watch it with me?"

"I sure would."

Why did his smile warm her up inside, the way sunlight blazed through the stained-glass vase?

Maybe she'd kept herself apart from everyone for

too long. She'd stopped shining inside—going through her life, pouring everything into her work and into her duties as a sister because she wouldn't get hurt. Not by her work and not from her sisters.

But from everyone else? Distant. Polite, sure, but even in this crowd, she was as lonely as if she was sitting on the back porch on a Friday evening.

Jerrod had taken more than her ability to trust. He'd taken away her will to *live*. She'd been stumbling along, surviving, existing, not living. She hadn't realized it.

Maybe that's why God had brought Cameron into her life. To remind her what she'd been missing, hiding away in her dutiful life. Without making new friends, letting old friendships slip away and allowing work to invade nearly every waking moment of every day.

"Are you all right?" he asked with concern, and she realized she'd been staring off into space.

"I feel almost perfect." For the first time in six years happiness sparkled inside her, bold like noontime sunshine through the glass. Like hope.

And all because of her new friendship with Cameron.

He felt like a man who'd been able to touch heaven for one brief instant. Cameron had the good Lord to thank as he carefully lifted the basket from the passenger seat. Maybe he should have called, made sure Kendra was home.

Nah. He remembered leaving her at her truck after the parade was finished. He'd asked her if she was in the mood for ice cream. She said she had to get back to the stables and relieve Colleen, who'd wanted to attend the rodeo—an informal annual event to raise money for the volunteer fire department and emergency services.

It was just as well. He'd wanted to kiss her goodbye, but he held back. He had big plans for her, for tonight. He watched her pull away, her pickup joining several of the other vehicles patiently waiting out the traffic congestion in their single-street town. He'd first put in some volunteer time helping over at the rodeo grounds before heading out Kendra's way with his surprise.

He lifted the vase carefully in his free hand and shouldered the vehicle's door closed. Nerves tingled in his gut.

Was he moving too fast? Or too slow? It had been all he'd thought about during the afternoon. Nope— all he'd *worried* about. She'd reached out to him. Laughed with him. Relaxed as the local fire trucks paraded by. The volunteer fireman tossed chocolate gold coins, and he caught a handful for her. With the little tykes there, getting the chance to watch over them, he got a good eyeful of what his future could be.

Would be. He couldn't let fear get the best of him now. He'd come a long way since Deb's passing. He'd crawled through a long night of shadow to stand here in the light of Kendra's affection. It felt like a smile from heaven as he strode through the long rays of the sun that carpeted the path before him.

The path to his new and future love. There wasn't a car in the parking lot, save for his. All the folks were in town enjoying the festivities. It seemed as if the angels were looking out for him—he just might have Kendra all to himself tonight.

There she was, standing in the main aisle of the big stable, a pitchfork in hand. Already he knew the curve of her face, the line of her back, the stretch of her arm as she worked. Tenderness fired through him. It hurt to love again, but he would not back down. He would not be afraid. *I know she's the one, Lord. Maybe you could open her heart, just a little. Help her to look at me in a whole new light.*

As if she felt his presence, the way he could feel hers, her stance tensed. She turned, not in fear, but in expectation, knowing exactly where he stood in the aisle. Like the moon always facing the earth, bound by a great force, she faced him.

"I told you I might be stopping by." As if that force pulled him now, moving him beyond his will, he strode toward her without remembering how he was suddenly in front of her. "I heard it's your birthday tomorrow."

"Heard? Who would have told you something like that? If it was one of my sisters, I'll have to ban her from Monopoly night for at least a month. Maybe more."

"Wow, you're sure tough. I'll have to remember not to get on your bad side."

"Your deputy saw my license. That's how you know."

"Guilty. We lawmen have our ways of getting any information we want." He handed her the flower-filled vase. "Happy birthday a day early, pretty lady."

She gazed up at him with big doe eyes, wide with an emotion he sure hoped was delight. "You picked sunflowers for me?"

"Yep. Look at the vase."

"Cameron." The generous arrangement of sun-flowers had caught her eye at first, but now she saw the delicate-cut glass horses galloping around the breathtaking vase. "No, this is too expensive. This isn't right. I can't accept this."

"Sure you can. I want you to have it."

"But—" And sunflowers, too. Images of last night surrounded her, the nodding flowers, the burning sun-set, how hard she'd held on to her faith. Relying on her belief to help her forget. To keep her standing alone and strong.

"I've got a basket here. Picked up a fried-chicken meal from the café. Even got Jodi to make you up a special birthday cake. A little one, for the two of us. If you want, we can have a picnic, and when night falls we ought to be able to see the fireworks from town. Even brought my telescope if you wanted to stargaze."

She *had* to be misunderstanding. "I've never had a client bring me flowers before, much less dinner."

"I'm a client, sure, but I thought I was more than that."

A slow tremble rocked deep through the scars in her soul. Her ears were buzzing. "We're friends. That's what we agreed on, right? Last night on the trail ride and today at the festival. You and I are just friends."

Why was her voice high and thin? Kendra took a deep breath and let it out. The sunflowers became a yellow-and-amber blur. "We're mostly strangers, Cameron. I don't think this is appropriate. I don't want this."

"I do. I just have to know. Is there a chance that you can love me?"

He stood as stalwart as the Montana mountains at his back, his heart in his hand.

She stumbled back, panic flooding her like a river at spring thaw. There was no way, no possible way. "I thought you understood. I appreciate your business—"

"My *business?* Sure, but last night wasn't business. Not today. Not now. I came here tonight because I thought I had a chance with you. I know what you're thinking. I'm not the best-paid man in these parts, but I'm honest and honorable and I'll treat you better than any man ever has. Or ever will."

"What? A chance with me?" She *couldn't* be hearing him right.

"Being loved by you must be like holding a fistful of heaven. Something a man knows he doesn't deserve by his own right, but by grace. That's what love is, a gift from above. I know. I thought my heart had died right along with Debra, until you came along."

"No, you've misunderstood, Cameron. I'm not in love with you."

He looked crestfallen, but undefeatable. "I know what happened to you. What you're afraid of."

"You don't know anything." There was no way, no possible way, she was looking backward. Only forward. To her future alone. That's the way it had to be. The only way she could keep going. "I won't talk about what happened, and you don't know, or you would never mention it around me."

"Jerrod was one man—"

"Don't you say his name." She thrust the flowers blindly onto the tack shelf and turned, seeing only the haze of sunset through the stable door and the smear of concrete at her feet. She wouldn't allow the past to rise up and drown her. She did not have to remember. She did not have to feel like that ever again.

"Kendra. I'm sorry." Cameron's footsteps pounded behind her, concern raw in his deep voice.

Cameron was a powerful man. He could stop her if he wanted. Hold her captive. Make her feel as defenseless as she had that horrible night and during the quieter, desperate times before that.

The years stripped away and suddenly she was helpless again, on the floor, blood mixing with the tears on her tongue, holding her broken arm to her ribs, curled up and waiting for the next blow to come.

"You're shaking." Cameron's voice sounded a mile away. His hand settled on her shoulder. "You're cold."

"It's the air-conditioning. I'm going outside. Let go of me, Cameron."

"Sure." He released her, looking confused. "You're safe with me. You know that?"

"Sure, you're the sheriff." She didn't think any man was safe, but what was the use of saying that to him? Cameron was a good man, she knew that.

So was Jerrod. Everyone said so. But good didn't mean without flaws. Every human on this earth had faults. Lord knew she had enough of her own, and she'd worked hard on forgiveness, but how could she forget? Every time she was alone with a man, every time she'd tried to date over the years, it was always the same.

She could not help feeling defenseless on that gritty, cold kitchen floor. Terrified and wounded and broken. No man was ever going to make her feel that way again. She'd make sure of it.

"You weren't going to ride Warrior tonight, were you?" she choked out, holding on desperately to the one purpose that had helped her through the days—her business. "I didn't saddle him. I'm going to close up early tonight. Maybe you could go home."

"Kendra." He followed her, climbing through the fence rails after her, radiating concern and strength and mercy, just as he had that night when he saved her from being hit one more time.

Would he follow her all the way to her house? Couldn't he see that it was his goodness she feared? Because it made her want and it made her wish and made her yearn to trust.

She would not run. She would not hide. She faced him, hands fisted, holding herself around the middle, defenses on full alert to protect what remained of her heart. "I can't do this. I can't start *dating* you."

"You say that like I've got the plague or something. Look, I know what this is about. You look at me, and you see him. You think one man hurt you, then any man can."

"I don't want any man. I don't want you. Not like that." She heard the edge in her words. Hated the sound of it. When had she become so hard?

It was too late to take it back. She wouldn't if she could. He had to understand. She had to protect herself. What she hated was having done it badly.

Silence like a startled slap stretched between them as larks whipped through the grasses, skimming on the last light before sunset. Jingles breathed out in an impatient "whoosh" at being ignored.

Goose bumps chilled Kendra's arms as she watched Cameron, a tiny part of her afraid at angering him.

Soldier-strong, as self-controlled and as noble as a warrior of old, he did not move. Long shadows of evening wrapped around him until he looked so alone, it made her want to reach out and pull him close. To kiss the pain away.

How wrong was that? He didn't need her, not really. How could he? He was a man. He was twice as strong as she was. What kind of heart did any man have, anyway? She was right in turning away. Right in leaving him standing there alone in the coming darkness.

She didn't need him. She didn't need anyone.

How long he stood in the field, she didn't know. She told herself she didn't care, but she did. She crunched through the bleached dry grasses toward home, the sunflowers bowing before her as the sun disappeared and darkness came. Fighting the urge to look back and see if he had remained. Or if he had fled.

The phone was ringing in the echoes of her empty kitchen as she burst through the back door. Let it ring, she didn't want to talk to anyone. She felt as if she was breaking apart inside as if it had happened all over again, as if all those years of rebuilding her life and protecting herself had been stripped away, and she was wounded and bleeding from the inside.

"Hey. It's Michelle," came her sister's cheerful voice through the decades-old answering machine. "*Somebody* I know is having a birthday tomorrow. Expect to be stolen away. No I-have-to-work kind of excuses, got it? Mom baked your favorite cake, that's all I'm going to say because it's a surprise, but I know how you can be bribed with chocolate. Be ready at noon, or I'll send the local sheriff to hunt you down! Later!''

The click echoed in her lonely kitchen. *Cameron.* Was he still standing outside? She pulled apart the curtain sheers. Twilight crept across the paddock, hugging the forest on the other side of the fencing. The firs cast shadows over the knoll where Cameron had last stood.

It was too dark to see him. She felt his pain in her soul, as absolute as the encroaching night.

She'd been too harsh, she'd handled the situation badly. Was there any way to fix it? No, if she went out there and spoke to him, apologized for her words and her rejection, it would only make it seem as if she cared.

She couldn't afford to care. Her life was safe. Isolated but safe. That's the way it *had* to be. She couldn't have a good man like Cameron coming around with more on his mind than simple friendship.

But he's hurting. Tears stung behind her eyelids as she sank to the floor. She was hurting, too. Why did her soul ache, longing for his tenderness?

There was no answer as the last shadows of twilight slipped away and left her in total darkness.

Cameron drove without seeing along the two-lane country roads back to the edge of town. Numb, that's what he was. Numb and shocked. He'd left the flowers, but the basket of packed food was on the passenger seat and the smell of fried chicken, normally appetizing, was making his gut twist.

I don't want any man. I don't want you. Her words haunted him. Her fear troubled him more as he slowed down for traffic at the edge of town.

Folks were heading in to catch the last of the rodeo and the firework display. Traffic congestion was a rare thing, but it bugged him mightily as he slowed down to a stall. Hurting bad, he wanted to go home and lick his wounds.

How could he have been so blind? He'd misread everything. Angry at himself, angry at Kendra for not understanding, he jabbed off the CD player. He wasn't in the mood for music, either.

He wasn't really mad at Kendra. He was enraged at Jerrod. What kind of man hurt a woman? Broke her bones? Kicked her when she was huddling on the floor in terror at his feet? How many times had he treated her like that?

Jerrod—the respected state patrolman who'd been captain of the football team his senior year, when Kendra was cheerleader. What a perfect couple they'd made, he remembered. Everyone thought they would marry as soon as Jerrod had finished his training with the state patrol.

How long had he been cruel to her in private? Cameron had his hands full during that time with Debra's sickness and taking care of her. Trying to be all that she needed. But he did remember how flawless Jerrod and Kendra had looked together in public, crossing the street to the diner. How happy her family had seemed with the match. How many years had Kendra said nothing? Maybe she'd feared no one would understand.

Yeah, he'd seen it too many times in his line of work. It saddened him, weighed on his soul.

He flicked up the fan and let the icy blast from the air-conditioning beat across his face.

Some folks who lived close by were walking along the gravel shoulders, and that made the traffic situation worse. He spotted teenagers ambling across the middle of the road. Families bunched together on the shoulder, slowing down the outgoing traffic.

He lowered his window to see if he ought to lend a hand. He spotted John Corey, the volunteer fire chief, heading his way. "Need any help?"

"No, we've got it covered. Say, you're sitting here alone. I thought you might have one of the McKaslin girls in here. Noticed you two have been together lately. Good for you, Cam."

Pain clawed through his chest. He clenched his jaw, refusing to let it show. "She's been a good friend to me."

"Sure, I get it. It's private. I know. You must be meeting her here. I'll keep my nose out of your business."

"How's your wife doing?"

"Alexandra's doing great. She's got the kids with her. I'll be glad when I can finish up here and get back to her."

"Let me take over. I don't have anywhere to be." Cameron had requested this evening off so he could be with Kendra, and that hadn't panned out. He didn't want to be alone. He might as well lend a hand, and this way he could help out John, a good friend.

"What about that pretty lady you're seeing?"

She doesn't want me. He bit back the words. Agony left him speechless as he shrugged. He had to clear his throat. "Don't you worry about me. Let me take over so you can spend time with your wife and kids."

"I'd appreciate it. Joshua is old enough this year to enjoy the fireworks. Cassie is still too little, but I'd sure like to be there with 'em."

"Then go. And take this." Cameron handed over the basket of food, and before John could say a word, nosed his pickup onto the grassland off the road. He'd keep busy, serving his town, helping out. Watching as other men with wives and kids came to enjoy the celebration.

He took the flashlight from John, sent him on to his family and tirelessly worked until the last car was off the road and parked.

Only then did he head home, driving away as bright bursts of red and blue and green lights flared in the sky behind him, glowing in his rearview mirror.

His rental house was dark and lonely as the winds gusted, and clouds snuffed out the last of the starlight. He couldn't face going in tonight. He hadn't realized how loving Kendra had put the spark of life back in him. What was he going to do now?

He sat on the top step and let the night surround him. There was comfort in the cloak of darkness that felt the same color as his soul tonight.

The faint noise from the carnival rides and the stadium's cheering drifted along with the gusty wind. The boom and exploding light of the fireworks blazed up high. Reminded him that everything he'd wanted was gone.

Kendra didn't love him. It didn't sound as if she ever would.

Defeated, utterly alone, he rested his face in his hands.

Chapter Eleven

❧

"Hey, who gave you the flowers?" Michelle waded through the grassy field, looking happy and relaxed and lovely in her fashionable summer maternity outfit. "Nice vase, too. Was it from any of the handsome lawmen in this town?"

"Stop teasing, please." Kendra gave her attention to the stallion easing forward to steal the garden-fresh carrot from her palm. "That's a good boy. See? I'm not going to hurt you."

The wild animal retreated, crunching the vegetable, his gaze fastening firmly on her, not ready to trust. But he already was. He just wasn't ready to admit it yet.

The older mare nosed her hand. "Hello, girl. I'm all out of carrots, but I've got one more LifeSavers."

The mare lipped up the treat, crunching gratefully. She'd lived a hard life surviving in the wild, but she was safe now. As if she knew it, the mare hesitated, almost trusting enough to be stroked. Tenderness for the animal filled her. Kendra knew she'd make a fine saddle horse in time, and would appreciate the companionship of the right person.

"You've got them looking pretty tame." Michelle hooked her arms over the rail and squinted, watching the horses. "Even the stallion isn't trying to knock you around."

"I'm charming him with food." At least Michelle wasn't wanting to talk about Cameron. Every time she thought of him, the pain behind her sternum intensified. Then stop thinking about him, Kendra!

"Everyone's up at the house." Michelle ran her hand over the curve of her tummy. "Karen has Allie up on Honeybear. She's having a great time. I haven't seen that old pony have that much sparkle in him for years."

"He misses having a little girl to love."

"Awesome. Only, when my little one is old enough, I get Honeybear next."

"There's still Michael and Allie ahead of your baby." Kendra ducked through the boards, suddenly struck with a grief so large, her knees buckled. She grabbed the fence for balance. She hadn't been this sad since she'd left Jerrod. Or rather, since she'd talked him into leaving her alone.

Being an aunt wasn't enough. She craved a better life. One filled with the happiness and love she saw on her sister's face. Michelle radiated joy, the peaceful, contented kind, and it wasn't only because of the baby she carried safe, beneath her heart.

"Can I ask you something?" Kendra dared to query as they hoofed it up the knoll toward her lonely cottage. "I remember how your first real boyfriend cheated on you."

"It's a small town. Everybody knew but me." Michelle shrugged. "Just like I can guess things weren't as good as they seemed with you and Jerrod."

"How did you know?"

"When you smiled, it never reached your eyes. And there was something cold about Jerrod. I always worried that he wasn't good to you."

"Sometimes it feels as if no man can be." A chill quaked through her. She'd said too much; she could not remember that horrible time, but she had to ask. "How do you know your husband will always be there for you? That you can trust him forever? That he'd never, oh, hurt you."

"Because of the man Brody is inside, down deep. He's a real man, and that means he's noble and honorable and faithful. That his love, when it's true, is forever. Why are you asking? Ooh, you've got it bad for the sheriff, but you're afraid to love again."

"No, I was just wondering. You know how I feel about marriage."

"I know you never dated anyone after you left Jerrod. That says it all, right? Cameron is such a great guy. I won't tease you anymore about it, I promise. I just want you to be happy."

Miserable, Kendra didn't answer. Michelle's words were no encouragement. Ever idealistic, ever romantic, that was Michelle. Kendra had made that mistake once, and she'd vowed to never do it again. Never trust a man who could hurt her, who could reduce her to nothing at all.

Yet Michelle had managed it. Their farm was prospering, their home beautifully refurbished, and Michelle looked truly happy.

You think one man hurt you, then any man can. That's what Cameron had said, when she'd just walked away from him. She'd told him to go home, after he'd been so wonderful. He'd left the flowers behind. If he were a horrible man, even one as smooth as Jerrod and quietly angry, it would be easy. Sending him away would be the absolute right thing.

But he was a good man, and that made it worse. She didn't want a good man. She didn't want any man.

That wasn't the truth, and she couldn't lie to herself any longer. She might wish for that once-in-a-lifetime love with Cameron, but it was simply not meant to be. She wouldn't allow it.

"Happy birthday!" Karen greeted from the fence, where she was holding little Allie's knee, as she was perched on the back of an indulgent Honeybear.

Kirby, sitting alongside her husband, Sam, clapped while little Michael tossed a ball and toddled after it.

As Kendra held the gate for Michelle, she spied her parents on the deck, cooing over baby Anna cradled in Mom's loving arms. One brother-in-law, Zach, lit the barbecue and the other, Brody, tenderly wrapped Michelle in his strong arms. They kissed so sweetly and affectionately that Kendra had to look away.

Not because she was embarrassed, but because she'd never noticed it before—the good men's love that made her sisters happier and their lives better.

Love. It surrounded her, one of God's most precious gifts, and somehow she felt isolated. As if something was missing inside her. Why did she feel alone with her family surrounding her? With their love everywhere?

"Kendra!" Gramma grasped balloon ribbons in one hand as she negotiated through the screen door, her gentleman friend tailing behind.

Just what she needed. Her grandmother's comforting affection, always there, always healing. Kendra wrapped her gramma in a warm hug, so grateful for her. For her family here, today.

She was just being foolish. See? She wasn't alone. She had plenty of love in her life.

"Happy birthday, my dear granddaughter." Gramma smiled at her boyfriend, who joined them on the porch holding several gaily wrapped presents. "Willard, oh, I see the gift pile right there on the picnic table. Thank you, sweetheart."

"Anytime, dear. Hello Kendra." The regal professor gave her a dignified nod and a warm, grandfatherly smile on his way to deposit the gifts. "Happy birthday."

"Thank you." Kendra liked the way Willard made her grandmother brighten. He clearly made her happy.

"It's too bad Kristin couldn't have made it," Gramma continued. "Seattle isn't that far away. I guess that express package must be from her?"

"Yes. She's the only smart sister I have. The others have been rendered blind by love and have married. It's terrible."

"Yes, isn't it." Gramma laid her left hand on Kendra's arm where the square-cut diamond sparkled on her ring finger. "Shh, I'm not announcing this yet, I'm going to wait to see how long it takes for someone to notice. Looks like the love bug's bitten me but good!"

"Gramma! Congratulations. I can't believe this." Kendra glanced at Willard, who was now supervising, along with Karen, Allie being lead around on Honeybear's back. "Did this happen last night?"

"I'll tell you all later. Right now I want to hear about you. A little birdie told me you've been spending time with our respected sheriff."

"Time, yes. But we're friends. Maybe not even that."

"My dear Kendra, you look so sad."

"It's nothing. Just—" Kendra couldn't say it. It was better to change the subject. "Willard seems like a kind man. I hope he makes you happy."

"He will. I know that for certain. Now, come with me and let's have a look at baby Anna." Gramma's hand on her own was firm and reassuring. "Now, I'm not prying. You know I would never do such a thing.''

"Of course not." Kendra rolled her eyes, trying not to laugh.

"I just want to point out that now that you've found a love of your own, I wouldn't mind attending another wedding. Welcoming more great-grand-children into the world."

Pain seared her like a burn that licked straight to the bone. "What are you talking about? You know I'm an independent kind of girl."

"Fine. Stay in denial, but you can't fool your gramma. Oh, look at how big our baby is getting. Alice, you've held Anna long enough. It's my turn to spoil her."

I'm not in denial. Kendra couldn't believe her grandmother's nerve. There's no possible way. I'm not putting my heart on the line. She'd been down that road and look how it had turned out.

But her sisters had taken the risk…and won.

Zach, done with the grill, had joined Karen by the back gate. They stood together, arm in arm, their love as tangible as the warm sunlight.

Sam had scooped Michael up to swing him in the air like a plane while Kirby watched, laughing with happiness as Sam pulled her against him and they all hugged. Their love as solid as the earth beneath their feet.

Michelle was snuggling in Brody's arms, as they talked softly together. Brody's wide hand spanned his wife's protruding stomach, and they smiled together. Were they wondering if she would have a girl or a boy? Their love for each other was plain to see in their honest affection.

That's what I want. The longing spilled up from her soul before she could stop it. Before she could block it off behind her defensive shields. Too late, the yearning remained a void inside her. An old aching dream that had been shattered, never to be made whole again.

I won't think of Cameron. She fisted her hands, steeled her courage, and still the wish remained. Love surrounded her.

Please, Lord, she prayed, hoping her sorrows would be heard, knowing the need in the world was so much greater than her heartache. But still, she hoped God was listening. *Please make this pain go away. I don't want to hurt anymore.*

The wind changed direction, whispering through the dry blades of grass and the maple trees.

Maybe that was her answer, she thought, determined to ignore the sadness within her that seemed without end.

Cameron had had better days. After a night without much sleep to speak of, he'd put in two long days while folks enjoyed the local harvest festival. Nothing had gone wrong; that wasn't what had him in a bad mood.

It was that nothing felt right. Sunday morning service hadn't brought him peace, as it usually did when he was in need. Peace eluded him. As the calm that came with the onset of evening settled over the town, the businesses closed, the vendor booths packed up and were hauled away; there wasn't a car on the street.

He couldn't put it off any longer. He turned off the lights, locked the door and ambled around back to where his vehicle was parked. Looking as lonesome as he felt in the shade of old maples planted decades before.

Thunderheads chased dry lightning across the sky. Yeah, that's sorta how he felt. Wasn't much in the mood to go home and try to fix something. Even a tuna-fish sandwich, his old standby. Maybe he'd swing by the drive-in.

Everywhere he'd gone today, Kendra had been on his mind. Roaming through the festival, keeping an eye out for trouble, he remembered how he'd spent the day with her. How she'd argued over buying him lunch, but he beat her to it. How right it had felt to have her by his side.

He pulled up to the drive-through menu. "Two bacon double cheeseburgers, onion rings and a huckleberry shake."

His regular order. Kendra had ordered the same meal the day they'd met in the drive-through lane. He'd taken that as a sign. How wrong was that?

"Hi, Cameron." Misty was at the window, ready to hand him back his change from the five he always gave her. "I haven't seen you in a while. I hear you're dating Kendra. She's been keeping you busy in the evenings, huh?"

He winced. This had been happening all day long, and it still hurt intensely. "I'm in the mood for your onion rings. The best anywhere in the whole state."

"I'm glad you think so. That'll be right up." With a courteous smile, Misty shut the window and disappeared into the kitchen.

Headlights flashed behind him in line. Kendra? No, it was Frank. A dedicated bachelor and a man who didn't cook, he was a frequent patron of the food establishments in town. Cameron returned the wave before accepting the bag of food and the milkshake from Misty, and pulling ahead.

Frank would have joined him inside the restaurant, but Cameron wasn't up for it. Frank would have predicted the outcome. After all, a woman who valued her independence so much obviously didn't need a man to love her.

What was he doing? He was heading north automatically, without thinking, when his house was in the opposite direction. Habit, to drive out to her place. When did he start thinking of her ranch as home? The answer was simple. Kendra was in his soul. He'd never fall out of love with her. So what did he do?

He was clueless. He munched on his burger, still heading north. The random lightning turned serious about the same time his phone rang. Seeing Kendra tonight—and trying to hammer out a solution between them—would have to wait.

If there was a solution to be had. How could Kendra see him and not the past? Could she ever love him with the wounds in her heart?

He didn't know. Helpless, all he could do was leave it in the Lord's hands as he pulled the truck around and headed straight into the storm.

"All settled in for the night?" Kendra asked her beloved mare over the top of the stall gate. Mom and daughter were snuggled together in the clean straw. Willow whickered low in her throat, a gentle, contented sound, while little Rosa slept. "I'll see you in the morning, pretty girl."

The snug feel of the stable was soothing. Kendra took her time ambling down the aisles, where horses drowsed, some waking enough to greet her as she passed by.

Cameron hadn't made it by tonight. Guilt stung like an angry yellow jacket. *I was too harsh. I hurt him. I shouldn't have done that.*

It was too late now. As much as she wanted to explain, it wouldn't change the outcome.

Warrior poked his nose over the gate, sad eyes beseeching.

"You're looking lonely." Kendra stroked his warm velvet nose. "I know, your master is a good man. It's my fault. I scared him off."

There was no choice. She had to talk to him. The

last thing she wanted was for Cameron to feel uncomfortable when he was here. With all he'd been through, he deserved the life he was rebuilding. She didn't want him to miss out on time spent with his new best pal.

"You are a good guy, Warrior." She scratched his ears. "Like that, do you?"

The big gelding nodded, leaning closer to give her better access. This was the first evening the sheriff hadn't come to visit his horse.

Longing filled her, sweet and aching. Why was she missing Cameron? He was a friend, that was why. And he'd come to mean more to her than—

No. She wasn't going to follow that train of thought. Heart thumping wildly, adrenaline kicking through her blood, there was no peace to be found.

Not even here in the stable. The past remained like a terrible whisper that would not be silenced. A whisper that followed her into the house, where her sisters were waiting with the Monopoly board set up and big bowls of buttery popcorn and glasses of soda.

A whisper that could not be silenced all through the evening and into the night where she lay, awake in her bed. A fear that followed her into her dreams and turned into nightmares of a man towering over her, his voice a thunderclap of anger, striking her with the fury of lightning while she cried, helpless at his feet.

Dawn came, and with it a cloud of smoke from the nearby forest fire. The dank smoke hid the surrounding mountains and cast a gray pallor over the sky. Like the gloom inside her, it remained, a gray haze that polluted the day.

"I've got next week's schedule figured out."

Kendra startled, realizing she'd been staring off into space again. She grabbed the hose, tested the warmth of the water and sprayed down Amigo. The horse thanked her with a sigh of pleasure as soap bubbles slid off his brown-and-white coat. "Amigo's owner is coming for your advanced class this afternoon. If that's a problem, then I can squeeze in a private lesson for her."

"No, I can do it. Hi, boy." Staying out of the spray, Colleen gave the pinto's nose a scrub. "What about Cameron? He didn't ride his horse over the weekend, did he? Will he be here today?"

"I don't have a clue."

"Really? Tell me he didn't leave those flowers for you. And that vase! I saw them in your office. They're beautiful."

"Cameron is way too generous."

"He's just about right for a courting man." Colleen waggled her eyebrows. "I'd go for it if I were you. He's a catch."

"He's not my type." Firmly, refusing to let the pain swallow her whole, Kendra moved to Amigo's hindquarters, where she hosed down his flanks. "I was wondering if you want to go over the bookkeeping with me later. You said you'd like to learn as much as you can about the business of running a stable.''

''That would be awesome. Wait—are you thinking of cutting back your workload? You know, like your sister Karen did at her coffee shop after she got married?''

''And just who would I marry?''

''None other than our handsome town sheriff.''

''Stop trying to play matchmaker. I think *you* should invite him for a trail ride sometime.''

''Me? No way. Don't try avoiding this one, Kendra. Cameron is a great guy, and anyone can see he's in love with you.''

''He's in *like*.'' It can't be love. She wouldn't let it be.

''Whatever. Here's some free advice. A good man doesn't come along like that every day. If I were you, I'd hold on to this one.''

''I like my life the way it is.''

Colleen looked so sad. ''I don't. I don't like going home every evening to an empty apartment. I look at the families who come here and the kids I teach, and I want that. But I'm not going to just settle for the first man who comes along and winks at me. Cameron is the kind of man you keep. There aren't too many out there like him. I don't want you to have regrets.''

I have them every day. Every evening. If there was one thing she could change about her life, it would be to go back in time and never date Jerrod at all. Never fall for the golden boy, town football hero, who'd been so perfect for her, or so everyone said. Nobody had seen the mean streak in Jerrod, and she certainly hadn't until it was too late.

Sure, he'd been good to her. Kind, at first. But over time there were changes. He was strong and brave and upstanding. He was the first person to ever hit her. He would be the last.

Finally alone, she squeezed her eyes shut willing away the memories of Cameron taking Jerrod down to the floor, rolling him over. In control, stronger than the abusive man and just as frightening in his calm, cool anger, he'd snapped the cuffs on Jerrod's wrists.

She'd seen what Cameron was capable of. Of taking down a man as tall as he was, as in shape, as powerful. How did she know he would never use his strength against her? Not only Cameron, but any man?

Why did she still ache to see him? To hear the low rumble of his voice, see the quirk in the left corner of his mouth when he grinned? Why did she feel as if he was a part of her spirit? She watched the parking lot for the first sign of his vehicle. Listened for the sound of his step on the path.

She missed his friendly presence. Friendly, that was all. Was it even possible they could still be friends?

No. She felt the answer soul-deep. It was impossible to go back to the serene companionship between them.

It's more than friendship, a quiet feeling within her whispered.

It *can't* be. She wouldn't let it be.

She felt his approach like the change in the wind, like the clouds skidding across the sun, dampening the brightness. In sudden shadow, she whirled Sprite toward the gate, knowing before she saw that it was him.

He was walking toward the stable, his back to her.

He hadn't stopped to wave. He didn't turn and his shoulders tensed, as if he felt her, too.

Sadness seeped into her soul, but it wasn't only her sadness. It wasn't only her soul.

Chapter Twelve

This was gonna be tough. Cameron had done a lot of soul-searching. He reached the same conclusion each time. He loved Kendra. He was in this for the long haul. He'd stood by Deb in her time of darkness.

A shadow of Kendra's doubt didn't scare him any. What she didn't know was that he was a real man, one who stuck when the going got tough.

The stable girl, who took care of Warrior during the day, handed him the gelding's reins. "I wasn't sure you were coming," she said. "Kendra's already started class."

"Thanks for keeping him ready for me." Work had gotten in the way and delayed him a few minutes, and he'd had to give himself a pep talk on the drive over.

He was sure. He was determined. He was prepared.

Warrior nudged his arm. Wise brown eyes studied him.

"Hey, buddy. I missed you, too." Warmth filled his chest at the horse's affectionate concern. Glad he'd chosen this fine animal, Cameron patted the gelding's neck and mounted up.

Kendra. He spotted her on the far side of the arena. She drew him like flowers to the sun. Hair down, rippling in the breeze, she sat astride her gelding, wearing a pink T-shirt and jeans.

Her lovely face brightened with a smile of encouragement as she coached one of her six little students who swung out of the saddle, touched the ground and sprang back up into place.

Feelings radiated through him, pure and bright and without end. Feelings that ran as deep as love could go.

He'd never felt this strongly for any woman. Not his dear Deb. Nobody.

A soul-deep yearning filled him. Gave him strength for the uncertain path ahead. *Please, Kendra. Just let me love you.* That's all he was asking. To have the chance to show her he would stand by her, protect her and cherish her through her doubt and through every day to come.

"Cameron, we're glad you could make it." She spoke without turning. Crisp and polite, but no more.

He didn't expect an easy road. "Sorry I'm late."

"Just fall in line. We're practicing quick dismounts. Sometimes while we're riding, situations pop up, and we have to be ready." Pleasant, but a very teacherlike demeanor toward him.

Fine. He wasn't discouraged. "Sure thing."

That's the way the rest of the hour went. With Kendra barely glancing at him. She kept her distance, commented on his improved posting skills the way she did with the other students.

He did his best, his palms sweating the entire time. Everything—his future and his heart—was on the line. This would work. He knew it. He just had to hang in there. Refuse to quit. Make her see that he would never waver.

"Our time is up," she announced. "Good job. All of you are working so hard, I think we're ready to take a short trail ride next time."

The class disbanded. The girls broke into twos and threes, riding and chattering excitedly. Cute little things. Cameron tried to hold back his hopes, but he couldn't. Didn't take much of an imagination to see his and Kendra's daughters riding just like that, sweet and precious and giggling as they rode side by side.

Daughters. Tenderness tore him apart. He'd like two girls and two boys. Children to celebrate the pure, ever-burning love he had for Kendra. A wife. A family. It all seemed too close, it surrounded him. They'd have to add on to the house, of course. Maybe an upstairs, make the living room big enough for all of them, and maybe a big-screen TV. Since he was dreaming, he'd make sure he'd add a satellite dish so he could watch Sunday football.

There it was, already formed in his mind. Big comfortable couches facing the TV, a fire burning in the stone hearth, snow falling outside the big windows he'd put in to take advantage of the incredible view. Christmas lights twinkling on a pine tree.

The little girls, with Kendra's beautiful golden hair and blue eyes, playing a board game with their mom. His sons shouting advice and encouragement at the game right along with him. The scent of a roast in the oven, the warm love surrounding them.

God's blessings of love and life and family, everything that mattered. And Kendra for his wife, his love. She would smile lovingly across the room.

"Cameron." Kendra dismounted outside the arena, and the firm line of her soft mouth was anything but loving.

His dream vanished.

"It was a fine lesson today." He'd start with a compliment. Maybe figure out a way to tease a smile from her. "I'm getting used to being the tallest student in the class."

"I'm sorry about the other night. I misunderstood things between us. I thought you wanted only a friendship and nothing more."

Determined, was she? She could push all she wanted, he wasn't going to give in. He would stick. Love was love, it couldn't be broken or dissuaded or stopped. "I scared you."

Her chin shot up. "You didn't. I have a full life, and running this stable takes all my time and energy. I don't have much left over, even for friends."

"Sounds like you're trying to tell me something.

Like you don't want to be friends with me from here on out.''

"That's right." Maybe this was going to be easier than she thought. She'd be honest, he would understand and they could at least be amicable and polite during classes or when they bumped into one another on the trails. "I'm glad you understand why I can never be friends with you, not after this."

"I can't be friends with you, either."

That was exactly what she wanted to hear. The perfect solution. Exactly the best thing for her heart and for her business. Why did his words sound so final? Why did she feel as if she'd lost the best friend she could ever have?

"I don't have friendly feelings for you." Cameron's deep voice rumbled in a way that made her hope. "I have romantic ones. I know you're not ready to hear this, so I'll wait until you are."

"No."

"You need time. Fine. Then as long as it takes for you to see that you can trust me—"

"No." Panic fluttered like a live thing in her chest, and she fought it. Glancing over her shoulder, she realized she wasn't alone with him. But she felt as if she were on the floor at his feet again, ashamed as he knelt to check her injuries. His voice calm and strong, dependable, as he called in an ambulance and she begged him not to. She was fine. That no one could ever know.

"Kendra." Cameron's touch to her jaw, cupping

her face. Tender. Solid. Infinitely comforting. "You didn't deserve how he treated you. You know that, right?"

She nodded, unable to say the words and admit that it had felt that way. That she should have known, should have seen it coming, and she hadn't until it was too late. "Everyone thought so highly of Jerrod."

"I bet they valued you even more." His thumb stroked her cheek, and he gazed at her as if she was the most beautiful woman he'd ever seen.

The shaking deep inside rattled through her, the raw and broken places from that night she'd fought so hard to protect. She'd tried so hard to cover it up so that no one could see what Jerrod had done. He'd taken more than her dignity. Done more than made her helpless. He'd destroyed her ability to love ever again.

How could she admit that to Cameron? With his heart of gold and his integrity like Montana mountains holding up the sky, he wouldn't know, he wouldn't understand. She had to go away. Wanted to run until the pain stopped hurting and her barricades were back in place.

Cameron's touch held her, not confining, but binding all the same. His touch, his love, felt like the most beautiful golden glow she'd ever felt, better than standing on the edge of the mountain with the beaming hues of the setting sun enfolding her. A light she craved with all the broken places in her soul.

And would never deserve.

She turned her chin, breaking away from him. Her skin tingled, already cold, already missing his gentle touch. Defenses exploded inside her, shields crumpled, she was surprised how calm she sounded as everything within her shattered. "This is hurting. You are hurting me."

"That's not what I want, darlin'. I love you. I'm not going anywhere. I'll back off. I'll be your friend. But I can't change how I feel. Nothing ever will. Like the flowers I gave you, I'll wait patiently until you're ready to love me."

"Don't you understand?" Cold settled in her veins. Pumped in her blood. Chilled the marrow of her bones. "I don't love you."

"Sure you do. A man doesn't marry a woman, stand by her during chemotherapy, do everything for her when she's too weak to do it herself and hold her hand while she dies without learning what love is. What it looks like. What it should be."

"There's no chance." She forced away the image in her mind of him caring for his dying wife, with his quiet strength. "Never. No."

"Don't say it like that. Give it time, Kendra. It's all I'm asking. Time for you to see I'm not like him."

"But you are." Couldn't he see that? "You're a lawman, you're stronger and bigger and you're used to being in charge—"

"Jerrod and I are nothing alike. A real man uses his strength to protect. You ought to know that's who

I am. I protect and I serve this community, and a wife, well, I would protect her with everything I am.''

''I can't.''

''I would protect you. You are a rare woman, kind and loving and like sunshine in my life. I want you. To marry you. To cherish and honor you for the rest of my life.''

''Those are words. How can I believe them?'' Kendra pushed away, choking, pain like rubble inside her soul. ''You say that now, but what about tomorrow? In a year? In ten years? Time changes people—''

''And so that means I'll hurt you one day? That is never gonna happen. People change, sure, times change, but not me. When I love, it's forever. You have no idea how hard this has been opening my heart again. How scared I am that I could get hurt. Lose you. Feel as if the sun has gone down on my world if something should happen to you. I never want to go through that kind of pain again, but do you know why I'm standing here?''

''No, I don't want to know. I want you to go find a nice woman and marry her. Someone who has a whole heart and has enough love to give you—''

''A whole heart? No one on this planet has a heart that is without a scar. Without a broken place. Life is both night and day, light and darkness, and it's a privilege to be here, walking the path the Lord has set before me. Don't make me walk it alone, Kendra. Please.''

He held out his hand, his wide palm tanned by the

summer in the sun, lined and callused and marked by a ridge of scars, like a deep cut long healed. ''Please.''

Yes, her soul cried out. She longed to place her hand in his, callused and scarred, too, and to hold on for dear life.

How could she? God hadn't kept her safe that night. How could this man? ''Maybe it would be best if you moved your horse to another riding stable.''

''No. I won't do it. You can push and push, but you can't change my heart.''

''You have to leave. I can't do this. I don't want you. If you're the man you say you are, then you'll respect that.''

''I can't walk away.'' Cameron couldn't believe it. Didn't she understand? His love was like a steel that could never be melted. A light that could never fade. ''I'll back off, fine. I'll even get into one of Colleen's classes if it bothers you—''

''No, Cameron.'' Her words were final, certain. ''You have to move Warrior. I'll call Sally over at the Long Horn and make arrangements for you.''

''Kendra.'' He wanted to haul her into his arms and hold her against his heart, take all her pain into him so she could be free. So the shadows would leave her eyes and the wounds vanish from her soul. So she could laugh the way she had at the festival, when their future together had been clear and easy to see. A future together, as man and wife.

He couldn't lose that. His heart was shattering as

she walked away from him. As if he were nothing to her at all.

It wasn't true. He felt her love aching within him, felt her hopelessness and her fear. Was there no chance at all? Lord, how could you have brought me here for no reason?

The only answer was a lifting of the wind, coming hard from the west, rattling the aspens shading the main pathway. Golden leaves drifted to the ground, the first fallen leaves of autumn.

Yep, that's just how he felt. Cameron did the only thing a good man could do. He left.

He never looked back. Not when he reached his Jeep. Not when he pulled out of the parking lot. He didn't look north toward the mountains that rose behind her ranch. He went inside, closed the door behind him and sat in the waning afternoon light. Darkness came and still he sat, his head bowed in despair.

Kendra worked past exhaustion. By the time every stall had been cleaned, every aisle scrubbed, her bookkeeping done, every corner swept and every horse cared for, twilight shadows were stealing the daylight. There was a nip in the air, making it too cool to ride. There was nothing left to do. She couldn't put it off anymore.

She didn't want to face the emptiness of the house where no one was there to greet her. Or her footsteps echoing around her as she closed the door and turned the dead bolt. The click of the old light switch grated like fingernails down her spine. Light spilled across the pictures on the walls of her family. She couldn't look away from the wedding portraits or the reminders of Christmases past gathered around the Christmas tree...from the precious captured memories of her newborn nieces and nephew.

She ran her fingertips over the framed snapshot of baby Anna. Gramma's words flashed into her memory. *She looks like you did. That little button nose. That round darling face. That's what your little girl will look like one day.*

I don't get to have kids of my own. No family. No wedding pictures. No Christmases filled with children's laughter and excitement, not in this house.

Her defenses destroyed, her shields nothing but wreckage, she could not hold back the dreams. Dreams she'd buried the next morning, when she'd opened her eyes in the recovery room, groggy and nauseous from the anesthesia. Dreams of little girls and a husband's unwavering love.

Dreams of everything that mattered in life. Everything she could never have.

Not because the Lord hadn't given her the opportunity. He'd led her to a perfectly wonderful man. Who could be better than Cameron? He was everything strong and noble. If she closed her eyes and imagined the perfect man, it would be him.

That's what your little girl will look like one day. The trouble was, her dreams had changed. She wanted

Cameron's love. Cameron's children. She wanted Cameron's steadfast love every day of her life.

She'd lost those dreams, too.

A knock at the back door startled her. Swiping at her eyes, she prayed, *Please, let it be anyone but him.* She should have uttered another quick prayer, *Please don't let it be Gramma,* but it was too late. Her grandmother was waving through the glass panes in the old-fashioned door.

This wasn't going to go well. How could it? It was hard to fool Gramma.

"What are you doing here, practically in the dark?" Gramma bustled in and flipped on a few more switches. Light spilled over the kitchen. "Goodness, has something happened? Are you all right? Oh, Kendra, you've been crying."

"No, I haven't. Just getting sentimental is all, over the photos. I need to hang baby Anna's picture."

"I see. Well, where's your hammer?" Gramma set down her handbag, pushed her red fall of curls behind her ear and dug through the drawer where Kendra had pointed.

Just pull it together, Kendra. What she had to do was pretend nothing was wrong. "Gramma, I can do that. Why did you drive out all this way?"

Gramma set aside the hammer. "We had a dinner date, you and me. Remember? My treat. The Sunshine Café."

"I totally spaced it. I can't believe I did that. I *never* forget."

"I know, dear. I just wanted to come by and check on you. I've called and called, and you haven't been returning your messages."

"I've been busy."

"My precious granddaughter. What is troubling you?" Concerned, she rubbed the wetness from Kendra's cheeks with the pad of her thumb. "Only a man can break a woman's heart like this."

"Only a man, but Gramma, I did the breaking." Baby Anna's picture lay on the table between them. A reminder of what she wanted so much.

How much did she love Cameron? Enough to forge through her pain? To put her past aside forever?

"Gramma? When did you know that Willard was a man you could marry? A man you could trust with your whole heart?"

"Why, that's the easiest question in the world. You know, I've been a widow a long time." Gramma wrapped her in a hug, gentle and sweet, and held on. "I know I can trust Willard completely. That he'll cherish me as I cherish him, because God put him in my heart."

Tears blurred her vision, not tears of pain but of truth. "In your heart?"

"Yes. I can feel Willard's presence before he enters a room I'm standing in. I can feel his thoughts as if they were my own. See his dreams as if he'd taken a photograph to show me. A love like that, so great and true, can only be from God."

That's the way it was between her and Cameron.

It was too much to hope, too much to be wrong about. She'd mistaken true love for something else once before. "I suppose a person could just want to love and be in love so badly, they could think that, but be mistaken."

"God doesn't make mistakes. Only people do."

"Exactly." She felt as hopeless as the coming night. "You can't look into the future and see how things will turn out."

"Yes, thankfully. Look at me. I never dreamed when Willard asked to share my table that I could be here, wearing his ring, happier than I've ever been. I want to see you happy."

Had she been happy? No. She'd been content and satisfied. Her life here had been comfortable and at peace. But she loved Cameron, and whenever she was with him, the sky was bigger, the sun brighter.

She was better when he was around. "The happiest I've ever been is with Cameron."

"Then open your eyes, honey. God is offering you the rare chance in life. I know you're dedicated to making your business a success, but don't be too busy to fall in love."

"It's already too late." She thought miserably of how she'd walked away from Cameron and left him alone.

Whatever chance she'd had with him was gone. She kissed her grandmother on the cheek, made plans for dinner later in the week. Alone, she sank to the top step, waiting, as night deepened.

Deer came close to nibble on the roses peeking through the lattice. The whoosh of Jingles exhaling as she bedded down for the night a few feet away. Pounce crawled out his cat door and leisurely curled around her ankles.

A few stars popped out as clouds moved, only to disappear again. The soothing feel of night, of her horses nearby, of her cat's company, brought her no peace.

Was there any chance that she could take that leap of faith and love Cameron? And if she could, was it too late?

Yes. She loved him. She wanted nothing more than to know his kiss and to share his life. Yet there was no way. She'd been afraid of getting hurt, but in truth, she'd been the one doing the hurting.

Her heart, like the night, turned cold. She shivered but didn't go inside. This was her world without Cameron.

It would never be the same again.

Chapter Thirteen

"I might as well get this over with." Kendra checked the lock on the tailgate. The big horse inside the trailer shifted his weight, restless. "I'd be nervous, too, getting a new home. Don't worry, big guy. Sally has a nice stall ready and waiting for you."

Warrior swished his tail, as if in protest.

"Yeah, I know how you feel. I don't want you to go, either, but it's out of my hands now." Sally had called first thing, and even though the morning was busy, Kendra needed to do this. She'd started this journey, and now she'd see it through to the end.

If she felt as if she were dying inside, well, no one needed to know that. She was a businesswoman. She would handle this professionally.

After a final check, including the tires, Kendra grabbed her wallet and her cell, answered a few questions for Colleen and headed out.

A quiet morning. Dew darkened the fields, and the earliest leaves were yellowing on the limbs, some showing a deep russet against the sapphire sky and amber meadows.

Kids huddled together in turnouts here and there along the main road to town, with backpacks and lunch boxes, waiting for the school bus. A few little girls from her classes recognized her and waved as she passed.

She waved back.

Odd how seasons changed. So gradual that she'd hardly noticed summer was ending and autumn had arrived in a quiet hush that left no doubt.

Just like her heart.

The main street through town was busy, for a small Montana town, anyway. She had to wait a few minutes while cars turning across the railroad tracks to the elementary school had to line up at the crossing for a passing train. While she sat there with a perfect view of the sheriff's office, she saw a figure move across the front windows. Cameron?

She imagined he was fetching more coffee as he worked at his computer this morning. Where was his cruiser? Maybe Frank was out patrolling the school zone.

The last toot of the freighter's air horn startled her. Traffic eased forward and she put her truck in gear. The deejay on the radio broke in to give the weather report—expect the first frost overnight—and she made a mental note to pick the rest of the squash and tomatoes from her garden.

A strobe of blue-and-red light flashed in her side mirror. A cruiser was behind her. It wasn't Frank. She felt Cameron's presence like an ocean swell inside her, pure tender emotion that hurt as much as it sweetened.

She lowered her window, watching in dread in the mirror as Cameron marched toward her as if he were a soldier facing execution. He didn't look happy.

Why would he? He wanted nothing to do with her, after the way she'd treated him. Shame weighed on her weary soul. "Hi, Sheriff. I *know* I wasn't speeding."

"Nope." He crunched to a stop in the gravel beside her. "It's more serious than speeding. I haven't checked the law book, but horse stealing used to be a hanging offense in this state."

"Like a hundred years ago, and I'm not stealing your horse."

"Looks that way to me."

Did he have to glare at her with his eyes so cold and hopeless? "I got the call this morning, and I assumed you'd approved the transfer. I should have called, but to be honest, I didn't want to talk to you."

"Didn't want to, huh? So, you just stole my horse, instead?" Cameron turned away, controlling his anger. She was never going to get it. Never going to understand. "I'd checked into prices at Sally's. I was going to move Warrior if you were going to make me. I see that you are. You didn't waste any time getting rid of us, did you?''

''You didn't ask Sally to take Warrior?''

''No. I believe *you* were the one. Didn't you call her?''

''I did.'' Through the haze of another night without sleep and the day of emotional agony, she'd forgotten. First, dinner with her Gramma, and now this. ''I'm falling apart. I *never* forget things like that, and now look at me. I'm a mess.''

''Me, too.''

She read the pain in his eyes, stark and deep. An echoing ache throbbed inside her. His pain was hers. She thought of Gramma's words. *I can trust Willard, because God put him in my heart.* And she knew God had put Cameron in hers, because she felt his pain. Bleak and hopeless.

It was impossible. He'd never want her now. God had changed her heart with the same quiet force of summer yielding to autumn, and as leaves swirled with the lazy wind along the empty park, she had to be honest with herself. Every dream that mattered to her was at stake. The rest of her life would depend on how she handled this moment. This last opportunity.

She trusted God with all her soul. If He'd put this bond with Cameron in her heart, then that was a miracle. Didn't all miracles come from love?

Cameron's jaw tensed. ''Would you mind stepping out of the vehicle?''

"Sure." Gathering her courage, she stepped down. He held the door for her, a gentleman to his core.

She led the way around the front of her truck to the privacy of the park. Every step felt as if she were marching closer to the edge of a cliff and the earth was crumbling beneath her boots. Would she fall? She didn't know. She could only have faith in God. In Cameron.

He fisted his hands on his hips. "What are we going to do about the horse?"

"A good question." Her fear fell away like an old coat she no longer needed, and the broken places in her were gone. Like dew vanishing with dawn's steady light. "Do you remember the flowers you gave me?"

"The sunflowers? What about 'em?"

"They stand with heads bowed all through the night, waiting for sunrise."

"Yeah. I know about that." Cameron refused to get his hopes up one more time. This was too important. Losing Kendra had hurt too much. He didn't want to come crashing down.

"It's morning. Is there any chance you're still waiting?"

Her question lingered on the wind, and she shivered. It was too late, she knew. She'd been too afraid to believe, and now she'd lost him. It was over, truly. Forever.

Then he cleared his throat. The corner of his mouth

crooked into a grin. "There's every chance in the world."

Joy surged through her, brighter than she'd ever felt. Made more sparkling by the bond connecting them, heart to heart, soul to soul.

"Come here, my love." He opened his arms to fold her close.

She snuggled against his steely chest for the first time. Laid her cheek against his sternum. A sense of rightness surrounded her, the wonder of this man's unshakable love. She'd been alone for so long, and now she'd come home.

"I love you." His confession rumbled through her, and when she met his gaze, she saw the enormity of it, the depth, the power of a good man's love. To protect and cherish and never to hurt.

"I know." She laid her hand over his hand, where she felt the amazing bond of affection that, like the sun in the sky, would light her world for all her days to come. "As I love you."

His kiss was tender and sweet, a warm velvet brush of his lips to hers. Their first kiss. A promise of a lifetime of kisses to come.

"Do me a favor?" He traced her bottom lip with his thumb. "Take my horse back to your stable. Take him home."

"For keeps?"

"Forever."

Cameron's second kiss left no doubt. Theirs was a forever love, forever strong and forever true.

Epilogue

"Good morning, beautiful." Cameron's warm baritone lit Kendra's heart every time she heard him.

Love glowed inside her, soul-deep, as she turned in the chair, balancing her cup of decaf in one hand. The sight of her husband in his flannel pj's, sipping from his steaming mug, was something she'd never get tired of. To think this man was hers to love, this morning and for every morning to come.

"Hey, it's snowing." He kissed her with a hint of passion and settled into the chair at her side.

"The first snowfall of the season." She felt as peaceful as those delicate white flakes floating to rest on the branches of the trees in the forest. "We won't be quite this happy with the weather after we clear the driveway so we can get over to Mom's."

"Baby, my Jeep has four-wheel drive. Nothing is going to keep me away from your mom's cooking."

"It'll be our first Thanksgiving together."

He cupped her chin in his hand. Affection shone in his eyes. "It's already the best one I've had so far. I get to spend it with you."

"As wonderful as this morning is, do you know what can make it better?" She brushed kisses across his fingertips, carefully watching his forehead draw into a frown as he thought. "I took a test this morning. Guess what it said?"

Hope trembled through him. She felt it as his hand gripped her shoulder.

"Are you…" He sputtered and tried again. "Are we…is there going to be…"

"Yes. We're going to have a baby."

With a victorious shout, Cameron abandoned his coffee and swept her onto his lap and into his arms. "I love you," he said, kissing her the way a loving husband should kiss his adoring wife. "What a good life we have."

"Absolutely."

Gramma was right. A love like this, so great and true, could only be a gift from heaven. Kendra wrapped her arms around Cameron's neck and kissed him in return, happy, as she would always be with him in the snug warmth of their little home.

* * * * *

Dear Reader,

Thank you for choosing *Almost Heaven*. It has been my pleasure to return to the McKaslin family and tell another sister's story. Kendra aches for a family of her own but believes an earlier tragedy will keep her from trusting a man again. Thankfully, Cameron enters her life, a man as stalwart as the Montana mountains. He teaches her an important lesson: that true love is strong enough to heal any wound and bring us into the light.

Wishing you peace and a life filled with love,

Jillian Hart